RICKY

A boy in Colonial Australia

SHEILA HUNTER

Pacific Wanderland Publication
3 Avoca Valley Way
Kincumber NSW 2251
Email: spowter@bigpond.net.au
(02) 4368 6723
www.sheilahunter.com.au

1st Edition 2014
2nd Edition 2015 printed by CreateSpace, an Amazon Company; available on Kindle
3rd edition 2016 - Large Print printed by CreateSpace, an Amazon Company.
This 4th edition published in Australia in 2017 by Pacific Wanderland P/L © 2017 Sara Powter,

National Library of Australia Cataloguing-in-Publication entry

Creator:	Creator: Hunter, Sheila, author.
Title:	Ricky : a boy in colonial Australia / Sheila Hunter ; Sara Powter, editor.
Edition:	4th edition.
ISBN:	9780994578211 (paperback)
Target Audience:	For secondary school age.
Subjects:	Australia--History--1788-1900--Fiction.
Other Creators/	
Contributors:	Powter, Sara, editor.

Cover Painting is of King Street, Sydney NSW looking East towards
St James' ca 1843- watercolour by Frederick Garling.
Original in Mitchell Library, State Library of New South Wales

Back Cover Photo is of a young Jake Cassar taken in the
Old Kodak Photo booth at Old Sydney Town Somersby NSW
Photo - used with permission. © Jake Cassar.

Cover design and text layout by Jenny Cowan
Printed in Australia by McPhersons

RICKY

A boy in Colonial Australia

SHEILA HUNTER

Co-Winner of 1999
NSW Premiers Senior Citizens Award

Editor's Note:-

While all the main characters in this book are fictitious, most the important buildings, places (although not Ricky's houses and store), and country settings are historically correct.

My thanks to Joan Harvey for help with proofreading and to Olive Eardley for encouraging me to get these fabulous stories printed.

My thanks also to my husband Stephen who has supported me through the highs and lows of finally getting these finished.

Sara Powter

Sydney 1830 [view of the Domain and Mrs. Macquarie's Point]

Dedication

To our family -
who come before and prepared the way for us today!

and to my children -
who have yet to travel the path that was made for them!

Let us learn from each other.

Sheila Hunter
1924-2002

SYDNEY DISTRICTS 1824

Sydney (Port Jackson) to the East
Parramatta is 20 kms (15 miles) to the west of Sydney,
Hawkesbury River is just North and runs around West,
joining Nepean River, thus encircling the Sydney Basin.

CONTENTS

CHAPTER 1: *Ricky meets a new friend*

Ricky shook himself, feeling very wet indeed. "I don't reckon winter's any good anywhere, but I guess I am happy that I'm not in England. I suppose Sydney town is better'n that. But I'm cold." He looked down at his very cold bare feet as though he wanted to comfort them.

The lad who muttered these things to himself huddled in a doorway and looked out at the pouring rain. The rain came down in huge drops and had soaked his meagre clothing right through. He thought about the situation and decided that as he was so wet he couldn't get much wetter so he may as well head for home. With a skip and a jump he went out it, singing quietly to himself one of the many lovely English songs that his mother had taught him. He always sang one of her songs when he was uncomfortable and he was very uncomfortable now. He wished he had had time to go down to the markets to scrounge some food, for as well as being wet he was very hungry. He sighed as he ran and thought that he could put up with another night of hunger if he could get dry.

He dodged through the few people who were about, keeping well away from the well dressed, who wouldn't tolerate an urchin who splashed them. He dodged and ran until he turned in at a high stable door. He quickly peered this way and that and slipped in, and up the loft ladder before the men could see him. He lay panting trying not to make any noise just before a large wagon came into the stables. Under cover of the noise of unharnessing the great horses he slipped off his wet clothes and covered himself with some sacks that he had secreted into his nest. He lay his wet things out on the hay and snuggled down under his bedding, a few sacks that his friend had lent him. He smiled to himself and lay there listening to the men working below him. He heard the chinking of the chains and the blowing of the lovely big beasts, the

1

soft whooshing of the groom as he rubbed his charges down.

Ricky tingled as he warmed up and was quite content to stay where he was knowing that soon the men would go home for the night leaving him to be free to roam around his domain until they returned to harness the horses again for another day's work on the morrow. One of the men, old Tom, lived in the stables in his room which was just a nook past the furthest loose box, but he took no notice of Ricky. He knew the boy shouldn't be there but had been such a lad himself years ago and so felt a great deal of sympathy for the children who roamed, homeless, about the streets of Sydney.

Old Tom had come as a child convict and knew what a terrible place this Sydney town could be to the young. He didn't encourage other boys to join Ricky, but he knew that Ricky was a reliable lad and would never let on that Tom was responsible for his illegal tenancy.

As Ricky warmed he drowsed, thinking of his life in this precarious place. He thought of Mam and felt a bit choked up. This wasn't what Mam would have wanted for him. He wondered where she was and if she could look down from that place she spoke about so much and could see his plight.

Mary English had voyaged out to the colony in the 1840's, with her much loved son, Ricky, to join her husband who had come to the colony to take land, twelve months before. Richard English prepared for his family before sending for them and thus started a new life that promised so many riches for them all. They were good, hard working farming folk who knew their abilities to do a job well and so knowing and understanding the difficulties they could expect, were full of excitement as their prospects.

Mary and Ricky enjoyed the voyage, and were fortunate that they were better sailors than some of their fellow passengers. Richard English had procured a good cabin for his wife and son and so they had a modicum of comfort, even being able to furnish their own cabin with some well loved pieces.

Richard had written of his joy at seeing his family again and his wife and son at least expected him to meet the ship, but, on their arrival there was no one to meet them and try as they did they could find no trace of the man. Mary found a room and soon set about searching for her husband. She asked the authorities to help her but to no avail. She was able to find the whereabouts of the farm he was buying, but as he had not paid in full the money due, the land was returned to its previous owner. Mary was heartbroken. Of her husband there was no trace, he just seemed to have vanished off the face of the earth. In the 1840's New South Wales was still a rough sort of place and so she soon realised that anything could have happened to Richard and she may never know what. But it was surprising that no-one knew anything about him.

Mary did not have a large amount of money with her and soon her meagre supply ran low. She was forced to sell some of her furniture so that Ricky and she could eat. She soon fell ill and was no longer able to search any more for Richard; soon she was past trying for some work that might have kept body and soul together.

Ricky, aged 11, knew that his mother was ill and did all he could to try to make a few coppers to help in their plight. Mary knew that she would not live long and so began to plan for Ricky's welfare after she was gone.

They were living in a rooming house run by Mr and Mrs Curtin. It was a decent enough place in the Rocks area and the couple seemed to be kind. She would often speak to them about what would happen to Ricky and on their assurance that they would keep him and care for him, she made over the little she had, money and furniture, just before she died. She had already been able to arrange for her burial and so when the time came she was decently interred, but the Curtins turned on the boy and almost before Mary was cold they took all they could from him and turned him out onto the streets.

Ricky didn't dwell on this very bad time often but when he was cold and wet and hungry it came to his mind before he knew it. The lad was quite a philosopher in his own quiet way. After the first few days on the streets he reasoned that if he didn't make the best of his situation he too would die, and that wouldn't do him or his father much good. For it was embedded in the boy's mind that his Dad was somewhere, and quite unable to get to his family, for he was a loving man fully conscious of his responsibilities. Not the sort of fellow who would leave without any word, or to drink away his savings. So Ricky was sure that his father was still alive somewhere, just unable to get to him.

Ricky was roused from a deep sleep by a prod from his friend Tom. "'Ere, matey, I seen you slip in soaked to the skin. I ain't got much, matey, but ere's a mug a' char."

Ricky sat up and grinned at Tom, "Gosh, Tom, that's great. Where did you get tea?" he asked. He sipped the scalding liquid, feeling the joy of something hot in his empty middle.

Tom answered, "Don' yer ask, young man. I ain't saying. Yer just drink it up. Lor' look at yer, yer starkers. I got me brazier goin' so bring yer clobber dahn 'ere."

Ricky stuck his head through a hole in the bottom one of the oldest sacks and wore it like a shirt. It wasn't much but it was something. He grabbed his wet clothes and clambered down the ladder to drape them around the charcoal fire in a brazier. He squatted in front of the coals and gloried in their warmth. He breathed a sigh and the old man looked down at him.

"Warmin' up?" he asked.

"Yes, thanks, Tom. Tom," he said hesitantly, "Tom, I don't know where I'd be if it wasn't for you and being here."

"Ah know, lad. Aht on the streets in the rain. It ain't much fun neither. Ah knows it."

"I can't stay here for ever, I have to do something about it. I could get you in strife. I try to be careful, but if they found me you'd lose your job."

The old man smiled. "Yer're a good lad, young'un. I wouldn' be takin' the risk if yer weren't. But it is tricky, ain't it? Like termorra. I gotta get yer out real early 'cos a load a' 'ay is comin', real early. Like as not it'll be rainin' again. Jes listen to it." He cocked his old head on one side and listened to the rain pelting down on the roof.

It was a constant worry to Ricky that he might get his friend into trouble but it was very hard for him to willingly give up the only haven he had found in the time of his street wanderings. He thought that if he could find anything at all, even just a fine weather place, then he would only come to Tom when the weather was at its worst, as it was at the present. There were so many urchins, many who belonged to gangs, that continually roamed the streets, but Ricky was not attracted to these. They were usually ruled by bullies who encouraged a life of crime and that was not the way Ricky wanted to go. During the last weeks of his mother's life, she had used her frail strength to stress again and again that he must keep decent and not let himself go. To keep the high standard that she had always set him. He tried to do this but it was hard, oh, so hard. If you were quick on your feet you could often steal a morsel here and there, but Ricky wouldn't let himself be tempted even when starvation was staring him in the face, but at the same time wondered how long he could last out.

Tom looked at the boy and saw the worried frown on the young forehead. "It ain't thet bad, matey," he said. "I won't toss yer out, yer know, and we're pretty slippy, ain't we?"

"Yes, we manage very well, Tom. But it isn't right and I know it. I'd never forgive myself if I caused you trouble."

"Trouble with yer, matey is thet yer've been brought up too strict by yer ma. Sorry, lad, but she jes' didn't know what it's like on the streets. Now did she?"

"You're right there, Tom. She didn't, and I'm glad she didn't. But she would want me to try everything before I got a friend in trouble. But gosh, Tom, its beautiful in here in the warmth. I'd hate to be out there tonight. I'd reckon I'd die."

Tom shook Ricky out of his loft before dawn and shared another cup of his precious tea with him. His clothes were dry and felt good. But on hearing the rain pouring down on the roof he wondered how long he would stay that way. There was no way he could stay in the stables during the day.

Tom said, "Off yer go mate, I'm sorry to send you out in this but yer must go, but 'ere, take this." Tom took up a piece of oiled cloth that he had been using at one time as protection, and draped it over the boy's shoulders. "You take it, 'cos I won't need it terday. I'll just be dodgin' in and out an' with luck I'll stay in 'ere to tend the 'orses, an' I can cover meself with a dry bag each time I 'ave to go out. 'Ere take it."

"Tom," Ricky said, "oh, Tom, are you sure? "

"Yers, I'm sure. You need it terday. Get aht quick, I 'ear a wagon. Can yer get out without 'im seein' yer?"

Before there was any more chance of discussion Ricky quickly ran to the far side of the high stable door and hid. Tom opened the door to let the driver in with the cart. As the vehicle came in Ricky slipped out and into the pouring rain. He ran up to George Street holding the piece of oiled cloth over him as best he could. Looking in at each doorway he at last found one deep enough to give him cover hoping that no-one would be about so early. If his luck was in he would be able to stay dry for a while anyhow.

Life was pretty hard for the waifs of the streets of Sydney. No-one seemed to care about them, they became quite adept at dodging the law and anyone else who may interfere with them living the only life they knew. Most knew little about their families, but a few had folks who just didn't want to be bothered with children and so had turned them out on the streets. Many of the girls became prostitutes at an incredibly early age and as they grew up, they in turn produced more children to become the next generation of waifs.

Ricky was getting to know quite a lot about his town. During the few months after the death of his mother he had found life extremely hard, for it had been a cold wet winter and no-one wanted to house a homeless, penniless boy. He was eternally grateful to Tom who was the only one to show him any kindness at all. He knew that the old man did have a need of the oil cloth but also knew that he would not last much longer if he had to live without a better haven than a doorway. He sat quietly trying not to move and give himself away, keeping himself tucked up under his protecting sheet. What could he do?

He became conscious of voices behind him and was afraid that someone would come to the door and so slipped out into the rain and waited, but as no-one came he went back to the shelter. Then he realised that the door was ajar. He had tried to keep his 11 year old self so quiet that he had not touched the door, but now he did and it slid open a little more. The voices were quite loud and without really intending he listened to the two men. It took a while for him to realise what he was listening to. The voices were quite cultured and so what he heard astounded him. These men were planning to rob the Bank of New South Wales in Bridge Street. He sat stunned. He soon heard the date, the time and the method they were to use. Obviously one person was to do the actual theft but the two men were the organizers of the deed. Ricky wondered who they were and considered how he may find out. One of the men had a very gruff voice, one that he would recognise again, the other he knew, would be harder to identify. He heard movement and decided that this was not the place to be discovered and slipped away and ran swiftly up the street before the men emerged. Ricky saw another doorway ahead, it was the newspaper office which had an awning over the main entrance. He slipped into the doorway, peeped round and looked back.

He saw a man in a great overcoat come from the door and turn to bid someone farewell. Hunching himself into his coat the man moved quickly up the street towards Ricky. He went to pass the boy and then stopped, sheltering under the awning. The man turned and spoke to Ricky. "Here you," he said roughly, "get that cab for me. That one up the street and get him to come down here. Go on, hop lively."

For once Ricky did not resent having to go out into the rain, for he had been able to get a good look at the man . He paused to take in the man's features, and he was sharply told to "get on with it."

Huddling under the protecting cloth Ricky ran up the road to the waiting cab. On finding the driver was a man he had a small acquaintance with, Bert by name, he asked Bert to let him know the address that his fare was wanting to go to. Bert reluctantly agreed to tell Ricky who hopped out as the cab pulled up and opened the door for the man to enter. The boy did not expect and got no thanks for the small service. Urchins were not to be considered according to this fellow.

Waiting there and watching the rain, Ricky wondered what to do. He considered whether a policeman would take notice of the information that he had and after a great deal of thought decided to try that out. He went to the nearest police station and looked in at the door. A constable at the desk was busy with some papers and glanced up as the boy entered.

"What der yer want, yer?" he was roughly asked.

"I want to tell you about a robbery I heard about," said Ricky in a soft voice.

"Garn, what would yer know abaht a robbery? More like yer want ter do one yerself," came the rough reply. "Come on wotcha want?"

"Well, I heard some men talking."

"Oo were they?"

"I don't know"

"What d'yer mean, yer don't know?"

"Well, I don't. You see I was sheltering in a doorway and I heard ..."

"What doorway?"

"Just down the street."

"Where? What doorway? There's lots 'a doorways."

"I don't know just which doorway, I didn't really look but the men said ..."

"Der yer know who the men are?"

"No, I did get a look at one of them, but I don't know who he is."

"Gunna rob a bank, I suppose," the constable laughed uproariously.

"Yes, that's right. That's what they said." said poor Ricky.

"Get aht o' 'ere. Jest gettin' out of the rain, yer are. Be orf wi' yer, and don' trouble me none. Ger on, 'op it."

"But, sir," Ricky appealed, "please, I did hear them."

"'Op it, before ah run yer in. 'Op it."

Ricky turned, covered himself with the oil cloth and went again into the rain. As the newspaper office offered the best shelter he ran back there and sat on the step, hardly realizing that the persistent rain was easing.

He was roused by a kindly voice saying, "Well, young fellow, are you taking root on our doorstep?"

Ricky jumped up. "Sorry, sir. I was sheltering from the rain. I don't want to be in the way."

"In case you haven't noticed, the rain has stopped and the sun is shining."

"Oh. I didn't notice," said Ricky ashamedly.

The man who had spoken looked down at Ricky and smiled. He saw a nice looking lad in dilapidated clothing who spoke a better class of English than one would expect from a street urchin. "What's your name, lad?" he asked.

"Richard English, sir," said Ricky.

"You were certainly deep in thought, Richard English. I spoke to you twice before you heard. I think you had better come into my office and explain yourself. Come on in, I work here."

Folding the precious oil cloth Ricky followed the man. He led Ricky into the news office where there were people rushing here and there being very busy. Ricky looked around and was fascinated by what he saw. He was led into a partitioned area of the office where the window showed that it looked out into the road, and was labelled, 'Editor'.

Ricky, still clutching the precious piece of oil cloth, followed the man and sat at a chair that was indicated.

"My name is Hughes, incidentally, and I am editor of this newspaper, as you see by that sign. Now that we know each other, what about telling me what is bothering you. I presume it isn't hunger, for I daresay you are used to that. Come on what is the story. Stories are in my line."

At this stage Ricky wondered whether he should tell this man what had happened for even though he looked trustworthy, he wasn't sure that that was the right thing to do.

Hughes saw that the boy was hesitating, and this caused him to think that a story was in the offing. He always prided himself that he could sniff out a story quicker than most. "There is a story isn't, there lad?" he asked.

Ricky sighed, put his oil cloth down beside him and relaxed into the chair. "Yes, sir, there is a story. You see I went up to tell the constable about it but he wouldn't listen."

"Right, "said Hughes, "let's hear it.

So Ricky related the conversation that he had overheard to the editor who became very interested indeed by the time Ricky had got half way through his story. When he had finished he said, "Tell me it all over again. Exactly who said what and which way it was said. Take your time."

So Ricky repeated the story, this time going through it with even more detail.

Hughes, stopped him at one point. "You didn't say that before. Are you sure?"

"Yes, sir. One man, the one with the soft voice, said that they were organising three men to start a fuss, a diversion, he called it, outside the bank and then he would slip into the bank and hold up the people in the bank and rob it. He mentioned the names of the men he was going to use. I didn't know any but one, and that was "Hank" who lives in a shed down near the docks. He was also going to have other men there to keep the fuss going until he got clear. The other man, this one with the gruff sort of voice said he would wait round the corner and down the street in a closed carriage and pick him up and get him away."

"Did you get a look at either one, lad?"

"Well, sir, when I heard them moving I shot off, not wanting to be caught and came up here and sheltered in your door. I watched and I saw a man coming out. He turned speak to the man who was left and then came up the street. He pulled his collar up and I thought I wouldn't see him, but he stopped and told me to get him a cab. It was raining pretty hard but I could see a cab up the hill, and I ran for it. But, when he spoke to me I got a good look at him and I asked the cabbie, his name is Bert, if he could tell me where he was taking him. I would know him if I saw him again, sir, and he spoke in a soft voice so the gruff man must live in the house down here."

"Good. You seem to be a bright lad. And the constable wouldn't listen, you say?"

"No, he wouldn't. He just told me to get."

"If we walked down the street could you show me the place?"

"Oh, yes, sir."

"Right let's go. Now, lad when we get there just look ahead and don't point whatever you do. Just tell me which one and walk on ahead. We'll go on a bit and then we will return here. Do you think you can find that cabbie again?"

"Yes, sir, I know where he often waits and I'll find him there if I can. "

Ricky soon pointed the house out to Mr Hughes who told him that it belonged to Mr Flint the solicitor. "He has a gruff voice, sonny, so it looks as though our scaly friend Flint is up to some nefarious practices. I think you had better cut along and see if you can find that cabby. Then come back to me and report."

RICKY

CHAPTER 2: *Ricky's Box*

After leaving Mr Hughes Ricky raced back to the stables and gave the precious piece of oilcloth to its owner while Tom was grooming a huge Clydesdale. Ricky had tried to slip in unnoticed but the head groom spied him and told him to "Git." Tom quickly assured the man that he was only returning something borrowed, so Ricky was told again to "Git" and he "Got".

Ricky searched most of the day for Bert, the cabbie, but was not successful until late in the afternoon. The man was reluctant to give out the information for he was quite sure that the lad had some ulterior motive. But however, after a considerable time spent in discussion he at last told Ricky that he had taken the man to a boarding house down at the Haymarket, one called "Sunrise".

"Silly name for a dump like thet," said Bert.

"You don't know his name, I suppose?" asked Ricky.

"Nah, I don,'" was the reply. "But I s'pose they'd tell yer dahn there, if yer really 'ave ter know. Leastways they mighn't tell yer." He added with a chuckle.

Armed with this information, Ricky ran quickly back to the newspaper office and asked for Mr Hughes. He had apparently been expected for the clerk took him straight in. Mr Hughes then told him to leave the rest to him but report back to him if any further information came his way, and also tried to interest the boy in coming and having a talk with him any time he wished.

The news office intrigued Ricky and so did visit his new friend. The editor was surprised that Ricky did not make a habit of visiting him, but was always pleased to give the lad a few minutes of his time. Ricky soon learned the best times to visit him and that was after the paper was 'put to bed' or printed. The man soon learned the boy's story and was most intrigued as to what had happened to Richard English. He sent out feelers in his own way and was as keen to get to the bottom of this mystery if he was to help the homeless boy.

"Did your mother ever try to go out to the farm to see if she could trace your father, Ricky?"

"Yes she did. I went with her. We went by coach to Parramatta and then on another one to Richmond. Then she hired a gig and we went to the farm. There were people there who had sold the farm to Papa, and who told all they knew. They said that they had expected Papa to pay the last of the money on the farm on a certain day but he didn't turn up. He had taken the money out of the bank, too, for Mam checked and we don't know where that is either. The people looked for Papa and when they couldn't find him, packed all his things into his trunk and left it there in case he came back. Then they told the constable in Windsor. We couldn't look any more because we needed all the money we had."

"Where is your father's trunk Ricky?"

"It's at the boarding house, Mr Hughes. At least it was when they threw me out. I suppose Ma Curtin has sold all the things out of it. But I did get Mam's little box with all her precious things in it. They didn't know I did."

"Where is it now? Have you any place to keep it?"

"Tom looks after it for me, but I worry that it isn't safe. But I don't know what else to do with it."

"Who is Tom?"

Ricky hesitated to tell about his friend, Tom, for he was reluctant to tell anyone how the old man had looked after him. He looked up at the man who smiled at him. Feeling that he could trust him Ricky then told him all about the terrible winter he had just gone through, and how Tom had found him one particularly bad night when he was wet through, freezing cold, starving and torn apart with the loss of his Mam. He had been thrust aside wherever he tried to get shelter but the old man had taken him into the warm stable, dried him out and fed him, sharing his meagre food and then letting him stay in the hay loft dry and warm.

"I am worried about staying there, sir, 'cos Tom would lose his job if anyone found me. Tom wouldn't be able to get another place and so I try to only go there when its wet like last night."

"Would you not go into an orphan home, Ricky?"

"No, sir. Mam told me to be independent and work for everything."

"But she expected you to be able to stay with the Curtins, lad. She wouldn't want you to be out in the streets."

"I know that, but I know I can work and if I could only find a place to live and keep clean, I would be able to make my way."

"Well, I would like to help you, I would like to think how, lad. In the meantime would you trust me to look after you mother's box for you, lad?"

Looking up at his friend Ricky said, his face beaming a big smile, "Yes, sir, I would and thank you."

Hughes had told the magistrate what Ricky had heard and they had quietly gone about their investigations, finding that the man the cabbie had taken was one, Alfred Perkins, an old lag, who had come out for stealing from the bank he had been employed at in England. The authorities thought that he had a grudge against banks in general and were very happy to think that they were able to set a trap to catch the perpetrators of this proposed plot. The solicitor, Flint, was not a trustworthy character either.

The 16th of August was the date that Ricky had heard. He was quite excited as the date arrived. Mr Hughes had suggested that he wait in his office for there they would hear the news as soon as the reporter assigned to the story returned. The editor had taken his senior man into his confidence and had arranged to plant him in the bank and so get a scoop with his story of the happening.

So there sat Ricky at the end of Hughes' huge desk trying to be quiet, be patient and be still. He was filled with suppressed excitement and so found sitting still quite an ordeal.

Hughes watched the boy out of the corner of his eye while he attended to other matters and saw that the excitement was almost more than the boy could stand. "Here, Ricky," he said, "What about you writing the story out in your own words and showing what you can do."

"I couldn't do that, sir. I'm no good at writing like that."

"Well, have a try, it will give you something to do. We can't expect to hear for at least another half hour."

So Ricky wrote his first effort for the newspaper editor, at first wondering how to start but soon warming to his task. He was just about to hand his effort to Hughes when the was a sound of swift excited feet and a tall man entered the office.

"Sit down and tell us about it Handley. How did it all go?"

"Very well, sir. It went just as they planned. Three men started a row outside the bank in Bridge Street with some other characters. While this was going on a masked man came into the bank and held up the teller. There were no customers in the bank, they'd all gone out to see what the row was. We stayed quiet in the manager's office watching through the glass door behind the curtains. We'd been told to do this. The teller gave the man the bag that had been prepared for him." At this he chuckled. "It was a leather bag full of paper and lead with a few notes and coins on the top of it. He had a gun but didn't use it for the teller gave the bag to him quickly so he had no need. He then walked calmly out of the bank and past the row that was still going on, round the corner to the coach that was waiting and hopped in. It was then that the police came out of hiding and nabbed them. Do you know, sir, that it was Mr Flint the solicitor who was driving the coach. I couldn't believe it."

"Yes, I never did think Mr Flint was a nice man. Well, Handley, I think that was a good morning's work. You'd better get to your story, now."

"Yes, sir. What a scoop. First hand information it will be. Sir, how did you hear about this. Can I know?"

"No, Handley. Just say 'information received.'"

"Yes, sir." He turned to go looking at Ricky, and seeming to see him for the first time, he said, "A budding reporter, eh sir?" At the same time wondering why an urchin was sitting at his boss' desk.

"Yes, a budding reporter, Handley."

Hughes turned to Ricky with a broad grin. "Mission accomplished, eh, Ricky? I think that is a good day's work. Let's celebrate and go and have some lunch at the cafe downstairs."

This cemented the friendship between this pair, of man and boy. Hughes tried unsuccessfully to take Ricky under his wing and at least pay for accommodation for him, but the lad was adamant that he must do it on his own and contented himself with running messages and earning a few pennies which kept body and soul together. After a while, Ricky himself came up with a scheme that satisfied both. He suggested that as he was out and about through the town, he often heard scraps of news that maybe even a sharp reporter may miss. He had learned the benefit of a 'scoop' to a paper and offered himself as a bearer of such scraps that may lead to such 'scoops'. Hughes was delighted at this and so often found Ricky coming into the office with news of happenings. He was extremely quick to pick things up and Hughes thought he saw reporter material in the lad, but Ricky was sure that he did not want that life, for he was going to be a merchant and sell things, he said. Bit by bit he was earning more and more and was concerned as to what to do with his small nest egg.

Hughes had been minding Ricky's precious box for some time now. It lived in the big office safe. Hughes had also taken himself to Curtin's lodging house and tried to prize Richard English's trunk from them. He threatened all sorts of things to them but was not very successful in getting it, but on taking Ricky with him one day he was able to get a few things from them that Ricky identified. But they obviously had sold most of the saleable items and so Ricky had to learn to live with the idea that they were gone.

Ricky was earning more money, now, and this also was added to the box in the safe. One day he was able to announce that he had found a small room in a lodging house and now was more comfortable. He eked out his meagre savings as carefully as a miser. He was so intent on being independent that he took nothing that he did not work for. But on several occasions he rushed into the office to Hughes, or Handley, if Hughes was not there, and tell them of something that was going on, at the docks, or the markets or somewhere else and that he had a cab waiting to take the reporter to wherever the incident was happening. He usually tagged along in the cab with the reporter to see what was going on. He would often get a tip from the reporter, as well as from the office which would always pays for news. So his nest egg was growing.

Hughes noticed that occasionally the lad would have a new

garment or new shoes, very cheap ones, but clean and tidy, and never more than necessary. He was also looking well and better fed. He was growing very quickly and he resented the way he grew out of his clothes and shoes. Hughes also spent time with him after hours teaching him some of the lessons that the boy would have had had his mother been still alive. The boy was quick and had been well taught when he had attended school, and so found his lessons were a delight. Hughes, a bachelor, became quite immersed in the welfare of his protégée. He admired his independent spirit and was pleased that he was so, for being independent himself he did not relish the thought of having to give up any of his own solitary life for the welfare of a stray boy. But he did like Ricky and was satisfied that their friendship was an office hours one and not at all demanding on the man's leisure time.

Ricky still visited Tom on occasions and was delighted that he could take him some extra food at times when they would sit around the brazier and munch away at whatever the boy had brought. The lad had a way of getting to know people well and he soon had friends in every sort of food store and therefore brought all types of snacks that were sometimes damaged, or stale, but tasted good to hungry people. He would talk things over with Tom and sometimes Mr Hughes. Neither of these gentlemen understood his ambitions well, Hughes being only interested in the workings of a newspaper. The thought of being a storekeeper was well beyond anything that Tom ever thought about. Ricky was sure that one day he would own a store and knew how he would go about achieving his ambition. When he was big enough and had saved enough money, he would buy a barrow and sell from that. He knew he couldn't think of owning one for some time for there was an ever the present fear that one of the gangs that hung about the streets might try to take the barrow. No, he had to wait until he was older and much bigger. In the meantime his nest egg grew, and it was in the safe hands of Mr Hughes in the office safe.

Ricky's room was on the ground floor of a lodging house, it wasn't much and it cost little, but for the first time he was able to claim that some place was a home. He now could look forward to having a warmer winter when that came, for he was also able to buy some thick blankets at Ma Farrell's second-hand shop. He had a bunk bed and a rickety table, and a few pieces of cutlery and a plate and a cup. As yet nothing but the bunk to sit on, but he would look round at his castle and think it was great. He wondered what had happened to all the household goods that came out on the ship with them. His mother put them in store but by now he thought they would have been sold as unclaimed goods. He decided not to dwell on this, but concentrate on thinking out how he could make the most of what he had and how to set about creating a life for himself that was what he would have had, had his parents lived. For by now he was feeling quite sure that his father must be dead. He had, at first, thought that something had taken his father away and would someday come back, but he had come to terms with the thought that he would never see him again.

Wherever Ricky went he took note of everything that happened, the things that he passed as he walked the streets, he took note of the people he saw. He watched when the soldiers marched past, the convicts in the chain gangs, the smart people in their carriages. He watched from afar the children in the parks with their nannies, he watched the ladies strolling down the streets, in the stores, in the parks. He noted what the men wore, how they behaved, with the ladies, and when they were with their cronies, as well as when they spoke to the servant class. He watched everything and everyone. Sometimes he would walk out to the suburbs which he labelled posh. To Elizabeth Bay and a few times out as far as Vaucluse. There he would wander looking through the gates that kept the population out of these wonderful places. There was never an envious thought in Ricky's mind, but he knew that someday he would have a nice home, not a grand one like those, but a nice home and a nice family, just like Papa wanted for him and his mother.

It was on the way home from one of these jaunts that he noticed something that he stunned him. He came across Hack, one of the large louts who was part of the diversion at the bank hold-up. Hack had a dray with a seedy looking horse to pull it and had been picking up rubbish from one of the houses. Ricky knew that Hack was an evil person and he usually kept his distance. As Ricky was on his way home and Hack seemed to be going the same way, he followed him. Hack seemed to be in a hurry and was forever casting furtive glances around as though he was doing something wrong and did not want to be seen. The huge man was sitting hunched up on the dray seat and Ricky chuckled to himself and thought, "Whatever he is doing why doesn't the silly fellow sit up and look as though everything is all right. He looks guilty and so he obviously is guilty of something."

Ricky kept out of sight as best he could and didn't think Hack had seen him. The big man's movements were so slow that the lad had plenty of time to duck into a doorway while the man was peering about him at intervals. The dray went down towards the docks to the shed where Hack lived. As he pulled up Ricky dived for cover and saw Hack lift something out of the back of the dray that looked like a big rag doll.

"What on earth is he doing?" Ricky asked himself. Then came a flash of understanding, the doll was a girl, yes, a little girl and that rotten Hack was taking her into the shed. Hack came back and took the dray and horse to the back of the shed where he unharnessed and let the horse go in the tiny yard, he tipped the dray up and emptied it of the stuff he had collected, and then returned to the shed. Ricky crept as close as he could and listened at the shutter. He could hear the man muttering to himself and then in a louder voice mention something about getting grog. Ricky shot away and hid.

Sure enough Hack came out shutting the shed door behind him. Again looking furtively round he set off towards the pub. As soon as he was out of sight Ricky raced to the shed door and tried to open it. It was wired tight, and it took some doing but eventually Ricky managed to open the door. He could hear the little girl whimpering by now and he found her lying in some filthy straw that was obviously Hack's bed. She looked about eight years old and was dressed in a blue floral dress which was now filthy from the dirt she had collected from the dray. She recoiled when she saw Ricky, but he tried to reassure her and quieten her. She wasn't very co-operative, he thought. She only wanted to cringe away from him.

"Come on. Are you all right?" he asked.

"Go away. Where am I? What do you want with me? I want to go home."

"Come on," Ricky said again. "Are you all right? Come on, we've got to get out again before Hack comes back. Come on, give me your hand."

The child only cried and tried to get further away from the strange boy.

Ricky realised that she thought he was responsible for her kidnapping and said, "Look you were taken away by someone called Hack, and I saw him bring you here. He has gone for grog and if you don't come quick he'll be back. Come on I'll help you but we must run."

He held out his hand and reluctantly she took it and he helped her to her feet. She was very wobbly and sat down again.

Ricky said, "I know you feel awful, but you've got to come. Hack'll kill us if he finds us here."

"I want to go home, I want Binksie."

Ricky picked her up and ran. She was a heavy weight for him but he staggered out of the shed and turned down towards the docks away from where Hack had gone. At first she struggled and then apparently decided that this boy was about to help her and she stayed quiet. When Ricky thought they were safe for a while he put the child down and straightened his back, panting heavily.

"Come on, you can sit down here for a while until you feel better. When you can walk a bit I'll try to get you home. I'm sorry I had to lump you about but I had to get you out." He looked along the road. "Even now, I don't really think we are safe, so as soon as you can we must go."

He took the reluctant girl by the hand and led her along gently until she stopped trembling. They climbed the hill towards the town, Ricky hoping to see one of his cabbie friends. He knew they would take him on trust and help him deliver the little girl to her home. He talked gently to her, telling her his name, and asked for hers. She told him it was Amabel Landon and that she lived with Mama and Papa and Binksie at Elizabeth Bay. As soon as he thought she could he tried to get her to run, for it was getting dark and he had an idea that her folk would be panic stricken by now. Besides he wanted to find a cab before it got to their busy time taking folk to the theaters.

As soon as they turned into George Street Ricky saw a cab. He said, "Quick, run," and pulled her by the hand. He was almost dragging her and she cried out.

Two army officers were walking towards them and Ricky dodged. Amabel cried out again and as they flew past one of the officers let fly with his stick and hit Ricky over the head. He went down like a stone. Amabel fell down by his side, weeping. Blood was pouring from a wound on Ricky's head and she dabbed it with a part of her dress.

The younger officer asked, "Was that necessary, Bob?"

The other man looked down and said, "Miss Amabel, what are you doing here?"

"Mr Saunders, what have you done? You've killed Ricky."

"What are you doing here?" he asked again.

"I was taken away and Ricky found me. He was going to take me home. What have you done?" she repeated, "Look at him, he's bleeding."

"I am sorry Miss Amabel, I thought he was hurting you. I don't know why you are here at this time of night." The officer looked around and saw the cab that the boy had been heading for and beckoned him.

The younger officer had knelt down and was tying his handkerchief round the boy's head. " Shall we put him in the cab and take him with us?"

"Yes, do," said Amabel, "I'll take him home and Binksie can look after him." She watched as Ricky was put on the seat of the cab and clambered in.

The two officers got in too but Amabel objected. "I'll take him home, thank you, you needn't come."

The second officer smiled and said, "Thank you, little lady, but I'm coming too. I wouldn't miss this for the world. You'd better come too, Bob, for you were the one who did the damage."

Captain Saunders got in the cab sheepishly and said, "Mr Landon's home in Elizabeth Bay, Cabbie."

CHAPTER 3: *The Landons and Tad*

A s the cab turned in at the Landon's gate Ricky roused a little and tried to sit up. The younger officer, who by now Amabel knew as Lieutenant Hinds, held him, supporting his very sore head. Amabel had explained in detail to the two men, how her adventure began. She was feeling very annoyed with Captain Saunders whom she knew as a frequent visitor to her home. She had never met Lieutenant Hinds before as he was a newcomer to the colony.

As the cab drew up Saunders ran to the door which was opened by the Landon's butler. The butler gave a quick exclamation when he saw the little girl he gasped, "Miss Amabel!"

There was a quick movement from inside the house and a frantic man came to the door. "Amabel, where have you been? What has happened? Did you find her Saunders?"

A woman pushed past him and clutched at the girl, "Amabel, we have been so worried, what happened?" She then saw her dirty state and held her away from her silken dress. "Child, you are so filthy. What has happened?"

The little girl stood imperiously before her parents, hands on her hips, "I'm all right Mama, but please Papa, let Ricky come in. He's hurt. Mr Saunders did it. Please let Lieutenant Hinds bring him in."

The Lieutenant was standing in the doorway holding the very wobbly Ricky close to him, just then Ricky broke from his grasp and staggered to the garden where he threw up as delicately as he could. He stood swaying and Hinds went to him and guided him indoors.

"I think he should lie down, sir. I must tell you it is owing to this boy that Miss Amabel has been returned to you. I do think he needs attention, Bob here, gave him quite a crack."

Captain Saunders, still looked rather sheepish, but drew himself up and introduced the younger man, and added that he only did what he thought was best.

Mr Landon, turned to his wife and said, "Sadie, dear, I think you should take Amabel to Miss Binks and I will hear the full story later. Off you go."

"No Papa," said Amabel, "no, it's my story and they might not tell it right. I'll tell you what happened and then I'll go."

"All right, child, let us all go into the sitting room and hear all about it. I am sure the gentlemen would like some refreshment, anyway. But what will we do with the lad?" He led the way into a large salon then turned to the butler. "Tonkin," he called.

"Yes, sir?"

"Take this lad ... what's his name Amabel?"

"Ricky, Papa," she answered.

"Tonkin, take Ricky to Mrs Tonkin and see what she can do for him. Tell her to fix up his head and do whatever has to be done. Look after him well." Turning to the men he said, "Now tell me what you'll drink and we'll have this story."

Amabel told her story admitting to her parents that she had run away from her governess and was caught by the man as soon as she went out of the gate.

"Amabel," her mother said, "I have always told you that your high spirits will get you into trouble and look where they have led you now."

"Yes, Mama," Amabel said meekly.

"Well, get on with the story, child," her father urged.

So Amabel told the rest of her adventures finishing by pointing her finger at Captain Saunders and accusing him of being cruel.

The Captain was moved to defend himself by saying, "But, Miss Amabel, if he had been forcing you to go with him and I hadn't stopped him, where would I have been then? I really don't wish the boy harm, but you see these street urchins are not really the class for you to be running with."

Amabel was about to object but her father interjected saying, "All right, all right," and then sent her to her governess assuring himself first that she was all right.

Soon the officers took their leave and Mr Landon sat wondering about it all. Wondering whether he should get on to the track of the man Hack, for he felt reluctant to involve his little daughter. He sighed and rang for Tonkin.

"Send a message to the police, Tonkin, to tell them that Miss Amabel is safe, "he said, "and ask one of the constables to call to see me."

"Yes, sir," the butler said, "and may I be bold to say sir, how glad we are that Miss Amabel is safe and sound, sir."

"Thank you, Tonkin. How is that lad? Fixed up all right? How bad is his head?"

"He has a nasty gash, sir, but he is much better. With your permission, sir, we will keep him for the night and send him off in the morning. A likely lad, he is, sir."

"Is he? Well, make sure I see him in the morning before he leaves. I have a lot to thank him for. In any case I presume a constable will want to see him."

When Ricky appeared before the man the next morning he was looking pale but quite steady. He had a nasty gash on his left temple that would probably leave a scar when it healed.

"Well, young fellow," Mr Landon said, "I believe I have a lot to thank you for. How do you feel?"

"Much better thank you, sir." Ricky said. "Thank you for letting me stay here."

At Ricky's words that man's eyes opened. He hadn't expected to hear good English from the lad. He was so surprised he forgot to ask him more about the rescue, for a moment. "Where do you come from, lad?' he asked, intrigued.

"I live down near the Haymarket, sir."

"No, I don't mean where do you live. Where did you learn to speak so well and where did you come from?"

So quietly Ricky told the story of his coming to the colony and his father's disappearance and his mother's death. He made light of his problems, not mentioning the cruelty of the Curtins who had taken his possessions.

"I am sorry you have had such bad luck, Ricky. I would like to help you."

"Thank you sir, but I manage very well."

"But how do you live? And where?"

Ricky told him of Mr Hughes and how he made money enough to keep himself by running messages and being useful to anyone who would let him. He told him a little of his ambitions to have his own business one day.

"Well, I can help you lad. In fact I can offer you a position in my business. Would you like that?"

"Thank you sir. But I have my own plans, and I can manage very well."

"A bit stubborn, eh, lad?" The man chuckled.

"No sir, only my Mam told me never to accept the easy way of life. I was to work hard and make my own way," Ricky said determinedly, trying not to think of accepting.

"But, lad, I am sure your mother would want you to accept a job if it was offered. Think it over."

"Thank you, sir, I will think it over, but I do not think I will accept. But may I ask, sir, what the job would be?"

"Oh, I could find something for you in my warehouse, I am sure."

"So, there really isn't a job, sir, you would only make one for me?"

"Yes. But lad, think, I owe you something for restoring my daughter. I am very grateful to you."

"No sir, anyone would have done it. She is so little and was so helpless."

"Hm, I know. We are very fortunate to get her back whole. Now tell me where this man is who took her. I want to report him to the authorities."

"If I tell you, sir, would you tell them about me? I don't want you to because if the word got around my life wouldn't be worth living. Couldn't you just say that some boy brought her back?" Ricky pleaded.

"You really make it hard for me, don't you, sonny?"

"Would you please, sir? Just forget about me."

Landon hummed and hawed but eventually agreed not do any more than tell the bare facts. No one need know that Ricky had anything to do with it. But he was sad for it seemed as though the man Hack would get away with it. He reluctantly let the boy go, too, but was determined that he would contact Hughes to find out more about him. So he told Ricky that as he was about to go to his place of business he would take him home, as it was near to where Ricky lived. Of course, he also wanted to see where and how the boy lived.

Ricky was not reluctant to accept a lift for to tell the truth he was still feeling a bit wobbly and had a headache. At his home he said a polite farewell and Mr Landon shook his hand, saying, "Will you promise me one thing, Ricky?"

"If I can, sir," Ricky answered.

"Will you promise to come to me if you are in any need or if you strike trouble at any time?" he asked.

"Well, sir," answered Ricky, "I will keep it in mind. But thank you all the same."

Mr Landon sat in thought as the carriage turned towards the warehouse, then he tapped at the panelling and called, "Gray, take me to the Herald office."

Mr Landon knew the editor, but not well. He knew he was a respected citizen and felt that he would get a sensible opinion of the boy who intrigued him so much. So it was that from then on, they shared an interest in Ricky. Landon catching sight of the lad at times, and Hughes passing on any information he thought may interest the man.

Meanwhile Ricky worked hard and by the time he was fifteen he had enough money to buy the barrow that he dearly wanted so that he could start his business career. He also acquired a few other things, first was a stronger and much bigger body, which indicated that he would be a big man when mature, and also made him realise that he would be a harder person to better when challenged by some of the street gangs which roamed the town. He also acquired a small boy who had come into his life one wet and cold winter's night.

Ricky's room opened straight onto the street and one night was awakened by a scuffling on his door. The wind was howling and the rain pouring down in torrents. The scuffling continued and Ricky assumed that it was a stray dog who was sheltering in his doorway, but something made him get up out of bed and look. There was a small boy curled up as small as a boy could trying to get his blue feet out of the wind and rain. He fell in when Ricky opened the door and what a wet, miserable little fellow he was. He was about ten years old and filthy, dirty. He spoke the language of the gutter, greeting Ricky with a foul expletive as he fell at the older boy's feet. Ricky remembering how many nights he lay in such a place almost crying for some sort of protection, bade the boy come in to shelter. He was tempted to ask the lad to share his bed but knew that he would be infested with lice, so decided to doss him down on the floor for the night and deal with him later. His offer was gratefully received and the funny little chap had a drier night. Ricky suggested that he take his wet things off but the boy refused saying, "What'd ah want take me things orf for? I ain't got any more an' ah'd get me deaf o'cold, ah would. Nah ah'll jes' doss 'ere, mate."

This began quite an interesting friendship. Tad, as he was called, found that his life had changed for the better, but not without some misgivings. Ricky insisted on complete cleanliness and many a battle raged before that state was reached to Ricky's satisfaction. He threw away Tad's collection of rags which he had called clothes and Ricky spent some of his hard earned savings to buy the boy some more. Tad was extremely pleased with the result but once clean could not see the purpose of having to continue in that state. He felt the minimum of cleanliness was much more desirable, in fact could not see much use of water in any form except for drinking.

Tad improved amazingly and was quite prepared to adapt himself to his new friend. Ricky found that he was an intelligent boy and thought that he must have had some decent antecedents, of whom Tad was very hazy. He had been "cared for" by some old woman he called "Gamma", but exactly who she was he was not sure. She had died some months before and he didn't seem to have many pleasant memories of her. She gave him enough food to exist but that was about all. He felt that he had fallen on his feet now and was quite co-operative and willing to fit in with Ricky's way of life.

Ricky felt that he had taken on quite a burden though, and had to shelve his plans to get a barrow. But Tad was quick to learn and soon he was able to help in running messages and even carrying stories to the newspaper and getting cabs for the reporters. So as Tad developed the day came when Ricky drew out of his store of money and bought a barrow and the business that went with it. He would go to the markets early each morning and buy the best quality fruit and vegetables that he could and proceeded to sell them to the passers-by in Martin Place. He was soon known as a good, fair business man and he built up quite a clientele. He later added flowers to his range of products and quickly learned how to present them in a way that made people stop and look and of course, buy.

Ricky's first winter as a barrow man was a very difficult one. It once more was a very wet season and he found that it was no fun to be standing out in the rain getting soaked to the skin. He got influenza when the cold was at its peak and had to depend on Tad to help him push the barrow to its usual place. He was later able to buy a driver's cape at Ma Parker's secondhand store which gave him greater comfort. He was determined that as soon as he could he would get himself into a shop, expanding his business greatly. But the thought of paying rent for such a place was a bit daunting to a lad of his years.

Tad was a much more in touch with the seamier side of life in Sydney than Ricky had ever been. He was the sort of boy who apparently knew everyone and knew about everything that happened. He had a real nose for a good story. So much so that Ricky thought he would have a good future as a reporter if he could only teach him how to read and write properly. Tad hadn't been willing to learn those skills. Ricky had found that if he could get an idea into Tad that something was worthwhile, the boy would work with a will, but the big problem was getting him to that state, and reading and writing so far had no interest to him.

The problem sorted itself out one day when Tad had found two stories for the newspaper at the same time. He was torn between running back to the office and reporting the first story and missing out on the second. He realised that if he had been able to get the first story down on paper he could have sent it to the office by cab. It made him think. That night he suggested to Ricky that he might be willing to give this writing stuff a try. He never looked back, and was soon proficient enough to get down on paper the bare bones of any scoop that might come his way. In the meantime he was always able to tell Mr Hughes a story with great lucidity, putting the facts together in a way that astounded the man.

Of course, Mr Hughes, knew Tad quite well by this time, in fact he saw more of Tad than Ricky. Tad was much chattier than Ricky and was forever prattling away to the editor and telling him everything that happened to them. The younger lad was encouraged by the editor to bring his writings to him and he would help in the basics of grammar. He became so interested in him that he offered to give him an hour's instruction each afternoon after he finished work. It was not long before Ricky joined in these lessons as he had usually sold his stock by that time in the afternoon and didn't want to miss such a great opportunity to improve himself.

Ricky's idea of renting a shop had to be put away once more for he soon acquired another dependent. The boys had noticed a lame boy hovering outside their door on numerous occasions. When Ricky spoke to him he would turn and hobble away. He asked Tad if he knew him, but Tad was a bit off-hand about him, and didn't really give a coherent answer. He told Ricky that his name was Will and that he seemed to eke out an existence by begging.

One night while they were eating their evening meal, which was cooked in the communal kitchen of the lodging house, there was a knock at the door. Ricky found Will there.

"Kin oi come in?" he asked.

"I suppose so, but what do you want? Will, isn't it?" asked Ricky.

"Yus, it's Will," was the reply.

"What can we do for you?" Ricky asked again.

Will pointed to Tad and said, "'E said, yer might take me in. Will yer?"

Ricky turned to Tad and said, "Did you say that? You said you didn't know him. What's all this about?" he turned again to Will.

"Oi ain't got no-where ter go," he said. "Kin Oi stay 'ere?"

Ricky looked from one boy to the other. Tad was sitting with his bowl in his hands looking rather sheepish. "Come on, Tad, say something."

"He's decent, true he is Rick. Give 'im a go," said Tad, putting his bowl down on the floor.

"But, Tad, I'm finding it hard enough to do all I have to do now, I can't take any one else on. You know that," protested Ricky.

"He don't eat much," said Tad.

"Oi done eat much," the small boy echoed, nodding his head enthusiastically.

Ricky looked at him and said, "He doesn't look as though he has ever eaten anything. But what am I supposed to be, some charity or something? Tad I can't."

"Oi don' eat much," said Will, again, "Oi don' really. Jes' a crust'll do."

Ricky threw his hands up in horror. "Did you cook this up between you?"

Tad stood up, looked at Ricky and said, "Listen Rick, I am bringing in some money now and we could manage it, true we could. And I'll work harder. Maybe I'll get a job or something. Maybe he could stay here and keep the place clean or something, or cook or something."

Ricky marveled at the way Tad spoke. He didn't drop an "h" and had chosen his words carefully to impress the older lad. Obviously his lessons with Mr Hughes were paying off. He must have rehearsed his speech well.

"You're a young rat, Tad. You schemer," and smiled.

The other boys relaxed but Will was still wondering what the outcome would be, when Ricky said, "Here you share your dinner with him as I've eaten mine, then you can go up and get some hot water and scrub him down. I'm not having any crawlies in here, and he looks as though he has brought plenty."

Tad shoved his bowl at Will and told, "Here. Sit. You're in."

Ricky played no part in the cleaning operations but lay on his bed reading while it was going on. When Will was as clean as Tad could make him the boy was red and shivering. Tad went through his meagre supply of clothes and shared them out. Ricky watched covertly and was pleased to see how the sharing went, for Tad gave him not his worst clothes but divided them fairly. The clothes hung loosely on the small boy but his beaming face showed his pleasure.

Will had apparently been on the streets most of his life. As he couldn't run messages or do anything useful he usually stole what he needed or begged for coppers. His thin little body was emaciated and as Ricky watched him he wondered how many more boys there were in that same state. He knew from bitter experience how hard it was to keep body and soul together and again mentally thanked old Tom for the many nights he had been able to shelter in the stable.

"There should be places where kids like us could live decently without being put into orphan homes," Ricky said to the others.

Ricky found that taking Will in was the easiest part. This boy had no morals at all. He had never had any teaching of any kind and thought that anything was fair game. Stealing was second nature to him and he didn't seem to be able to learn that you just couldn't help yourself, even if you weren't caught doing it. He ate like an animal and had no idea of hygiene at all. Truth was something quite foreign to him. He was a trial.

Tad and Ricky had their work cut out trying to keep Will on the straight and narrow. Nothing Ricky could say made any difference, Will just didn't understand. He looked upon Ricky as general provider and thought it was fair game to steal anything removable in the room and hock it at any of the dubious shops that abounded that would give money for such goods. He certainly was a trial.

In the end Ricky left him to Tad to deal with, for when Tad dropped his newly found grammar and spoke to him in his old gutter language it had some effect. Ricky found it very interesting to watch the education of Will proceed and noted after some time that there was an improvement, but it didn't happen over night.

"Blimey, Will yer'll be the death o'me," said Tad one evening when Will had been particularly trying. He had been so tried that he had dropped into his old speech, which always seemed to happen under duress.

The older boys thought that Will would be a lot better if they could find something to do, but they racked their brains and so far had not come up with anything. Will was quite jealous of the other's sessions with the editor and couldn't understand why the boys were so keen to attend, but Ricky and Tad knew that they couldn't trust Will to sit tight and just listen, they knew he would help himself to anything that was lying around. They usually had a frisking session after they had been anywhere, such as in a shop where they bought food.

One day after Will had performed once more at being left on his own, they took him with them, introducing him to Mr Hughes, and warning him that he mustn't touch a thing. He promised, but the others knew just how much they could believe that and decided that if they made a proper search of the boy before they left, it should be all right.

Will was made to sit in Mr Hughes office in a big chair, which really pleased him, for he had never sat in an upholstered chair before. He sat quite still listening to the lesson that was going on for a time, and then, as the other three had their heads down working hard he slipped out of the chair and wandered around the office. He walked over to a tall sloped desk where he was surprised to find a man working. The man was sketching things on paper in lightning strokes which fascinated the boy. Will stood open-mouthed as the man seemed to make the pencil marks come alive. He was so still that the man was not conscious of him for a time. But slowly the consciousness of being watched came to him and he turned to find a scraggy urchin taking it all in.

"Where did you come from?" he was asked. "You shouldn't be here."

Will's eyes were still glued to the drawings. He just pointed to Mr Hughes office. "I comed wi' 'em, over there," he said. "Ow jer do thet, Mister. "Ow jer do them pichers?"

"Haven't you seen anyone draw before?" asked the man.

"Nah, wot's draw."

"That's what I am doing. I am drawing. You see I take some paper and then a pencil and I draw what I need to draw. For the newspaper, you see." The artist took a fresh piece of paper and drew a few lines on it and built up more and more until he had drawn a cat with a mouse.

"Caw, ain't thet grand. Do some more," Will said.

"I am not here to draw for you, my lad. I have work to do. I have to have something ready for tomorrow's paper. Here. Here's some paper and a pencil. You have a try. Sit over there." The man pointed to an empty desk. He lifted the small boy onto a tall stool before the sloped desk and put some sheets of paper down and gave him a pencil. Will settled himself down and the man watched him for a while, and then said, "No don't hold the pencil that way. Do it this way and hold it lightly. Now look what you've done, you've broken it." He took a knife from his pocket and proceeded to sharpen the pencil. "Look, sonny, hold the pencil like that, softly. So soft that you can pull it through your fingers. Then put soft strokes on the paper. See."

Will bent over the paper with a forceful expression on his little sharp face and his tongue protruding from his mouth and drew some lines on it. His mentor said, "That's no good. Look, sit up a bit and relax. I mean, loosen up and let the lines flow. Here, let me hold your hand and get the feel of it. Just stroke it like a cat. There, got the idea?"

Will did as he was asked and soon was putting soft lines and then hard lines all over the paper. He had a glorious time and forgot to notice that Ricky and Tad were finished their lesson. They walked over to him with the editor.

"Got a pupil of your own, Colin?" Mr Hughes asked.

"Yes, sir. The lad has never seen anyone put pencil to paper before, I do declare. He's making his way now, though. Is it all right if I send him off with off-cuts and some pencils, sir?"

"Yes, certainly. I was going to give some to Tad and Ricky anyway. By the way, I don't know if you have met my pupils." He introduced the boys to Colin Fraser.

"Are you Mr Fraser who does those wonderful drawings of people?" asked Tad.

"I am glad you like them, lad. You're the one who wants to be a reporter, aren't you?"

"Yes, sir, I am," answered Tad.

Fraser looked at the editor, "Seems as though we have a budding artist here, Mr Hughes. Look what he's done first off, and he hadn't seen a drawing before today. Not bad for a first effort. Keep it up, sonny. If I can help you at anytime, I would like to. Is that all right, sir?"

CHAPTER 4: *Ricky, Tad and Will*

It was still very hot at 5 o'clock when Tad joined Ricky at the barrow. There was still quite a lot of fruit left on Ricky's barrow, but he had had a good day and was packing up as Tad joined him.

"Had a good day, Tad?" Ricky asked.

"Busy," said Tad. "Look what I made." He held out his hand and Ricky saw that he had not only coppers but quite a few silver coins.

"You sure did," said Ricky. "What did you do to earn all that?"

"Everyone seemed to want messages taken this morning. An' you know thet solicitor, thet I told yer ..."

"Told you, Tad," put in Ricky.

"Well, all right. You know that solicitor fellow I told you about?" Tad mouthed carefully.

"The one in Pitt Street? Yes, what about him?"

"He's given me a job. I have to go to him every morning and deliver things for him. You know papers an' things. An' then he'll tell me if I have to go back in the afternoon. What d'yer think o' thet? What's more he pays me each message I run. He pays me for each one an' he says I'm quick and reliable."

"Great, Tad. I can see us being able to eat like lords if we are both earning."

Tad helped Ricky pack the remaining fruit into the boxes that Ricky kept under the barrow and together they pushed it back to their room. They parked the barrow in the back yard and carried in the boxes, where they were stored until the next day. They nudged their way through the door and stood gazing at the scene before them.

"What's going on, Will?" asked Ricky.

"Have you used all that paper, you young devil?" demanded Tad crossly. "Come on have you used it all? What am I going to do my work on?"

Tad put the box that he was carrying down on the floor and looked at the crippled boy. Will was sitting on the floor surrounded by sheets of paper that were covered with all sorts of pencil marks. Apparently the boy had spent the day drawing continuously. Gone was the pile of off-cut sheets that they had collected the night before, which Tad had left neatly on the rickety table.

"Lok wot ah done, Ricky. See Tad, I bin drawrin'. It's good, drawrin.'"

The older boys bent down and picked up some of the used sheets. Will had been drawing all right. Some were covered with scribbles, but on some there was a real attempt at making the lines mean something.

"You enjoyed it, did you, Will? Its good to see that you had something to do," said Ricky. "But you'd better go carefully with the paper. We don't get it easily, you know."

"But the little blighter 'as used it all up. 'ow am I going to do me work?" asked Tad indignantly. "You could'a kept some for us, Will. In any case did yer get anything for us to eat? What did yer get with the money we left for you?"

"Gee, Tad, I didn' think abaht thet. I jes' bin drawrin'"

"You mean you've been drawing all day, Will?" asked Ricky.

"Yus, an' I bruk the pencil and a' didn' know how to fix it. We ain't got a sharp knife like thet Mr Fraser, but I did it."

"How?"

"Look I took it ahtside on the stones and rubbed it." Will held out what was left of the pencil and the others laughed. He must have rubbed most of it away.

This was the beginning for a budding artist. Will accompanied the other boys to the newspaper office when they had their lessons with Mr Hughes. Sometimes Fraser was there and those sessions were a delight to the lad. At other times when the illustrator was away Will would leave the drawings he had done on the desk, and then live in a state of excitement until he could hear what his teacher thought about them. He tried drawing everything, as Mr Fraser had told him to. One day he took in a drawing of a boot and Mr Fraser was able then to give him a lesson in perspective.

"What do you think is wrong with this boot, Will?" Foster asked.

"It's nearly wore aht," said the boy.

"No, lad I meant the drawing. Can you see what's wrong with it?"

"Nah, it's orright, ain't it? I loike it."

"Yes, it is a good drawing, as far as it goes. But it is really all wrong, for it has no depth," answered his mentor. "Look, I'll show you."

Foster put his foot up on a stool and unlaced his boot. He put it up on the desk in the same pose as the one Will had drawn. " Now," said Foster, "What's the difference?"

Will grinned at him and said, "Your boot ain't worn."

"You young scallywag, you aren't thinking. Look at this. Can you see how far it is from here to here?" Foster held his pencil up to the top of the boot and measured it from side to side. Then he showed Will that it was a few inches wide. "See," he said, "it is about three inches and your drawing looks flat, doesn't it?"

"Yeah, but the paper is flat. 'ow can you make it inches wide?"

"Here, I'll show you." Taking up a new sheet of paper Foster sketched the boot quickly putting in the lines of shadow skillfully, giving the boot depth and life. Will watched fascinated as the boot seemed to take on real proportions. The pencil flew over the page and Will absorbed it all.

"Caw," he said, "Ow 'je do thet?"

"Just be putting lines in the right places," said his teacher. "Now just do this."

Foster soon had the lad learning to look at his subject and get it down on paper quickly. Will was quick to learn and he was certainly eager to improve. The artist kept him supplied with pencil and paper and found that he was becoming very fond of this little urchin. He told him of the stories he was called upon to illustrate and showed him some of his huge stock of sketches. So nowadays Will filled his days easily and found it hard to break away from his everlasting sketching in order to get the food needed for his friends when they returned home each evening.

The boys had many friends in the town and had come to some good arrangements with the various shop keepers. Of course, they always had enough fruit for they ate the overripe pieces from the barrow that would not sell, the baker along the road was always happy to let them have bread and sometimes cakes and pies that were damaged or less than perfect. One eventful night they came home to two dozen squashed meat pies that the baker's boy had dropped when he was taking them out of the oven. They had to eat them quickly for they knew the meat would not keep well in their hot and stuffy little room. The butcher let them have scraps that they could eat. Ricky was adept at making a stew from scraps, cooking it on the stove shared by other residents. They found it very palatable after he had let it set and taken most of the fat from the brew, it was always full of good vegetables, and so they did eat quite well, most of the time. But there were lean times and then they had to spend more than they wanted to keep themselves healthy. Ricky was still fiercely independent and had instilled into his two charges that they must either work for their money and food and not expect charity or take it when offered.

They had settled down to a pleasant life, they thought. Their quarters were very cramped. Hot in the summer and very cold in winter. Ricky and Tad had paliasses to sleep on and blankets to help them keep warm. They had given Will the bed for he was very prone to catch cold and after seeing him try to keep warm when that first winter started, Ricky made him take the bed which was certainly warmer for it was away from the continual draught that blew in under the door, and the thin mattress on the floor was no great protection.

In the summer the room was hot and stuffy and so the door was kept propped open to catch any breeze. This had its drawbacks in many ways for the various louts of the streets thought nothing of bursting in and upsetting things greatly. They seemed to take demonic delight in rushing in and tearing up Will's precious drawings, kicking the beds around and upsetting the boxes of precious fruit. It worried Ricky greatly but felt that their finances were not such that they could move into anything better as yet.

They were all getting on well with their studies. Tad now spoke well and had proved himself to be a hard working lad. Mr Hughes thought he was nearly ready to be offered a permanent job as office boy, but he kept this idea to himself until he felt certain. Will had blossomed under the tutelage of Mr Fraser. He, too, was learning to speak better and they all had hopes that he would one day be a credit to them. The two men were fascinated by the three lads. They often talked about them and concluded that there must be a lot of wasted talent among the street urchins of Sydney town.

John Landon kept up his friendship with Charles Hughes. At first so that he could keep track of Ricky's progress and later for the quality of the man himself. Charles spoke often of the boys and of the progress they made. John, not wanting to interfere, but being very interested, asked Charles if he could drop in one evening while the learning sessions were on and see for himself what was going on. He did this on several occasions and sat silently while watching and listening. He said little to the boys but was always ready to greet them cheerfully. He was ever mindful of his great debt to Ricky but rarely made overtures to the boy for he respected his independence and was content to watch and wait.

Mr Landon surprised the boys one evening when he appeared at the door of their room. The door was ajar but was barricaded so that it could not be opened wide. He rapped on the door with his cane and Will looked up from his drawing and then peered through the aperture, and said, "Caw, it's a nob."

Ricky came to let him in removing the boxes that stopped the door from opening, and asked their visitor in, explaining about the barricading of the door, and saying, "There's not much to sit on, sir. Just a fruit case. Here I'll put a pillow on it. Is that all right?"

"That's fine, Ricky. I am sorry to barge in on you like this but I thought I would like to pay you three a visit and see how you are managing. I hope that's all right with you?"

Tad and Will were quite tongue tied, for it is one thing to speak in the news office but the man seemed very out of place here and was it rather intimidating.

"Are you drawing, Will? May I see what you are doing?"

Will handed his effort to John wordlessly, feeling rather frightened that the man had come to criticize.

Landon sat looking at the three pairs of eyes that were gazing at him, obviously wondering why they had been so privileged. He smiled at them, knowing what they were thinking, but lifted his eyes to peer round the room. Will's many drawings were strung neatly onto cords that were suspended from the cornices of the ceiling. He could see that the boy was certainly an able artist. He thought about the small lad who was so crippled and thanked the Lord that he had found such a refuge from the cruel outside world. He looked beneath the ruffled blankets with eyes that were seeking any sign of dirt and laziness and did not see any. The place was very clean, amazingly so. But then Ricky was in charge. Yes, he could see signs of Ricky's hand in a lot of things. He looked down again at these three pairs of eyes that were still wondering about this invasion.

He asked, "How do you apportion your tasks? Please tell me."

The boys seemed to relax a little, but it was Tad who answered. "We each have our jobs, sir. At least Will and I do the housework in the mornings because Rick has to go early to the markets. Will does the shopping unless it's wet and then I do between messages because we are tired of Will getting wet and sick, so he's not allowed in the rain. We've got to watch him 'cos he forgets when he gets to do his drawing, and if we aren't careful there's nothing to eat when we get home."

Ricky laughed. "He doesn't seem to need to eat, Mr Landon, when he is drawing. He just loses himself."

The boys relaxed as they spoke and finding the man casual and friendly soon told him all about their way of life. And indeed he was relaxed, and enjoyed sitting on the upended fruit case with a hand on each knee listening to what he was being told and thinking what a good job these boys, who had so little to help them, were making of their lives.

After some time he suggested that Ricky escort him to his carriage which was waiting outside. He called to his driver, who was waiting at the horses heads, and told him to remain there as he was going to stay for a while. He then turned to Ricky and suggested that they sit inside the carriage and talk. Ricky climbed in after Landon and sat opposite him as he was bidden.

"Tell me lad, how are your plans going in achieving that ambition of yours to have a store?" he asked.

Ricky sighed and said, "Not as fast as I hoped, Mr Landon."

The man chuckled. "Didn't plan on having dependents, did you Ricky?"

"No, I didn't, sir. But I wouldn't tell them that for anything. They are my family, sir, and I feel I have to look after them. I'll get there in the end even if it takes a bit longer."

"I have a proposition and I hope you will think about it seriously."

"I don't need any help, Mr Landon. We are managing quite well, you know."

"Do you want to stay in that room for ever, boy. Have some sense and let me help a little."

"No, really, we are all ..."

"Now wait and hear what I have to say." John Landon raised his hand to silence Ricky. "Son, I have just bought a building adjoining my warehouse and intend to make it my headquarters and so extend the warehouse into where the office is now. This new building has two shops on the ground floor and I want to offer you one. How old are you?"

"Nearly 17, sir. But I couldn't accept charity, sir."

"Now you listen to me you silly fellow. I know what your mother told you about accepting charity and I admire you for sticking to that. But enough is enough. She didn't expect you to adopt two waifs to look after. I have been watching your progress and I am pleased with what I have seen. Now be sensible. If you are interested in the welfare of those boys you will do what is best for them."

"But, sir ..."

"No, listen. I am not giving you something for nothing. This is a business deal. I will rent the shop to you for five shillings a week and between the three of you you can keep the yard at the back of the building clean and tidy. There are stables there but we will not be using them. The shop that I am offering you has a residence behind it with three rooms and a kitchen and would be far more comfortable than that hot place you are in now. I will also put furniture in it that you can use so you will have better comfort than you have now. Now what about it?"

Ricky sat thinking then he looked up at the man opposite and said, "I must admit it is tempting, Mr Landon. But I feel as though I am letting myself down."

"For goodness sake, lad, don't be so stiff necked. I know you value independence. I do myself, but think. Apart from anything else, you must remember that I owe you a debt that I have not been able to discharge. Please, let me help you to this extent. Let me tell you more."

They talked and talked and eventually, reluctantly the boy agreed to come the next day and look at the shop in question, but asking Landon not to say anything to the other boys until a decision was made. So Landon had to agree to that.

Ricky went back to the room, finding that he was more than ever conscious of the heat in the confined place. "I wish people would leave us alone to make our way," he stubbornly thought and at the same time wishing that he could accept the wonderful offer.

The other boys greeted him with lots of questions but he was able to brush them aside and tell Tad that he needed him for a time the next day to look after the barrow so that he could go and see Mr Landon again.

"Gee, maybe he's going to give you a job, Rick," said Will. But Tad just looked at his friend and saw that he was deep in thought and was not communicative and so said nothing, nudging Will to be quiet.

Ricky met Landon at the warehouse the next day as planned. He was surprised at the size of the large offices, and asked Mr Landon what he kept in the warehouse.

"I import all sorts of things," he was told. "But it is mostly materials that I deal in. Materials that range from heavy canvasses to fine materials for ladies' dresses. But also all sorts of other things. I will show you our stock some time. Now come and look at this shop."

After seeing the shop, Ricky found that the decision was harder than ever. "Why are you really hesitating Ricky?" asked the man. "Do you find that it is too daunting? If you will let me I will help you?"

"Thank you, sir. I just don't know. Maybe I've been dreaming about a shop for so long that I am frightened of making a mess of it. Yes, I think I am a bit scared."

"Bigger men than you have been scared of a new venture. But you have admitted it and that's something. If you take it on you must promise me one thing."

"What is that, Mr Landon?" Ricky asked.

"If you find yourself in sticky waters you will come to me for help before you get in too deep."

"Sir, do you think I am letting Mam down?" asked Ricky, wistfully.

"No, lad she would be proud of you, as I would be if you were my son."

"Thank you, then I daresay I'd better try it and hope I can make a go of it. And yes, I will come to you if I find things getting ahead of me, I promise."

"Good, I think you are learning to accept at last. We will shake hands on the deal."

Tad and Will were ecstatic when he told them the news that they would soon be able to move in to new quarters. Ricky was, however, in no hurry to get going. He was heavy of heart and this the younger boys could not understand. But it seemed to the lad that his responsibilities were growing apace and he wondered, now that this opening had come about, whether he wanted to take on any more. But giving himself a good shake he decided that he mustn't shirk it, but make the most of it.

They all went along the next day to look at their new home and were rather stunned at the bareness of the place. They walked around and peered through this door and that noting that the shop area at the street level was large and commodious. So much so that Ricky agreed when Will said, "Gee, Rick. Will you ever have enough fruit to fill all this?"

The place was quite empty but clean and the walls were a rather nasty dun colour. They wondered whether they would ever be able to get enough furniture in it to make it cosy. After living in such close quarters as their present room, this place seemed huge, cold and unfriendly. Mr Landon had told Ricky that the place would not be available for two weeks and Ricky felt pleased that he could put off the day. He had a great deal to think about and plan. He could see that he would need a lot of shelves, but when he had asked Mr Landon about this he had been told that shelves would be put in place before they moved in. Also Ricky knew that he would have to dig deeply into his store of cash to finance the amount of stock which would fill those shelves. There was so much he had to decide and it worried him that he may not be able to get it all done. He talked it over with his fruit wholesaler at the markets and found that the man was prepared to help him by giving him credit, but this was just another thing to frighten him for he was very afraid of getting into debt.

They could not put off the evil day any more and according to Mr Landon's instructions the boys prepared to move in one very sunny, hot day. They loaded the barrow with all their possessions and trundled it down to the new shop. They pulled up in front of the shop and immediately saw that the interior had been painted and new shelves put in place. Leaving the barrow at the door, Ricky went up to Mr Landon's office to collect the keys. The man was looking very serious and handed the keys over with a few stern words, showing not much encouragement, which rather concerned Ricky, for he felt that this was all Mr Landon's idea anyway and that he needn't be all that stern about it.

So with a rather heavy heart he went below to start this new life. He couldn't help but be excited while he had two lads such as Tad and Will with him. They were jumping up and down with impatience, saying, "Look through the window, Ricky. We think we can see some furniture. Come on quick, let's get in."

Ricky was amazed at the transformation of the place. The shop had pleasant cream walls. There were shelves all round the shop. Some which sloped to show the fruit off to advantage. There was a very good counter that was big enough to be able to be able to store all sorts of things underneath. Ricky stood, feeling the top of the counter and then ran his hands over the shelves, while the boys pushed through the door into the living area and their shouts of joy beckoned the older boy through to see for himself.

There was a passage along one wall which had three rooms opening off this. All had been painted the same cream as the shop and each had two beds and a cupboard with drawers and a curtained corner for hanging clothes. The passage opened into a large living area the full width of the shop. This was kitchen and workroom. An old black iron stove was at one end, which the boys greeted with delight for they knew that this would warm them during the winter nights, there was a large white pine table and six pine chairs coloured green. There was an old kitchen dresser with some cutlery and crockery in it and below these they found a well stocked store of groceries. There was an old sofa and more pleasing there were three slope-top desks with closed store space under the top. It would not come into the category of luxury but to these boys it was the nearest thing to heaven that they had ever experienced. They just stood and looked and one by one they moved to the desks and each sat at one. No-one spoke. They were far too moved.

Someone came in through the shop but the boys hardly heard, until Mr Landon called, "Boys, where are you? Are you here?"

They came to, each answering the man's call. "In here." "Here, sir." and Ricky's "Come in, sir. Thank you. What can we say?"

"I don't want you to say anything at all, Ricky. I just had to see you, you looked so downcast up in the office."

"I thought you were annoyed with me or something, sir."

"No lad, I was just excited. I daresay I am like a boy myself and just wanted to please you."

"Oh, we are pleased, aren't we boys?" The others were keen to say how pleased. "But, sir," said Ricky, "we can't accept all this. How can we pay you back?"

"Look, Ricky. None of it cost very much and I couldn't in all conscience let you move in here with the amount of furniture you had. It would be like tying a millstone round your neck, to expect you to have to pay for your stock and furnish the place as well. Really there is only basic stuff here and it was no trouble. One of the workmen painted the place and got the things so I didn't have to do much. You'll find stove wood in the shed outside, too. Now is there anything else you need? Can I leave you now?"

"All we can say again is thank you, sir. Can't we boys?"

"Yes, thanks, Mr Landon." "Thank you sir," they said.

When the door closed on John Landon the boys suddenly whooped and laughed and danced. "Gee," said Tad, "I reckon we're the luckiest blokes, don't you Rick?"

"Yes, I sure do," said Ricky. "What a great gun he is. We'll have to look after this place really well and show him that we can. That'll be mostly you, Will. Can you do it?"

"Sure thing, Rick," said the smallest lad.

"Let's go out and look at what's out the back," said Ricky.

There was a bit of a verandah out the back door with a washstand, dish and bucket; a backyard toilet along the end of a short path and a large stable across the back with a double gate leading out to a lane. There was a huge pile of wood in one of the loose boxes but nothing else. The back yard was cobbled and quite a decent size. There was a high fence separating them on each side from the stables behind Landon's warehouse and the big factory on the other side. The boys looked around at it all and stood in the centre of their backyard and grinned at each other with delight.

CHAPTER 5: *An Arrest and some Drawings*

The boys settled into their bedrooms, one to each, that night, but it was not long before Will crept into Tad's room and asked, "You asleep, Tad?"

"No, what d'yer want?"

"That room's awful big. Kin I come in wiv you?"

"Sure thing, Will. I was just thinkin' the same thing. Bring your blankets into the other bed."

"What's all the noise?" Ricky asked from the other room. "Can't you fellows sleep?"

"No we can't," said Tad. "It does seem strange, don't you think, Rick?"

"Well, get going and try to get to sleep. I've got to be up very early. Goodnight and get to bed."

Ricky found sleep didn't come easily. He was too worried about how it would all work out, but eventually thought, "Oh, well, I suppose we can go back to what we were." With that he slept.

It was still very dark when Ricky set out to get his new stock. He knew that he would have to make several trips so that he could fill his shelves, and he wanted to be ready to open when the people started moving in the morning. He had paper and bags to get and all sorts of things. He found that he was able to do all he planned by that time. When he returned after his first trip he was surprised to see that Tad and Will had a fire going and a kettle boiling ready for a cup of tea. They had found tea and sugar in the cupboard and were delighted with that luxury. They had begged some old newspapers from the store-man from the factory next door and had even lined the shelves with some. Ricky could see that they were beside themselves with excitement.

The first customer came while Ricky was away for his second load, and Tad served the woman with great seriousness while Will told her that they would stock all the things that their neighbours would need. When she paid for her two apples Tad wondered then where they were going to keep the money they took, for Ricky had his cash bag with him for his purchases. The boys decided that there was a lot in this storekeeping business.

Ricky, too found that there was more in running a bigger business than he ever dreamed and to Tad and Will he seemed to be forever wearing a serious look and wasn't full of the usual smiles. There was so much to learn and no-one to learn from. Tad suggested Mr Landon, but Ricky refused that as he wanted to feel no further obligation. However Mr Landon was watching from a distance and could see that the weight of it all was somewhat overwhelming, but kept away from the lad knowing that he wished to make his own way. But two weeks later when the shop was really going Mr Landon came down to see Ricky on his way home one day.

"How is it going, Ricky?" he asked.

"Very well, thank you, sir," came the answer.

"Business good, is it?"

"Yes, sir. More than I expected." But Ricky said this with a frown.

"Can I help in any way? You seem to have a worry."

"Thank you, sir. I just have to get used to the book keeping and banking and everything and I feel rather that I have jumped into deep water and I cannot swim. But I'm learning."

"I thought you may need some help in that line, son, and so I have asked Mr Summerland, our head clerk to give you some time. He can help you a lot. Just tell me when you can come and I'll arrange the time. He is a very pleasant chap."

"Thank you, Mr Landon. I would like to talk to someone about some of the things and I don't want to worry you, but I don't want to take up your head clerk's time. Are you sure it will be all right?" Ricky asked.

"Yes. Quite all right. Call at the front desk and make the time with Summerland."

Ricky looked forward to his session or sessions with the head clerk of the firm, but it didn't reach the boy's expectations. He found that Mr Summerland was pretty old, at least in his eyes, but he was a rather jolly looking man. He sat at a high sloping desk which was piled high with impressive looking books that were dark green in colour, their backs and corners with leather binding. He was received with a grunt and told to, "Sit there." The man pointing to a high stool beside him. The clerk wore gold edged glasses and peering over the top of those he spat at the boy, "What right have you to wheedle your way into Mr Landon's good graces? He shouldn't be troubled by the likes of you. He is far too important a man to have more worries than he has."

Ricky looked startled and began, "I am ..."

"Yes, you are ... all right. Just full of you own importance. I know."

"Thank you, Mr Summerland. I will not trouble you. I thought Mr Landon said you would help me, but I will not be spoken to like that." Ricky looked up and saw that others in the office had heard and that some were sniggering.

"You'll sit there and do what your told. Now listen to me."

Ricky could hardly take in what the man said and of course this made Summerland presume that he was quite dumb and unable to comprehend. However he did look at the big books and learn a little about what a ledger was, a balance sheet and cash book, but it was hopeless to take in what they really meant, for the man was clearly reluctant to spend more time than he had to on them, and Ricky could see that it would take more than the cursory run through that Summerland was prepared to give him, to learn more than the bare basics. So after sitting through a humiliating half hour he slid from the stool and thanked the man as politely and patiently as he could and left the office. Looking back he found that the man was smirking with satisfaction and hearing some laughter from the others he quickly went down the stairs vowing that he wouldn't put himself in that position again.

Ricky realised that Mr Landon hadn't explained their relationship, and indeed was glad that he hadn't. But he had expected some sort of co-operation from his staff and had been surprised and hurt by their attitude.

He was happy to get back to the shop to relieve Will who was manfully trying to hold the fort. He smarted all the while and was upset to see that as the office workers left the building some actually looked in at the shop and grinned knowingly. Some people could be cruel.

Just before the shop was due to close one of the men Ricky had noticed upstairs came in. He greeted Ricky and immediately apologised for the reception he got. He told Ricky that he was leaving the office and would be glad to be free of Summerland and his cronies. The man, Gosling, appeared to be a pleasant man. He was a slight person with a rather rat-like face, but when he smiled he seemed to be quite friendly.

"I think I can help you young fellow-me-lad. I am going into business with a friend of mind and we will be selling first class fruit and we would deliver it to your door, if you would care to buy from us."

One thing that troubled Ricky was the everlasting carting of cases of fruit. His turnover was greater than he had had when selling from his barrow, and he found that he was unable to get enough fruit on his barrow to keep his shelves stocked, without making several trips each morning to the markets. His enquiry of one carrier had not been a success for the man had wanted to charge an exorbitant fee for the cartage and so the boy had given up that idea. This did seem to be an answer to his problem.

He liked the look of this man and asked, "Can you guarantee the quality of the fruit you sell and at the right price?"

He was assured in this, and so after much further discussion he came to an agreement with Mr Gosling. He was to commence buying from him on the following Monday and gave his order. Gosling also offered to help him with his books.

The boys were very interested in hearing all about Ricky's adventures, and were happy that Ricky seemed pleased with the forthcoming arrangements. They were too used to abuse to take much notice of Ricky's experience in the office. Ricky made light of it anyway, he was not one to grouch about adversity, but it still rankled.

Will was the only one to throw cold water on Gosling's proposal by saying, "Mind him, Rick. If 'e's the one I think he is, 'e could be a bit slippy." Will still missed an 'h' or two occasionally. He suggested that Ricky check him with Mr Landon, whom Will thought was nearest thing he knew to God.

But Rick assured him that he would be careful, and in any case Ricky was in no mood to consult Mr Landon any further. He was determined to stand alone in future.

They spent a pleasant evening, as their evenings were usually. Tad was always full of the news of the town, and this day he had an extra bit that pleased them all; one of the office boys was leaving and Tad had asked Mr Hughes if he could get the job. Mr Hughes had said that he would think about it, but as he now spoke well, wrote well and dressed tidily he had good prospects of getting it.

Ricky was very pleased, of course and told him so. "Will it mean you will have to be inside all the time, Tad? Will you like that?"

"Yes, I'll just be inside all the time, but it is the way most of the reporters started and so I know I'll have to start that way, too? I'll just have to make myself so useful that they will give me a better job quickly. I'll get proper pay, too, Rick. That will help, won't it."

"Yes, you'll have to have a bank account and save all you can."

"But, Rick, I'll share it with you and Will. You share all you have."

"No, Tad I don't share all of it, I put as much as I can in the bank for a rainy day."

"Yes, but you use that for us when we need it. I think we are your rainy day. Any way I've got to give you some, I've got to help you with costs and things. You have bought these clothes for me so I can look decent and now it is my turn." insisted Tad.

Ricky was very pleased with his protégée and smiled at him. "Well, I guess we'll see when you get that job."

Will looked wistfully at the two older boys. "I wish I could earn some money. I just don't seem to be able to do anything to help."

"Yes, you do, matie," said Tad. "You clean up and do all sorts of things, doesn't he Rick? Anyway, one day your going to be a famous artist and get more money than the lot of us."

"You do help a lot, Will. You look after the shop when I'm busy and do all sorts of things." He smiled at the eager boy, thinking how hard it was to get flesh on those pinched cheeks and how frail looking he was. Will was always keen to try to keep the place clean and do what he could to help, but the others knew what an effort it was for him everlastingly dragging a lame leg, and so Ricky had found that it was better for the boy to be in the shop and Ricky himself do the hard cleaning. He was always able to make Will feel that he preferred to do it.

Gosling arrived on Monday morning with all that Ricky had ordered. He was careful to scrutinize all the cases before taking delivery. Gosling watched him carefully standing with the man who owned the cart. He smiled at the care of the boy and nudged his companion and said, "There's a man who knows what he is after, George. He's going to be a good man to do business with."

Certainly Ricky was pleased with the quality and amazed at the low price. He was happy to give a further order, but at the same time wary. Somehow it all seemed too smooth. However he would be careful and be alert.

For two weeks all went well. The fruit arrived on time, it was very good quality and a good price. Ricky felt that things were going well for him. But on the third Monday morning just as the cart arrived and unloading was taking place, suddenly there was a rumpus outside the shop and several police appeared at the door.

"Where's that fruit thet was brought in 'ere, lad?" A burly policeman demanded.

Ricky showed him the two cases that George had placed inside the door, and asked what the trouble was.

"Stolen fruit, that's what the trouble is, my lad. And I arrest you for receiving stolen goods."

Ricky couldn't believe his ears. Now what had he got himself into?

"But sir, I pay for these. I didn't know they were stolen. What am I going to do?"

Outside the shop he could see that George and Gosling had already been arrested. He looked around helplessly.

Will had heard all this and he edged himself to the door while the arguments were going on. He hurried up the stairs to Mr Landon's office as fast as his leg would let him, cursing all the way for making him so slow. He went to the main counter and asked to see Mr Landon, "Quick," he said. But was told not to be a nuisance.

Will was not be put aside and just stood there yelling, "Mr Landon, come quick. Ricky needs you." The clerk who had tried to shoo him away was aghast, but the door of a glassed in office opened and Will was relieved to see Mr Landon.

"What is it, Will? What's wrong?"

"Quick Mr Landon, go to Ricky." Then he whispered as the man caught up to him, "The police are arresting him."

Landon raced down the stairs. Will marveling at the speed the man went. He was very slow and on arrival in the shop found that Mr Landon seemed to have the situation well in hand, just as Will had expected him to. He heard his god say to the policeman, "Come on officer, are there any of the marked cases in this shop?"

"No, sir, I will admit that there ain't. But I must take this man to the station for further questioning, for he must have been conspiring with these known felons."

"No," burst out Ricky. He turned to John Landon. "No, I didn't know they weren't straight. Really I didn't. You'll believe me, won't you Mr Landon?"

"Yes, I do, son," replied John, and addressing the policeman he asked, "Have you found any stolen goods on the premises, officer?"

"No, sir, I haven't. We knew that these fellows were stealing from the markets and so we marked some boxes and they are all there on that wagon. But that doesn't mean he wasn't consorting with known criminals."

"Are they known criminals, officer? If they are then I have been associating with them, for until recently I was employing Gosling. I am afraid you will agree that there is no evidence that this lad has bought anything suspect. You honestly haven't, have you, Ricky?"

"No, sir, and I never would. I stand by my honesty," pledged Ricky.

"And I guarantee it, too, officer. I really cannot see that you have any need to question this lad any further."

Ricky stood looking first at his mentor and then at the policeman, listening to what was said and he breathed a sigh of relief when he heard the officer agree that he would not proceed further in the matter and turned to say, "Let this be a lesson to you, my lad.

Buy your stuff from recognised dealers and don't go through any back doors or you'll get yourself in more trouble. I'll be watching you and if there's any more nonsense you'll hear from me."

"Thank you, officer, I assure you I never intended to do any wrong and as you say it has been a lesson to me." Ricky looked sheepish.

After the police left taking George, Gosling and all their goods, John Landon looked at Will and asked, "Can you make tea, Will?"

"Yes, Mr Landon, I can."

"Well run off and make some, then could you look after the shop while Ricky tells me how he got mixed up with these fellows?"

"Sure, I can." Turning to Ricky he said, "I telled yer," with a big grin.

Ricky ruffled his hair, "You did, too, Skeeter. You did warn me, didn't you? I'll listen next time."

Over a cup of tea John Landon heard parts of the story, but Will piped up and said, "You tell Mr Landon about that nasty Summerland man, Rick."

"Summerland? What's he got to do with it? Tell me lad."

"All right," said Ricky. "But Will, you'd better watch the shop."

"I'm going, I'm going, but mind you tell him all about it."

"Come on Ricky, what is it that I have to hear?"

Ricky reluctantly told of the reception he had had from the head clerk and how distressed he had been about it and how he had agreed to buy from Gosling when the man had come with his easy offer. "It didn't occur to me that Gosling was crooked, Mr Landon. I thought that if he worked for you he must be all right."

"Yes, I am sorry about that Ricky, but we had to sack him because we didn't trust him. We found him to be a very slippery customer. I am surprised at Summerland, though. I thought he had more sense. I will certainly give him the edge of my tongue."

"Sir, I don't want to get him in to trouble. He apparently thought I was just a nuisance to you and he was getting rid of me for you."

"Well, you leave that to me. When I give orders I expect them to be carried out. Now, what are you going to do about stock, today? Can you go back to your old associates and buy from them?"

"Yes, I can do that. I'm good friends with one particular man. As a matter of fact I didn't like leaving Charlie, but these fellows offered such a good price and they delivered to my door. Perhaps I'll have to buy my own horse and cart for cartage costs a lot."

"Yes, I am sure that it won't be long before you will have to do that, but in the meantime, as you are buying so much more stock now you should be able to find a carter who will deliver at a reasonable price."

"It's being so young that's the trouble, Mr Landon. They all want to take advantage of me, but I'll get the better of them, I will. And I'll never get into strife like than any more, I assure you."

"I know that, lad. Off you go and sort things out. I'll have to go back. My people will be wondering where I disappeared to." He chuckled. "That young Will certainly is quite something. They wouldn't listen to him when he asked for me, so do you know what he did? He just stood there and yelled for me. It was most effective."

"Golly, did he do that? Gee, I am sorry, sir."

"Think nothing of it, Ricky. I am sure my daughter will like to hear about Will's effort, when I tell her tonight."

"Miss Amabel, sir? You won't tell her about what happened, will you, sir?"

"Well, some of it. Especially about Will. She is always interested in what you boys do. She remembers you got hurt on her behalf, lad." Looking intently at the boy he added, "And so do I."

On returning to the office John Landon walked to Summerland's desk and said, "Come to my office."

The head clerk followed into the glass office and carefully closed the door. John Landon spent the next few minutes telling Summerland just what he thought of servants who did not do as they were asked. He had raised his voice so that everyone could hear what was occurring and Summerland felt smaller and smaller, every now and then trying to get a word in to excuse himself. John Landon finished by saying, "I don't need to tell you why I am interested in those boys, that is none of your business. But if any of them receive anything but complete courtesy from any of my staff the person responsible will be sacked. You can tell them that."

Judging by the complete silence from the outer office Summerland knew he would not have to pass that word around, he knew that they had heard it. At the same time he wondered why the boss was so interested in a trio of stray boys.

Summerland valued his excellent job and decided that the best way to get back into the boss' good graces was to apologize to Ricky for the treatment he had meted out to him. He found that too hard a pill to swallow, but decided that perhaps he could try to quietly make up for it in some way without losing too much face. So Ricky was surprised when he came in to the shop one day and made a half-hearted offer of friendship. Ricky was wary but realised that the man was trying to get out of a sticky situation so without a show of enthusiasm replied in kind. After a few encounters they both lowered their defenses and Ricky at last found the helpful man he had expected to find when he first made contact with him.

In the meantime Ricky had come to an arrangement with his old wholesaler, Charlie, who after chaffing him about being taken for a sucker was able to put him on to a carter who would charge reasonable prices and deliver when it suited Ricky. So the business thrived and grew to such an extent that Ricky could look into the future and see that he would one day have to employ helpers and he was already making plans for extensions.

So life moved on apace. Tad was now installed as office boy at the news office, not liking the change, for he was ever an outside person always wanting to know what was happening in the town he knew so well, but with a knowing eye to the future he was content to work hard and wait for the opportunity he knew would come. He was saving a small amount each week and depositing it meticulously, each pay day, in the bank. Will called this his "horse money", for when the great day came that Tad would be a full blown reporter, he wanted to have enough money to buy a horse so that he could ride faster to and from his assignments.

Mr Landon had learned his lesson. He now kept the boys in sight at all times, not that they knew that for he respected Ricky's need to keep his independence, but from afar he watched over them. He saw the business grow and noted that Ricky had added to his stock and also to the variety of his stock, he was now not a fruiterer alone but had gone into such a variety that one could call his shop now a general store. Many a time, Landon chuckled over the appearance of a new line. Over some, shaking his head knowing that they wouldn't sell, and watching them disappear from the shelves never to appear again. And others, adding quality to the place and therefore enhancing the shop. There was now a continual stream of customers and Landon stood by, sharing his thoughts with Summerland, who had now become quite an ally of Ricky's, waiting to see the next move from the up and coming lad.

Landon did visit openly at times. Usually at closing time when he was on his way home, sometimes buying flowers for his wife. He used the excuse of having a cup of tea with the boys while seeing what progress Will was making with his drawings. He had become very interested in the youngest boy and could see his potential. He had not really taken much notice of Will's interest until the day he found Will alone in the kitchen and wanting to speak with Ricky, who had slipped out for a time, he got chatting to the boy and discovered what he thought could be a mine of talent.

He asked Will if he was still intending to be an artist. Will's face lit up in a way that surprised the man. This small lad, although he must be about 14 now, thought John Landon, seemed to glow. He looked at Will while the boy showed him some of his work, and saw a slight lad with a very pale skin and dark straggly hair. He looked very frail, and he was, according to what Ricky had indicated. He knew that Ricky and Tad took great care of him and would not allow him out in cold or wet weather. Will limped badly as he had a twisted foot, or something of the sort, so he knew that Will found it difficult to walk any distance.

Landon was thinking all these things and only half listening to what the boy was saying, he missed looking with any great interest at one of the several folders that the boy had, but as Will took out one labelled "Church", he focused on what Will said. Inside this folder were heads, noses, eyebrows, eyes, ears, mouths and other bits of the human face and then there were faces, full heads, hats, bonnets, and all sorts of things that immediately took the eye.

"What are these, Will?" he asked eagerly. "Did you do all of these? Where did you see such people?"

"In church," answered Will nonchalantly.

"Do you go to church?" the amazed man asked with a smile.

"Oh, yes," Will replied. "You see as soon as we moved here and were able to get some better clothes Ricky said we had to go to church. He is great on church, is Ricky."

"I didn't know that," said Landon wonderingly. Thinking with appreciation of the little dead woman who had had such an influence on these boys. "Do you like going to church, Will?"

"Oh yes," he said honestly, "there are such interesting people, and I can get to draw them because they sit so still. The trouble is that Ricky won't let us sit in different places each week and so I don't get to do all the ones I want to."

"Where do you go, Will? Actually I think I can tell you. St James, isn't it?"

"Yes, sir, St James. But how do you know?"

"I don't think there would be more than one nose like Macgillicuddy's in Sydney."

"Yes, it is a good one isn't it?" They both laughed over a sketch of a man's head that was decorated by the biggest and most bulbous nose that one could ever find on a human being.

"Do you like the Chaplain's sermons, Will?"

The boy looked up and he flushed, took a deep breath and said in a rather muffled voice, "Well, I reckon I miss a lot, Mr Landon, 'cos I am so busy drawing that I forget to listen. Ricky gets mad at me."

"I am surprised he lets you draw. You shouldn't, you know."

Will looked more sheepish than ever.

"A bone of contention, is it, Will?"

"I don't know what a bone ... what did you call it, sir?"

"I called it a bone of contention. That means that he has one idea and you won't move from yours."

"Yes, that's it. A bone of con ... conten ..."

"A bone of contention." John Landon made sure he spoke to Ricky about Will. Up until now he hadn't given much thought to

Will's welfare. He just accepted the fact that Ricky and Tad looked after him and was their responsibility. Will had suddenly become a person in the man's eyes. He waited until the day that Ricky was due to pay his rent and told the clerk on the front desk that he wished to see the lad when he came. As Ricky was extremely punctual he knew when to expect him and was waiting .

After a few preliminaries he said, "Ricky, I feel as though I am only getting to know young Will. What is to become of him. Tell me your thoughts."

"I am glad to have the opportunity to speak of him Mr Landon, for Tad and I are rather worried about him."

"How old is he? And all of you for that matter?"

"Will is 14, Tad is nearly 16 and I am nearly 19, sir. We are getting old," he said with a grin.

"You are indeed."

"At least I know how old I am but the others don't really know for no-one ever told them when their birthdays were, but that's what we have worked out."

"And I hear that you are all called English?"

"Yes. That was Tad's idea originally, for he didn't really know what his name was. Will, too, made such a mull of working out what his name was that Tad thought it would be a good idea if they both used my name. It makes us feel like brothers."

"What is Tad's name, Ricky, is it Thaddeus?"

"He doesn't know." Ricky laughed. "I tell him it is Tadpole, but we all decided that it should be Thaddeus. It sounds good, don't you think?"

"Yes, I do. Now, back to Will. You've made a good job of him Ricky. He speaks well and seems quite bright. Can he get any sort of work, do you think?"

"We hoped he could be a quick sketch artist like Mr Fraser at the newspaper office. But Will wouldn't be able to keep up the pace, sir. He can't hurry or go far and so he couldn't rush out on assignments like Tad does. I find it's a bit of a worry. I would like him to be independent but I can't see how. I know it worries him, too, Mr Landon, because he is such a willing little bloke, he helps me a lot. He can't stand for long in the shop though, so I try to get him to do other things, so he feels useful. He writes a very good hand so I use him to copy letters and accounts. He likes doing that. `He is all right if he can take his time and rest between jobs, but he could never keep up with anyone else."

"What about his art work. Do you think he could develop that?"

"He just loves it. I have hoped that I could get him real lessons. I'd have liked him to go to school, too, but he wouldn't have stood the bullies, sir."

"Quite a responsibility, eh, lad?"

"Yes, sir, it is."

"Would you let me help, Ricky? I would like to think about it and see what I could do. But if I do think of anything, would you let me help?"

"Yes, sir." Ricky smiled. "I know you think I'm pig-headed, but where Will is concerned I would be glad of your help, for I don't know what to do."

"I can see that school wouldn't help. In any case I daresay he wouldn't fit in with school children, with the life he has led. Incidentally, I think he is quite bright."

"Yes, Tad is a wonderful teacher. He makes Will sit down and do all sorts of work, but even Tad is limited. I would like to get someone to help both the boys, and me as well, but I don't know anyone who could help. I had thought of getting someone to come in a few hours a day to give him lessons."

"Leave it with me, Ricky."

But John Landon didn't have to find a teacher for Will. One appeared in the shop. Or at least, he didn't just appear, for Ricky knew Mr Fishbon, who called in at the shop regularly for supplies. He knew Mr Fishbon was married and lived not too far away. The old man seemed always to have enough money, so Ricky had often wondered why the man of the house shopped and not left it to a servant. One day Mr Fishbon explained.

Geoffrey Fishbon had been a well-known teacher at a famous English boy's school and when the Kings School started in Parramatta he was asked to join the staff. So he and Mrs Fishbon agreed to come with great happiness, for their son wished to emigrate, too, and become a landowner. They all came together, Mr and Mrs Fishbon, their son Anthony, his wife and three children. Anthony had bought a beautiful property on the Hawkesbury and was prospering very well indeed, his two sons being educated at the Kings School, where Mr Fishbon was a master. It was a happy situation for all concerned until Mr Fishbon fell and broke his leg. He was never able again to resume his teaching for his leg did not heal well and he was unable to stand before a class. Anthony was only too pleased to supply his parents with such an adequate income that they would never be in want, and had bought them their present house, in Elizabeth Street, and the older couple settled down to a happy retirement. But even though Mrs Fishbon was completely busy with her household matters and a certain enjoyment in a little social life, her husband found that time hung heavily on his hands. He missed the liveliness of the pupils he had loved. He took on the job of shopping for the household so he could keep in contact with 'people'.

He had liked and admired Ricky from the start, had always taken an interest in the boy's progress. He hadn't spoken to Ricky very much but being a student of human nature he was able to sum up the situation without much prompting. Given the opening, Ricky one day found himself telling the tale of his concern for Will to this very good listener. He was surprised to find that the man was a teacher and one who was more than willing to take on the lad. In fact it pleased Mr Fishbon so much that he almost danced from the shop. He had made Will's acquaintance on the occasions when he was in the shop and had discovered that he was a lad of some potential.

Will on the other hand was not all that pleased when he heard the news, but being of sound good sense, it was not hard to talk him into accepting this new experience that his mentor had arranged for him.

Soon Mr Fishbon seemed to be part of the family. Will learned to respect his new teacher, for Mr Fishbon was one of those men who delighted in broadening a youthful mind, and Will's was

61

like one he had never come across before. He was so ignorant of some things of life, but very far advanced and mature for his age in others. At times it even seemed as though Will was teaching the teacher. It was not long before Mr Fishbon exceeded his duties by sometimes spending an evening with the boys and discussing things like literature and history. He delighted in their passion to learn, finding that each had different skills and were sincere in their need to develop those.

John Landon was very pleased that Mr Fishbon had come into the boys' lives for he knew the man slightly, better knowing his son, who was a well thought of pastoralist.

CHAPTER 6: *Life Skills and Finding Tom*

It was not long before Mrs Fishbon decided to come in to the boys' lives. Her husband was forever speaking about these pupils of his who were so different and so she accompanied him on one of his shopping excursions to meet them. On that occasion she met Ricky and Will, for Tad, of course, was away at his job. She liked what she saw and suggested to her husband that they invite the boys to dinner, pointing out that a little social polish would do the boys a great deal of good.

"But, my dear," Mr Fishbon replied, "I cannot see those fellows enjoying an evening being polite to two old fogies like us."

"Precisely, Mr Fishbon. I am surprised that you cannot see that those young men are going to make a mark on this town and will need some social graces before long and who better to teach them, but you and me." Mrs Fishbon nodded to emphasize her remark.

"Yes," mused her husband, "you are quite right, my dear. I must admit I did not think of that. Yes, by all means let us have them to dinner. But at first let it be a simple affair, nothing to frighten them off, and then put the proposition to them that they can look to us for some polish."

"But we won't put it like that," said his wife sagely. "No, we must not. We must be very diplomatic. Geoffrey, it will be such fun. I can think of all the things we can teach them. I know they will learn easily, from what you tell me."

"Yes, indeed. They pick things up very quickly and will not need telling twice."

When Mr Fishbon suggested that the boys dine with them, Ricky and Will were at first rather non-plussed, but Mr Fishbon used the diplomacy suggested by his wife and the boys found themselves agreeing to attend on the stated date. At first Tad was very reluctant to attend, but on thinking it over he, too, decided to accompany his friends.

The first problem appeared when they started to dress for the night out. Tad was all right for Ricky made sure he was always dressed well enough for his job, but Ricky had always been happy to just get by in enough clothes to work in and one set good enough to be able to slip into the back of the church on Sunday or to see Mr Landon. But this was different. Ricky had remembered the sort of clothes his parents wore when dining out and he felt that his and Will's clothes were not what one should wear to grace a lady's table. However, they wore their best.

Then came the problem of how to transport Will to the Fishbon's house. In the end Ricky decided to call a cab. It was such an adventure for them all, but they were very nervous as well. Will had never been in a cab and sat quite silent throughout the journey. The Fishbon's maid received them at the door, taking their hats and laying them carefully on the hall table, before showing them to the sitting room where Mr and Mrs Fishbon awaited their guests.

"Come in, come in," greeted Mr Fishbon. Turning to his wife he said, "You know Mr Richard English, and his brother William, but allow me to present Mr Thaddeus English." This startled the boys, for they were not used to being addressed so.

Mr Fishbon was a tall man, almost 6 feet, his hair was snowy white and quite abundant. His wife was a plump little lady who knew how to put the boys at their ease. She was wearing a dress of deep plum silk and over her shoulders she wore a cream shawl with a long fringe, best of all she was wearing a wide smile and it seemed right from the start that she intended to make her guests feel comfortable.

She came forward extending a friendly hand and bid them all to sit and take their comfort. The three perched on the very edge of their chairs and looked decidedly uncomfortable, for so far ladies' drawing rooms had not come their way and it was quite terrifying.

Their hostess gave a small chuckle to herself, thinking of the task she had before her. She set about trying to ease their pain and as she was a lady skilled in dealing with bashful and frightened boys, she soon had them, eating out of her hand, so to speak. She offered them some cool refreshing drinks and over these she concentrated on talking small talk to Ricky, whom she knew was the 'father' of the group. Mr Fishbon did not make a great effort to ease the discomfort of the other two boys but was willing to let his wife handle the situation, for he knew of old her wisdom in such matters. She was very experienced in dealing with the boys whom he had found difficult, when he was a house master in England, and he knew she would not find these Australian boys any different.

Dinner was a quiet meal served in a small room with a fairly small table. The boys did not know it but this room was Mrs Fishbon's sewing room. She had thought that the formal dining room would be a little too much for her raw recruits. She planned well. She found that Ricky had taught the others well, for when something cropped up that the boys didn't know about, such as, which were the fish knives, they just waited, hardly breathing, until they could see what their host and hostess did, then they quietly followed.

They retired to the sitting room again after dinner and Mrs Fishbon surprised her husband by coming out in the open with her plans.

"Richard," she addressed Ricky, "I know and understand that you are ardent in your desire for education, not only for Will but for Thaddeus and yourself as well."

"Yes, ma'am, I am, and Mr Fishbon is helping us very much indeed. We are very grateful, aren't we?" he asked Tad and Will. They agreed.

"Yes, well, that's all very well, but you should have your education rounded off. Did you know that?"

"I am sorry. I don't quite understand." Ricky replied wondering.

"Richard, you are going to be one of the leading business men of this colony. I gather that Thaddeus will become a leading journalist and that Mr Hughes will have to watch his position one of these days. And I hear that William is a rising artist and with the right tuition he will be also someone of note. Do I surmise correctly."

The three boys had chuckled loudly over her summing up of their capabilities, this seemed to break the tension that had accompanied their visit. She went on, "To be successful you need more than academic skills, native wit and ambition. You need a certain amount of social skills and I am here to provide it."

"But Mrs Fishbon, but what do you mean? Have we done anything wrong?" blustered Ricky. Tad and Will looked quite embarrassed.

"No, you have done nothing wrong, and I am surprised you haven't." said their hostess. "But you will find yourselves in much more difficult situations that this. Do explain to them Geoffrey."

Now Mr Fishbon took over, explaining to them how pleased and happy they were that the boys were able to handle themselves with the skill that they had shown that evening, but offered the services of his wife and himself to teach them all the nicer points of etiquette, to learn not only how to be guests but also to be hosts, to dress well, to talk social small talk and all the other things that one needs when one 'goes up in the world'. At first Tad and Ricky got a bit hot under the collar about it. Will by this time lad lost interest in the conversation, so it went on over his head. Before Ricky could speak Mr Fishbon went on in his quiet way and smoothed them down until they could see the reasoning behind it all.

This was the beginning of a new life for the boys. They learned to live in a different world. The Fishbons were wonderful teachers, they were true to their word, they taught them not only to be guests, but also to be hosts, in other words they gave the boys some polish. At times they thought their teachers went a little far, especially when Mrs Fishbon insisted that they learn how to properly set a table, serve food and wine and all the other things that a good servant knew. At the look of dismay on their faces she laughed and said, "A servant is no better than his master. If you want good servants you must know what to expect of them." Tad laughed when he thought of his having a servant.

There followed some evenings which were full of surprises. At first alone with the Fishbons where they took to their lessons quite well. But one evening when they arrived expecting it to be the same medicine as before they were surprised to find some friends of Mr and Mrs Fishbon, who had been invited for dinner. They were a couple, Mr and Mrs Reeves, who were much of an age as their hosts. They gathered that Mr Reeves had been a teacher at The Kings School at the same time as Mr Fishbon. The boys presumed that they had been told of the lessons but were surprised when the Reeves asked how long they had been in the colony and had they attended The Kings School. When answering in the negative to the last question Tad looked a bit bewildered, not knowing how to answer at first. So Ricky took over and said straight out that they were very much of the Sydney scene in that they had had to make their own way in the world and that Mr and Mrs Fishbon were helping them acquire a little town polish. The astounded pair were most impressed and Ricky went on to tell them how they filled their days and what their ambitions were.

The boys remained after the Reeves left for home, waiting to hear the comments of their teachers, for Ricky was rather wondering if he should have told straight out what he did. But he needn't have worried for Mr Fishbon congratulated him on being so forthright, saying, "I am pleased that you told our friends your story, Ricky. I think you handled that very well. I did not tell Mr and Mrs Reeves anything about you. I wanted you to learn how to handle being asked and I thought it would be better to spring it on you."

"Well, sir, it did give me a start, as it did Tad, I could see. I think he thought as I did that I would shuffle past that, then I thought, why shouldn't I say what we did. It is no use telling people we are gentry when we are not. I am not ashamed of us and so I went ahead."

"Yes, I agree," said Mr Fishbon. "Many people have come to this colony and tried to make out that they are other than what they really are. Answer in like manner when asked, and do not be ashamed of what you are, for we are very proud of what you have achieved, and you should be too."

From then on the boys did not know who would be at their hosts home when they dined, and they very rarely had to explain who they were or what they did, for Sydney was full of people whose lifestyles had changed, some for the better and some not. Transportation had stopped in 1841 and so there were no new convicts in the colony, but there were many folk who had come as convicts and were only too pleased not to be asked their background. But mostly the guests they met were families who had young people much their age. So their circle of acquaintances grew.

Will was the least interested in all of this than the other boys, as his ambitions were not of the social kind. Not that Ricky or Tad had social inclinations either, but they did realise the worth of what Mr and Mrs Fishbon were teaching them. Will always thought a lot of Mr Fishbon for he had the knack of making lessons very interesting and always seemed to be able to use examples for his lessons that brought in things which he knew Will was particularly keen about. But as for all that Mrs Fishbon said, well, he agreed to go along with it because Tad and Ricky wanted to, but all changed when he found that Mrs Fishbon had at one time produced some very passable water colour sketches.

Mr Fishbon showed him these one evening when he could see that Will was particularly bored with proceedings. The boy's delight knew no bounds. "Can you still paint like that, Mrs Fishbon?" he anxiously asked.

"Yes, dear," she said, "I still do paint at times. Would you like me to teach you the little I know?"

"Oh, yes, please," said Will, "I just dream of colour. I do want to paint."

"Well, you shall. Mind, I'm not much good and I cannot draw as well as you, but I can teach you the technique and you will soon pass me in skill."

Will was in seventh heaven, and before he left that night was able to pin his hostess down to making a firm appointment to come during the daytime and have his first lesson.

Transport was always a worry. Ricky was coming to the conclusion that they would soon have to invest in something that would get them from one place to another. Left to the two older boys, this would not be a worry, but getting Will around the town was quite a difficulty. There were horse drawn buses but they were far too difficult for Will to cope with. However Mr Fishbon suggested that he take Will home with him after some of the academic lessons and send him home by cab when his painting lessons were over.

John Landon was most interested in his young friends' progress. He often caught up on their welfare from Mr Fishbon and Mr Hughes of the newspaper. He was concerned that Will was not able to take his painting along quicker than he was and so was pleased when Mrs Fishbon agreed to teach what she knew of the art.

In the meantime, Ricky's business was flourishing. It was past being called a shop and was in the category of being a store, having a greater variety of goods. He had put on two staff, a lad called Jackie and a man who was a clerk as well as shop assistant. This allowed Ricky to spend more time buying and getting around the town to learn ideas of how to enhance his business. He had his eye on the area beside his own shop, the part that Landon's used as a sort of storeroom. He knew it was not essential to Mr Landon's business for he had enough store space in his other building. So one day while paying his rent he asked if he could have an appointment to see Mr Landon.

Mr Landon noted with pleasure that Ricky was dressed in very neat, well cut clothes that showed the mark of an up and coming business man. He bade Ricky sit and then wanted all the news of the boys' doings. Then he asked how the business was progressing. Ricky was rather reluctant about wanting to take over more of the man's accommodation, but knew that he must expand and so put his case.

"I am very pleased that you are doing so well, Ricky. How do you aim to use the other shop?"

"Well, sir, I have a lot of ideas, but at first I would like to buy materials from you and sell them there. I thought of having seamstresses to make them up there and all sorts of haberdashery lines and various other things that seem to interest the ladies. I have been looking in the other shops and looking at magazines that I have had from England and I think I can give the customers what they want."

"A very good idea, Ricky. I have often toyed with the idea of going into the retail business myself, but have no real inclination for it. Let us discuss it more."

They did this at great length to their mutual satisfaction. Then John Landon asked how Will was developing his painting skills.

Ricky was amused at this, knowing that they had not told him about Will's painting lessons, he knew that Mr Landon must surely be keeping a weather eye on them all.

"Will loves his lessons, but he is certain that water colour is not his way of painting. He is mad keen to start in oils, sir, and I am a bit dubious about how to go about that. But for all that he is producing some very good paintings."

"I think we have a true artist there, Ricky. Does he draw or paint all the time? Does he do anything else?"

"Yes, sir, he does. He helps me a bit in the shop, but now that I have help he is very keen to go out and about to draw and paint as soon as he does his housework. He still insists on doing that, and I must admit I am glad. He keeps the place pretty clean, too."

"He's a good lad. What does he do when he goes out? He can't walk far, can he?"

"I wish you would call in, Mr Landon and see some of the painting and drawings he is doing. I think they are really something. Can you come sometime, sir?"

"Yes, I'll call in this afternoon, if that's all right."

Will was out when Landon called at the shop. Nodding to Jackie and George Parker the senior assistant, he went through to the residence, where Ricky was making afternoon tea. He was surprised to see that Ricky had even put a cloth on the table and set out some decent cups and saucers. He started to say something and changed his mind, being caught open-mouthed as Ricky looked up at him.

Ricky laughed and said, "We promised Mrs Fishbon that we would never let our standards down and always make a point of doing things correctly. She's a hard task master, Mr Landon. If we find we are doing something she says we are not to, we get a guilty conscience. Would you care for a cup, sir?"

"Yes, my boy, I would, thank you. You seemed to have fallen on your feet with the Fishbons, Ricky. I was thinking of asking him to help you for I know him slightly, but you got in before me. Mrs Fishbon takes a hand, too, I take it."

"Yes, she has us to dinner one night each week, usually Saturday, and we have to turn out in proper style. She is giving us a little polish, as she calls it, and introducing us to various people. She's rather wonderful, Mr Landon, we all like her very much," he added wistfully.

"You are very fortunate, lad, to have such a pair of teachers. I feel that you will go a long way in your career and from what Hughes tells me of Tad, he will too, and a little town polish will stand you in stead as you get older."

"I know and appreciate it. Will was not very interested in it all until he found that Mrs Fishbon could paint. Now he thinks the world of her and will do anything she wants him too."

"Where is he now?"

"He has taken to going along the lanes and streets near here and drawing all he sees. At the moment he is in next door at your stables drawing the horses as they come in. Mrs Fishbon wanted to show him how to paint trees, but he was not interested. He mainly does people and town streets and houses and people working, look I'll show you."

Ricky took out some paintings from Will's large folios and put them up one at a time on the easel that was standing against the wall near Will's desk. John Landon was amazed at the quality of them. He found it very hard to realise that a stripling of a boy did them. Will obviously loved painting heads and he had done quite a variety of them. He just didn't draw the features, he seemed to get right into his models and bring out their character. Then Ricky put up some of his street and working people drawings. His line was very strong and fluid, he caught the movement and life of the people and the streets around him. Then finally Ricky showed his water colours and John immediately saw what Will wanted to do. The water colour was too weak for his strong subjects. He could see what some of them would be in heavy, strong oils. They were magnificent. He liked several of the local smithy. The whole painting was dark, as dark as one could get with water colour, the light coming from the forge shone on the sweaty skin of the smith.

John Landon felt breathless as he gazed in, almost, awe. "Ricky, he must be taught properly. He must! And we must set him up in a place where he can be free to do what he wants."

"I agree, sir, but don't know where to start."

"Well, I do. I hear that Patrick Thomas is taking pupils and I will go and see if he will take Will. Thomas is a portraitist but does other things and I am sure he will help Will a great deal. What do you think?"

"That would really be something, sir. But I wonder whether I could afford that. Would he charge much, Mr Landon?" asked Ricky anxiously.

"That is my responsibility, Ricky. I told you I would see to Will." As Ricky was about to protest he went on. "I can see that Will has amazing potential and he will need a sponsor. I will be very glad to take that on. But he will need somewhere to spread his wings. I wonder where."

"Well, I was going to suggest that he has one of the rooms behind the new shop, Mr Landon. If the door through here from the kitchen was opened up, I think one of the rooms like these would do fine. I think it would be suitable, at least until he is older and can get a place of his own. What do you think?"

"Yes, it may do. We'll wait until it is cleaned up, then we can see."

Ricky thanked him and added. "Mr Landon there is another thing that worries me, too. I would like you to tell me where we could get some experience driving and riding, please. Which stables should we go to? You see Will is very restricted and I feel he should be able to be more mobile. I would like to get a gig or sulky or something so he could move around a bit. In any case we all need to be able to move more freely. We should ride, too. Tad especially needs to when he gets his new job as reporter, which will be soon. He does ride some of the horses at the newspaper office, but I am sure he should be taught properly. So should I really."

"My dear boy, I am so sorry, I should have thought of it before. Ward, the head groom at our factory stables is just the man."

"Oh, no, Mr Landon. I didn't mean that. I wasn't asking for that."

"I know you were not, Ricky. But nevertheless I will speak to Ward. He will teach each of you to ride and drive. There is no better teacher, I'll speak to him in the morning. You go and see him tomorrow and make the arrangements."

Things moved quickly, then. The storeroom next door was cleaned out and the new shop set up. The double door dividing Ricky's shop and the new one was opened, as well as the ones that divided the living quarters. They found there was a very reasonable room for Will to use as a studio, and he was delighted. Another room was turned into an office for Ricky. At the same time all this was going on Ward taught them all to drive and ride. Later when the time came he was able to advise them about purchasing a decent horse and a sulky and a small horse for riding, which Tad used. So they set up their stables and used their newly learned skills, which under Ward's tutelage, included the grooming and feeding of their stock.

It was not long after this that Ricky was driving Will through town when he pulled up suddenly calling to a stooped figure outside a public house. The old man looked up at the voice and came to the sulky.

"Why it's young Ricky come up in the world."

"Tom, what are you doing here. I've never seen you anyway but at the stables, and you were there last time I called."

"They give me the push, matie. A couple o' munce back. They says I wus too old, so I'm aht on the street like yer were. They got a young'n there in my job nah."

"Well, Tom, you just get up here, we'll take you home with us. We'll look after him, won't we, Will? Oh, Tom, this is Will." Will looked a little non-plussed at this but moved over as he was bidden.

Tom objected though, saying. "Yer've no call to take on the likes o' me, matie. I kin manage."

"Tom, you gave me shelter when I needed it badly and I am not going to refuse you. You just come on up and we'll take you home."

"Well, matie, I'll come with you but I won't stay wiv yer. I ain't going to live on yer."

"I'll tell you what, Tom. We've got a stable and two horses. We could make you comfortable there in the stable and you could have that."

"A stable, eh?" said the old man wistfully. "Would yer do thet, matie? I miss me 'orses."

"You come and see, Tom. You needn't stay if you don't want to." Ricky was sad to see his old friend so wobbly on his legs as he got into the vehicle. "When did you eat last, Tom?" he asked.

"A while back, matie," came the reluctant reply.

"You'll get a good meal tonight, Tom. Will here is a great cook."

So another person joined the family. Will and Tad were quite dubious about taking him in, but Ricky had known that Tom wouldn't live in the house, for he had never lived anywhere but stables or the street. The boys settled him into the quarters at the stables and they dubbed him their groom. He ate with the boys but slept out with the horses and thought life was grand. He was able to cut the wood and do all sorts of jobs when his strength returned but spent most of his time keeping the sulky, and the gear and of course the horses in tip-top condition.

John Landon had great pleasure in making himself responsible for Will. When the new shop was painted in the same cream colour of the other shop, he insisted that Will's studio be painted white so that there could be as much light as possible in there. He had picture rails put all round the room on two levels so that Will would have plenty of hanging space for his pictures. Will watched the proceeding with great interest and on the day he entered his new domain, finished and ready, he found two easels, a palette, a wonderful box of oil colours, canvas and stretchers, all the brushes he would ever need, knives, and palette knives and the other things a budding artist desires, like turpentine, varnish for finishes and even a few frames to hold against the finished product to get an idea of what they would be like. There were small tables, a few chairs and last of all a sofa to rest on when he wanted to sit and think. All he needed now was a teacher to tell him how to mix his paints and lay them on as thickly as he wanted to do. He found he could not keep his fingers off all his new treasures and was most anxious to begin his lessons.

Patrick Thomas, the artist who was to teach Will his art, came as a rude shock to Will. He came home after his first lesson saying that he didn't know whether it would be worth it for a more insulting, rude man he had never come across.

"If I hadn't seen some of his work while Mr Landon was talking to him, I wouldn't go back. But his paintings are really wonderful, so I suppose I'll have to put up with him. If I end up by painting like him, I daresay it will be worth it."

"What are his paintings like, Will?" asked Ricky.

"Just grand," answer Will. "I don't think I could explain, but I will show you, you just wait. I can see that he will teach me a lot, but I sure will have to take the insults with the lessons."

"Why, what does he say?"

"Well, he calls me 'limpy', for a start. He tells me I am not worth teaching and he said I am just a runt that no-one wants, and if he wasn't being paid for it he wouldn't give me house room."

"I wouldn't take that from anyone, Will. Would you like me to deal with him?" asked Tad, ready to go to his brother's defense.

Will laughed. "No, Tad, I'll fight my battles my own way. In any case there are two more learning from him, one told me that he is often like that and not to take any notice of him. They told me he is a very good teacher and to let it just go over my head, and I will."

"Well you tell us if you can't take it, Will," said Ricky. "I won't have you put up with too much."

They heard little about what Will had to take, but they saw plenty of the results of the lessons with Patrick Thomas. He became totally immersed in his painting. At times he even forgot to do his share of the housework. But what he produced was simply grand.

One of the first series he did was those of the smithy that Mr Landon liked so much. John's remark about how much better they would be in oils was quite correct, the resultant four paintings were the best the young man had done up to that time. One day after they had dried and were framed, Will asked Ricky to help take them up to John Landon.

On being invited into the man's office they set them up for him to see. The first one was, as they all were, quite dark but the light on the sweaty shoulders of the smith drew your eyes to that. The smith was standing at the anvil and was raising his hammer to strike a red-hot bar. The second one showed the smith at the forge. Beside him was his striker. The light shone on their faces and they looked down on the dull embers. The next showed the smith's boy pumping up the bellows to burn the coke at the forge. Sparks were showing up from the glow and the light shone on the boy's face. The last one showed the smith shoeing a horse. He had just placed a hot iron shoe onto the horse's hoof, the smoke coming off where the hot iron touched. The smith's bare back glistened in the filtering sunlight and the hind quarters of the big roan horse just showed in the sun through the door. The contrast of the sun on the horse, the filtered sun on the smith and the glow of the forge in the background was beautifully achieved.

All John Landon could say was, "Oh, Will."

Will smiled and said, "That's the first installment, Mr Landon. I did want you to have my first big works, for you have made them possible. This is my thank you."

"Do you mean I am to keep them, Will? I couldn't take them, lad. You must not give them away."

"Yes, you are to keep them. I painted them for you and they are yours. One day I will do much better but they are my first real and I want you to have them."

CHAPTER 7: *Ricky's Business and Bushrangers*

Ricky was kept so very busy with the expansion of his business and Will was taken up with his painting, that Tad wondered where his lovely long companionable evenings had got to. Ricky always seemed to have his head in an account book and Will doing his 'homework' in his studio, that Tad found it difficult to have a conversation with his brothers. He had not been given the promotion he longed for and was rather despondent about it. Ricky was so busy with his own things that he didn't realise the strain he was putting on the boy. Tad sometimes tried to get a conversation going with Ricky, but he received only half answers, and so began to be rather tetchy with the older boy.

It came home to Ricky when Tad burst into the kitchen in great excitement, one evening, and announced that he was heading for the gold fields. Ricky stood up, the books he was studying sliding to the floor, and said, "What?"

Tad suddenly realised what Ricky thought and with a grin strung him along for a while. "Well, why not?" said Tad, "no-one ever notices that I am around anymore. I will go off and seek my fortune."

Old Tom was sitting by the stove smoking his rotten old pipe, which he removed from his mouth and turned to look at Tad. The gleam in his eyes and the faint twitching of the boy's mouth gave him away and so, content, he turned back to the warmth of the stove.

Ricky was quite conscious that gold had been found in the country around Bathurst, indeed that had been very good for business; he really wasn't interested on a personal level, not really believing half the stories that came out of the fields. But for Tad to entertain the idea of giving up all his ambitions, well … he just couldn't take it in. It was unbelievable! He stood there, grabbing at his books, half of which were on the floor at his feet and stared at Tad. "You can't," he said.

By this Tad realised that he had gone far enough. He was shocked at Ricky's face. Ricky was deeply shaken and quite a nasty colour. Tad was sorry that he had been so precipitant and went over to his friend, putting a hand on his sleeve.

"It's all right, Rick. I'm not going to make my fortune. You know I wouldn't be so silly. I am going with Mr Handley and Mr Fraser, we've been sent up to get some stories of the diggings. It's my first big chance."

Ricky breathed a big sigh of relief. "Don't do that again, you rotter," he said with a grin. "You had me on there for a while. Tell me about it."

"Did you really think I would leave my job, Rick? I wouldn't, you know. I am not stupid."

"Tad, old fellow, there are more experienced men than you who have dropped everything and gone looking for their fortune. I must admit you scared me for a while, but I honestly could not see you down a dirty hole digging all your life. Any way tell me about what you are going to do."

"Mr Hughes called us in and asked if we would like to go. Mr Handley to do the stories and Mr Fraser to do some sketches, and me to learn all I can from Mr Handley. We are to go up by coach on Monday. I have to be ready packed and be at the coach depot at 7 on Monday morning."

"I daresay you'll need some rough clothes and boots. Let's go into the store and see what we can find for you."

Tad chatted away merrily while they went through the dungarees, shirts, and socks, boots and all the other gear that Ricky had recently been selling to the prospectors. Ricky making him try on this and that. Then he realised that Ricky was piling things on to him and said, "Hey! Stop! I'm only going for a week and I won't be digging. I won't need all these."

"Maybe you won't, Tad, but if what I hear is true and you run into some wet weather, you'll be going through lots of mud and you'll need heavy boots, especially if you are going out on the field talking to miners. It seems they almost live in mud. And ... if it is so wet, you'll want a change of clothes. I don't think it will be the place for wearing your best."

"But we'll be staying in a hotel, I believe," said the ignorant Tad.

"From what I hear any country hotel out west is bad enough, but anything you will find on the diggings will be pretty horrible," Ricky assured him.

Tad opened his eyes and said, "Will it? Gee I thought it would be good to stay in a hotel, I was thinking of one like the Soldier's Arms up the street."

"Not a hope, matie, as Tom would say, you'll be going out to rough it."

"Oh, well, it will all be an adventure won't it, Rick, and an experience that I can chalk up?"

"Yes, you keep your eyes open and your mouth shut and learn all you can, and yes, it will be quite an experience. I am happy that you are going with Mr Handley and Mr Fraser, I am sure they will look after you. I must admit, though that I cannot see Mr Fraser out in the bush, he seems to be a real townie."

"But he is only going out to do pictures, I don't suppose he will wander around too much."

Ricky was reluctant to let Tad go on such an adventure on his own. He knew he wasn't really on his own, but couldn't help feeling that Mr Fraser and Mr Handley wouldn't be all that much protection. Tad was so excited, though, he didn't have the heart to dampen his spirits. When they arrived at the coach station they were amazed at the number of men who wished to go to the diggings. The three from the newspaper were all right for they had booked seats, but there were about twenty men, loaded with picks and shovels and all sorts of implements who were demanding to get on the coach and beware anyone who would stop them. Tad and his companions were inside the coach with three others. There was a wild scramble as the driver announced that he would take six on top and no more. The first to get on and find a place could do so, the rest had to stop. There was almost a brawl. But eventually, as the driver yelled that he was going off, those who could grabbed a place and those who couldn't were left behind. As the coach went off down the street, there were still some legs and arms waving in the breeze while trying to get a toe-hold. Ricky could see an arm waving from the inside of the coach and presumed that Tad was waving his farewells.

Ricky missed Tad, thinking of him a great deal, wondering how he was getting on. He hadn't realised how much he depended on him for companionship, and suddenly realised that he had neglected him of late. He was determined he would do something about this when he returned. Will, now, was so immersed in his painting that he didn't seem to need as much companionship as he used to. Every now and then he would appear and want to talk and talk and talk to Ricky and Tom, as though he had been in isolation for months.

Old Tom was usually sitting by the fire each evening. Not that he had to come to the kitchen for that, but he, too, liked the companionship of the busy boys. Ricky had spoiled him, he insisted, for he had had a pot-bellied stove installed for Tom's comfort in his room at the stables. Tom could not believe his luck. But these evenings spent listening to the old man made Ricky feel that he had been very fortunate and could never complain about anything that had happened in his life. Tom was certainly no trouble to anyone, he was so used to living a lone life that he just pottered around and fitted in with what everyone else was doing. He rather felt that Ricky was some sort of god, the way he treated him, and could not do enough for him.

Ricky was surprised how little of Sydney Town Tom knew. Then he realised that there was little he knew, or Will. Tad got around more than they did and was their usual means of finding out interesting tit-bits, but as for the knowing the outlying parts of the town, well, they were very ignorant.

"Tom," he said one night. "I think I'll be very rash and buy a buggy that will take the four of us. Then each weekend we can go exploring. Have you ever seen the Macquarie Light? or the water supply or anything like that?"

"No, matie, I ain't seen much o' the town but right 'ere. I never wus much o' a walker and never 'ad no call to walk very far any ways," the old man said.

"I haven't, either. We must go and see them. What sort of vehicle should we get? Now that Will is using the gig so often I find I need another one anyway. What do you think?"

They discussed this at length and finally decided to ask Ward, Mr Landon's man at the stables next door. As a result there was a new double buggy in the stables and a nice pair of horses that were the pride of old Tom's eyes. He had gone with Ward to buy this turnout and so felt really responsible for it. He was so happy to be working in the place that he had a continual grin on his face. Ricky was a bit concerned that it would be too much for Tom and thought that he would look for a boy to help him.

Tad didn't turn up the day he was expected, and Ricky was quite worried but half way through the next afternoon there was a yell and a 'hoy' and there he was. He was full of his adventures and insisted on sitting Ricky, Tom and Will down to listen to what had happened to him.

"I've had such an adventure, you'd never believe, Ricky," he said, his eyes shining. "We've been held up and shot at by bushrangers, and Mr Handley is hurt and I have to write the story up and everything."

"Now, hold hard, Tad, get your wind and tell us. Is Mr Handley hurt badly?"

"No, not badly, he was shot through the shoulder and we had to leave him with the doctor at Penrith. The doctor said he would be all right. But he can't write and so Mr Hughes told me that I am to write the story up. Isn't that great?" Tad asked.

"Yes, it's great," said Ricky and Will together, "but tell us what happened."

"Well, I'll tell you about the bushrangers first, will I?"

"Yes, don't keep us in suspense."

"Well, you saw how crowded the coach was when we left, Rick. Everyone seemed to want to go to the goldfields but hardly anyone was travelling back in this direction so, not long after leaving Bathurst we had the coach to ourselves. It was much better than going up, which was awful. It made me feel sick. The driver said that all the people on top made it top-heavy and it swayed like mad.

But on the way back, we could spread out a bit and it was more comfortable. Well, just as we got to the bottom of the ranges just near Emu Plains, there was a shot and the coach pulled up. Three men were riding hard at us and leveled guns at the drivers. I must admit, I was scared and Mr Fraser didn't look too happy either, but Mr Handley pulled a pistol from his pocket. Can you believe it? I wouldn't have thought he would own one, let alone shoot with it. He pulled the trigger but it apparently didn't hit anyone, but the bushrangers got mad and shot him. Gee, he bled all over the place."

"What happened then?"

"Well, the bushrangers yelled at us to get down, but Mr Fraser told them that he would have to attend to his friend, and he knelt down and started to fix him up. They told him to hand over his wallet and then fix Mr Handley and he did that. The drivers were sitting on top with their hands up, and the bushrangers could see that they didn't have anything and neither did I, they looked around to see if we were carrying gold and when they didn't find any they just wheeled their horses and went off into the bush. As they were galloping away one of the drivers jumped down and grabbed his gun off the ground and shot towards them. We think he hit one, but they didn't stop. Then Mr Fraser got his bag out and tore up his nightshirt and bandaged Mr Handley up as well as he could. I'd been holding a handkerchief tight over the wound. He lost a lot of blood. We got him fixed up and told the driver to go as fast as he could. We got to Penrith after such a long while, at least it seemed like it and found a doctor there. He has arranged to have him looked after."

"I do hope he is all right. I like Mr Handley," said Will.

"The doctor said he would be, as it hit high and didn't go right through, but we helped the doctor while he pulled the bullet out. I didn't like that, but I stuck it. Poor Mr Fraser couldn't look and had to go out and get sick."

"Good lad," said Ricky.

"Well, someone had to, there was no-one else. Besides," added Tad sheepishly, "I realised that I would have to write the story up and I was so excited that I didn't think much about what the doctor was doing."

"What a mercenary brute you are, Tad," said Ricky.

Tad was full of more stories about the diggings, and how they had to go to Mr Hughes and tell him. Mr Hughes had been most concerned about his reporter and was sending Mrs Handley out in his own coach to look after her husband and bring him home when she could.

The diggings held no lure to Tad. He thought it was a very poor place. When Will asked him if he saw any gold he pulled a tinderbox from his pocket and in a screw of paper he pulled out a small piece of gold as big as a pea.

"Do you know, a man gave it to me. Just after we arrived, there was a terrific fuss, someone had found a pocket of gold and one of the nuggets he found was absolutely huge about as big as man's fist, and lots of little smaller ones. He gave it to me and asked me to write up all about his finding it, and I will. Isn't it great?"

Tad handed it round for his friends to see. Each one took it in his hand and felt it. It was almost smooth and extremely heavy. Will immediately asked what it would buy, but Tad couldn't answer that.

"Do you think I could keep it, Ricky? Or should I sell it and keep the money. I would rather keep it for I don't suppose I will ever have another one."

"Don't you want to go back and dig for some more Tad?" asked Will.

"Not on your life. I reckon that would be beyond everything. Of all the rotten places. I couldn't think of worse. It was so dry and dusty when we got there, it was awful. But after it rained it was worse. Those poor people up there are living in terrible conditions and as far as I could see very, very few of them ever find more than a few specks of gold. No, it's not for me. Gee, I am glad you gave me those rough clothes, Ricky. Poor Mr Handley teetered around in his town shoes and wasn't able to see nearly as much as me. I reckon I'll have some great stories. I'm to go to the office in the morning and start writing it up."

Tad could not stop talking about the diggings, the country, the bush, the coach and all he had seen. The others were quite sure after listening to all his stories that they knew what a gold field looked like and decided that they wouldn't have to 'go bush' to find out. He quietened down a little by the time he had worked hard on his articles and rewrote and rewrote them, finally producing enough by the end of the week to satisfy his demanding editor. Mr Hughes was secretly very pleased with his efforts, but was reluctant to give Tad anything but the barest praise. Mr Fraser had also filled him in as to the great help Tad was in their shooting incident, and had greatly praised him for his coolness and readiness to help in a nasty situation.

When his first article was published, with illustrations by Mr Fraser, Tad felt that his cup was full. He bought six copies of the paper and rushed home when he could to show his friends. His exuberance was infectious. Even Tom caught some of the excitement, though he couldn't read, he admired the pictures and was pleased when Will read the article to him, especially pointing out that it was headed "by Thaddeus English, our special correspondent".

"Matie, I feel real honoured ter know yer. Shake!"

Tad shook the old man's hand and beamed at all and sundry. Mr Landon came down to offer his congratulations, and then Mr Summerhayes. A phaeton drew up at the door and Mr and Mrs Fishbon asked if they too might come in and congratulate their protégé. Altogether it was a day of wonders for Tad.

By the time the whole series had been published, and with very little alteration from the editor, Mr Hughes called Tad in to tell him that he could now consider himself as being on the writing staff permanently. Now his cup was overflowing.

"It's all due to you, Rick," he said that night.

"Nonsense," retorted Ricky. "I couldn't write like that. You did it. It's not my field at all. Look how hard you've worked to get there."

"Yes, but you started me off," Tad said. "If you hadn't taken me under your wing, I wouldn't have got this far. Anyway, thanks, Rick."

After the big series of articles were written, Ricky felt that he could take his family out in their new vehicle. Up until then Tad had not been much interested in it, but now that he had time to think about it it seemed to have a great deal of potential. As they all wished to drive and as no-one could decide, Ricky told Tom to take the reins. The old man grinned and took over. With Tad sitting beside him he asked, "What are you going to call these beauties, matie?"

"Oh, I haven't thought, have you, Rick?" Tad asked turning round to address him.

"No, I suppose we'll have to think up names for them. We are getting quite a stable now, and we must have their names on their loose boxes. Will can do that."

"Oh, can I," said that gentleman. "Well if I have to put their names on their boxes, I'll have to name them. Now. What about Spic and Span?" asked Will.

"Well, not bad, I suppose," said Tad. "What about Rise and Shine or High and Mighty?"

"Terrible," said Will. "For a literary man you've got bad taste. I still like Spic and Span. What do you think Ricky?"

"I think Tom should choose. You look after them, Tom. What do you think?" asked Ricky, knowing that he had to be sage about this decision.

"Well, maties, I like to 'ave a name thet suits a 'orse and as I keep 'em Spic and Span, I reckon thet'll do. After all young Tad, yer named the pony, Lancer, as its yers and Ricky calls the other horse, Brownie, well, I reckon young Will ought ter name these. 'Ow abaht it, matie? Wotcha think?" he asked.

"All right, I agree. Anyway they are spic and span, you do keep them very well, Tom, so I do agree." Looking around he added, "Hey, Tom, where are we going?"

"Well, I reckon'd we'd go dahn to Darlin' 'Arbour and work rarnd ter the Rocks 'n then out ter thet Mrs Macquarie's Chair, which I ain't ever seen, an' hev a look at all thet. I ain't seen much o' this 'ere town and I reckon this is a good enough time ter do it. Wotcha say?"

They all agreed and spent the rest of the day poking in and out of all these things that Tom had said he had never seen. They went down to where the new railway station was being built and wondered what the engines and carriages would look like.

"Mr Handley tells me," said Tad, "that a steam engine is a very big thing, that is even bigger than a big coach. He has seen them in England."

"Yes," said Ricky, "I can remember seeing them, too. I daresay it will cause a great deal of interest when the engines arrive. We'll be able to travel to Parramatta by rail, I believe. In fact, why don't we go down there by ferry next weekend. We could do the journey there and back in a day."

"Wouldn't we get sea-sick, Rick?" asked Will.

"No, stupid, it will be in the harbour and wouldn't be rough. It should be good to do it, what do you think of that, Tom? Would you come?" answered Ricky.

"Yer don' want ter be draggin' me orl round with yer, matie. Yer go orf on yer own. Besides ah bin there." said the old man.

Not wanting to intrude into the man's past but wishing to please him, Ricky asked, "But wouldn't you want to come? We want you, don't we, boys?"

"Yes, sure, Tom. Why don't you come?" Tad said.

"We want you," put in Will.

"Kinda yer," said Tom. "Orl right, I will. Besides I ain't bin in a ferry."

By this time they had pulled up at a rise overlooking Darling Harbour. There were houses and buildings of commerce built near the water, wharves and warehouses below them. Overlooking these they could see all kinds of ships. A steamship with auxiliary sails was just berthing, one that they were not at all familiar with. Most were sailing ships, though, and some ferries which served all the places on the harbour and up to the Parramatta River. The whole place was a hive of industry. There were several ships unloading cargoes. The men working them looking rather like ants, from the top of the hill.

The roads in Sydney were on the whole not good, in fact at times quite horrific, but their new buggy seemed to take them quite well. They threaded their way between ruts all the way along the waterfront to the Rocks, where a great number of people lived. You could see St Philip's Church up on the hill. The Rocks area was not at all a savoury place to live at that time, for it was where deserters from the ships and criminals of all types lived, in fact it seemed to be a place where misery and disease abounded. The houses were quite small and were crowded together allowing many people to live in a small area.

Circular Quay was as busy a place as Darling Harbour seemed to be, ships to be seen everywhere, activity all around all the way to Bennelong Point.

"What does Bennelong mean?" asked Will. "Is it an aboriginal name?"

"I dunno, matie," said Tom. "I think there were a old house there or summat. I did 'ear tell thet it belonged ter blacks or the like."

"I think I know," said Tad. "I believe Captain Philip, who was here at first caught one of the blacks, called Bennelong, and got him to try to live like a white man. He even took him to England, I think. And later he built him a house on that point. Am I right, Ricky? Have you heard?"

"Yes, that's the story I heard, too, Tad. I think there was another black who went with him. I fancy his name was Arabanoo or some such, but I don't know much about it. I think one of them died of too much drink. Let that be a lesson to you young Tad."

"That's something I won't die of Rick. I saw too much of it when I was a kid."

"Me, too," put in Will. "I've seen too much of it, too and right now with Mr Thomas. Gosh that man's at it all the time. He gets awfully bad tempered when he's had too much."

"You didn't tell us that, Will. I hope he isn't a problem to you. I don't think I like the sound of Thomas," Ricky said.

"He isn't so bad first thing in the morning, but as the day goes on he's had enough to make him rotten. I agree, he isn't a nice person, but he paints well and is a good teacher, I think. Can I drive now, please Tom?" asked Will wanting to change the subject.

"What say Tad drives until we get to thet Mrs Macquarie's Chair and then yer kin take over after?" asked Tom, handing the reins over to Tad.

"All right," said Will.

"Look," said Ricky, "there's Government House.

Government House could be seen with the Botanic Gardens, and the road that led to Mrs Macquarie's Chair. They left the buggy and walked down to the point. Tom saying that it wasn't all that much to see anyway. He did admit that one did get a good view of the harbour from there and you could see over Woolloomooloo.

Will drove back past the Domain and the Rum Hospital whose real name was the Sydney Hospital and back home past St James' Church.

They all called it a great day and felt that they knew their town a little better than they had previously. They decided to make this a habit in future until they knew their home territory well. They could take a ferry to Parramatta, of which several a day now ran. They could take a ferry to North Sydney from Dawes Point. This was a steam ferry with two paddles and it was said that one did not even have to leave one's vehicle during the ten minute ride to North Sydney. The roads on that side were not well developed, but there was a move afoot to improve that.

That night on reaching Mr and Mrs Fishbon's house they found that the people they first met there, Mr and Mrs Reeves, were to dine. After the gentlemen rejoined the ladies, the boys were surprised to find that the drawing room carpet had been rolled up and an expanse of polished floor exposed. Trying to be polite and not remarking on it, they each took surreptitious looks at it and wondered what was in store for them for they knew their hosts did nothing without a good reason.

Their hostess smiled at them, remarking to herself that their restraint was commendable, and said, "Tonight, gentlemen, we learn to dance. Mr Reeves, you may take your place at the piano."

There was an audible gasp from the three. "That counts me out," said Will, happily.

"No it doesn't my lad," said Mr Fishbon. "You may never be an expert, but you can learn just as the others will."

"But sir, my leg. I could not do it." Will protesting.

"Yes, you can. You probably will not be able to dance for long, but you must learn the steps. You can do it if you really try," persisted his tutor.

"But, sir, does a newspaper reporter need to be able to dance?" asked Tad. "I really don't like the thought of it."

"Yes, my lad, it is not only necessary, but desirable." Turning to Ricky, he said, "You do not protest, Ricky, as do your brothers?"

"No, sir, as a matter of fact I would like to learn. We might be able to meet some nice young ladies if we can dance and be sociable. Thank you for thinking of it."

"Now, there's a philosopher. Take heed, young Will, and Thaddeus, take heed of your elder."

"Who wants to meet young girls, anyway?" said Will.

"You will one day," said Mrs Fishbon. "Now Mrs Reeves if you will allow Thaddeus to partner you, then I will undertake to escort Richard. We will then take turns with the boys and Mr Fishbon will direct the proceedings. Now Geoffrey tell us what you wish us to do."

After two hours at this pastime the boys at least felt they knew what was expected of them on a dance floor, but they realised that dancing was not as easy as they had thought. There were a lot of steps to learn, but agreed that it had been a very pleasant evening, and they thanked their teachers sincerely.

CHAPTER 8: *The English Stores*

The new shop opened on the stated date. Ricky had asked his various friends to come to share in the actual opening, so Mr and Mrs Landon, Mr Hughes, Mr and Mrs Fishbon and Mr and Mrs Reeves all came to breakfast with the boys to see the opening of the new door which led to the new shop. All of Ricky's staff were present, too.

Across the building above the new verandah a big sign said, "THE ENGLISH STORES". Ricky had thought very carefully about the name, and he chose that for he felt that it included Tad and Will in it. He knew that one day he would move from this present site and maybe one day it would be changed to "THE ENGLISH EMPORIUM". He was a young man with ambitions.

The new shop was mainly clothing and materials for men and women. He had appointed three new staff for it and thought that they would be very successful in promoting its growth. Ricky was very proud of it.

The breakfast was a great success. He had hired a woman to come and cook and serve the meal. Tad and Will were very excited, too, being included in their first social event as hosts. They were happy about those they knew but all were very wary of Mrs Landon whom they had not previously met. However, that lady was a pleasant surprise for them for she was most enthusiastic about the venture, and pleased them no end by asking them to come and visit her and her family at their home.

In due course the ribbon which was stretched across the doorway was cut by Mrs Landon and the door of the new shop was opened, and the first of their customers came.

There was always a great call for men's clothing and so selling those were no trouble. Their stock ranged from all kinds of working clothes to gentlemen's attire, the latter having a very pleasant area set aside for it. But for some reason which Ricky could not fathom, the ladies section was not doing well at all. There was no want of customers and the items for sale could not be faulted and so Ricky presumed that Miss Jones, who was in charge of that section, was the problem. He watched as carefully as he could but whenever he was in the vicinity he could find no fault in her treatment of the customers. It was a problem that he could not solve.

One evening when he was returning home late he was surprised to find someone sheltering under the verandah in the shop doorway. At first all he could see was a huddle sheltering from the rain. He could hear a whimpering sound, and so presumed that there was a child there. He nudged the form and he could then see that it was a woman with a small child. He was wet from the rain and it was very cold. He was unable to pass through the door and so asked the woman to move aside so he could enter. He caught sight of her white face and then the child coughed a terrible croupy cough.

"Have you nowhere else to go?" he asked.

"No, sir I haven't," came the reply.

"Is your child sick? Can't you find somewhere to go? Perhaps you should take her to the hospital."

"It's my little boy, sir. He is really sick, but I haven't any means of getting to hospital. I have no money at all."

Ricky looked down at her. She spoke well and looked as though she ought to have somewhere to go. "I think you had better come in with me, at least I can give you something to eat and a bed for the night. It will be warm, too."

"No, thank you sir, I would not accept taking that from a gentleman. We will just make do here." The little one was coughing badly.

"I am not offering anything to you but shelter for the night. There are only my two brothers and an old friend and we will not harm you. Come in and see. Come, be sensible, we will not harm you and you must have care for your son," Ricky said. He opened the door as she stood up holding her bundle tightly. "Have you no possessions?" he asked.

"They wouldn't let me get them," she answered.

"Who wouldn't?" he queried.

"At the hotel. I was working there and they threw me out because Phil was sick and they didn't want to have him there. I couldn't take my things anyway for I didn't have the price of a cab. In any case I had nowhere to go." She didn't speak in a complaining way just spoke straight out telling her plight.

Ricky ushered her in through the shop to the residence at the rear. For the first time he could see what she was like. She was still carrying her child, who was so wrapped up that you could not really see what he was like. He appeared to be quite large, but she didn't stoop in her carrying of him, she was quite a tall woman and very upright in stance. She clutched him to her almost fiercely, as though she was preventing anyone from removing him.

But Ricky didn't attempt to remove her big bundle but led her to the kitchen where Tad was reading by the fire and Tom snoozing gently. Tad jumped up at the entry of the woman and said in an amazed voice, "Who have we here, Rick?"

Ricky motioned the woman to a chair and said, "Put the stew back on the fire Tad, this lady is in need of some."

"I thank you, sir. I do not want to be any trouble to you." The child had another terrible paroxysm of coughing.

"My goodness," said Tad, "your little one sounds very sick."

"Yes, he is sir. I would like to have had a doctor to him but I cannot see my way to doing that. I will just have to manage. I can look after him, thank you," she said.

"Tad, I think we might do something about that little room next to Will's studio. Can we make it habitable, do you think?" Ricky asked. Turning to the woman he said, "We have a room behind the next shop that I think will be all right for you to use until you can make other arrangements. Would that do?"

"Thank you, sir, you are very kind. Anything would do, just as long as it is dry and warm. It is very good of you."

Tad went along to look at the room which Ricky had mentioned and soon came back with Will who was looking a bit put out as was Tad. Tad said, "Come and look at it Ricky and see if it is all right."

Will and Tad told Ricky in no uncertain terms what they thought of his latest find. Ricky stood with hands on hips and said, "You're a fine pair. What would have happened if I hadn't dragged you two out of the rain on certain nights some time ago? What would you expect me to do when I found someone in need on our doorstep? I am surprised at you. She won't worry you, Tad, you should have more sense. Will might see her more often, but I should say she will keep to herself if she can. Please get this room ready." With this Ricky walked out and left them.

After some minutes Tad and Will returned looking sheepish. Will announced that the room was ready for occupation. The woman was sitting at the table eating a bowl of stew and trying to entice her sick little boy to have a mouthful or two.

"I thought that I might go and fetch the doctor, Ricky, if you think our guest would like that," said Tad.

Tom, who had been serving the stew, smiled to himself and winked at Ricky as he said, "Good idea, matie."

"Yes, I was just suggesting that I should go, Tad, but you go if you will." Turning to the woman, he said, "Mrs Yates, may I present my brothers Tad and Will English. Boys, this is Mrs Yates and Phil. I believe she has had a very rough deal from Paddy Flynn at the Shamrock."

"I'll go an' saddle Lancer, matie. Take a coat, it's wet." With that, Tom left for the stables.

Ricky explained to Tad that Mrs Yates had been working at the Shamrock as a maid. But when young Phil became ill, Flynn had told her to go because he disturbed the patrons and he didn't want any sickness in his hotel. At this Tad laughed grimly for he knew that the Shamrock was a pretty tough place and he didn't think a few coughs would harm the place.

"Was it the only place you could get a job, Mrs Yates?" he asked.

"Yes, Mr English. I did not have anywhere to go for my husband died on the ship on the way out and we have little money. It was all I could do to find a job where I could have Phil," she said.

"You'll be all right here," assured Tad, "My brother is a great one for helping people. I'll go and get the doctor."

"Here, Tad, put on the old riding cape, it's pretty wet outside," said Ricky.

The doctor told the worried mother that the little boy only had a bad run of Bronchitis and provided that he was kept warm and was fed nourishing food he should be all right. He seemed to take it for granted that she lived there. She didn't attempt to tell him that she was homeless, just nodded and assured him that she would do all she could to look after him. He gave her some medicine and left after telling her that he would call in the next day.

She looked up hopelessly at Ricky and he said, "Don't worry, Mrs Yates, you can stay here until Phil is better. We'd be very happy for you to use the room we have. But I was thinking that while it is so cold it might be a good idea if you let him sleep here on the sofa until he is better. What do you think?"

"Thank you, Mr English, you are very kind. I don't know what I would have done if you hadn't come along. I was at my wit's end."

Tad and Will brought a second sofa into the kitchen, the one from Will's studio, and made the mother and son as comfortable as they could. They stoked up the fire and left them for the night.

The boys were rather uneasy about a strange person in their home, but made the best of it. Mrs Yates had the fire going well in the morning, the table set and the breakfast ready, when the boys appeared. They were all rather quiet wondering what would happen and how different their life would be if Mrs Yates stayed for long.

At the table she said, "I am very grateful for your letting me stay. I do not want to interrupt your lives. I cannot think what is best for me to do, but believe me I am willing to do whatever you want. Do you know of anywhere I can get help? Please tell me and I will go as soon as I can. If I could only get the money owed to me and my things from the hotel, I could move somewhere else. Please, can you tell me what I should do?" she asked.

"How long have you been in the colony, Mrs Yates? asked Tad.

"Only four weeks, Mr English," she answered.

"What were you planning to do when you came?" he asked again.

"My husband was coming out to work on the new Cathedral. He was a stone mason, who specialized in making stone lace. He would have been very well paid and so we would not have had any worries, but he died on the ship and now we are left. I have a little money but not enough to live on and all my papers are at the hotel and Mr Flynn wouldn't give me leave to get them, he just threw me out. It was so unfair."

"What were you working at there?" asked Ricky.

"I was doing housework. I didn't really care what I did as long as I was able to keep Phil with me, and was pleased to have it," she said.

"I will go down to the Shamrock with Tom and bring back your luggage. Would you come with us? Will could look after Phil while we are away, wouldn't you, Will?" said Ricky.

Will swallowed hard, but not wanting to be difficult, said in a small voice, "Of course, Rick. But you wouldn't be long would you? I don't know much about looking after children."

"No, Will. I wouldn't leave you if I could avoid it but I am sure Flynn would not give me the money owed to Mrs Yates. She must come with me, that is if Phil would be happy for you to come, Mrs Yates. I could try Flynn on my own," suggested Rick.

"Thank you, Mr English, if we are not long I am sure I would be happy to leave him. I'll tell him and he will understand. He is used to me leaving him in our room at the hotel, I would never let him roam from there and so he is used to being alone."

Ricky and Tom took Mrs Yates to the Shamrock and suggested that she goes in to Flynn and try for her things, Ricky would not be far behind and if there seemed to be any trouble, he would take over and deal with it.

The Shamrock was not the type of place that Ricky would wish any of his new family to be associated with. He was loth to let Mrs Yates go in to speak to Flynn, who was a small wizened Irishman with a very unsavoury reputation, but thought that if she could manage without his intervention it might be better. By staying in the background he was far enough away to be near and listen and not be too obvious. He soon realised that Flynn was going to be as difficult as he had feared.

Ricky, at twenty, was quite a large opponent for the little man, and when he sauntered in, he stood looking with disgust at the publican. "What did I hear you say to Mrs Yates, Flynn? Did I hear you refuse her property? I would think again, if I were you. I have no doubt the magistrate would be glad to find some reason for invading your territory. You do have a very unsavoury reputation, you know," he finished witheringly.

Flynn hastily said, "Good morning, sir. I am sure you heard no sich thing, sirr. I was just explaining to the leddy that I find it difficult to bring her things right now as I am alone."

"Well, you had better think again, Flynn. My man can help you with anything Mrs Yates has left here, and I believe there is the matter of money owing to her. See that you get that, too. How is it that I hear your barman here, if you are alone? We are waiting," Ricky said in the haughtiest voice he could muster.

Within a very short time Mrs Yates trunks were loaded onto the buggy. Flynn had given her the money owed and they were able to make their way home again. The publican was not at all pleased with the episode and as they drove off made a filthy remark about the cheapness of some women and how they dragged a decent man down if given the chance. Ricky made Tom pull up again and hopped down ready to take issue with the Irishman, but Tom restrained him saying, "Fergit, it matie. Don' let 'im get ter yer." So Ricky turned his back on the man and got back into the buggy.

This made him more conscious of the position he was in regarding Mrs Yates, and wondered whether he was wise to have given her shelter. He would speak to Mr Landon about it.

They found Will talking to the small boy, Phil, when they got back. Phil was propped up at the end of the couch he slept in, looking very pale and wan, and every now and then was racked with a terrible fit of coughing. Ricky was surprised to see that he was bigger than he had thought and asked how old he was. Being told he was eight, felt a little happier about that for he had imagined that Mrs Yate's little boy was about three or four. He knew very little about children.

Phil and his mother disturbed the boys and Tom much less than they expected. As soon as Phil was well enough, in less than a week, they confined themselves to their part of the residence, and apart from finding meals ready and beds and house tidy, there was little evidence that there was anyone else in the house. Will saw more of them than the others and a firm friendship gradually grew between the two lads, one small and the other thin and frail-looking, as Will always was.

Phil had a great ability to make himself even smaller and so appear like a shadow in unlikely places. He went into Will's studio one morning after he was better and crouched against the couch, there watching the older boy paint. It was only that he had to cough suddenly that made his presence felt. Will turned to find him down on the floor trying not to cough, but hardly managing it.

"What are you doing there, young' un?" Will asked.

"Just watching you. Can I please?" Phil asked.

"How long have you been there?"

"Oh, a long while. I like to watch you," came the reply.

"Well, as you are quiet enough about it, you'd better come up and get on the couch or you'll get sick again. But you be quiet, won't you. I don't like chatter."

So the little boy often sat watching the young artist as his work and a strange friendship developed between them. One day, without really understanding what it meant, Phil told Will that he was going to be a stone mason like his father.

Ricky was constantly concerned about his new shop. He could not find the root of the problem in the ladies' apparel department. He thought the staff was good for he tried to watch them carefully, and as a stream of women seemed to be forever browsing through, he could not work out why it did not pay. One evening after supper, as Mrs Yates was washing the dishes, he was busy perusing the sales book and mumbling to himself, with a furrowed brow.

Will, who was wiping up for Mrs Yates, asked, "What's the worry, Rick? Something seems to be concerning you. What's wrong?"

"It's the new shop, Will. It just isn't going as well as I hoped. At least it is the ladies' department that isn't paying. Anyway, don't you worry, I'll sort it out."

Mrs Yates, with soap suds up her arms, turned and looked at Ricky. Then seemed to think better of it and turned back again. Ricky caught her movement and looked up in time to catch a look that spoke. "What were you going to say, Mrs Yates? Did you have an idea to offer?" Ricky asked.

"I am sorry, Mr English, I don't want to intrude," she said.

"No, please. If you have anything to say, please say it. I will admit I am at my wit's end to solve this and I wish you could help me. Maybe a lady could tell me where I am going wrong."

Mrs Yates was obviously concerned that she may speak out of turn. Knowing what a private sort of person she was, the boys knew that she would not speak unless persuaded, especially if it concerned something that she didn't consider was her business. But after some persuasion she came over to Ricky, wiping her hands on her apron. Standing at the table opposite Ricky she said, "Mr English, it's none of my business, but you've been that kind to me that it has been on my mind to speak, but didn't like to. It's Miss Jones. She hasn't the right way of speaking to customers. She doesn't encourage them. She stands there like a rock and doesn't talk to them about what they want. And then sometimes when she makes up her mind what she wants them to have she tries to force things on them and that's not right. It upsets the ladies, sir."

"I had no idea she did that. Have you seen it, Mrs Yates?" he asked.

"Yes, sir. I sometimes slip into the shop and I notice what she does. I know it isn't any of my business sir, but you could do better, I know. She doesn't teach the girl, neither. She just lets her do what she wants and that's not right ."

"I am surprised that Mr Parker hasn't picked that up. Are you sure, Mrs Yates?"

"Yes, sir, I am," she said, looking rather embarrassed about it.

"Thank you. I will have to look around for someone to take her place then. She came with good references, too." Ricky looked more worried than ever.

"Hey, Ricky. Maybe Mrs Yates would be the one. You could do it couldn't you, Mrs Yates. Go on tell Ricky that you have worked in a ladies' shop," said Will excitedly.

"Is this right, Mrs Yates? Have worked in a shop like mine?" Ricky asked, but feeling at the same time he was being pushed into something he didn't want to get into.

"Yes, Mr English. I am a seamstress, and I worked in a big shop when I was younger. I could train girls well, too. I know what's needed. But, sir. Please. I don't want to cause any trouble, really I don't. But it makes me fair boil when I see ladies come into the shop and go out again without buying. You're losing good business, Mr English," she said.

Ricky had learned to trust the woman. He thought she was honest with them. She certainly worked hard to make them comfortable. He realised that her motives were probably that she wanted security for herself and Phil, but he didn't blame her for that. She had a good appearance and spoke very well. Much better than one would expect from someone of her class, but then if she had been trained for that sort of position, that is probably where she learned to speak so well. He hadn't really thought about it before, he was only too glad to help her, and then she had made herself so useful that they all felt she was indispensable. She certainly was not intrusive, and neither was Phil. It was amazing that such a small boy could remain almost invisible at times.

"Thank you, Mrs Yates. You have given me something to think about and we will speak about it later." Will smiled encouragingly at the woman as she returned to the sink.

Will was not surprised when, some two weeks later Mrs Yates was given a trial in place of Miss Jones. Ricky asked Mr Parker to watch carefully and see that she was as good as he hoped. They were very pleased to see that the sales figures improved almost immediately and Mr Parker gave a glowing report on her customer conversation. The salesgirl who had been employed since the shop opened began to blossom a little, too, and Ricky felt that he had solved a problem.

But another problem was looming. The boys had reached an age when they needed more housekeeping care. When Mrs Yates was working in the kitchen and doing general housekeeping, they could see what an improvement their meals were and how much better the house was looked after, so Ricky knew he would soon have to get a housekeeper. He also thought that as their various interests had developed, living behind a shop was not satisfactory any longer, besides the shops were doing so well that they could now look for a place of their own and set up living in a better style. He needed their living space for offices, for the business had grown so. He wondered what he could do about housing Mrs Yates and Phil. He didn't want to lose them altogether, but now that she was working in the shop, he didn't think it was suitable for her to be living in the back room. He had lots to think about.

Mrs Yates loved the work in the shop. She was in her element and of course, because Ricky had been kind to her when she was so desperately in need, she wanted to do all she could to pay him back. She set about her work with a will, and was soon producing garments for sale that were very popular, and quickly make alterations to suit the customers. She had an ability to please them in helping them to choose materials and make suggestions as to style and mode. She took a pride in the girl, Annie. Annie was learning a great deal about the shop and how to handle customers. She was also sewing well and Mrs Yates could see that Ricky would have to set up a dressmaking business as well as selling the materials. Soon they would need extra staff. The business was growing very fast indeed.

Ricky found himself going up to the office upstairs, quite often, to consult John Landon. He had often made mistakes about the business side of the shops and knew that he could have got himself into a great deal of hot water, at times, if he had not consulted his friend when he had. Under John's guidance he had appointed a good business manager who was proving his worth. He found himself wandering in Landon's office direction again one day and asked for an appointment.

By this time, of course, the Landon staff knew that Ricky was a close associate of their chief and would always arrange an appointment as soon as possible. This day John was in the outer office when Ricky entered and asked him in immediately.

"You caught me at a good moment, Ricky. How are things progressing with you?" he asked.

"Well, thank you Mr Landon. But I wonder whether I could make an arrangement with you that would allow us to talk things over at length. I have some problems that I would like your opinion on, and I am a bit fearful that I might be rushing ahead faster than I am able. Could you spare some time for me, sir?" Ricky asked.

"You want a lengthy talk, I take it Ricky?"

"Yes, sir. I would also like to take you out and show you a project I am thinking of. Could you spare the time, please?"

"Yes, of course. You intrigue me. Big things in the offing?" Landon asked.

"Yes, big things for me, sir."

Landon drew his appointment book towards him and said, "I'm busy tomorrow, Ricky, but what about the next day, Thursday? Say 10 o'clock? Would that suit?"

"Yes, sir, that would be fine. I would like to speak to you first and then take you out. We should be finished all I want to do by lunchtime. I look forward to seeing you then." Ricky stood to shake the man's hand.

"I will be most eager to find out what all this is about." He shook the young man's hand and then asked anxiously, " It isn't trouble is it Ricky?"

"No, sir, nothing like that."

CHAPTER 9: *Ricky's Three Houses*

On Thursday morning Ricky was anxiously waiting for 10 o'clock to come. He arrived at the office just as the office clock struck ten. He was motioned to a seat and John Landon lay back in his chair and said, "I am consumed with curiosity, Ricky. How can I help you?"

"Well, sir," he said, "I suppose I should say straight out that I am making a great deal of money."

The man laughed. "And here was I wondering what the problem was. Don't you know what to do with it, Ricky? Do you want me to help you spend it?"

Ricky joined in the laughter and said, "Well not quite, sir, but I do need your advice. Or rather I think I want your approval. I hope I am not intruding on your time over this."

"Go ahead. I am most interested, as you know. I rather feel as though you are a sort of foster son. "Landon looked at the young man, "Do you know, Ricky, I am very proud of knowing you."

Ricky flushed. "You are, sir? I don't know why."

"Yes, I am and I do. I've admired your way of doing things. Not always right, of course, but you have learned by your mistakes. You have always been able to accept advice, and I take it that you are reaping the benefit of this."

Ricky smiled. "Well, the benefits are rolling in, Mr Landon. It seems as though I am a successful storekeeper."

"How can I help, you? I think you know more about storekeeping, as you call it, than me."

"Well, it isn't really about the store that I want your opinion, but it all fits in. You know how I have always wanted to help the young street boys. Those who are like we were."

"Yes. I knew you had some scheme in mind. Have you reached a decision about it?"

"I want to begin training some boys so that they become useful citizens and I have some thoughts in mind."

"You must bear in mind that they are not all Tads and Wills, you know Ricky."

"I know. But I want to be able to give a chance to those who would benefit by it. I thought that I would set a scheme going whereby they will be able to use the skills they learn. I will be needing a continual stream of boys to work in the shops, the office and the other places that will appear as we grow. My biggest problem to begin with is to house them. I might say, at this juncture, that we have thoroughly outgrown our residence here, Mr Landon, and we must move out. I want the space for offices in any case."

"What are your long term plans, Ricky?"

"You mean for the store?"

"Yes, I am sure you know where you want to go."

"Yes, I know where I want to go, and I hope to get there one day. Do you know that land at Durham Street, where the old inn was?"

"Yes, a good piece. I would say about the best part of an acre. Do you want to buy that, Ricky? A bit ambitious isn't it?"

"I have bought it, Mr Landon, and paid for it too."

"You amaze me. Business must be doing well, Ricky." the man said.

"But that's not all. I have another scheme, too. I do want to build a store on the Durham land, but not for a while yet. It is a good site, isn't it? Right near the heart of the town and fairly flat."

"I hope you haven't gone too deep with spending, Ricky."

"No, sir. If I can't pay cash I won't buy. I will stick to my father's principle of not borrowing. I have plenty left over, enough for my boys' scheme. Do you know the new terrace houses in Pelton Street, Mr Landon?"

"Yes, I pass them on my way home and have been interested to watch their progress. Is that what you have your eye on?"

"Yes. I would like to buy three of them."

"Three! Good heavens boy, are you going to start a hotel or something?"

"No, I wouldn't do that." Ricky said chuckling. "But I would like you to come and look at them and see what you think."

"But why three, Ricky?"

"I thought I would have one as a sort of hostel for the boys, with a housekeeper to feed them well and for staff to teach and encourage the boys. As well as give decent accommodation for some of my store staff like George Parker, who lives in a room. Then I want another for Tad, Will and me. I could turn the top floor into a studio for Will. It faces south and Will assures me that a studio should. Then Tad and I could share the rest. The boys are too old, now, to live in the small rooms we do. No reflection on you, sir. We thank you for the opportunity you gave us. Do you know it took me a while to realise that you let us in at a ridiculous rent? I am glad we pay better now. We have been very happy there, they have been marvellous years but we all seem to be too big for them, now. The third house would be for the girls."

"Girls, Ricky? You aren't going to take on girls are you?"

"I had no intention of doing it, Mr Landon, but I can see the necessity. I want to be able to train girls to sew, sell, dress well and have the opportunity of making something of themselves."

"I can see what you mean with boys, but how are you going to manage a girls' hostel?"

"I wouldn't do it myself, of course. Mrs Yates, who runs my lady's department seems to have a natural gift for training girls and I am sure she would jump at the chance of living in a new house. She seems to be a loyal and good woman and I could trust her. I would like to find someone like Mrs Fishbon, but I would not ask her to do it. She is not well and I don't really think it would be suitable for her. I was thinking of someone who could take an interest in the project. There are apparently lots of girls who come here to the colony and cannot find anywhere decent to work or live and they are in great danger of being caught up in wrongdoing. You know what I mean... So I would need someone to teach them to learn the skills that a lady knows. Am I too ambitious, Mr Landon?"

"I don't know. I'll have to think that over, lad. I don't think it is really proper for you to have a household of women."

'That's one of the things that worries me. I would like to hand the whole thing over to some kind, understanding, competent lady.

I would appreciate it if you could think it over, in the meantime I would like it if you could come and look at the terraces."

By this time Tom was waiting in the street with the buggy and Spic and Span. Tom in his best suit for he knew that this was an important occasion. Ricky nodded to him as he and John Landon were seated in the buggy and Tom sent the horses off.

The terraces were being built on a side street that promised some quiet for the residents. They were three stories, with large windows looking out to the north, which gave glimpses of the harbour. The small front yards were apparently to be fenced but they were at that time filled with rubbish. Ricky led the way into the first one, which appeared to be the most closely finished. The plasterers were working just inside the front door and they threaded their way past them to walk along a passage from which several rooms opened. The passage as usual, opened out into a living room with a large kitchen in the rear. There was a verandah at the back and quite a large yard. As yet there were no fences dividing the yards, they were to come. Back in the house Ricky led John upstairs. Wooden stairs that were being polished by an industrious looking man. The next floor had several nice rooms and further stairs leading to spacious living and bedroom areas on the top floor.

They found that each house was the same except that Ricky had asked that the top floor of the next house be left until he decided whether to buy or not. This was to be Will's studio. They walked all over the three places and at the end Ricky enquired anxiously of his friend whether he thought them worth buying. Landon said that he thought they were very sound and that if Ricky was determined on his project they could probably not be better for his purpose. However he shook his head over the thought of the whole thing and stated that Ricky was about to take on more than he could cope with.

"That is what worries me, Mr Landon. Somehow I have the urge to get on and do it, but I don't want to make a fool of myself."

"Ricky, I suppose you are going into this with your eyes open, so if it doesn't work, you will still have some good real estate and with that I don't think you could lose. But, I do feel you are taking on a lot. And you must be careful how you handle that Mrs Yates. You could get into complications that you haven't thought of."

Ricky smiled wryly at his friend. "You mean my reputation could be damaged, sir?"

"Yes, I do. Be careful. You have to think of Tad and Will, too. It could get you into a situation that you would find it hard to get out of. People talk, you know."

"This is why I want a sensible female to live here with Mrs Yates and anyone else we can find. I am not attached to her in any way, please be assured."

"I didn't think you would be, but be careful. I might talk this over with my wife. She is always interested in what you are up to. I rather think she will be a bit startled at this one though. By the way, she is always asking when you are coming to have that tea with us. Better make it soon."

"I will, Mr Landon. Thank you for coming."

"Now I must get back to work."

That night John Landon told his family about Ricky's latest ideas. As they sat around the dining table they asked questions of him, about the training plans, the houses, what Mrs Yates was like and other things that was of great interest to them.

Amabel sat quietly thinking about what her father had told them, and then said, "Father, I have met Mrs Yates. I've spoken to her at the shop and she seems to be a very pleasant person. I think she would do well in that scheme."

"Is she the person who served us when we bought the muslin, Amabel?" asked her mother.

"Yes, I think so. That's who it would be, isn't it father?" she asked.

"Ricky only has the one woman in that department, Amabel, so I should imagine it is. I have not really spoken to her, but Ricky seem to think she is very reliable. He does find the most amazing people on the streets, doesn't he?" John said.

This brought a great clamber of questions from his three daughters. "Do you mean she is a street woman?" asked Betsy.

"Betsy, you don't know what you are talking about," said her mother.

"What do you mean, Father?" asked Amabel.

"She apparently lost her husband on the ship coming out and had to find a job. As she has a small boy this was difficult. The only thing she could find was as a maid at an inn, not a very savoury one, either. When her boy became ill she was told to go, without her money or belongings and where should she end up but on Ricky's doorstep." He chuckled. "He seems to attract them, doesn't he?"

"Is she decent John?" asked his wife anxiously.

"Ricky assures me she is. She looked after them until he found that she could run the department better than the woman he had there, and so she went into the shop and it hasn't looked back. Apparently it is very profitable. There's a young man with very big ideas."

"Your very fond of him aren't you, Father?" asked Harriet.

"Yes, I am, dear. He has proved to be very stable. Never will I forget what a sad looking boy he was when Hinds carried him in that night. I have a lot to thank him for," he said looking fondly at his oldest daughter.

"I am sure I have, too, Father," said Amabel.

The three Landon daughters knew the story of when Amabel was taken away, but they had had little to do with Ricky. Their father kept them informed of Ricky progress in life and that, too, of Tad and Will. They all knew him by sight, for they often, nowadays, went into his shop. There was little intercourse except that of customer and storekeeper. Ricky felt he could not intrude into their private lives and so remained distant. This was probably why he had not accepted Mrs Landon's invitation to take Tad and Will to tea. He always felt that perhaps the boys would be made to feel their start in life and he would never put them in a position which might hurt them. He was very protective of his 'brothers'. He felt that perhaps he was of a lineage that would match the Landon's, but was not really sure of that as he knew little of his background, but he would not take the risk of a snubbing. But he did know that he would not get that from the Landon's for they had always been a friendly family, and this colony was a funny place. With some colonists there was no barrier between classes, but with others there was just as much as he knew existed in England.

"Father," said Amabel, as she finished her breakfast the next morning. "May I speak to you and Mother before you leave for the office?"

"Certainly, my dear," said her father, "come into the drawing room." Turning to his wife he added, "Sadie, my dear, I see thoughts dashing round in Amabel's head. We must attend." He put an arm round each and escorted them to the large front room. "Now," he said, sitting Amabel on a sofa.

She looked up at her father, and using the name for him she used when little, "Daddy, I have an idea. What about Binksie?' Wouldn't it be a good thing for her, Daddy? Mama what do you think?"

"Binksie, Amabel? What? To go to this hostel of Ricky's you mean? What made you think of her?" asked her father.

"Binksie?" asked her mother. "Whatever would Binksie think, Amabel?"

"I think she would like it, Mama. Now that Betsy is out of the school room and Charles is at the Kings School, you know she hasn't any reason for stopping here. You know it was worrying you. I think she would like it. She loves teaching and she always said she would hate to go to another family," said Amabel.

" I wouldn't want Binksie to leave us, Amabel, but really I think it is not really what I would suggest," said Mrs Landon.

"Don't you think she would be good at it, Daddy?"

"Oh, yes, she would be good at it. None better, girl, but I don't think Binksie would dream of doing it," said her father.

"Well, I am sure she would. I think she'd love it. Why don't you ask her, Mama?"

"I don't think I could, Amabel. She would probably be insulted, don't you think?" replied her mother.

Amabel smiled, thinking of all the hours she had spent with her governess, and knowing that she and Harriet and Betsy knew her better that anyone, except, probably, her young brother Charles. They all loved Miss Binks very much and it was very sad for them to think that she would have to leave them and find another post.

Miss Binks was not looking forward to it either for she had been with the family ever since Amabel was a tiny girl.

"Well, if you think she would be interested I daresay we could ask her," said John Landon. "I'll send Tonkin for her."

"John, you wouldn't suggest it, would you?" asked Sadie Landon anxiously.

"Yes, my dear. I daresay Amabel has mentioned it to her already and knows what Binksie will say. Is that right, minx?" he smiled at Amabel.

"Yes, I did mention it a little. Daddy, I will go and get her, don't bother Tonkin."

With that Amabel ran from the room without waiting for her parents to say anything further. She was very soon back with her old governess who wasn't old at all. Miss Binks was in her late thirties. She was not very tall but carried herself well. Her hair was light brown and her countenance very pleasant. All the family adored her, she was such a jolly person, she loved teaching, and she had that wonderful gift of making learning a joy. Amabel knew that she had been concerned about her future and had been quite interested in this different venture about which Amabel had told her.

She came into the drawing room, taking a seat on a sofa, as Mr Landon indicated, saying, "Has Amabel told you what she has already told us, Binksie?" he asked.

"Do you mean about this new girls hostel, Mr Landon?" she asked calmly. "If you mean that, yes, she told me of it, and what Mr English was planning. It sounds a good idea, doesn't it, sir?"

"Yes, a good idea. But what about you? Would you be interested in being part of this?" he asked.

"I would like to know more about it, Mr Landon. But I am rather reluctant to look for another post as governess. I have been very happy here and I cannot say that I know of another place in Sydney that I would like to go to," she answered simply.

"I am glad you have been happy here, Binksie," said Mrs Landon, "we just love having you and can't really think what we will do without you."

"But would you go to a girls hostel, Miss Binks?" Mr Landon asked more formally.

"It would be a challenge, Mr Landon, and I like a challenge. I know Mrs Yates already, a little, and she seems to be a pleasant person." She smiled at them. "Don't worry, sir, it is just the sort of thing I have been thinking of but didn't know how it would ever come to pass. The girls wandering around Sydney town are a worry to a lot of people, and this is a chance that I may be able to take to help them a little."

"Well, I wouldn't have believed it," said Mrs Landon. Turning to her husband she said, "John, before we let Binksie go there, you must find out all about it and whether it is a suitable place for her to go."

"Don't worry, dear, I will keep watch and see that she is well looked after," he assured her.

"Father, do you think Harriet and I can help with the girls, too? We would love it and Binksie will look after us. We could teach them all sorts of things. Couldn't we, Binks?" asked Amabel.

"My goodness, what next. You'll be wanting to join the force soon, my dear," he said to his wife.

"And why not, John. That might be a good idea." His family roared with laughter.

"See what you started, Daddy." Amabel laughed.

***

Mrs Yates heard a small noise in the shop. She did not think anyone was in that department then and so continued her sewing quietly, listening intently. There it was again! A small shuffle. She stood up and quietly moved round a table that had upright rolls of pretty velvets on it. On the other side she found a girl who was just about to finger the pure white of the nearest velvet. "Don't touch that with your dirty fingers," she said, kindly.

"They ain't thet dirty," came the reply. The girl, about 12 years old, looked down at her fingers. Then looking at Mrs Yates she said, "I weren't gunna 'urt 'em. I jes' wanted ter see what they felt like.

Honest I did. I jest come in ter see 'em up close." Holding out her hands she said again, "See they ain't reel dirty."

"They are," said Mrs Yates, "they are quite filthy."

"Well, Ah'll go aht an' wash 'em in the 'orse trough. Thet'll do won't it?" The girl asked.

"Indeed it won't," said Mrs Yates. "I can't have my materials getting dirty, especially the velvets, they are so hard to clean again and wouldn't look nice for the customers."

"Are they yours, Missus?" the girl asked. "Gee you're lucky ter 'ave sich a lot."

"No they are not mine really, but I am responsible for them. People won't buy the things if they are dirty. I think you had better go, now."

"If I go and wash 'em proper, will yer let me feel them?" the girl insisted. "Mebbe I could borrer some soap," she added.

Mrs Yates looked at the ragged figure before her. She obviously was a street urchin. She had seen them often enough looking through the window of the shop, but none had ever ventured in before. This girl was dressed in poor clothes, she wasn't very clean but her dress was not in rags as so many of them were. She was a pitiful sight, but her eyes were quite clear and she looked straight at Mrs Yates. There was something about the child that was quite appealing. "I suppose I could take you to my room where you could have a wash, then you can feel the materials," she said.

"Gee Missus, ye're grand. Would yer?"

"Yes, but just wait." Mrs Yates turned from the girl and went to the back door of the shop and called, "Annie. Could you please come to the shop?"

Mrs Yates took the girl through to her room and poured some water into her washstand basin. She handed her some soap and stood waiting with a towel. The girl was stuck in one place looking at the pretty things that Mrs Yates had around her bedroom.

"Ain't it lovely?" she said.

"Come on wash yourself properly," said Mrs Yates. She watched as the girl took the soap and washed her hands.

"Kin I wash me face, too?" she asked. "The soap smells thet lovely."

Mrs Yates laughed, "Of course. Go ahead." She nodded her approval and when the girl was finished she looked a great deal better. "Your thorough, anyway."

"Yer bed is ever so pretty. It must be lovely ter sleep in thet."

"You like pretty things. Don't you?" Mrs Yates asked. "What is your name?"

"I'm Martha an' I does, too, I luvs pretty things. Now, kin I go and touch them things?"

That was Martha's first visit to Mrs Yates. From then on she became quite a constant visitor, but she was very well behaved and was never intrusive. Mrs Yates found that she just wanted to watch and take in all she could see. Mrs Yates was quite concerned for her appearance, for she was certainly no ornament to the shop, but as she would stay well in the background when a customer came in she was not very noticeable. If Mrs Yates was with a customer Martha had the sense to keep away.

When asked about her home conditions she was very cagey. Apparently her older sister Josie looked after her and they shared a room somewhere. This room was not available to Martha during the day and so Martha would stay longer on rainy days, trying to be as quiet as a mouse in case they should send her away. She became quite adept at shrinking behind the rolls of material. Mrs Yates would often find her sitting carefully fingering some pretty material. The girl certainly loved them. Maria Yates was careful not to ask too many questions of the girl and it was not until many weeks had passed that she got the whole story.

Maria had asked Martha whether she would like learn to sew. She had noticed that there had been a marked improvement in the girls appearance. She was no longer dirty, and as best as she could she kept her dress clean. It seemed to be the only one she possessed.

Martha had looked up to her with glistening eyes and told her new friend, "Yes" breathlessly, but then was concerned that she had nothing to sew and that she had no money. Maria had assured her that there were some samples and other pieces she could learn on and so the lessons began.

Mrs Yates had always sewn, it seemed to her. She could not remember not sewing something. For she was a tiny girl when her mother started her on sewing cards, and was not much older when she started her first sampler. So it came as a shock to find that as Martha had never handled anything as small as a needle that the exercise was almost more than the girl could cope with. Maria realised then how fortunate she had been by learning to be dextrous with tiny dolls and small toys at an early age, but this child had never had anything to play with and so using her fingers for tiny things was an effort.

Martha's mother had died when she was small and Josie, her sister, was all she'd had for a mother. Josie, Maria learned, was fifteen, 3 years older than Martha. Their father had worked on the roads as a navvy. He had been a taciturn sort of fellow but had brought in enough for them to eat and have a home of sorts. He was quite disinterested in them except for providing for their creature necessities. He had died some months before and Josie now had the job of providing for her sister. When asked about where she worked Martha became incoherent, so Maria didn't push her, but she had her suspicions. It was some time later that Martha admitted that Josie was "on the streets".

Maria said, in a disgusted voice, "Oh, Martha, no, surely not."

Martha looked up at her friend and said, "She didn't 'ave no choice. Yer see, me dad, 'e didn't leave us any money and we were near starvin'. She tried ter get a job, true she did, but it wern't no good. There was the rent ter pay of the room. We 'ad ter live somewhere, and so she went aht, and she 'ates it loik poison."

"Well, don't you be tempted, Martha."

"Don' worry, Missus, she'd skin me alive if I did. She wouldn' 'ear o' me doin' sich a thing. She's sich a good gel is Josie. Thet's why I can't go 'ome of a day, an' sometimes at night, but not often."

"You poor girl. I think I would like your Josie. Why don't you bring her to meet me, Martha? Will you?"

"My word, I will, Missus. I tell 'er all abaht you an' what yer done fer me and she's reel grateful. I didn't bring 'er 'acos she thought yer wouldn' want ter mix with the likes 'o 'er."

"Well, you see that you bring her and soon. We'll have tea together in my room and leave Annie to look after the shop," said Maria.

Mrs Yates was surprised to find Martha at the shop early next morning with a sad looking girl who was obviously Josie. She had no idea that the promised tea party would happen so soon. However she took the girls in and as it was so early there was no one in the shop. Leaving it with Annie she took Josie and Martha to the kitchen and there she sat them down to eat. She made toast and tea and the girls devoured it as though it was manna. "They probably think it is," mused Maria. She chatted away trying to draw Josie out a little. She could see she was very unhappy, but Josie had hardly said a word all the time. Martha had been chirping along merrily, but at the same time watching her sister very carefully.

Maria said, "Martha it is time you went out and did some sewing, Josie will help me wash up. Now, off you go," she hustled her out.

"But Missus ..." said Martha.

"Off you go," said Maria. She turned towards Josie and looked down at her. "My dear girl, tell me what's worrying you?"

"Oh, Missus," she said and burst in tears, putting her head down on the toasty plate, "Oh, Missus. I'm so bad. What'll yer think 'o me?"

Maria came round and took her in her arms and held her tight. "I think you are fine, Josie. I think you are brave and fine and I am proud to know you."

"Oh, Missus. Ah'm thet un'appy. I dunno what ter do."

"Tell me what worries you?"

"Missus, Martha told me she told yer abaht me an' what ah'm doing, an' I jest 'ate it. Me mum would be thet mad at me an' I don' know what Pa would'a said. Least I do, 'e would bash me one, 'e would. But I got ter look after Martha, and I dunno 'ow else."

"You poor child." Maria sat looking at her and thinking hard. Then she said, "Josie, would you stop what you are doing and live a good life, if I found somewhere else for you and Martha to live and learn to be useful girls?"

"Oh, yes, Missus, I would. I ain't cut out ter be a falling woman. But where could you find a place like thet? I'd do anything, I promise, Missus."

"All right. Now dry your eyes. Will you promise not to go with any men if I give you enough money for a few days. I want you to come an see me again. I have to speak to someone first. Promise, Josie?"

"Too right, Missus. I promise. But there ain't no call fer you ter give us money. I got enough fer a few days, I 'ave. Oh, Missus, is it true? Could yer find somewhere fer me'n Martha? We'll be good, reel true we will."

As soon as she could Mrs Yates found Ricky and asked him if she could move in to the new house quickly with two girls who needed help fast. She explained in detail and so it was that the new venture began quicker than they had expected.

CHAPTER 10: *Tad meets Amabel*

The promised tea party at Landon's was a great success. Old Tom insisted on driving them as though he was a groom. He even suggested that Ricky provide him with some sort of livery for he wanted to show people that he was proud to serve such young gentlemen. However he was laughed to scorn, the said young men assuring him he wasn't a servant but a good friend.

"Well, you be careful when we get to this place. Don't you treat me like no friend. I'll just drive round to the stable like I was a servant and don't you mess it up."

Ricky could see that the old man was determined to do the best for them and so let him have his way. Tom, sitting upright and looking straight ahead, drove to the front door of the mansion, not looking at his passengers, then he drove off when they had alighted, to find his way to the stables somewhere at the rear of the house.

Tonkin took them inside and Mrs Landon came bustling to meet them and held her hand out to Ricky and Will. She had not met Tad before and Ricky introduced him. She took them out to the side lawn where afternoon tea was set on tables with chairs on the lawn under the shady trees. The three laughing Landon girls made a charming picture. "Blossoms under the trees," thought Ricky, as he went across to meet them. Mr Landon made the introductions and to the other lady who Ricky presumed and found that it was Miss Binks.

Ricky was most interested to see the look on Tad's face as he was introduced to Amabel. Poor Tad was trying to be rather nonchalant but kept having quiet peeps at that pretty maiden. They all chatted happily, even the youngest Betsy having her say. These Landon girls were not shrinking violets but daughters of their wise and very pleasant parents.

After tea they all wandered through the gardens which were quite extensive and lovely. Ricky noticed that Tad was skillful in maneuvering himself nearest to Amabel with Harriet on his other side. Will, on the other hand, was happy to walk with Mr Landon, leaving Ricky to walk with the others. They eventually retired to the drawing room where the ladies began to ask questions about the proposed hostel for girls. Ricky was surprised to hear that they all wanted to be involved with the project and soon they were immersed in plans.

Tad, it was noticed, was quite content to sit and unobtrusively gaze at Amabel. Will was, as usual, busy with his sketch pad, not noticing the turn in the conversation. Ricky quietly suggested to Will that it was not a polite thing to do, but Mr Landon laughingly hushed him by telling him that one could not stop a genius from doing what he wished.

The idea that the Landon ladies wanted a large share of his latest project surprised and delighted Ricky. He was very taken with Miss Binks and felt that she would get along well with Mrs Yates. So Ricky came away feeling that his hostel was already staffed. All he had to do now was wait for the houses to be finished, supply enough furniture to set them up and his hostels could begin.

Ricky had thought that it would still be some weeks away before they could think of looking for girls who would want to take advantage of the opportunity of living in the hostel. Choosing the right girls would be a problem and he had not known how they would go about that, but now, here was Mrs Yates wanting to put two girls in right away before the house was even furnished. "Perhaps I should speak to Mrs Landon and Miss Binks," he thought. With this he saddled his horse and set off immediately for the Landon house.

Mrs Landon was not at home but found that Miss Binks was and so he was able to talk it over with this practical lady who was able to put his mind at ease. In a short time she planned furniture and the use of the rooms which were already finished, stating that it would be part of the girls' training to be in on the planning and preparation of it all. She would take up residence the next day as would Mrs Yates, if possible, and then with the barest of preparations they could take the girls in the following day.

Ricky was able to go home with a mind at ease knowing that there was someone at the helm who would take all the little things out of his hands. All he had to do was pay for it all.

This wasn't a worry for Ricky as he was fast becoming a well-to-do man. He seemed to know by instinct how to trade, and make it pay. He had very good and sensible ideas but was never backward asking for advice and assistance. Probably his greatest asset was his ability to assess people. He rarely made a mistake with his staff, Miss Jones being his most notable one, in that direction. There was, of course, his terrible mistake in getting involved with Gosling early in his storekeeping life. But it must be said that he was not as experienced in dealing with women as he was in dealing with men. So when interviewing the few women he employed he usually asked George Parker to sit in on the interview and found that it always paid dividends.

George had proved to be an able man who grew in competence as the business grew. He was a loyal man who thought a great deal of Ricky, and who only offered advice when asked for it.

John Landon had recommended an accountant to Ricky who was of very good repute and so became Ricky's man of business. So with Parker who dealt with most of the personnel and Johnson who watched over the money side of the business Ricky was able to relax somewhat.

Within the next few weeks Ricky was to see them all established in their new homes. George Parker and Jackie Smith in house number one, Ricky, Tad and Will in number two and the girls' hostel in number three. All were very satisfied with their lot. George Parker was so keen about his role in choosing and training boys that Ricky was happy to leave the choice of training staff to him. They had a cook/ housekeeper who had been such in a boys school in England and who had recently lost her husband. She had a son who was very willing to learn to work in the store and so number one acquired it's first trainee. Their house was divided into large bedrooms holding four beds each, with separate rooms for George Parker and Mrs Gibbs and her son Bert. The furniture was simple and useful, the furnishings plain and washable.

Mrs Gibbs was considered to be a gem for she was skillful in making her menfolk happy and contented. She was not a notable chef but was able to serve good plain wholesome food to her charges.

The girls hostel was furnished in much the same manner but Miss Binks and Mrs Yates were very keen for the girls to do as much as was possible so that they would feel they had a real stake in their home, and so many of the curtains and cushions etc were made by Martha and Josie, under the guidance of Miss Binks and the Landon ladies.

Martha and Josie loved their new home but life was not all soft and gentle for them. They had only ever lived in small squalid quarters and all the cleaning and scraping that was asked of them now was very foreign and at times very hard to take. The two girls often had a cry together and wondered whether it was all worth it. Josie was the one who kept them going. Martha was all for the soft life. She loved the good food and the pretty things which were now surrounding them. She was very proud of her pretty sprigged bedcover and had been most excited when told she could choose what she wanted from the cottons in the store. She had laboriously hemmed it with stitches carefully placed and now it was her pride and joy. When she was feeling miserable over her lack of freedom she would go to her room and sit on her bed feeling the pretty stuff.

Each morning they had housekeeping duties which kept them scrubbing and cleaning until everything shone to Mrs Cook's idea of perfection. Mrs Cook being the new cook-housekeeper who looked after the female part of the enterprise. She had worked at the Shannon Hotel and had kept in contact with Mrs Yates while she was at the store. When offered this position she jumped at it for she knew that it would be far better than the job she had and in much more pleasant surroundings .

After the cleaning was to this hard taskmistress' satisfaction there was a cooking lesson for both girls. Mrs Cook loved her work and considered that cooking was an art. She was delighted to find that the girls responded well to her training and knew that they were "coming on fine". They learned to set tables and do all sorts of housewifely things. In the afternoon there were sewing lessons,

lessons in speech and deportment, writing, calculating and general knowledge, all taught by Miss Binks and at times the Landon ladies when they were not otherwise occupied.

So life was very busy and Martha and Josie had little time to have to themselves. But on Wednesday afternoons they were permitted to go to the store and look around, wander up the streets of the town and look at other shops. But at four o'clock they were back at their tasks again. They looked forward so much to their weekly outing for they now had "real clothes", as Martha called them. In the house they wore and had indeed made their utility dresses which they wore with an overall, when doing their chores. But on Wednesday they wore their "pretties". Mrs Yates had made muslin dresses that delighted the girls. She was a skillful dressmaker and knew just the colours to bring out some real prettiness in these little waifs. The delight on their faces was all the reward she needed.

The girls felt somewhat overwhelmed by adults telling them what to do. It seemed to be work, work, and nothing else. But one day a woman appeared at the door and asked for the lady in charge. Martha had answered the door and showing the visitor into the drawing room she scurried off to find Miss Binks.

The visitor introduced herself as Mrs Summers, who had an interest in the girls who arrived on the ships coming in to port. Some not being able to find a place to work or live fell into living unsavoury lives of prostitution and crime. She asked Miss Binks if it were possible to bring several of the better girls to the hostel for training.

Miss Binks was able to assure the woman that they would be interested and that they only wanted to have girls who wished to be trained. Miss Binks was adamant that the desire had to come from the girls themselves. Mrs Summers understood and agreed with that principle. They discussed the merits of this training, Miss Binks stating what her methods were.

Over a cup of tea, which was served very well by Martha, and who was introduced to the visitor, they discussed plans. Mrs Summers was able to tell Miss Binks that her Society would be able to subsidize some of the cost of training the girls. Binksie gave no information about how the hostel was funded but only said that she would pass on that information on to her principals.

Binksie showed her visitor over the whole house and encouraged her to speak to Mrs Cook and the girls. She left with the assurance that Miss Binks would accept two or three girls at a time until all their fourteen beds were filled.

Three girls arrived the next day and life at the hostel changed considerably. The new girls seemed to be intruders to Martha and Josie, for they felt that this was their own home and were a little resentful of the changed conditions. But when they realised that the work was now shared life seemed a little rosier. They felt that they were the seniors and that they could tell the new girls what to do. Mrs Cook had to watch Martha at first for she was, for all her 12 years, inclined to "be a bit above herself", as she reported to Miss Binks.

However they all settled down and soon each girl was rostered to do daily tasks and one day of the week each was free of household duties and could spend that time studying or doing whatever she wished. Miss Binks had a variety of extras that the girls could be interested in, and when they had been there for a short time could work out what interested them most, be it sewing, millinery, specialized cookery and cake decoration, knitting, embroidery or any other handcrafts that would never have come their way in any other life they lived.

It was not long before more girls arrived from Mrs Summer's association and Miss Binks had to ask for more teaching staff. But Mrs Landon stepped in here for she had been spreading the word to her friends and because of this there was considerable interest among the ladies of society. Soon three of the women of her circle came to her with genuine offers of help with certain skills and Mrs Landon and Miss Binks was able to report to Ricky that the hostel was humming with activity. The women not only brought skills but they brought ideas and some of them very useful indeed. Soon the girls of the hostels were being trained, not only as maids and shop girls but nursery maids and other more skilled positions. Their handcrafts of embroidery, especially their white work, and their patchwork quilts, won great commendation and some of the girls were able to sell their pieces.

The boys hostel grew slower than the girl's but nevertheless it did grow and soon there were several men who came in to teach the lads and there were eventually ten who were there to train. They, too, learned various skills, but most wished to learn to be effective clerks and managers, buyers and salesmen. They had made a very good workshop in the yard at the back where most of the boys could learn carpentry and joinery, especially working on furniture restoring under the tutelage of Mr Brown, a rotund man with a great sense of humour.

The main house was furnished carefully and slowly by Ricky. He was particularly interested in the cedar furniture made by Andrew Lenehan[1], which was made in the colony of local timber. Also Ricky had been able to acquire some lovely furniture which had been brought from England and had been battered on the voyage out. Under Mr Brown's guidance these pieces were being restored by the boys in the hostel and were either for use in the houses or for sale. The boys working on these projects being rewarded with some of the money these pieces brought when sold. It was a great incentive for them.

Ricky's house gave him a great deal of satisfaction. He was able to decorate it in a particularly lovely way using soft furnishings and furniture which he had never had in his young life as a street urchin or for that matter had even seen. He often wondered who had the furniture and other stuff that his mother had brought out on the ship and had been sold by the unscrupulous Curtins who had thrown him out of their boarding house. He often wondered, too, whether he would ever find one of the pieces and sub-consciously was ever looking for them, but knowing that it was doubtful that he would ever recognise them if he saw them.

However the main house was getting to the stage of pleasing its owner. Ricky had made a large room which faced south, (as Will assured him it should) into a studio for Will, with his bedroom beside it. Ricky's room was also on the first floor beside Will's. Tad had been given the top floor to do what he liked with, for Ricky had decided that three flights of stairs would be too much for Will.

---

[1] Andrew Lenehan (c1815-1886) who was a cabinet maker in Market St Sydney

Tad was learning a little about how to and how not to furnish his rooms. He made some terrible mistakes and his colour sense was not all that good, according to Will. The colours he had chosen were too strong and before he had been in residence for long Tad was wishing he hadn't been so adventurous and hoped his fabrics would wear out quickly and then he could have newer and quieter ones, not the red and purple he had.

Ricky's business was growing at such a pace that he decided to make it into a private company with Tad and Will as shareholders. He had always given the boys an allowance. Tad somewhat reluctantly taking it and saving it, for he never did like spending money irresponsibly. But since meeting Amabel Landon Tad did all he could to work harder and save harder for although he had not told Ricky or Will, he had his heart invested in that young lady and knew that unless he had some substance behind him her parents would never allow her to come his way. At moments of sane thinking he didn't really think he had a chance anyway for knowing that he had no 'background' he didn't see that they would let their precious child go to a chancy fellow like him. But she was his goal and he would at least try to win her, but also try to be sensible at the same time. In his moments of madness he felt that she may be attracted to him, and her lovely shy smile made his heart do peculiar things, but he told himself not to hope.

Ricky on the other hand never seemed to have his heart involved in anything but business. Tad considered that he was growing quite dull and that he was only interested in making money. Ricky objected to this and knew that it was just his skill in knowing how to make that commodity, not his desire for it, that was the truth. There was no doubt about it, his store was thriving to such an extent that he would soon have to think of the new large store that he planned for the land that he had bought in Durham Street.

Ricky had no idea when he could start building, so thought deeply what he should do and set about having some plans drawn up. He didn't know whether he should build in stages or wait until he could build the whole. He would have to borrow to be able to build it all now and was loath to do that. So until the plans were drawn by the town's architects for the whole thing he would bide his time.

Will was still painting with Patrick Thomas. He always told Ricky and Tad he disliked the man intensely, but seemed unable to break away from him as he knew he was a great teacher even though he was an unpleasant man. Ricky thought that Will was painting very well, and was interested to hear that Mr Landon thought so too. That gentleman told Ricky that he thought he would send Will to Paris when Ricky felt he was mature enough to be able to take the life there. This startled Ricky a great deal, and disturbed him too, enough to protest to John Landon and say that he really thought Will ought to stay home and be content here, and anyway he wasn't strong enough to fend for himself. John replied that Ricky hadn't noticed that Will was maturing fast and would soon be a grown man. "You can't keep him tied to your apron strings forever, Ricky."

"I don't intend to, sir. Anyway, I don't," he said indignantly.

"I think you do a bit," said Landon jokingly. "A good thing too, if you ask me. Goodness knows where he would have ended up if you hadn't. He knows it, too."

"He's a good lad. But he's awfully one-track-minded, Mr Landon. I don't think he ever thinks of anything but painting."

"You would be surprised. He looks as though he is in a dream half the time, but deep down he knows what is going on around him. He is very fond of you, Ricky, and would do anything for you."

"He shouldn't feel that way. But I am very fond of him, too."

"He considers that it was because of you that he has his painting. He wonders if he ever would have found it if it hadn't been for you."

"I am sure it would have found an outlet somehow, don't you think Mr Landon? It is strange when you think of it, just how our lives could have taken different turns. I can look back and say ... if this had happened, or if that hadn't happened. What then?" mused Ricky.

"Yes, son," said John Landon, looking closely at this young man who meant so much to him, "I look at you and think, what would have happened to my girl if you hadn't been there when she needed you most."

Ricky just managed to look rather sheepish at this, for he rarely thought of his episode with Amabel, and was usually startled when the older man reminded of it. Amabel always gave him a shy smile as though she shared something secret and special with him, but Ricky just looked to her as he would his own sister and she to him.

Will had acquired a sort of pupil. Young Phil Yates spent as much time as he was allowed with Will. Phil attended school now that they were settled in their new home. He told Will that he was crowded out with females and he disliked it intensely. He had asked his mother if he could go and live in the boys' hostel but, of course, she was adamant that he should not. But he hoped when he was older she would let him do so. In the meantime he spent as much time as he could curled up in the corner of Will's new studio watching that young man paint, and sketch and model. Phil was a quiet boy who tried not to intrude more that he need. He often sat for hours watching Will. Will sometimes forgetting he was there. But when Will began to model with clay he found that Phil could hardly keep away.

Will did not do much modeling, but sometimes did it to roughly get an idea where shadows would fall in a painting he was doing. Patrick Thomas did some sculpture and so Will had picked up the rudiments of the art, not having a real keenness for it but finding it an interesting medium for what he wanted. But young Phil could hardly keep his fingers off the clay that Will had brought home from the studio. It was kept in a wooden tub with a damp cloth over it and at times Will was surprised to find some of the pieces that Phil had used and replaced in the tub. He was sorry that some of the little boy's efforts were destroyed for he could see that Phil had an eye for it. He tried to encourage him to model while Will was there but the little chap was reluctant and so Will just had to be content to know that Phil was using the material at all. He was surprised that a ten-year-old could stay so still, watching, watching all the time.

But one day Will came home to find Phil hard at work, the boy so intent that he was hardly conscious of the older one being there. Will, understanding the mood, just lightly picked his way across the studio behind Phil and sat down with a book. It was quite a long while after this that the boy looked up and smiled.

"Hello, Will. Are you home?" he asked.

"Yes," said Will. "Can I look?"

"I suppose so. But only if you really want to," he answered hesitatingly.

"Only if you really want me to, Phil. It's your business and it is up to you."

"All right," said Phil and stood up, leaving his clay on the board while he washed his hands at Will's sink.

Will went over to the table and looked down at the boy's model. There, on the board, was a lovely little cat, lying on her side feeding four fat little kittens. All very beautifully executed. This perfect little tabby mother cat, complete with stripes, had lifted her head and was looking up, just as though she was watching her creator. The satisfied look that a mother cat has when feeding her babies was quite evident. You could almost hear her purr. Will stood looking at this wonder, he was so still he forgot Phil standing beside him until he spoke.

"It's Nittens, Will. I wanted to make her stand but I couldn't. I don't know how to make her legs keep her up. So I made her lying down." He looked up at his friend. "Is it all right, Will? Do you like it?"

"Yes, Phil, it's all right. And yes, I do like it."

"Good. I'm glad. I tried before, you know, but I couldn't do it right. But today I felt I could."

"Yes, you did, old chap. We must keep it. I'll get a wire and we will lift it up off the table and put her on another board to dry. We'll cover it with damp cloths and let her dry slowly. All right?"

"Yes, all right. Do you mind if I do keep it, Will? Because I rather like it you know." Phil looked up anxiously.

"Help me put it away in the cupboard and we'll think what we should do with it. I think we should have it baked so you can keep it always. What do you think, Phil? An artist should always keep his first major work, you know."

Phil's small chest expanded with pride. "Yes, I must keep my first major work, mustn't I, Will? Then I can do lots of other things, can't I?" he added.

"I can see that you will do lots and lots in the future, my lad. We'll have to see about you taking lessons someday."

"You could teach me, Will."

"No, lad, I can only teach you to draw a little but I fancy you are more interested in modeling and such like. What are you going to be, I wonder? A mason like your father?"

"My mother tells me he wanted to be a sculptor, that's carving things, you know, but he had to be a mason. I'd like to be a sculptor, too. Do you think I could be, Will?"

"You never know Phil. I didn't know I wanted to paint until I saw it done."

"If I could carve then I could have made Nittens stand up, couldn't I Will?" asked the small boy wistfully. Will looked down and the serious face and agreed. Phil then asked, "How could I carve her legs in stone, Will? Would they break easily?"

"I've wondered about that sort of thing myself, and it must be a bit tricky, but I daresay you could learn how."

"There's something else I would like to do, Will. If I tell you you won't laugh, will you?"

"You know I won't. What is it?"

Phil sat down and thought for a minute and then cocked an eye up and looked bravely at Will. "I want to make a boy," he said.

"You mean a statue?"

"Yes," Phil said stolidly, "I do."

"Who's the statue to be of, Phil?"

"Henry," he said.

"Henry?" asked Will. "Who is Henry?"

"Henry was at my school and he was nice. He died, Will. He was nice to look at, I liked looking at him. I would like to make a statue of Henry to give to his mother. I think she would like it. She could look at it and see Henry. Do you think she would like it? I remember what he looked like."

"You are an amazing fellow," said Will sitting down suddenly. "That's quite an ambition. I've never heard of anyone wanting to do that. Did you like Henry a lot, Phil? Was he a special friend?"

"No, I didn't know him much at all, but I liked looking at him. He was sort of put together right. Do you know what I mean?"

"You mean he was handsome?"

"Yes, " he said eagerly, "that's it. I was going to say he was pretty, but you can't say that about boys, can you? Yes, he was very handsome and I think it is a shame I can't look at him any more."

Will tousled the boy's hair and said, "You know young man, you are quite someone to have round the place."

CHAPTER 11: *Mr English*

The boat drifted down the river quietly. The four soldiers watching the banks carefully. Two men were at the oars and one at the rudder, the officer at the bow crouching on the forward seat.

The sergeant, who was steering, said, "They can't have got this furr, sir."

Major Hinds looked around and softly said, "I think they could have, sergeant. They had a lighter boat, you know, and they were quite fit. If they had rowed hard they could still be ahead of us. We'll keep going. Put your backs into it men, and lets see what's around that bend."

The men dug the oars in and soon they were skimming down the waters of the Hawkesbury. It was a lovely spring day, a bit hot for rowing in heavy uniforms, and soon the men were sweating freely. They rounded the bend and the full vista of a long stretch of water lay before them. Not a sign of the boat they were seeking with the three deserters.

Major Hinds peered ahead and said, "They couldn't be that far ahead, sergeant. We must have missed them, but I don't know how unless they were hiding in a patch of thick scrub. We'll turn back."

"Sir," said the sergeant, "I thought I saw something. Let's go on a bit and look at that bank over there."

"All right, sergeant, but its a long way back upstream, remember," Major Hinds said. A muffled groan came from the oarsmen. "Pull over there, men."

As they neared the western bank an aborigine appeared. He was a tall black man, carrying some spears and other weapons. He appeared to be alone and was waving wildly.

"Blacks, sir," came the yell from the sergeant, picking up his rifle.

"Put your arms down, sergeant," Major Hinds said.

"But he's got spears, sir."

"Yes, I see them. It's when I don't see them that I worry, sergeant. Pull in, men. We'll land and see what he wants."

They drifted towards the bank. "What do you mean, sir, when you say it's when you don't see them that worries you?" asked the sergeant.

"If they want to attack and not show their arms, sergeant, they often hold them with their toes and drag them through the grass so you cannot see them. They are usually safe when the arms are apparent." As the boat neared he landed, the black man making welcoming noises to him. "Stay here with the boat, men, and sergeant, come with me."

"Will I bring the gun, sir?" the sergeant asked anxiously.

"No, I am sure all is well."

The native gestured to a place not far from them and obviously wanted them to follow him, he turned and they found that he was leading them towards a patch of bush near some rocks. "White man," he said, "longa dere."

Major Hinds turned to his soldier, "You'd better bring the gun it may be one of those we are after."

The black man must have understood what he meant for he said, "No, no. Sick." He took them through the bushes and they were surprised to find a man lying on some leaves near a shallow cave. He was a sorry sight, very bedraggled, with long dirty hair and beard. What was left of his clothes were just pitiful rags. The man was very ill indeed and was certainly not one of the men the soldiers were seeking. He looked as though he had been in a bad way for some time.

"Who is he, sir?' asked the sergeant.

"You may well ask," Major Hinds said kneeling down beside the man. He was burning with a fever and was very weak. His lips were very dry. "Sergeant, give me your water." The sergeant unclipped his water bottle and passed it to his officer. Hinds held it to the man's lips and he drank greedily. He spoke to the man who just looked up at him silently.

"No talk-talk," said the native. "Sick. He finish."

"What's your name?" The major asked.

"Me Durren."

"Where did you find him, Durren?

"Dharug[2] men find. They come Dharug country," he said pointing along the river. "They find him long time, long time. Him in boat, they get boat and him in. Him sick." He bent down and showed them a very old scar along the man's scalp where a ball from a rifle had made a deepish groove. "They take him, fix him. He live longa them in their country. Dharug country. He no talk-talk ever. Now he sick they bring him back."

"Who is he Durren? What's his name.?"

"Me not know. Him hab box in boat. Dharug leave here." He pointed to inside the cave. Durren led the way in and pointed to a ledge up above their heads. They could see nothing in the murk of the cave and the major told the sergeant to climb up and look. The man didn't look happy about it and asked, "Will there be snakes, sir?"

"I doubt it, sergeant. Come on man."

The reluctant man climbed up and peered into a deep cleft in the rock. "I can't see anything, sir. It's black dark up here."

"Well feel around , sergeant. Come on man."

"Yes, sir, I've got it. It's a tin box. Here sir." The sergeant passed a small tin chest down to his officer and jumped to the ground. "It's been there for years, I'd say, sir. But it's sealed all right."

Major Hinds knelt on the ground and tried to open the lid but found it locked. So he took it to the sick man and asked him if it was his. The man looked fixedly at him and then there was a slight movement that could be a nod. "I am going to force the lid. I hope you don't mind," he said, and as there was no obvious upset from the man he took it that he was agreeable. The sergeant produced his bayonet and with this they forced the lid open. In it were papers and a wad of bank notes that were in amazing preservation, there must have been several hundreds of pounds. The sick man watched but took little interest, so the major took the papers and read the

---

[2] Dharug people are a group of indigenous people of Australian Aborigines that were united by a common language, strong ties of kinship and survived as skilled hunter–fisher–gatherers in family groups or clans scattered throughout much of what is modern-day Sydney.
http://en.wikipedia.org/wiki/Darug

top one, then the others below this. They all seemed to be in the name of Richard English and to do with buying a parcel of land from one Thomas Smith.

"Richard English? Are you Richard English," he asked the sick man. A slight nod was the reply.

"Do you know him, sir?" the sergeant asked.

"No, but I know his son whose father was reported to have gone missing, oh, some ten years or so ago." He looked down and found that Richard English had fallen asleep or had become unconscious. "We'll have to take him back with us, sergeant. Go and get the men."

They cut two saplings and with their coats threaded through these they were able to make a simple stretcher. They lifted the sick man on to this and carried him to the boat. Major Hinds turned to Durren and taking his hand, thanked him for taking care of the man. The black man turned and disappeared into the scrub.

"Sergeant, I think it would be better if we carry on to Mr Forrest's place and unload Mr English there. I know he will see that I get Mr English to Parramatta as quickly as possible. It will be better to take him in Mr Forrest's carriage than an army cart. We could make the journey much more quickly."

"Yes, sir. Is it far from here?" asked the sergeant.

"To Forrest's place, you mean? No, not far. You can unload there and then make your way back to Captain Saunders and tell him what has happened," said the major.

"Do you mean to go with him, sir?"

"Yes, indeed, and to Sydney tomorrow if I can get him there in time. I would dearly love to deliver his father to young English, even in this state."

"Do you think he'll make it, sir?" the sergeant asked anxiously.

"I sincerely hope so, sergeant. I will know better when a doctor has seen him in Parramatta."

Round the next bend of the river they saw a small pier jutting out into the water and quickly drew up at it and moored the boat to it. The major sent one of the men to the homestead and soon was back with the farmer.

"Good day, Major. Your man has told me the story and I have

given orders to have the carriage put to. My wife is anxious to do what she can for the poor man before we take him away."

"I think there is little we can do Mr Forrest, except have some water for him if he comes back to consciousness again."

"Well, we have some of that, Major. I will take a flask of brandy too in case we need it." Mr Forrest watched as the men took the stretcher ashore. "My, he looks bad. Poor man."

"I only hope we can get him to his son alive, Mr Forrest. Did Johnson tell you who he is?" the major asked.

"Indeed he did, Major. Young Mr English will get a shock. I daresay he never thought to see his father again. It always was a mystery. You know he was going to be a near neighbour of mine and I was looking forward to having him here. He must have been going to Tom Smith's place to pay him for the land when he was hit by someone unscrupulous." He tut-tutted as he trotted beside the stretcher and was quite breathless by the time they got to the stables, where some workmen were putting the last of the harness on the horses. Mrs Forrest was hovering nearby and handed her husband a hamper.

"Hurry Edward. I've put everything in the basket that I can think of that you may need," she said and added as she looked down on Richard English. "Poor dear man. What he must have been through all this time. Wouldn't you let me clean him up a bit before you go, Major?"

"Thank you, Mrs Forrest, I think we must go. I am sure the hospital will do all that. It is a long way and I feel we must go. Thank you, again."

"God speed, then. I will be most anxious to hear how you get on. I won't worry Edward, you stay with the major as long as he needs you," she said.

The long trip seemed even longer, the sick man waking at intervals and taking some milk and brandy which the major mixed up from what was in the hamper. They had lain him on the squabs of the very comfortable carriage and Major Hinds thought he was as comfortable as he could make him.

"I am glad you thought to bring him to us," said Mr Forrest, as he watched the major taking in the comfort of the carriage.

"He is far better off in this than an army wagon.

"I was thinking the same thing, Mr Forrest. It is a lovely carriage," answered the major.

"Well, as you know our roads are none too good and its lonely enough for a woman in these parts and a good well-sprung carriage is an essential in my eyes. Nell likes a trip to town and this allows her to have it," the farmer said.

It was dark by the time they reached Parramatta and as they drew up at the hospital Major Hinds sighed with relief that they had made the journey with his patient still alive. They soon had him taken into the hospital and bedded down in a ward. The nurses cluck-clucked over the dirty state the man was in, but the Major was happy to leave him in their hands, which he hoped were capable. They assured him that the doctor had been sent for and suggested that he take himself off and come back later if he must. Mr Forrest took him aside and suggested that he take him to the Duke of Wellington for a meal and leave English with the staff and come back later to see their patient.

Over dinner Major Hinds told Mr Forrest that he had known Ricky since he was a twelve year old urchin and admired him immensely. Even at 12 he thought there had been something really good about the lad, and was happy to say he still thought so.

"He's built himself a grand store, Major. It should be a great asset to the place. But I believe Mr John Landon is behind his venture," the farmer said.

"They have been quite close, Mr Forrest and I know that Mr Landon has been a guide to him all these years, but I feel sure that Ricky has done most of it on his own, gathering in some other young men as he's gone along," the major said.

"I see that you know him well, Major."

"Yes, I do, sir and admire him greatly. I sincerely hope I may deliver his father to him so that he may have him for at least some time, however short it is."

"I join you in wishing the same, Major. Shall we return now and see how he goes?"

"Thank you for dinner, sir. I doubt whether I would have thought of it if you hadn't been here."

"Well, no, I didn't think you would, under the circumstances. I am going to suggest that we stay here for the night, for I have no intention of returning home until morning," stated the farmer.

"Yes," said Tim Hinds, "I imagine that is a good idea, I am not thinking."

"I can see that you are most anxious. We'll book rooms as we go out."

At the hospital they found their patient looking better. He had been washed and most of his matted hair had been cut off, he looked a deal cleaner anyway. The doctor was about to leave when they arrived and stopped to speak to them, assuring them that he was anxious to do so.

"Mr English is in a bad way, gentlemen, but I think with care he will pull through. Apparently he has had a bad head wound at sometime which seems to have put a stop to his ability to speak. I think his fever is caused from that old wound but he should get better. That is as well as he ever will," stated the doctor.

"Will I be able to take him to Sydney tomorrow, doctor?"

"I would not advise it, Major. Is there any real need to do so?" the doctor asked.

"Yes, there is. He has been missing for over ten years and his son must have the opportunity of having some time with him. If I take him on the ferry would he not be all right? I would have him taken straight to the hospital there." The major asked anxiously.

"I do not recommend it, Major. But if you insist, of course I cannot stop you." Came the reply.

"Would it really hurt him, doctor. I feel very anxious to get him near Ricky."

"Well, I'll tell you what. If you take two nurses with you, I will let him go. I will give them strict instructions and he will be in their care. I daresay the ferry would be the best way to travel as the road and rail would be too rough. All right, I agree," the doctor said reluctantly.

There were not as many ferries running since the rail was put through to Parramatta. They took Mr English, with the two nurses, to the wharf on the Parramatta River, in Forrest's carriage, and were able to claim the quietest and most secluded area they could find on the ferry. Major Hinds thanked his farmer friend and promised to tell him of Richard English's progress.

The major saw little difference in the condition of the patient, on the trip. At times when he looked at him he found that Richard English's eyes were open, and once he even turned his head as though to see where he was going. Tim Hinds sat beside him all the way and whenever he found the man's eyes open he spoke softly to him telling him where they were taking him. He didn't think he ought to mention Ricky to him at this stage and in any case there was no way of telling whether he had taken anything in. At Darling Harbour they were able to get a conveyance to take him to the hospital.

The doctor who saw him was quite encouraging and suggested he leave him in their care to go and find his son. "I don't think it can harm him, but he is in a pretty bad way and may not even be able to understand who the lad is. It's some years since they met, you tell me?"

"Yes, doctor. Mr English doesn't even know that his son has arrived in the colony or indeed that his wife is dead."

"Well, I would tell the lad not to go into details. He needn't tell his father about anything that would worry him, like his mother's death. I daresay he wouldn't understand, but he just might and I would like to see him much better before he is told anything serious."

"I'll tell Ricky that."

"Do you mean this is Ricky English's father. I didn't think about the name. He's not a lad, he's a grown man," stuttered the doctor. "I thought you said the boy was twelve."

"He was eleven or twelve when he saw his father last and that's about 10 or more years ago," explained the major.

"What a story!" said the doctor, "and what a country! This wouldn't have happened in England." He went away tut-tutting.

Tim Hinds was not looking forward to telling Ricky about his father. He wondered why, for he knew he had been very fond of him. Then he thought that finding half a father might be worse that none at all. "Ah, well, it must be done." He wondered where he would find him for Ricky was in the process of moving into his grand new store and could be in either place, the old or the new. He opted for the old and called in to Landon's office for support on the way.

"May I see Mr Landon, please?" he asked at the front desk of Landon's office.

"I am sorry, Mr Landon is not in," answered the clerk.

"Will he be back soon?" asked the major.

"That I cannot tell, Major. May I take a message?" the clerk asked.

"Well, if he comes in in the next 15 minutes, could you please ask him to meet me in Mr English' office?"

"Major, that's where Mr Landon is. You will catch him if you go right down."

"Thank you, I will," said the major already on his way down.

He was shown into Ricky's office, carrying the tin box, to find the two friends talking over a cup of tea. He was welcomed warmly and Ricky sent for another cup. "Sit down, Tim. Draw up that chair," he said.

The major sat looking worried. He put the box on the floor beside him. John Landon said, "What's wrong, Hinds? You look as though you have something on your mind." The major didn't know how to start.

Ricky laughed, then said, " Come on, Tim. What's the trouble?"

Mr Landon asked, "Is it something private? Shall I leave you?"

"No sir," said the major hurriedly. "No, sir, I went looking for you so you could help me."

"All right, tell us man," said John, pouring the tea.

The major could hardly get it out, then took a breath and said, "Ricky, I have something to tell you." He hesitated once more.

Ricky realised that something was wrong and was suddenly serious. "Tim, what is it? Get it out, man, and tell me. Now you're worrying me."

"Ricky, I have found your father."

"What?" "Where?" asked the two men.

"Is he alive?" asked Ricky.

"Yes. I'll tell you all about it." He proceeded to do that and his two companions sat stunned while the story unfolded. When he had finished telling, Ricky jumped up to get his coat and set off, but the major restrained him and said, "They told me not to let you see him for an hour or two. I know it is hard but he has been having a rough time and he is pretty exhausted. I'll tell you all I can and then we'd better work out what is best to do."

Ricky sat down again, saying, "I can't believe it. Tell me more, Tim. Start again, please."

So Tim Hinds started all over again, filling in the bits he had missed out and telling gently that he didn't think that Richard English could speak. Ricky and John questioning him so that they could get the picture in full. It took Ricky all his strength not to go straight to the hospital but was taken by his friends to lunch while they tried to keep his mind busy.

Early after lunch they accompanied the young man to the hospital and Tim was pleased to see that Richard's hair and beard were now neatly trimmed and he looked a great deal better that he had when he had arrived. He was asleep and so Ricky just went in and sat by the bed. He took his father's hand and put his head down on the emaciated body. The sick man's eyes opened and he looked rather startled, not knowing, of course, who the stranger was.

"Hello, father. I am Ricky grown up. Can you believe it is me? I've missed you so much." Richard continued to look and didn't show any sign of understanding, but Ricky felt a slight pressure on his hand and thought that he may have had some glimmering of recognition.

This was the beginning of many long vigils Ricky had at his father's bedside. He had long talks with the doctors who could give him no definite answers to his queries, but kept telling him it was just a matter of waiting, eternal waiting. They knew that the ball that had come from the gun which shot his father years before was responsible for his lack of speech, but they had no means of knowing whether he had been able to lead any sort of normal life apart from speech. The very fact of his not returning home indicated to them that he had been unable to or had forgotten how to. However they thought that with patience Ricky might be able to teach his father to recognise him. If he ever reached the stage of Ricky being able to take him home they thought his father would eventually learn to accept the rest of Ricky's household as well, and at least be comfortable with them. By the hour Ricky would sit by him and hold his hand and when he began to feel better he told him about his mother's death and how he had grown up and was now a wealthy business man. He received very little response but Ricky told himself that he was improving.

Tad and Will visited his father with Ricky, but they were quite unused to the conditions and found it hard to just stand there telling someone about a life that they obviously knew nothing about. Tad tried so hard to be patient and keep the vigil with Ricky, but Ricky realised that it was something he had to do alone. He could not expect the lads to share this with him and so sent them off to carry on with their own lives. However, Will still accompanied Ricky whenever he could and it was not very long before he was sketching the sick man.

After many weeks the doctors told Ricky that if he could arrange for someone to look after Mr English he could take him home. They told Ricky that there was little hope of improvement but the man seemed to derive a great deal of comfort from Ricky's visits and they thought it would be a good thing to give him a life in his home away from hospital where there was always noise and busy-ness. At the same time telling him that as he probably had a ball somewhere in his head he could succumb at any time, and so Ricky must be prepared to have him for only a limited time.

Ricky found a young man who was willing and able to look after his father. He vacated his own room and turned that into a place of comfort for the patient and his attendant. His sitting room gave them a place where they could spend their days. Ricky moved up to the top floor into a room beside Tad's.

Henry Job grew very fond of his charge. He was a very patient young man who was quite content to attend to someone who showed little response to his ministrations. As time went by Richard recognised them all and would even smile at them when they did anything for him. It was about all he ever did.

Will's studio was on the same floor and at times Henry would wheel Richard in on his chair with wheels which Ricky had ordered to be made especially for him. At first it was because watching Will paint was a pleasant pass-time and as Henry was content to sit and watch, Will didn't mind him being there. They were surprised to see how interested Richard apparently was. His eyes seemed to be glued to every stroke that the young man put on canvas.

Will drew and painted several good pictures of Richard and one day fell to wondering what he had looked like when he was younger and in full health. He decided to try to reconstruct what he imagined him to have been, and painting from the side which was least affected by his illness, that is the side that didn't have the scars from the gunshot, he set about producing a portrait which he would give Ricky.

It was finished and sitting on an easel when Ricky came to see his father one day and it nearly took his breath away. All he could say was, "Will, oh, Will lad. You have caught him just as I remember him as we said 'goodbye' to him in London."

"Is it right, Ricky?" asked the artist. "Is there anything you can think of that I haven't got right?"

"No, I think it is just perfect. Will, thank you. Thank you very much. It is the way I had remembered him all that time. You are good to think of it."

"He seems to have been very interested in what I've been doing, Ricky. Henry and I are amazed at how he keeps watching all the time. He never seems to go to sleep while he is in here."

It was just three weeks after that that Henry roused Ricky one night with the news that his father was ill and he thought Ricky should get the doctor. Tad heard the disturbance and volunteered to go for him. Ricky found his father very restless and hot and knew that the fever caused by his old injuries had come upon him again. He'd had several of these episodes in the time he had been in the house but this was a very severe attack. Ricky didn't need the doctor to tell him that his father was dying and to their dismay he passed away just three days later.

It was a sad mourning household when this happened and he was laid to rest in the cemetery at the south end of the town, just near his mam.

Ricky went back to his new store after playing truant on so many occasions during his father's illness, but with no regrets of wasting any of the precious time he had been able to spend with his dad after all those lost years.

CHAPTER 12: *Ricky's trip to the Hawkesbury River*

It was on Ricky's mind that he would like to and indeed, should, go out to the Hawkesbury to thank Mr Forrest for all he did for his father. He had written to the man, of course, but this time he wanted to thank him in person so he wrote again and arranged to visit him one weekend. He asked Tad and Will to accompany him, telling them that he expected to stay at the hotel where Mr Forrest and Tim Hinds had stopped in Parramatta. Tad refused, but was torn, for he wanted to see more of that country, but he had promised to visit the Landon's that weekend and wanted to keep the appointment. Ricky wondered why it was so important, for Tad saw quite a lot of Amabel and it was not like Tad to miss an opportunity for any kind of adventure. However, he accepted the excuse, and in any case Will was anxious to accompany him, so he would not make the journey alone.

They went to Parramatta by train[3] and checked in at the Duke of Wellington Hotel in time for dinner. They strolled out into the streets while it was still twilight and walked along to the hospital where Ricky's father had stayed. They didn't go in for they knew that Richard had not been there long enough for anyone to remember him.

Ricky hired a carriage and driver the next morning and they set off at an easy pace for the Hawkesbury River country. It was good to relax and enjoy the countryside, so different to their usual scenery. Ricky asked Will if he felt he wanted to paint scenes like these, but Will explained that he had no real thoughts about it and it was people and streets that interested him.

"But I like looking at it, Rick, and I wouldn't mind living out here some time, but I want to paint my kind of things, for people

[3] Sydney's first rail line connected Sydney and Parramatta Junction near Granville and opened on 26 September 1855. It was extended to the current Parramatta station on 4 July 1860

and streets have filled my life and ... well, I daresay I don't know any other life. Maybe if I lived in the country I might be moved to paint landscapes. But I daresay I won't be anyway so I don't think about it." Will pondered over the idea.

"Have you thought any more about Mr Landon wanting to send you to Paris, Will?" asked Ricky.

"Not really, Rick. I daresay I'll think about it sometime, but it just doesn't seem to fit in with what I am doing right now. Do you think I ought to go Ricky?" he asked rather fearfully.

"It isn't what I want, Will. I would miss you, as you would right well know. But it isn't up to me, you are the one to make up your mind, and I am happy to go along with whatever you want." Ricky smiled at him.

"I daresay lots of people would jump at the chance, but ... oh well, Mr Landon hasn't mentioned it for a while, so I don't really have to think about it, do I?"

Ricky chuckled. "You're too comfortable, that's your trouble."

"Well, I must admit Paris seems very far away, Ricky and I don't remember any life but Sydney and I'm not all that anxious to leave it. Yes, I daresay I am too comfortable. Sorry if you're disappointed." Will looked sheepishly at Ricky.

"No, I'm not disappointed, Will. I want you to do just whatever you wish and you're old enough to make your own decisions, goodness knows. And as I know nothing about the art world except what you have taught Tad and me, I daresay I haven't any knowledge to advise you one way or another."

They passed through a great deal of wooded country and after some time they came out into lovely farming land. The drought which the farmers had just been through for some time was over and the paddocks looked grand in their mantles of green. Sleek beasts were grazing in all the paddocks, mostly dairy herds, Ricky thought.

"Sometimes I could think I was in England, except for the eucalypts," Ricky mused.

"Is it all that different, Rick?" asked Will.

"I think it is. Mind you my memory is not all that good, but I think it is quite different."

The driver knew where Forrest's farm was and Ricky was interested to see it as they drove up the long avenue of poplars which led to the house. Without knowing much about farming, Ricky could see that it was very tidy and neat and quite prosperous looking. There was a herd of Jersey cows grazing in the nearest paddock and Ricky was quite surprised that he remembered what they were. His father had them in England and he felt sure that his dad would have approved of these.

Edward Forrest heard the carriage and came out to greet his guests. "Welcome, welcome," he called as the carriage pulled up. He told the driver where to take the vehicle and ushered Ricky and Will into the house. Calling to his wife he took them into a huge living room in which was scattered large comfortable sofas built for size and comfort. It was easy to see that the man of the house had a say in their purchase for he was a big man who appeared to like his comfort. A fireplace stood on one side, the mantle made of the local sand stone, which was very popular in the colony.

Mrs Forrest came in bustling to meet their guests. Ricky saw a pleasant, smiling woman of medium height who had a bright complexion as though she had been running. Ricky was to learn that she always had that swift way of doing things, he thought she was forever rushing here and there. However she was pleased to sit and talk to them and soon was pouring tea and plying them with superb scones dripping with melted butter.

"I know you will be famished, Mr English, "she smiled at both men, "so eat up, for it will be a while before we sit down to luncheon." She continued to pass the scones around until they could eat no more.

"They are lovely scones, Mrs Forrest. I would never tell her so but our Mrs Keen doesn't make them like that," said Will.

"Thank you, Mr English, I don't do much cooking nowadays, but I do like to make the scones, for most people seem to like them. The children do in any case."

Then they spoke of generalities and Ricky found himself asking intelligent questions about the land and after a while admitted that he had thought he had forgotten all he had ever known about a farm.

"You know farming, then Mr English?" asked his host.

"Until I was 11, we had a farm in Sussex. I thought that was what I would be, a farmer. I really had no thoughts of doing anything else. It was just accepted that I would work with my father. It was not to be."

Mr Forrest steered the conversation away from what he thought might be a painful subject but Ricky spoke his thanks again to the man who insisted that he had done no more than anyone would have in the circumstances. "Besides, young Hinds had the matter in hand. All I had to do was provide the transport," he said.

"And very much more," said Ricky. "I do thank you both. In fact I wanted to come and personally do so, for you have no idea what it meant to me to have my father with me if only for a short time, and I am sure if you had not been able to help he may not have stayed alive long enough for me to see him again."

"How long did he live? Was he able to speak, Mr English?" Mrs Forrest asked.

Ricky told his interested hosts about his father's last weeks, telling of the happiness he got watching Will paint and the contentment that had shown in his father's face during that time. "It was as though he knew he was at home, wasn't it Will?"

"Yes, Mrs Forrest. Henry, the man who looked after him would wheel him into my studio in his chair and there he would be watching everything I did. I got so that I would have long conversations with him and forget that he couldn't answer. Every now and then he would heave a large sigh and smile as though he was as happy as could be. He must have been a wonderful man. I wish I had known him before the accident."

"Can't you remember him, Mr English?" she asked anxiously.

Will looked at Ricky and said, "Please tell Mr and Mrs Forrest, Ricky."

Ricky chuckled, "All right Will. You see I adopted Will and Tad as my brothers, Mrs Forrest, because I was rather lonely and we were all at a loose end."

"What a way to put it, Rick! Thaddeus and I were just little strays, Mrs Forrest. We were homeless and quite miserable. Ricky found us and looked after us, he has done everything for us. I would never have learned to paint if it hadn't been for him. We owe him everything."

Their hosts looked rather startled at this and looked at Ricky for confirmation. Ricky looked rather embarrassed and said, "What we did we did together," he laughed.

"He adopted us and we took his name because we had none of our own, or at least if we did we didn't know. That is great isn't it?" said Will.

Ricky was quite startled at this because Will rarely opened out to this extent. He just smiled and said, "Well it has suited us and it makes life easier if we have the same name. I am sure if my parents could have chosen they would have given me brothers like Will and Tad."

Ricky was very pleased that at this stage a maid came to announce lunch and he thankfully got to his feet and followed his hostess to the dining room.

This room was furnished with colonial Lenehan cedar pieces. The large table shone with the effort of much polishing. It looked quite new and indeed was for Mr Forrest asked, "Do you like our new table, Ricky. I am going to call you Ricky, I do hope you don't mind."

"No, I will be pleased if you do, Mr Forrest. And yes, I do admire your lovely table. Is it locally made, sir?"

"Yes. We are both very interested in the furniture made from colonial timbers. We feel that they are as good as we had at home in England. The table we brought out was damaged and we always promised ourselves a good replacement when we found one that suited. Lenehan does a good job, don't you think?"

"I have furnished our home with all local timbers and we are pleased with it, aren't we Will?"

The door opened and a young woman entered holding a small boy by the hand. She was followed by two young girls. Ricky thought she might be a governess but seemed more familiar than one would expect from such a one. Mr Forrest introduced them saying, "Jenny, my dear, come along and meet Mr Richard English and Mr William English who have come to visit. And gentlemen these are our three colonialists, Amanda, Nellie and James. Miss Elston came to live with us in this unknown land just three years ago. Wasn't she adventurous to come out all alone?" They both agreed that she was and was introduced to the children, Amanda, Nellie and small James.

"Come along then," said Mrs Forrest, "If you will sit here Mr English and here Mr English."

Ricky and Will laughed, then Ricky said, "Truly it would be much easier if you would call us Ricky and Will. Please do this Mrs Forrest."

Mrs Forrest smiled and said, "Thank you my dear boy. I do feel I want to and having heard about you from Mrs Landon I have wanted to meet you. "

It was a happy meal. The children were obviously used to dining 'en famille' as they behaved as children do when doing something familiar. It was a relaxed time and the boys felt very much at home with these friendly people. Ricky took note of Miss Elston who was very much part of this remarkable family. He was able to watch her without anyone seeing, he hoped. She was of medium height with crisp brown hair. Ricky would not have called her pretty but she was a pleasant healthy looking girl. At this thought he was surprised at himself for he thought it rude just to think of her as pleasant. She was a very attractive person, not because of beauty but she had a vitality and happy countenance that made her quite ... Words failed him at this stage and he found that he been addressed by his host. He was quickly able to catch enough of Mr Forrest's question to be able to make a sensible answer and decided that he must keep his mind on the conversation and not get caught again.

They all sat on the wide verandah after lunch and then Mr Forrest suggested that they all walk to the 'Folly" and look at the river view before it was time for his guests leave them. On being told that the Folly was a summer house or gazebo that Mr Forrest had built with his own hands Ricky and Will stated that they indeed wanted to see this marvel. As they set out Mr Forrest asked Ricky quietly whether the walk would be too much for Will's crippled leg and was happy to be told that Will could manage very well.

Miss Elston and the children went with them, the children running ahead joyously calling out and playing 'tag'.

The extensive lawns ran right up to a knoll on which stood Mr Forrest's folly. It was a circular building as such often are, made of oiled timber, looking as though it was happy nestling in amongst some beautiful shrubs. There were six steps up to the floor level and this enabled one to get a full view of the surrounding country from the windows which were set in place right round the building. Below them the ground sloped to the green banks of the Hawkesbury River. There were some very handsome horses grazing in the nearby paddock and they could see Mr Forrest's Jersey cows further down. The property was on a slight bend of the river and so gave river vistas on three sides. The Blue Mountains seemed to be at their bluest on this sunshiny day. In the other direction one could look over the rest of the farm which, on being shown where the boundaries were, Ricky could see that it was very extensive indeed. There were lovely orchards of what Ricky thought would be several different kinds of fruit. The house nestled in amongst beautiful trees and the artist in Will approved of it all.

"It is almost too beautiful to paint, Ricky. Remember what I said coming out here? Well, I take it back. I can see lots of things I would like to put on canvas. Mr Forrest may I come and paint from here sometime?" Will asked Mr Forrest.

"Oh, do you paint, Mr English?" asked Miss Elston.

"Yes, I do, Miss Elston, but nothing like this has come my way before. I must admit I have not attempted anything like this superb scene. Whenever I have been out into the countryside it had just seemed to consist of fields and cows."

"Most of it is, young Will. But I must admit I am proud of this particular view," replied his host. "This was all thick scrub when we came here and I almost had to burrow my way through, but I did want to see what one could see from here and I found this. That's why I built my folly."

"It wasn't folly to build it, sir," said Ricky, "It is a work of art in itself. He's an artist in his own right, isn't he Will?"

"Well, we enjoy it," said Mrs Forrest, "We often come up here for tea in the summer. Please sit down, do."

"I'll go down after the children, Aunt Nell. They are getting too near the creek and will end up by falling in," said Miss Elston.

"All right, dear. Bring them back and we'll go down for a cup of tea before our visitors have to leave."

Ricky managed to seat himself in a position where he could watch the muslin clad figure without making it too obvious. He saw her run to catch up to the children who had wandered down to a line of small trees that apparently lined a creek. James saw her getting close and run fast to get away from her. He ran fast and then suddenly jumped as though he jumped over a hurdle, yelling something that the adults could not catch. They saw Jenny stop where he had jumped, giving the girls instructions to get their little brother and go away she grabbed up a stick and began to flail the grass. Ricky jumped up realizing that there must be a snake there and hearing his movement Mr Forrest, who hadn't been watching asked what was wrong, looked down and gasped, running out and down to the group as quickly as he could. But by the time he got there, with Ricky hard on his heels, Jenny had dispatched the wicked looking thing.

Mrs Forrest had taken the scene in and knowing she could do nothing she had waited, fingers in her mouth, hardly breathing, until she heard relieved voices, then she let out a long sigh of joy. She turned to Will who had started out after them, but realizing he would not help, returned to the gazebo, "I hate those things, Mr English. I don't think I will ever get used to them. If it wasn't for snakes, I think this country would be perfect."

"I've never seen one, Mrs Forrest. I wouldn't know what to do with one if I did see one," he replied.

"Well, I daresay you should go down and look at it for you never know when you will come across one." Mrs Forrest rather shooed him off, and he walked down to meet the group.

He was surprised to find that Mr Forrest was carrying the snake up to him looped over a stick. "I brought the snake up William because Ricky tells me he has never seen one and thought you hadn't either." He lay it on the ground. "This is my brave heroine who very neatly killed it in the correct place." He smiled at Jenny.

"I've never killed one on my own before, Mr English. I did do it once before but Uncle Ned was with me and told me what to do," she said.

"Well, I think you're brave, too," said Ricky. "I wouldn't have known what to do." He looked with great admiration at the girl. She had made light of it, but looking down at the snake which was still writhing now that it was on the grass. "What a wicked looking thing it is. Do you get many, Mr Forrest?"

"Yes, we do. That is why I taught Miss Elston what to do, Ricky. You never know when you will come across one here, and they are all bad ones. To my mind there is no good snake and I kill them all. This is a brown and quite lethal. Look I'll show you what to do if you were to meet one. Children, it is good for you to have another lesson with it, too."

They all watched while he lay it down in some longer grass and Ricky and Will were amazed that a thing five feet long could look so inconspicuous. He showed them how to keep watching it while searching around for a stick, then using the one he had he thrashed it, and showed them just where to aim.

"It is still moving, Mr Forrest. Is it really dead?" asked Will.

"Yes, son, it is. But still dangerous so ..." turning to the children he asked, "What do we do?"

"We keep our distance," they chorused.

"Yes, we do. Lesson over. Let's go and get some tea." As he turned he gave Jenny a squeeze on her shoulder and said, "You're getting to be a good Australian, my girl."

The children raced up to their mother telling all about the snake. She sent them on towards the house and with Jenny on one side and Will on the other walked off down the hill.

Ricky walked with Edward Forrest, saying, "That was a brave thing to do, Mr Forrest."

"Yes, she is a plucky lass is our Jenny," he said.

"I take it she is a relative, sir."

"Not a close one Richard. Her mother was Mrs Forrest's cousin.

Her parents died about four years ago and after her brother married she was made to feel rather de trop, I think. My sister-in -law thought she was unhappy and told us about it and we invited her to come here. She courageously jumped at the opportunity and came out by herself. Or rather she came with another family who have daughters, the Bradleys. Do you know them?"

"Yes, I have met them. Miss Elston is going to stay out here in the colony then, Mr Forrest?"

"Oh yes. We are very fond of her and would only let her go with a fight," he said with a laugh.

They walked along silently for a moment. Then Ricky said, "Mr Forrest, there is one thing I would very much like to ask you."

Forrest looked up sharply and stopped. Ricky was rather startled at the look on the man's face as though he expected Ricky to say something outrageous. Ricky stopped, too, and stared in wonder at the man. "What have I said, sir?"

"Go on," his host replied, "say it. What do you want?"

"Well, sir, I was wondering whether you might advise me as to how I should purchase a property near here."

"Oh," said the man relaxing a little. "What do you want a property for?"

"Well, knowing that my father was buying one and as I have the money he was going to use to do that, I thought I would go ahead and buy one and use it to train some of my boys."

"Your what?" he demanded, "Explain yourself."

Ricky was rather taken aback at the change in the man's attitude. "I am rather keen about training boys to be well equipped to hold down good jobs, and I have a scheme in operation in Sydney which enables young fellows, perhaps unfortunate ones like we three were, to be trained."

By this time his host was smiling and at the last of Ricky's words, burst in to laughter. This non-plussed Ricky even more. He asked, "Whatever have I said to upset you, Mr Forrest?"

"I am sorry, lad. I was imagining all sorts of things. I really am sorry I jumped ahead of you. Please pardon me?"

"Of course sir, but won't you tell me why I upset you?"

Ricky asked anxiously.

"One day I will, lad, one day I will. When I know you better."

Ricky expostulated to no avail, his host could not be drawn.

"Give it up lad, I won't tell you how I jumped the gun. But now you must tell me more of this training program of yours. Tell me all about it."

Ricky was still explaining when they reached the house. He found his host much interested in his ideas and gave some very constructive ones in return. However he was still baffled by Forrest's unexplained behaviour. "Maybe he is unreliable or something," he thought, "but he doesn't seem to be. Or perhaps thinks I am."

Forrest led him to the dining room from where they could hear voices. "Come along, there will be tea ready and you must replenish your inner man before taking to the Parramatta Road again." As they entered the room where the family sat eating, he said, "Nell, Ricky tells me he wants to be a neighbour of ours. He wants to buy a farm."

"Mr English, that would be nice. But I thought you were a town business man," she said.

"Yes, I am, Mrs Forrest. I would not try to run it myself." When he sat down he told them about his training plans for farm workers, explaining about his father's money. They were all very interested in what was planned and made many suggestions.

"I think you must come back, Ricky, with time to look around. I will make some investigations about farms and write to let you know. But I have just the right man for the job of training the boys, here on the farm."

"Who, dear?" his wife asked.

"Rob Martin, of course, Nell." He turned to Ricky. "Martin and his wife had a farm near here. They lost their only child, a son. Then Mrs Martin became ill some time ago and needed hospital care. So he sold up and went to live in Sydney near the hospital to be near his wife. She died, poor soul and he has come back here. He hasn't enough money to buy again and not long ago asked me for a job. I only had a dairy hand job vacant but as he was desperate I put him on. He is a good man and I am sure he would jump at the chance. You couldn't do better."

"Of course, dear. I should have thought of him. He is a good man, Mr English. Very honest, and kind. They were quite distraught when their son died. They planned so much for that boy. When he died, I think that is when Mrs Martin gave up trying to live. He would be good with boys, Mr English. I am sure."

"It looks as though I have come to the right people to advise me then, Mrs Forrest. I thank you for thinking about my ideas."

"You must do as my husband suggests and come and stay when you want to look around. There is always room for visitors in this rambling place."

"Thank you, I will accept your kind offer. There is one other thing, though, Mr Forrest, before we really must start on our way back."

"You are full of surprises, young man, what is it this time?" asked Forrest, with a mock scowl, but with a laugh.

"Have you seen anything of the aborigines who helped my father, sir?"

"Well, that's quite another question. You see we don't seek them or encourage them, but, yes, I do see them when I go up river. The place where your father was found is quite a well known camp for them. Next time you come we'll go along and see if we can make contact."

"Thank you, sir. Are they safe to visit?" Ricky asked anxiously.

"Yes, quite safe. There hasn't been trouble here for years. Only we don't encourage them because they are rather apt to hang around. But if they do come over this side of the river we give them tucker[4], when we think they need it, and indeed they usually only come when they do need something."

"I would like to meet that man who was looking after my father and so will take you up on your offer, sir."

"Hinds told me that it was a man called Durren. I have heard of him through others, too. He seems to be a good type and has worked on the farms at times. But you know, they are not given to working on farms much and the farmers don't encourage them, but when we are short of labour we have tried to utilize them,

[4] food

154

without a great deal of success. It's just not their way of life." Mr Forrest added, "I will try to find Durren in any case Ricky, before you come again if possible."

"Thank you, sir, I would appreciate it and look forward to meeting you again soon."

The Forrests led the young men out to their conveyance and said their goodbyes, assuring them of a welcome when they cared to return.

Ricky sat in a brown study not realizing that Will was as silent as he. He lay back on the squabs thinking of Miss Jenny Elston. Thinking of her and thinking of the effect she had had on him. "Is this love?" he wondered. "I am sure I do not feel like Tad does, or I don't think I have shown it if I do. There was no mistaking it when Tad fell head over heels in love with Amabel Landon. Tad showed it with exuberance. But I don't feel exuberant, I just was to hold the thought of her as one would a precious jewel, in my hands. Precious, yes, that's the word to describe what I feel. She is so precious that I don't want to share it with anyone. I just want to think of her. I wonder if she is thinking of me."

Ricky came to earth to hearing William say, "so perfect in form. So lovely it took my breath away."

Ricky's heart turned over. "Not Will, too. No I couldn't bear it if she had that effect on Will too. She's mine," he thought. He sat up and asked, "What did you say, Will?"

"Weren't you listening, Rick? I was telling you about the form and how I wanted to draw it. You know I think I could have been wrong about the country, there are a lot of things I could paint, I see that now." He looked at Ricky, startled. "What's up Rick? You all right?"

'What are you talking about Will? Explain yourself." Ricky asked anxiously.

"I'm talking about that tree, Rick. Didn't you see it. It was on the slope where the girl killed the snake. It was a gum tree. Did you see it? It was standing by itself and was all gnarled and twisted with a big top and filmy leaves against the blue of the sky and the mountains. It was really lovely. What are you laughing at? I know

I said I didn't want to paint out here, but that tree was special." Will added indignantly.

Ricky had burst into gales of laughter in sheer relief. "Sorry, Will. I wasn't laughing at you, but myself. I was half asleep and you got all mixed up in a sort of dream."

"Well, you looked really odd, Ricky as though you were scared or something."

"Don't worry old man. I wasn't thinking properly.

After a while Will asked again, "Hey, Rick, did you mean it when you asked Mr Forrest about buying a property out here?"

"Yes, I did, Will. You know I have been thinking about it, because I want Father's money to be spent on the land. He had no use for town life and I want it to do something useful. I am sure he would like that. What do you think?"

"Well, if it is the success the other training houses are I would think it would be most successful. The Forrests seem to want to help, too."

"Yes, they are nice people aren't they? Miss Elston seem to be all right, too, wasn't she, Will?"

"Yes, she was all right. Easy to talk to. Is she the governess or something?"

"No. Not really, but then I suppose she really is."

"Whatever do you mean?" Then Ricky spent the rest of the journey relating all that Forrest had told him of the girl. He felt it was safe to do so, but as he did he felt a lovely warm glow as he spoke of her.

CHAPTER 13: *Ricky, Mr Forrest and Jenny*

It was late in the evening when Ricky and Will reached home. Mrs Keen was waiting to serve supper and Tad was pacing the passage aglow with excitement.

"I've got to tell you, Ricky. I've had the most marvellous day." Tad burst out as soon and Ricky walked in the door.

Ricky mildly said, "Have you, Tad? I'll want to hear about it but wait 'til I've washed up and sit down to supper."

"I want to tell you now, Rick. Mr Landon ..." said the impatient Tad.

"Wait a while, Tad," said Ricky eyeing Mrs Keen and trying to hush Tad.

"All right," said Tad, "but hurry won't you," he called as Ricky disappeared up the stairs.

Tad had to curb his impatience while dinner was served and it was not until the meal was over that the three were alone and able to talk.

"Now, Tad, tell us all," said Ricky, "what was it that Mr Landon said?"

"Ricky, Mr Landon will allow me to pay my addresses to Miss Landon. Isn't that great?"

"Well, yes, it is Tad. But I thought you were doing that all this time. I imagine that if Mr Landon didn't want you, he would have rid the family of you a long time ago."

"That's what I've been hoping, Rick, but I didn't really know. Just hoping."

"Well, go on tell us what happened, Tad," said Will.

"Mrs Landon and the girls were going out and so I thought this would be a good time to speak to Mr Landon. I asked him if I may and he took me in to his study. Gosh, I was nervous." Tad hesitated.

"Well?" said Ricky.

"Yes, well. I told him what I wanted and he asked me to sit. Then he asked my what my prospects were and how I would be able to support a wife and everything. Mind you I assured him that I didn't want to marry for a while. Just to have an engagement. He questioned me and questioned me. He wanted to know how much I earned, and what other money I had. I was able to tell him what I do with the money I do earn and how I buy shares in the newspaper with it. I told him, too, about the shares you gave Will and me. He seemed to be a bit surprised that I do save."

"Was he happy about that, Tad?" asked Ricky.

"He ought to be," put in Will. "You never seem to think of anything else but newspapers and how you can make enough money to be able to marry Amabel. I want to do more with my life than marry someone. Seems to me that once a man is married he never has time for anything else. Look at us. Ricky and I are free to go where we want and do as we please."

Will missed seeing Ricky colour at these words. He tried to cover his mild confusion by asking more about the interview and then they fell to discussing what Tad's future plans should be. Ricky offered him the top floor of the house for when they married and they discussed how that could be modified to suit their needs.

At the back of Ricky's mind he wondered how all their lives could alter in the next few years. Will seemed to be content to be just Will, painting when he felt like it and enjoying the life he led. He was selling quite a few paintings nowadays so he was not as dependent on Ricky as Ricky had thought he would be. In a way Tad and Ricky took a small part in Will's life but they were always there when he wanted or needed them. He had a careless regard for anything serious in life and was content to just let it all slide. Ricky wondered how he would get on if his interests took him out to the Hawkesbury often, perhaps even settling out there at some time, with or without someone like Miss Elston. He was afraid that Will would miss his brothers and Ricky made a pact with himself to see that Will was not left bereft.

Mr Forrest wrote telling Ricky of two properties that may suit and so he went to stay at "Claremont", the Forrest property, and enjoyed himself immensely. He was very careful to watch Miss Elston from afar, not wishing to hasten things along too quickly, but was very pleased when opportunities cropped up which allowed him to have some conversation with her. By the end of that first weekend he knew that his heart was telling him aright that he was in love. Not just with a sweet girl who had nothing much to commend her but her looks. No, he felt that his Miss Elston was a young lady of character and good sense. Not that she was not attractive, indeed she was, but her beauty was more of a wholesome type rather than the extreme prettiness of some of the town girls he had met. He hoped that he would be able to make many a visit and get to know her very well. He was delighted when Mr Forrest, casting a wary eye on the young man, suggested that Miss Elston accompany them on their inspection of a dairy farm nearby.

"Not that I wish for her expert opinion," said Mr Forrest, with a laugh, and looking down at the young lass, "but Jenny wishes to visit Mrs Ormsby who is looking after her father."

As they drove off down the avenue of trees, Mr Forrest told Ricky about the man they were to visit. "John Raynes is an old man now," Mr Forrest said. "He had a stroke not long ago and so is now unable to get around. He has been a wonderful dairy farmer all these years that he has been in the colony. About thirty, I think. I would say it is about the best dairy I have seen out here. He has a large herd of Guernseys and has specialized in producing butter and cheese. Unfortunately he has no sons to follow him but has six industrious daughters who are also married to farmers. His wife died some years ago, and my goodness, she was a worker. His daughter, Mrs Ormsby, lives quite near and has come to be with her father until he sells up. Then she will take him to her home."

"I look forward to meeting him, sir. If I cannot manage to buy his farm, then, perhaps he can advise me about some other," said Ricky.

"He could at that," said his host. "He is well thought of around here."

Jenny Elston sat in the phaeton looking around her and waving to this one and that. Mr Forrest sat beside her and pointed out the various farms and other interesting features of the countryside.

He was quite a knowledgable man and was apparently keenly interested in the doings of his district. He was on the roads board and noted any part of the road that they were travelling on that was less than par. He showed Ricky where the road changed considerably and said that Mr Raynes had taken it upon himself to keep his section of road in good order at all times.

"Is this the farm then, Mr Forrest?" asked Ricky.

"No, not until you get to that stand of trees, so obviously Mr Raynes has spread his care further along the road than he need. See this line of trees." Forrest indicated trees which grew along a fence boundary. As they drew near he said, "Here. The property begins here." He told his driver to pull up. Standing in the vehicle he showed where the farm ran down to the riverside and right along this to a ridge that cut down from the hills right to the banks. It was a wonderful sweep of lush green pasture that was breathtaking in beauty. Across the river were the thickly covered mountains where the bush came right down to the river flats. "It is something to delight in, isn't it, Ricky? And that isn't all. Raynes has more farmland over that ridge. It is harder country than this and that is where he keeps his Hereford herd."

"I didn't dream that it was as good as this, Mr Forrest. It seems to be very extensive, too. Do you think it is in my range, sir? I do have a limit, you know?"

"Well, lad you did say you were looking for two properties, and here I present you with two properties in one. It has everything you will ever need and if you could manage to buy it I can see that it will provide you with all the challenge you will ever want."

"And the price you told me, Mr Forrest, is that for all this. It seems to be a very good offer. How big did you say it is?"

"Over 500 acres, lad. Take your time, but in the meantime we'll go and see Raynes, for he will be expecting us."

Ricky sat down and found himself looking at Jenny opposite him. She had said little during the journey and nothing while they had been stationary. "Why so silent, Miss Elston? What do you think of it all?" Ricky asked.

"There is little that I can say, Mr English, for I do not know about buying properties. But Mrs Ormsby is my friend and I know she holds her father in high regard, both as an honourable man and as a farmer. I have heard Mr Ormsby say that his father-in-law is the best farmer he has ever met. I believe the dairy is renowned."

"Indeed, yes, Ricky wait until you see the set-up there. He has a wonderful dairy and an excellent staff who produce the best butter and cheese in these parts."

"Would the man Martin be able to manage a place like this, Mr Forrest? It would be beyond me for I would never pretend that I know how well or otherwise the farm should run. I would have to trust him to have complete control."

Forrest smiled and said, "I am happy to recommend him to you. I know him to be completely trustworthy. I would not say so unless I had that confidence. He is an excellent farmer and would still be on his own farm if it hadn't been for his tragic family life. He is a likeable chap, don't you think? I feel sure you would suit each other admirably."

"Do you know Martin, Miss Elston?" Ricky enquired.

"Yes, Mr English. My aunt and I visited his wife when they were still on their farm and often saw him when we did this. He appears to be a caring man and would I think be completely trustworthy," Jenny answered. "Of course, I know nothing about his farming methods but I do know he is well thought of in the district."

Ricky smiled his answer to her and sat gazing around him at the lovely piece of Australia that could become his own. They drove up a long well kept track and pulled up before a wide squat house that seemed to nestle into the hillside. The front was elevated and wide wooden stair ran up to a wide verandah that must look across the river to the mountains.

As they climbed the stairs a woman came out to greet them, "Good morning, Jenny, Mr Forrest." Mr Forrest introduced Ricky. "Welcome to "Rocklea", Mr English. Come along, Father is waiting to meet you. Jenny lead the way, Father is along on the east balcony, its warmer there in the morning."

They were taken round the corner of the long verandah and Ricky found that this wonderful building ran most of the way around the house. They found an old man lying on a lounge chair looking up anxiously at his daughter. Introductions were made and Mr Raynes bade them sit. Mrs Ormsby left them and soon re-appeared with a tea trolly loaded with tall scones and pikelets loaded with jam and cream, and a huge teapot. Soon they were sampling this repast and Ricky decided that "Rocklea" cream was the best he had ever tasted.

As soon as morning tea was over the two women disappeared and the men talked business. Mr Raynes wanted to know what a young town businessman wanted with a farm. He sounded a little scathing and so Ricky settled down to tell him a little of his own history and what his ambitions were for helping the young people in the colony. He was questioned closely and Ricky soon learned that Mr Raynes' body might be deteriorating but his mind obviously wasn't. There were questions that Mr Raynes also asked Mr Forrest about his guest and Ricky was surprised to find that his host had been making quite a few enquiries of his own. He felt as though these two men knew him through and through by the time the session had finished.

After a long while, it seemed to Ricky, a man arrived on the verandah, asking Mr Raynes if he may enter. On being asked in, he was introduced. Ron Fells was the manager, who Mr Raynes had asked to escort the two visitors to look over the farm.

"I must tell you now, that Ron does not wish to stay on the farm. He had given notice some time before this wretched stroke came upon me and has kindly stayed to help until I can sell the place. Ron now has his own farm and is keen to work on it. Now, go along. I will be anxious to hear your verdict."

Ron Fells took them to a buggy which was drawn up at the front steps. "We'll drive over to the far paddocks, Mr Forrest, and look at the pastures there."

"Right, Fells. I am looking forward to it for I haven't been over the ridge," replied Mr Forrest. "In you get Ricky."

The track from the house led straight to the huge ridge of rock that ran down from the hills to the riverside. At first Ricky could not see a way across this but as they drew near he saw a wire gate, which Fells opened after throwing the reins down casually. Edward Forrest moved to take them but Fells assured him that old Betsy would stand.

Ricky could see a track running along the fence and into the trees, they soon drew into higher ground and then the track turned up over the ridge itself. Fells drew up to look across the farm.

"This part is what we call the home farm. This is the dairy section. The beef cattle are over in the valley. That's where we are going," he said.

They sat looking at the lovely scene before them. Ricky drew a sharp breath at the sight of it all, wondering if it could ever be his. The thought was rather daunting and hard to take in.

"Seen enough, sir?" Ricky turned to face the man. Fells looked at him in his town clothes and Ricky felt rather surprised at the expression on his face. He knew that Fells was thinking that he was just a run-of-the-mill town farmer or perhaps had ambitions to be one. He was about to explain but then decided that if Fells was to be a near neighbour, he would soon find out what Ricky's motives were, so he stayed silent. Forrest had caught the expressions on both of his companions' faces and making a good guess as to their meaning he chuckled and said nothing.

"Yes, let's get on, Fells," Forrest said.

The track was surprisingly flat on the ridge as the actual ridge was quite wide. They rounded a corner and there before them was a lovely valley. The ground was sloped and quite extensive. Along the far side of it ran a creek that obviously came down from the hills. On the far side of the creek was thick timber and this formed a natural barrier. The cleared paddocks ran for some way up towards the hills and here and there stands of trees had been left to give the sleek cattle good protection, although in this sheltered area one would presume that they would not need it for it was a shelter in itself.

"Down this way," Fells said, pointing to their left, "the paddocks go almost to the river. You can't see the river for the trees, but we will when we get down there." He click-clicked at Betsy and she moved slowly down the track, which was quite steep but manageable.

The horse trotted comfortably when they reached the track that lay at the foot of the ridge and soon they were looking over the river at the hills on the other side.

As they turned to go back Fells asked if they wished to go the full length of that paddock to look at the cattle which were sleeping under the trees.

"Can we see all of the paddock from here, Fells?" asked Mr Forrest.

"Yes, sir. You can see it all. There's just bush further on and some very pleasant swimming holes. The young ladies used to like to go up there where Mr Raynes has had it cleared and they picnic beside the creek. Very pretty, it is," he explained.

"Are you anxious to return, Fells?" asked Ricky.

"Not if you wish to see more, Mr English, but I was instructed to get you back at the house for lunch at half after twelve and it has gone noon now. We could come again this afternoon, sir."

"It it possible to drive over to the cattle there under the trees? If it is I would like to see them and then we could return," said Ricky.

"Yes, we can go straight over now. The ground is level and we can drive anywhere in this field, Mr English. You'll find they are in fine condition. May I ask, sir, if you know cattle?" queried Fells.

Forrest and Ricky both laughed. "I daresay I know as much about cattle as you do about running a store," said Ricky. "I hope to learn a great deal in the future and I also hope that Mr Forrest and Rob Martin can teach me. But in any case I would like to see the cattle," he added happily.

"I would guess you would learn all right, Mr English, and if you have Rob Martin here to teach you, you would not go far wrong. Is that not so, Mr Forrest?" the man asked.

"And I would imagine he would be a quick learner, Fells," replied Forrest, "I haven't noticed that he is a slow top."

Fells drove slowly across the paddock so as not to disturb the beasts, and indeed they just stayed quietly in the shade as the vehicle drew near. About a dozen young Herefords turned to look at their visitors. They stood lazily gazing at the men while slowly chewing away as is usual in such animals.

"They are in excellent condition, Fells," said Mr Forrest.

"Yes, sir, they do well out here. It is good pasture."

Fells turned towards home and they quickly scaled the ridge and through the gate to the home paddocks. "After luncheon, I believe Mr Raynes wants me to show you the dairy and the herd over here and so I will collect you when you are ready, Mr Forrest."

"Thank you, Fells," they said.

Mr Raynes was waiting anxiously for their return but refrained from asking his questions. He called, "Ada. Ada, where are you? Our visitors have returned."

Mrs Ormsby came to her father and greeted the men. "Come in, gentlemen, lunch is served. Father has his out here so we will be seated."

She led them to a dark paneled dining room where they found Miss Elston waiting. "Please sit. Jenny will show you where."

"What do you think of the farm Mr English?" asked Jenny.

"Very beautiful indeed, Miss Elston. But I believe we have only seen a portion of it. I am rather surprised at its size," Ricky replied. "You must have felt that it was a delightful place to grow up in Mrs Ormsby?" he remarked.

"I will be very sad to see it leave the family, Mr English. I was born here and I must admit it does seem to be part of me, but none of our family wish to take it on and it is far too much for Father now, so we are sensible and know that it must go. You see, all of my sisters have other interests, my family and I are the only ones near to here. Father is quite resigned to letting it go and I think he is quite keen to come to me so that I can look after him. He is very thoughtful."

Ricky made few comments during the meal, leaving the conversation to the others. Apparently Mr Raynes was anxious to hear what he thought of the place and asked straight out, when they returned to the verandah. Ricky shocked the man by telling him that he thought the place may be a little large for what he needed.

"Needed?" asked the invalid, "you need a property? Why would you need a place, Mr English? I thought you were just looking for a country property and I was rather dubious about that. Why do you need a property?" he repeated.

"Well, sir, I wish to train farmers by bringing boys out here and have them taught farming. I am sorry I though I had explained."

"What? What did you say?" The old man nearly exploded and looked quite offended.

"Well, sir. I am interested in giving young fellows a chance to make themselves useful citizens. We have training schemes for boys who want a city life but there are many who don't fit into the town scene and I want to establish a place where boys who have no country experience can learn farming," Ricky explained.

"You mean you would bring a lot of town scum to work on my farm? I won't have it, sir. This is a prize farm with prize herds and you want to turn it into a school or something." Clearly the old man was very upset and Ricky could see that Mrs Ormsby was becoming agitated.

"Father, stay calm and listen to what Mr English says. I am sure it isn't as bad as you think," she said.

"No sir, please, I don't want to upset you. I am sure I can explain what I want. You could help me so much for I will need a great deal of advice."

"Explain yourself then, young man," Ricky was told, tersely.

"Well, you see, Mr Raynes, there are a great number of people coming to the colony whose children don't seem to fit into the lives their parents have. Some are farming folk who have lived in one place all their lives and do not understand conditions out here. Many of them come from farms that have done one thing always and do not understand the diversification that our farms here in the colony have. Take for instance the Scottish farmers who have been thrown out of their farms because of the enclosures ..."

"What are the enclosures, Mr English?" asked Mrs Ormsby.

"Well the farmers in western Scotland, and I am thinking of the Western Isles as much as anything, have always farmed by grazing their beasts on common pasture, but since many of the farms have been sold to English landowners they have enclosed a great deal of the pastures and evicted the farmers. Crofters they are called. Some of the Scottish lords or lairds, have been very worried about their people and have developed a scheme for re-settling them in the colonies. This is fine and has saved the lives of many families, but the farming here is so different that the young fellows are quite at sea. I have found quite a few who just wander the streets not being able to find work. So my plan is to find a place that will be suitable to train fine farmers with men who can be trusted to train such boys."

"And you think this is the place for that, young man?"

"Well, sir I must admit that I had no thoughts of buying a place so grand. I haven't seen the dairy as yet, but if it is anything like the part I have seen, well, then I think it would be too expensive for me." Ricky then explained about his father's money and how he wished to use that.

"Don't you want the best for these lads of yours?" challenged the old man.

"Of course, sir," replied Ricky. "I want the best I can get for them, but, sir, I am not exactly made of money."

"How do you expect to keep this scheme of yours going then, young man?" Ricky was asked.

"It would have to pay for itself, Mr Raynes. The boys would be trained to be experts, I would not have shoddy work. I plan to ask Rob Martin, who Mr Forrest recommends, to manage the place and I would employ the best men I could, but once the scheme is established it must run itself," Ricky explained.

"Well," said Mr Raynes mildly. "You had better get yourself to the dairy and look that over. Come back after I have thought about all this. I imagine Fells is waiting for you. Are you there Ron?" he called.

The dairy was an amazing eye-opener for Ricky. He had no idea that a dairy could be as clean or as large as this one was. He vaguely remembered the one on his father's farm but it had not interested him and it was not the main interest on the farm anyway. This dairy was built along the hill line above the milking sheds so that all the drainage could run freely down into the grassy paddocks and so remain moderately dry underfoot.

The inner walls of the dairy itself were whitewashed and everything was spotless. The dairymaids were just tidying up and so there was not a lot of activity there, but they had just finished their washing for the day and one woman was hanging up the cloths and towels used for the day's work. There were many large bowls on scrubbed shelves which contained the rich milk setting under their cheesecloth covers in preparation for the morrow's skimming for butter. On other shelves were well scrubbed wooden pails and bowls, churns and other dairy implements. Butter pats were sitting in water to keep moist. In the room adjoining but quite separate were dozens of moulded cheeses hanging by their cloth coverings and next to this was the smoke house and cold room where carcasses of smoked pork, ham and bacon were hung.

"I have not seen a dairy as extensive as this, Mr Forrest. Ours at home was just a small one suited to our own needs for we were not a cream dairy but sold milk only," said Richard.

"There are not many as large as this, Ricky. This is really a specialist organization. Tell Mr English about it, Ron."

"Well, you see, Mr English we supply very special customers, most of the leading hotels in Sydney buy direct from us. It has taken Mr Raynes a long while to build up their very satisfied custom and I am sure he would be distressed if it was not carried on."

Ricky realised that this man was certainly not in favour of the property going to him. He understood his feelings and sympathised with him and with Mr Raynes. In fact Ricky was not at all sure that he wanted such a show place of a farm. It seemed so specialized and so top quality that he wondered whether paid staff could keep the quality up without a 'live in' owner. It would take a great deal of thought to come to a decision. He would have to have his man of business look over things and he would find a stock and station man to advise him. Mr Forrest would help, of course.

They looked over the rest of the farm with Ricky thinking hard and not showing a great deal of enthusiasm. He was so tied up with his thoughts that the other men presumed he was not interested. Fells left them as they returned to the invalid obviously showing his distrust of the city man. It was a great surprise when Forrest heard Ricky asking very intelligent questions of the old man and he could then see that it was not disinterest on Ricky's behalf, just very deep thought.

Mr Raynes was very pleased when Ricky said, "Sir, I am very impressed indeed with the quality of your farm and I am loth to take on something that will deteriorate under my care. If I were a full time farmer I would have no hesitation in taking this over but I just wonder whether an absentee owner could expect this quality to remain."

"Well, young man, I, on the other hand, would not like anyone to take over this farm and let it deteriorate. I love this place and I have spent many years building it up to its first class state and would raise thunder if anything second rate was produced here. I was horrified to hear that you were thinking of bringing young ragamuffins to the place. I might be selling my home, sir, but I insist that its standard is kept up."

Ricky could see that the old man was getting quite worked up. He said, "I quite agree, sir. I would hate it of all things. If you did let me buy it I could promise you that I would aim to have the best people available to run it and already Mr Forrest assures me that Rob Martin would be excellent as a manager. I would see that he would have hand-picked staff. But above all, sir, I would wish you to be happy about it."

"Forrest speaks highly of you, lad, and I trust his word. But is there no opportunity for you to come here and live? Are you so tied to the city?" Mr Raynes asked.

Ricky unconsciously looked towards the sitting room where Mrs Ormsby sat with Miss Elston and said, "Well, sir, in all honesty I cannot say that I would never come here permanently, but at the moment I make my living at my store and must tend to that. I would always have an apartment here and I imagine that I would spend as much time here as is possible and would enjoy learning as much as I could about what goes on here."

"Then, young man, go away and think about it and come back again and tell me more about your plans." Turning to Forrest he said, "I can trust him, you think, Forrest?"

"I think you can," said Ricky's host. "We must make tracks, Ricky. It will be late when we get home."

Ricky sat silent as they drove away. Miss Elston thought him far, far away and was reluctant to break into his thoughts. She watched his face because she thought he wasn't conscious of her but suddenly he looked up and caught her at it.

"I beg your pardon Miss Elston. I am sad company, but I have much to think over."

"Did you like the farm, Mr English?" she asked.

"Indeed I did. I could not do otherwise, but it isn't what I expected. It seems too polished and more like a show place than an everyday farm. Don't you agree, Mr Forrest?" he asked.

"You would be taking something on if you did buy it, Ricky. Do you contemplate it?"

"I don't know. I really don't."

"Are you really going to set up a training scheme, Mr English?" Jenny asked.

Ricky smiled, "Yes and an orphanage, too, but I must admit I wasn't brave enough to tell Mr Raynes that," he answered with a grin.

"An orphanage?" "An orphanage, did you say, lad?" Ricky's companions asked.

"Yes, an orphanage. Don't you see lots of poor little town brats enjoying life out at 'Rocklea'?" he said with a chuckle. Then more seriously, "How wonderful to give the children a chance of living in such a place."

"I think you must be serious, Ricky. Is it true?" queried Forrest.

"Oh, yes, true enough, Mr Forrest. It has long been a dream of mine. You see some of the street children would find it very hard to adapt to living in the country for they only know the slums, but if children were brought here when they were tiny they would grow up with it and love it and be able to be better farmers."

"Well I never," said his host.

"I didn't know gentlemen had such ideas," said Jenny wistfully.

CHAPTER 14: *Mr Falconer-Mead*

R icky decided to take the farm and Tad and Will were to become quite used to seeing less of Ricky over the weekends. They knew little of Jenny Elston, though, and did not realise how much Ricky had thought of her. Ricky seemed to see her in everything he did whether at home, at work or at the Hawkesbury. He knew he was deeply in love.

When negotiations became intense he visited 'Rocklea' during the week with his man of business and Jacob Warrender the Stock and Station agent from Windsor. The property would soon be Ricky's and Mr Raynes would take up his residence at Ormsby's farm, Rob Martin was already working at 'Rocklea' for Mr Raynes wished him to become conversant with the working of the farm and would not leave until he was sure that the new manager knew his job. In fact the old man would not sign the final papers until he had watched Rob Martin in action for some weeks. Ricky was pleased with this for he knew that Raynes could tell him whether Martin would be suitable or not for he knew he had not enough experience to judge. He signed all the papers with John Raynes and was able to come home to tell the boys that he now owned a farm.

He returned one Thursday evening expecting Tad and Will to be there but found that Tad had sent a message that he would be eating out and would see Ricky and Will later and would they wait up for him. They were used to Tad having assignments at odd times and so were not very surprised, but it was unusual for him to wish them to wait up. They presumed that he and Amabel had at last set a date for the marriage.

It was with a great deal of surprise that Tad was looking rather glum when he came in. Will, who was ever rather eager to jump in impatiently, said, "What ho! old chap, you look as though the troubles of the world are on your shoulders. Come and unburden yourself. But hurry I would like to go to bed."

Tad came in and sat looking at them both. Ricky said eagerly, "What's up Tad? You look really troubled."

"I am Rick. I ..." he stopped and then said, "I suppose I really should start from the beginning."

By this time the boys could see that Tad was very disturbed indeed and Will asked anxiously, "Are you all right Tad?"

"Yes," he said. "I suppose it's because I have had rather an amazing experience."

"Well, get on with it," said Will impatiently.

"It was while I was on a job this afternoon. I had to go to the King's Arms to interview Gertrude Hamley. You've heard that she's here to play at the Theatre Royal. I was going up the stairs, and you know there's a divided staircase to the next floor. I realised that someone was walking beside me going up the stairs but didn't take much notice for there were others on the stairs too. There's a big mirror on the landing, do you remember? and you feel as though you are walking towards yourself. You can't help but watch yourself approaching, I've done it lots of times. But, you won't believe me. I could see two of me. It took me a few minutes to realise what had happened, that there were two figures looking at themselves in the mirror. The person who had come up stairs with me was standing there. He realised what he saw at the same time as me and we turned to face each other. He just looked like me, but in different clothes, though. You couldn't imagine the surprise we both got. The likeness is amazing.

He asked me who I was and on telling him it didn't seem to mean anything to him. He asked me some more and I told him a little. Then he asked me if I would go and meet his grandfather who was in the hotel, and I agreed. He left me outside a door while he went in to see his grandfather and tell him I was there."

At this Tad sat quietly, his breath came in a sob. Will said, "Go on, what happened?"

"He came back for me and I went in to see a very old man. He gasped when he saw me and asked me to sit and tell him all I knew of me. You see he thinks I am his grandson. Ricky, Will, can you believe it. I think I have a family."

Neither Tad or Ricky saw the colour drain out of Will's face. The lad sat back in his seat and listened to the rest of the story.

Tad went on. "His name is Joshua Falconer-Mead, and so is his grandson. The old man persuaded his son to let his grandson come to the colony to search for his other son, who came out here with his wife over twenty years ago. The last they heard of him was that he and his wife were going out to a place where they were to take up land and that they had a baby son whom they called Theodore. Mr Falconer-Mead was so distressed about not hearing from his son, whose name was Matthew and his wife Martha, that he sent someone all the way out here to search for them. He did this not once but three times and even though he had tried to investigate through the authorities, too, no-one could trace them. You know how it is out here, and with the great influx of people coming for the gold rushes. Anyway they got no help and Mr Falconer-Mead became ill because they could find out nothing. So young Joshua decided to come with his grandfather who was most anxious to search for himself. They only arrived last Monday."

"So they think you are the missing one, do they?" asked Will roughly.

Ricky glanced quickly at Will, but Tad seemed to notice nothing, he was too interested in what had happened.

Ricky said, "Well, do they, Tad? Do they think you are Theodore?"

"They think there is a distinct possibility, Rick. But I'm not building on anything, I don't see how they could find out any more than I know myself. I've tried, goodness knows," said Tad shaking his head.

"You have?" asked Ricky sharply. "You never told me. Has it really worried you, Tad?"

"Of course it has. I have always wanted to know who I was. You are lucky Rick, you know," the young man added wistfully.

"Sorry I didn't realise it, Tad. What about you Will?" Ricky asked.

Will stood up, "Congratulations, Tad. You always were a lucky dog. If you don't mind I'll go off to bed now. I'll hear more tomorrow."

His limp seemed more noticeable than usually. As he reached the door he turned a gave a salute, then left.

Ricky thoughtfully gazed at the closed door. Tad said, "Funny chap, Will. Ricky, let me tell you what they want to do."

"Yes, sure Tad. What is Mr Falconer-Mead going to do to make sure you are his grandson?"

"Well, first thing they are going to try to check from this end, trying to trace anyone who knew anything about me and all that sort of thing, and of course they want to talk it over with you. But I told them you wouldn't know any more than I do." Tad looked quickly at Ricky. "You don't do you Rick?"

"No I don't, Tad. You know that. If I ever found out anything about you I would have told you. I really think we left it a bit late. I don't think it occurred to us at all when we first met up, did it? We just got on with living."

Tad looked rather quiet at that. Ricky caught his mood and asked, "Did it worry you even back that far, Tad? " He could see that it had and said, "Sorry, old chap, I didn't know. I suppose I have been blind."

"You knew who you were, Rick. You didn't have to think that out. The only thing you worried about was where your father was, you knew who you were and who he was."

"I am sorry. You must have felt that I was very hard."

"No I didn't. I knew it didn't occur to you, and in any case, I must admit that I didn't let it worry me much. But recently when I have wanted to marry Amabel, you would expect me to do all I could to rake up a family tree, wouldn't you?"

"Yes, I must admit I have thought of it a little in regard to Amabel."

"Gosh, Ricky, wouldn't it be simply splendid if I did turn out to be his grandson."

"Yes, I would be very happy about that, Tad. Have you thought how it would change your plans? If you are their missing one, what would they want to do about it?"

"Mr Falconer-Mead spoke about that. If my father was his son he was the third, and so there would be no property to come to me but there would be money. He didn't say how much, but I gather he is rather wealthy. In any case I can't see how they could prove it one way or another, so I really am not thinking about that. But at this stage it would be just nice to know that I really belong somewhere. Don't you agree?"

"I certainly do. Now let's have a toddy to send you off to sleep for I feel you are rather wound up. What will you have?" asked big brother Ricky.

"I think I will have some of that port you got from the last shipment. I suppose I am rather wound up Ricky. I just can't wait to tell Amabel."

"I am surprised you haven't already."

"No, Ricky. I felt that I owed it to you to tell you and Will first."

"Thank you Tad, I am grateful for that."

"Well, no matter what happens you are my brother and as far as I can see you always will be. We've been through a lot together, Rick, and I owe you so much. In case I never thanked you, I do, Rick, I thank you for what you have done for us both."

"Come on now, lad, drink your drink, you are getting senti-mental. Come on we'd better go up."

Ricky tapped lightly on Will's door, but receiving no answer he went to his own room to think of his two lads and all they had been through together.

A hotel footman came the next morning with an invitation for Ricky to lunch with Mr Falconer-Mead. He had a previous engagement but decided that he should do all he could to put this aside and deal with Tad's problems first, so hurried to his office and had his secretary dispatch messengers to those men he had been engaged with.

Tad had described Mr Falconer-Mead as old, but even so Ricky had not been prepared for one so frail. He immediately felt drawn to this man who had suffered much in the loss of a son of whom he was obviously fond. He first told Ricky about his family, how close they had always been, how sad he was when his son had decided to come to Sydney Town.

"I could not blame him, though, for he was my third boy and there would be no land for him at home. I would have done as he did.

He told me that as he could not live at "Mead Park" forever he would go and seek one of his own in the new world. He was a good lad and a good correspondent, as was Martha. They never let a mail go without letters to his home or hers. Her family were near neighbours, Stanthorpe by name, and friends of long standing. Our properties march side by side in Sussex and all our children grew up together. Matthew and Martha were of an age and had loved each other from the time they were tots, I think."

"You must have wondered at not hearing, sir, when the mail stopped."

"Yes, I did, and the Stanthorpes, too. James Stanthorpe and I got together and sent three lots of people here to find out what happened. All we could discover was that after selling their house so that they could settle in the Bathurst area, they moved into lodgings, for Martha's time was close and they wanted her to be in the town when the babe was born. They expected to move out west when the child was old enough to travel. We heard of his birth and that it was not an easy one, which makes me think that Martha may have been ill with that. But the last letter from my son told us of the little one's birth and that they had named him Theodore, and Matthew remarked, "He is a little tad". But I did not tell your Tad that."

"I am glad of that, sir. But really I imagine that Tad feels that he does belong for apparently there is a remarkable likeness with your grandson."

"Yes, Mr English, it is remarkable. I may have to depend on that likeness to guide me for I believe it will be hard to prove anything else."

"I did try to find out a little, when I first met Tad but even then I couldn't find out much. Tad had spoken of an old woman he called "Gamma" but as she had died before I met Tad I was not able to trace anything of his story. We did go to where she had had lodgings but no-one knew anything about her. I must admit, sir, it did not seem to be important to us at the time, for it was much more important to find enough to eat each day, and antecedents didn't matter in the scheme of things."

"I suppose not, young man, I suppose not," said the old man. Ricky could see that he had upset him. But he went on to ask Ricky, "Will you tell me all you can about that life of yours when you were growing up together?"

"I will sir, but I daresay to you it will not be a pretty story. But in our own way we were happy. You see our life was spent striving to keep body and soul together and to then try to gather enough to better ourselves."

"I want to hear, and about the other boy Tad told us about."

Before Ricky could start on the story there was a tap on the door and a young man entered. Ricky gasped. Here was Tad's twin. He had never seen two men more alike. It put all doubts out of his mind. No two such people could be unrelated. They shook hands and Mr Falconer-Mead explained that Ricky was about to embark on the story of Tad's life as he knew it.

Ricky tried to be as truthful as he could telling what a scrubby little fellow Tad had been, but even though he tried to belittle his part in the story Mr Falconer-Mead said, "Mr English, I want you to know how sincerely grateful I am to you. I shudder to think of what hands Tad may have fallen into if you had not found him."

"No sir, don't feel like that. Tad actually found me and we did things together. He always had good stuff in him and so I didn't have to do much," protested Ricky. "It was also Tad who brought Will into the family. I am not responsible for him. In fact we all did things together. We felt like a family and still do."

They all talked more and more until Mr Falconer-Mead realised that luncheon time was passing. He asked Joshua to pull the bell for service and they set about choose a meal that would be served in the room.

"I do not get about as easily as I used to, Mr English, and usually eat in my room when I can," he said. "Young Joshua is my legs and I only have to sit and wait to hear what he has been doing. Eh, Joshua?"

"Are you not well, sir," Ricky asked.

"Shall we say a little old, young man," he answered.

"I admire you very much, Mr Falconer-Mead, for taking such

a journey. It makes me realise just how very keen you were to find your grandson," Ricky said.

"I am fortunate that I am an excellent sailor and so was able to take the voyage well. But I did spend most of the time in my cabin but was well looked after. My grandson seems able to cope with one so old," and smiled at his grandson.

"I didn't have to do much Mr English as my grandfather brought his valet with him and Burton knows how to look after him. But I must admit poor Burton is not a good sailor so we had to exchange cabins for some of the way, and I was able to be with Grandfather for those times. We spent many a pleasant hour playing chess for we are well matched."

"Indeed we are, lad. I taught him to play and at times I am sorry for it."

"But many times you are glad, Grandi," the young man rejoined.

"Especially when I beat you Josh, eh? Ah, here's lunch."

A man who was obviously not of the hotel staff entered the room pushing a trolley. He deftly brought a table towards the men setting it up neatly and quickly. He announced that the meal was ready and served them silently. Joshua helped his grandfather to the table and smiled at his and the man's assistance.

"Mr English, this is Burton. We've been talking about you, Burton. We told Mr English that you did not enjoy all of the voyage. Not too good, was it Burton?"

"No sir, not all of it," smiling at his master.

Ricky enjoyed these two men and no matter where the conversation started it always seemed to finish up with the subject most on their minds.

Young Mr Falconer-Mead seemed to voice their thoughts when he said, "Grandfather, I wonder whether we would ever have found Tad if he hadn't happened to meet me on the stairs."

"I wonder that, too lad. I just wonder that."

"Do I take it then, sir, that you really are convinced that Tad is your grandson?" asked Ricky. "Have you made up your mind so quickly?"

"What would you think if you were in my shoes, Mr English. Eh? What would you think?" the old man asked.

"I wouldn't attempt to answer that Mr Falconer-Mead, I have no evidence but the resemblance to justify my opinion. So I will not say."

"You are very sensible, young man, and I will not tell you just what I think, yet. Nor will I stop trying to search for further clues. In fact I will not say anything to Tad one way or another until we have been here some months and I get to know him well. I wish to meet Mr Landon and his family, especially Miss Amabel, whom I am told on good authority is very beautiful."

"I daresay you will wish to check up on me, too Mr Falconer-Mead and see what kind of fist I have made of my life." said Ricky. "I would expect you to do that."

"Indeed I will young man. I hope to know you a great deal better by the time we leave for home."

"I look forward to that, sir. I hope I can be of service to you in some way and will always be as co-operative as I can."

Ricky pondered over the problem and wondered how it would end. Did it mean that Tad would have to go back to England, change his name and take up a life that would be so different to the one here? How would Amabel like this new life away from her family if this happened? What a change could come over them all. What did Will feel about it? His manner was rather strange last night.

When Ricky got home that night Mrs Keen told him that Will was not coming home until late and Ricky was to be the only one to dine. "All right, thank you, Mrs Keen," he said. "Remember that I am going to the Hawkesbury tomorrow and will be away until Sunday."

"Yes, Mr English, I remember that you are to take over the farm this weekend aren't you? I do hope it is all you wish."

"It is a lovely place, Mrs Keen. I will be able to take you out to look at it soon. I will need your advice about how to set up the house for the boys. I hope you will help me."

"I'll be glad to, sir. I grew up in the country and at times I miss it very much. Of course the country here is not like mine at home, I'm sure. It is probably very lonely."

"No. I don't think you would find this so. It is beautiful country and you can see your neighbour."

"I look forward to seeing the place," she said. "How soon would you like dinner, sir? It could be ready anytime for I made it simple seeing that Mr Tad and Mr Will are out."

"Thank you Mrs Keen. I'll start to pack my things and you may call me when it is ready," said Ricky.

He had hoped to be able to speak to Will before he went away for three days but he left a note for him telling him that he would return on Sunday evening. He caught the early train to Parramatta and was able to get to Windsor to complete his business in good time and have a late lunch at the hotel with the lawyer who had completed the contracts. He had asked Rob Martin to come in and collect him after lunch and was able to chat to the man all the way to his new possession.

Rob told him all the news of the place. He had never seen the man so animated about the prospect of the amazing venture he had got himself involved in. Rob had been rather reticent about taking it on but when he found that he was to have good help to aid in the training of the boys he agreed to enter in to the project. He now asked eagerly when the boys would come, telling Ricky that the young man he had sent down to meet Rob appeared to be quite satisfactory and he thought would be a good leader for the boys. They talked about the way they could train the five boys who were chosen to start the scheme, and how to accommodate them in the house.

"I thought, Mr English, that we could get young Perks to knock up some petitions along the big side verandah to make cubicles for the boys. This would give them some privacy but not isolate them from each other. This way we can see that they learn to live tidily. If they were all in one big area they could mess up each others places but having them divided would make each boy responsible for their own area. What do you think, sir?"

"Yes, you do what you think, Rob. We now have a free hand to go ahead and do what we want. You are completely in charge and you may do what you wish, but I would like to be consulted if you plan anything radical," said Ricky.

"Of course, sir," Rob answered. The house is so big that it will easily accommodate a number of boys as well as give me a good place to call my own and an apartment for you, too. The rambling old place would almost house a regiment, I think."

"Yes, I was surprised at its size. It is much bigger that it looks. Where have you decided to take as yours, Rob?" Ricky asked.

"Well, sir, you have first choice, of course. But I thought that I would have a room off the side verandah that Mr Raynes used. There is quite a suite of rooms next to that that I thought you would want for yourself and your brothers. I don't think I would be in your way. I hope that is all right."

"Yes, of course it is, Rob. It is just where I wished you to be. I daresay my brothers will not be here often, but Will may be. My brother Tad will be marrying soon and he and his wife may wish to visit on occasions."

Ricky spent a pleasant weekend planning things with Rob. He was pleased to see how well he got on with the staff and soon realised that he was all Mr Forrest said he was. He obviously had given a great deal of thought to the planning of the whole project and Ricky was amazed to find that he had also been planning where to build the orphanage when the time came. Rob had also spent some time seeing all the customers of the renowned dairy, assuring them that the quality would continue and supplies would remain constant.

Ricky was just sitting down to tea on the verandah when he heard a vehicle come to the gate. He was pleased to see Mr and Mrs Forrest and Miss Elston.

He called to the new housekeeper to make more tea and ran down the steps to greet his very first visitors.

"I hope you don't mind the invasion, Ricky, but I couldn't keep my women folk away. They were determined to be your first visitors," said Mr Forrest.

"You are very welcome, sir, and Mrs Forrest and Miss Elston. I am so pleased to see you. You see I am feeling rather overwhelmed and I was just sitting down wondering what I have done and whether I can cope with it all. I need you to boost my morale."

Ricky helped the ladies down and called for a hand to take the vehicle to the stables. "Please come up and have tea. I've asked

Mrs Smith to bring more. I am sorry we haven't very much furniture. We did manage to get Mr Raynes to part with enough for us to get by, but we are not overstocked with chairs I am sorry."

"Never mind, Ricky," said Mrs Forrest. "As long as we have tea I will stand for it and then we must see everything."

"Well, dear, I hardly think we will see everything. Poor Ricky has only just arrived and we can hardly expect him to have the place organised yet," said Mr Forrest, "or to take time off to show us."

"I have you both to thank that things are as good as they are, sir. Rob Martin is a marvel. The place is running as smooth as silk," Ricky laughed. "There isn't much I can do right now."

Jenny chuckled. "We did think you would find Rob useful, Mr English."

"Yes, Miss Elston, he seems to be very good. He has entered into all my plans, including orphans, to such an extent that I think I will be 'de trop.'"

"Not if I know you, young man," Mr Forrest put in.

"After tea you must help me plan and look things over in the house, at least." He led them round to the verandah where he first met Mr Raynes. Mrs Smith had found enough chairs that were suitable for them to sit on. "Oh, thank you, Mrs Smith, you shouldn't have carried them. I forgot we have a full set of chairs in the dining room. That is something we inherited from Mr Raynes," explained Ricky. "This is Mrs Smith, who has come to look after us and doesn't seem in the least intimidated at the thought of looking after a lot of men and boys." He smiled at the buxom woman.

"And why not, sir?" she asked. "Didn't I always work in boy's school back at home, to be sure?"

"How did you find such a treasure, Ricky? She seems to be just what you need here." Mrs Forrest asked, as Mrs Smith went into the house.

"I didn't find her, Mrs Forrest, Rob did. She certainly had glowing references. So good that it makes me wonder. However we will see."

They wandered all over the house, finding many of the rooms empty. Ricky talked about Rob's idea of turning the other side verandah into cubicles for the boys. The women had some good ideas for this and Ricky started to write things down as they went, realizing his limitations.

"Wherever are you going to get enough furniture in Windsor to furnish all this?" Mrs Forrest, not thinking about what she said.

Ricky laughed, "That is one thing I do not have to worry about Mrs Forrest. I can send what I need from the store."

"I am sorry, I didn't think," she said. "What fun to go into a store and say, I want this and that and send that."

"Well, I can't exactly do that, but yes, it is rather easy to do. I have to answer to my other share-holders you know. My brothers may not like the idea of helping to furnish this place," he said.

"Will they come out here, do you think?" she asked. "I still have to see Mr Tad English out here yet."

"Oh, yes, Tad is quite excited at the prospect, but he's rather occupied at the most. He has visitors from England. But Will finds he likes the bush after all and wants to paint some gum trees. I hope he makes a better job of it than some of the artists so far. They make gum trees look like English trees."

"Is Mr Will a good artist, Mr English? Or is it right to ask you?" asked Jenny.

"I probably am a bit biased, Miss Elston, but I do think he is really good. He does seem to paint people more than things, though. In fact he is getting to be quite popular as a portraitist. He could have all the work he wants, but is rather particular about his subjects, he likes painting character rather than beauty and so misses out on painting all the young ladies their fond parents would like him to do. Will's hard to budge when he makes up his mind." His guests noticed a quick frown appear on his forehead, but did not comment.

"Would you mind if I took my wife to see the dairy, Ricky? "I have been waxing lyrical about it. Jenny has seen it and I would like to show Nell," asked Mr Forrest.

"Will I get my feet muddy, Edward?" she asked.

"No, Mrs Forrest, there is a good path," Ricky answered for her husband. "I hope you enjoy it. I can never find a better place to spend time. It truly fascinates me. It also worries me to think that I now own such a famous one. If Miss Elston would care to see it I will point out where my orphanage is to be, or at least where Rob wants it to be."

"I, too, will ask, Mr English. Will I get my feet muddy?" Jenny asked.

"No, Miss Elston, we will not leave the verandah, you can survey all from here," Ricky assured her.

Ricky spent a glorious half hour showing his new love the plans that he had for his schemes. He was so pleased that she asked intelligent questions and really seemed interested in it. He had an overwhelming desire to tell her how he felt but knew that it was not yet time and so tried to keep his mind on the plans and not the sweetness who stood beside him. She asked him when his orphanage plans would go ahead, and he explained that he could not give a date yet as he had so much to think about and plan. There was no hurry, for his present children were well housed for the moment.

"Your present children?" she asked. "You mean to say that you have some already?"

Ricky laughed. "You sound just like my brothers when they heard about it. You know I am sure they must have thought I was quite demented. But I assure you, Miss Elston, that I am quite sane. I just cannot bear the thought of little children having to go through what Tad and Will went through in their early days. Do you realise how many there are roaming Sydney's streets?"

The colour drained from Jenny's face. "I am sorry to say, Mr English, that I do not. I know that there are children there but I do not see many of them when I am in Sydney and those I have seen have not interested me one whit. You make me feel ashamed."

He took her hands. "I had no intention of it Miss Elston. I know that I have only come to the knowledge because I have made it my business to find out. I did not tell you to make you feel any remote responsibility. Please accept my apologies."

"No, I know you did not. I didn't mean that but I am truly sorry that there are so many little ones whom I could perhaps have helped and did not."

"It is very difficult to help them. Mrs Landon and her daughters help in the girls hostel, but I do not see how you could help with the street children. They are a difficult bunch to assist."

"And yet you do," she challenged.

"Yes, but my circumstances are very different. I live in the town, I have the resources to do it and I am a man, which makes it so much easier," he turned away from her. "Besides I told you, I was a street boy myself and they know it and accept it from me." He didn't think she would realise what a wrench it was to say that straight out to her.

Jenny stood looking down at the place where the orphanage would be. "What a good thing you were. You must have a goal in life, Mr English, and that's your goal, isn't it?" she said turning to him.

She looked up to him with such compassion that Ricky's heart seemed to turn over. He wanted to pour out to her all he felt. He got as far as saying, "Miss Elston ..." When a 'halloo' came from Mr Forrest who was leading his wife towards the house. Ricky gave Jenny's hand a gentle squeeze and took her to the steps to greet his guests. Trying to compose himself he asked, "And what do you think of my dairy, Mrs Forrest? But don't give me credit for it, for I really haven't done anything towards its workings as I have only acquired it today." He felt rather confused and his cheeks were a little flushed.

Mrs Forrest looked at him with interest as she had seen them gazing at one another. She was sorry they had returned when they did for she was sure that she and Edward had interrupted something.

"Will you have some more refreshment, Mrs Forrest, before you leave. Perhaps you would care to stay for dinner. I am sure Mrs Smith could supply it," said Ricky.

"Thank you, no, Ricky," said Mr Forrest. "We will get along now. We told them at home we would be in before dark."

Mrs Forrest smiled a knowing smile and asked, "Will you be here for the whole weekend, Ricky?"

"I must return on Sunday, Mrs Forrest," he said, "but I shall probably be here most weekends."

"I am sure you will be," she thought, but said, "Would you care to come for dinner tomorrow evening."

"Thank you Mrs Forrest. Yes, I think I could manage it. I have to go round the place pretty thoroughly with Rob tomorrow, but dinner should be quite all right."

"It shouldn't take you all day to look at your new possession, Ricky," said the farmer. "Come as early as you can."

"Thank you I will. I'll ride over, sir. I believe there is a shorter way if one rides."

"Yes, Rob will put you right. He knows every nook and cranny of this area."

"I'll do that," Ricky said avoiding looking at Jenny.

"I asked your man to bring around the carriage. Oh, here he is," said Forrest.

They walked to the phaeton, Ricky helping the ladies in could hardly contain himself when Jenny gave him her hand. They smiled at each other as though no-one existed but them. Mr Forrest gave his wife a quizzical look. She was frightened he might make some remark so gave him a quick frown.

Jenny didn't turn to wave just sat still seeming to be in a dream. The Forrests smiled to one another chatting over the afternoon's events. But Nell couldn't help saying as they neared home and noticing that Jenny had uttered not a word, "Mr English is a fine young man, Jenny. He seems to have some great plans."

Jenny looked up and said, "I think he is the finest ever made, Auntie."

Nell leaned towards her and said, "Jenny love, I am so happy."

CHAPTER 15: *Jenny*

Three o'clock the next day saw Ricky riding helter-skelter along the lanes to "Claremont" to see his love. Rob had given clear instructions how to find his way and Ricky had been surprised to find how easy it was. In his eagerness to get there he forgot for a while that he should arrive looking cool and not full of the excitement he felt. So he pulled his horse up and walked him for some time and so cooled himself off as well as his eager mount.

He was disappointed to find that there were visitors taking tea with the Forrests and so had to compose himself to being patient until he could get his Jenny alone. Mrs Forrest smiled to herself as she noted that he could barely look at Jenny for fear of giving himself away. He was certainly not the usual attentive guest who was quick to take part in any inane conversation, but had even to be spoken to twice at times. The Prices were dreary guests at the best of times and never seemed to know when to go and Nell cudgeled her mind as to how she could gently hint them away, but could not come up with any thoughts in that direction. So she said, "Jenny, dear, I wonder whether you could go and gather those long stemmed pink roses for me that I promised Mrs Whitlaw. Ricky, I am sure Mrs Price will excuse you if you go and carry the basket for Jenny."

At this her husband opened his eyes and looked at her then shook his head imperceptibly with a smile. But Ricky said, "Of course, Mrs Forrest. Come, Miss Elston."

Nell leaned back in the chair with a contented sigh as she saw the young couple go into the garden.

"But, dear Mrs Forrest," said Mrs Price, "whatever are you thinking of. Mrs Whitlaw is away. You told me so yourself."

"How silly I am," said Nell, "I mean Mrs Cross, of course."

Ricky led Jenny out along the path to the summer house,

dropping the basket and shears on a garden seat as he passed. "But, the roses," protested Jenny.

"I don't think we should worry about them, Miss Elston. Mrs Forrest must have forgotten that it is far too hot to pick roses. I am sure she was just taking pity on us having to listen to Mrs Price go on and on."

"Yes, she is a trial isn't she?"

"I do hope it is not too hot for you to walk to the summer house, Miss Elston?" he asked.

"Not at all Mr English, I am quite used to the heat."

Ricky put her hand through his arm and led her along through the lovely garden. It was very hot and they were pleased to sit in the shade of the little house where they could catch some breeze.

Ricky turned to the lass. "Miss Elston, Jenny, I do love you," he said. She looked up at him. "Jenny, I would think it a great honour if you could consider marrying me. Would you?"

Jenny looked down and nodded her head sweetly.

"Oh, my darling, darling Jenny." Ricky lifted her chin and kissed her.

The small Forrest girls crept into the sitting room and tried to speak to their mother. "Girls, girls, where are you manners?" she asked. Amanda and Nellie said their polite pieces and then tried to whisper to Nell. "Hush, now, that can wait," she said.

The Prices were obviously about to depart and so the children had to be content to wait until the carriage drove off. Nellie was dancing on her toes and cried out, "Mama, Mama, do you know that Mr English is in the summer house cuddling Jenny. Isn't that awful?"

"He's kissing her as well as cuddling her, Mama," chimed in Amanda.

"How nice," said their mother, "I thought he might." The children were aghast.

Mr Forrest said, "It was all rather pointed, wasn't it dear? You are not usually as transparent as that." He chuckled.

"My dear, what else could I do. Those dreadful Prices just would not go and poor Ricky was almost exploding with impatience.

I just had to do something. I don't think either of them heard one word of the silly conversation."

"Mama, did you want them to cuddle?" persisted Amanda.

"Of course dear. Now run along and see where they left the flower basket. I would think they would have left it on the first seat they came to. Run along and see who finds it first." The little girls ran.

"What a match-maker you are my love," said Mr Forrest.

"No dear, the match was already made. I just assisted a little. I must admit I was almost as impatient as they were." She turned to her husband, "You are pleased, aren't you, Edward?"

"Oh, yes, of course, Nell. I don't think she could have a better man. We are going to miss her though." He looked up towards the summer house. "I did think he would have consulted me first though."

"I daresay he would have, my love, for I heard him ask Barnes for you when he arrived and was quite non-plussed when he heard that we had those wretched Prices. So I just helped them along a little," Nell assured him.

"You certainly did. According to the children he didn't wait to consult me. Nell, I daresay dinner will be late now. How long will it be before they come down to earth long enough to realise that some men can be hungry?"

"I imagine it won't be long now, Edward. In any case you ate such a huge tea that you couldn't possibly be hungry."

"Well, I am. It must be romance that makes me extra hungry," he said with a grin, and slipping his arm around his wife's waist he led her back into the house.

Indeed they did not have to wait long but Nell did find the waiting tiresome as she wanted to see these two people she loved so much. She was so happy in her own marriage that she wanted the same for her Jenny, and over the past months she had become very fond of Ricky, feeling that he was an unusual and benevolent man, as well as being a good looking one who was well able to keep her Jenny in the style she was used to.

Ricky brought Jenny into the sitting room and announced that they were to be married. Jenny went over to Nell and they shed a few tears of happiness together.

"I thought you at least would have asked my consent, young man," Edward said, trying to look stern.

"You didn't need to, Ricky, Jenny is her own woman," said Nell.

"I am sorry, sir, I did mean to but Mr and Mrs Price were here and I did not have the opportunity."

"Pests, weren't they, son? That's all right, only next time do it in the right order," Edward slapped Ricky on the back, grinning. "My dear, I think this calls for champagne. I shall tell Barnes."

"I have already, Edward," Nell told him.

"What a managing woman you are, Nell. See what happens when you get married Ricky. Think hard before you take the plunge." Then turning to his wife he asked, "You told Barnes, Nell? When, may I ask?"

"At luncheon, dear. I thought we would need it."

"Well, I never," he said and the company burst into laughter.

Nell turned to Ricky and said, "I hope you can come back tomorrow, Ricky, when we have all got used to the excitement and we can talk about weddings and things."

"No, I am afraid I cannot, Mrs Forrest," Ricky replied, "I must return home tomorrow for I have much to do. But I will be back next weekend. This will give you and Jenny time to work out what we should do and when we should plan to do it. I hope that is all right?"

"How can you two bear to be parted for a whole week?" she asked, burbling with laughter.

"I know," Ricky said seriously. "But I will write, I promise, Jenny." They all laughed at this.

"Ricky, I don't want to hurry you but I think it would be best if we had an early dinner and you went on your way before it gets too dark, for you won't know your way in the dark and those lanes can be deceptive," Edward said.

"You are quite right, Ned," said Nell. "Do you think you know your way, Ricky? If you get lost you would ride around all night before you found your way home or even back here."

"Nell's right, Ricky. I think I'll get one of the men to ride back with you, at least as far as the pound, for there are several lanes that lead to the pound and the stock route and are quite confusing."

"In that case, sir, I would appreciate it if someone could put me on the right track. But, I must admit I do not want to leave early, but on the other hand I don't fancy a night riding up lots of lanes. I must get back to Sydney tomorrow for I have a few things that are needing my attention."

"Ring for Barnes, Edward, I must tell him to put dinner on early," said Nell.

Of course, the conversation at the table was about the engagement. The children, allowed to dine with the adults as it was early, were very ready to ask all about it.

Amanda, who was the elder of the two girls was fascinated and couldn't stop asking about what it all meant. "Does this mean that you will come and live here with us, Mr English?" she asked.

"No, it wouldn't, silly," said her mother. "Jenny is going to live in Mr English's house. Won't that be nice?"

"You mean Jenny would leave us and go away?" she asked anxiously.

"Yes, dear. Jenny will have a house of her own to look after."

"No, Mama," she cried, with many tears. "What will we do without Jenny? How would we do our lessons? You wouldn't take Jenny away from us would you Mr English?"

Poor Ricky was quite non-plussed over this, but Nell smiled calmly and told her daughter not to be so selfish and didn't she want what was best for Jenny. Jenny came into the picture by suggesting that the little girls might want to be flower girls at the wedding. This brightened things up again and the time was spent telling the children all about weddings. The girls were appeased when they heard that they would wear pretty frocks that reached the ground. So the tears were turned to happiness in the discussion of where the wedding would take place and the whensoever and howsoever of it all.

"I'll go and tell Green to saddle up and go with you, Ricky," Ricky's host announced after dinner.

They were surprised to see Forrest's own mare saddled beside Ricky's, Nell calling to him asking the reason. "Well, on the way over to the stables, I thought, why shouldn't I go? It is a lovely evening and I would like the ride."

"Good idea, Ned," said his wife. "We could have done the same but it is a bit late to change into riding gear, isn't it, Jenny?"

"Yes, I suppose it is, Auntie." Jenny said reluctantly.

Nell laughed at her. "Never mind, Jenny. We'll all go next time when we think of it earlier."

They watched the men canter down the track and turned back into the house, chatting all the way and loving the prospect of all the arrangements to be made.

Edward Forrest rode with Ricky until he was certain he couldn't get lost and turned to canter back in the lovely summer dusk. "See you next week, Ricky, and many a one after that I'll bet." With a wave he was gone.

"Good to see you home and safe, Mr English." Ricky found Rob waiting for him on the verandah. "I thought I might go looking for you if you did not come soon, for I know how easy it is to get confused at the far opening of those lanes."

"That's very kind of you, Rob. But no worries. Mr Forrest saw me part of the way. So I found it quite easy."

"I might have thought he would do that, Mr English. He would see that you didn't take a wrong turn."

"He did indeed. I seem to have friends everywhere. Thanks Rob."

"What time do you plan to leave tomorrow? I think you said you would want to leave early." The man asked.

"Yes, I do have to get back to Sydney, but I thought I would get you to take me in to Windsor early enough for church at St Matthew's, then I can catch the coach to Parramatta in good time."

"Good," said Rob. "I can go to church myself and then drop you at the coach. It'll save you a walk."

"Thanks Rob, that would be good. Well, I'll see you in the morning."

Ricky let himself in through his own front door well before dinner the next day, and was greeted by a worried looking Mrs Keen. "Everything all right, Mrs Keen?" he asked.

"I hope so, Mr Ricky," she answered.

"You hope so? Come now, what is wrong?" By this time Ricky was getting worried, too.

"Well, it's Mr Will. He's in the studio. Please go and see him."

Without a word Ricky took the stairs two at a time, paused on the landing and walked quietly into the studio. He had expected trouble but the scene that met his eyes shocked him. There were pieces of drawings and paintings that had obviously been torn apart in anger. Will was sitting at the table and before him was a half full bottle of whisky and a glass. It was easy to see that he was very drunk indeed. He looked a little self-consciously at Ricky who asked, "What's all this Will? Since when have you taken to drinking?"

"What's it too you if I do?" he answered rudely

"It has a lot to do with me, as you must know. It's the sort of thing I hate and you know it. What's got into you, you silly fellow?"

"I'm drowning my sorrows. I can do that if I wanna," said Will belligerently.

"You don't look as though you have drowned much else other than yourself. In fact you look positively miserable," remarked Ricky. "What's got into you Will? This isn't like you."

"I'm miser ... miserab..b.ble," Will at last got out.

"You look awful. I can't think it is giving you much pleasure. Will, really, are you all right?"

"Oh.h.h, Ricky I feel terrible." With that Will looked as though he was about to be sick, so Ricky tipped a bucket up depositing a lump of clay on the floor and handed it to Will.

"I think you'd better take yourself off to bed and I'll talk with you tomorrow when you've come to your senses."

Ricky looked at him distastefully and then helped Will sheepishly leave the studio and go to his bedroom. Ricky got rid of the evidence of the rather unusual day that Will had 'enjoyed'.

By the time Tad came for in dinner there was a certain amount of normalcy apparent. Ricky had time to sit and think about Will's unhappiness before this but decided that he would tell Tad what had happened for Tad had always felt very responsible for the younger man. Until Tad had told of his recent experience with the Falconer-Meads there had always been a great deal of openness between them, even Amabel's appearance in Tad's life had not interrupted that.

Over dinner Tad told Ricky that he had told the Landons his news and that Mr Landon had called for Mr Falconer-Mead and Joshua on Saturday and had taken them to spend the day at his home. The visit had gone very well and Amabel, of course, had impressed the visitors.

Ricky, in his turn, told Tad about his proposal to Jenny and her acceptance of it. Ricky's experience with Will had somewhat dulled the news but on speaking of Jenny his heart glowed with happiness.

"This really calls for a celebration, Rick. Let's have a bottle of champagne? Won't Amabel be pleased about it?"

"Certainly tell her, Tad, but it is not to be announced as yet. The Forrests want to make a formal announcement at a ball. I must admit I will find it hard to keep it to myself for I really feel as though I could yell it from the housetops."

"Rotten you had to come home a find Will's trouble. But anyway let's have some fizz," said Tad.

"I don't think so, not tonight, Tad. Alcohol isn't my favorite thing of the moment. We'll celebrate later when a few things have settled down."

Ricky visited Will's room before he retired and finding him asleep went off with less worry. Neither did he speak to Will before he left for the store the next morning as he was still asleep but left a note for him saying that he would try to get home for lunch to be able to talk to Will, but if not, would appreciate it if Will could be home for dinner as Tad would be out and they could have an uninterrupted time together.

Ricky had to be content with that and went off with a heavy heart. Later as he went through the shop before luncheon he saw John Landon there. "Hello there, sir, wanting to buy my shop out?"

"Hello, Ricky. No, just wanting to buy a trifle for my wife, and I spied these pretty shawls. Do you think Mrs Landon would like this?" He held up a fine gossamer wool scarf in a lovely shade of pale blue.

"I cannot say that I am an expert in that field but I do think she would like it. Miss Fox would advise you much better than I. But they are a fine line that came in the last shipment and I think they will sell quickly when the ladies see them." Ricky called the attendant over to help his friend. "Mr Landon," he asked, "would you have time to talk to me for while? I have something I would like to share with you."

"Yes, I was about to go to lunch, Ricky. Why not come with me?" Mr Landon suggested.

"I'd rather not, sir, if you don't mind. I know what lunching is with you, I can hardly get a word in with all the people who see you and wish to speak with you," Ricky laughed. "But, I am on my way to order some sandwiches to be brought up to my office. Will you join me there?"

"Gladly, Ricky. I'll finish my purchases and come up then."

Ricky was able to tell John about Will without feeling disloyal to him for he knew that Will had always been a special concern to the man. He told him that he was pretty sure he knew what the trouble was and was rather at a loss to know how to cope.

"You mean about him not having a family and now it looks as though Tad has. Yes, I think you are right about that, and Tad feels it too."

"Does he? I didn't think Tad had noticed it when he told us about the Falconer-Meads."

"Yes, he did and not knowing what to say about it decided to leave it work itself out. Leave it to me, lad, leave it to me. I won't tell you what I'm going to do, I will let Will tell you but I have a scheme that I think will work."

"You're good to us, sir. But then you always have been. Do you really think there is something we can do?"

"Well, there is something I can do." With that he took leave of Ricky. Soon he was knocking at the door of Ricky's house. "Good morning Maria," he said. "Is Mr Will at home?"

"Yes, sir, he is."

"Is he is his studio?"

"Yes, sir."

"I'll go straight up. No need to announce me."

Maria looked as though she would like to protest but decided against it as she knew Mr Landon was a close friend of the family.

John opened the door of the studio without knocking. Will looked up, a picture of misery. He stood up to greet John, "Hello sir, did you want to see me?"

"Yes, I did Will. Shall we sit down?"

"Would you like tea, Mr Landon?"

"That would be good, Will. I didn't have time for much lunch today."

"We'll go downstairs then, I'll call Maria."

John looked around him and saw that the studio was not its usual neatness. "What have you been doing here, son?" he asked.

Will turned his back on the room and leading the man out he said, bitterly, "I suppose Tad's been talking out of turn?" He stumped down the stairs.

"What's wrong, Will? Aren't you well? As a matter of fact you don't look very well. Are you all right?"

"Yes, I'm all right. But tell me, Mr Landon, has Tad been talking about me?"

"No, I cannot remember that he mentioned you this weekend. You know that we had the Falconer-Meads out on Saturday and I have hardly had private speech with Tad. What is worrying you? What should he have said to me?" asked John, in all innocence.

Will ushered his guest into the living room and rang the bell for Maria. "Maria, bring tea for Mr Landon and me, please," he said when the maid appeared. "Please sit, sir, and I will tell you. I suppose I may as well before you see Ricky. He might and I don't think he understands."

"I think you are unfair there, my lad, for I think Ricky sees a great deal that neither you or Tad have credited him, now tell me what has happened? What's all the mystery?"

Now that Mr Landon was listening Will began to feel that after all he didn't want his friend to know just what he had been doing.

"Come on, Will, tell me."

"I daresay I'm not very proud of it, Mr Landon. I wouldn't have mentioned it but I thought Tad would have told you. I ..." Just at that moment Maria came in with the tea so Will had to wait. "Thank you, Maria. Serve Mr Landon, will you?"

When the girl left Will started again, he seemed to take a deep breath and said in a rush, "I got drunk," he said defiantly. Then told of Ricky's home coming and what had happened when he saw Will.

"A bit unusual for you, wasn't it, Will? Not the normal thing, was it?"

"No, sir, I've never done it before, and I can't say that it did me much good," said Will wryly. "I'm a bit sorry now."

"Anything in particular worrying you, son?" John asked kindly.

Will looked a bit ashamed and said, "I was very upset about Tad's new relatives."

"That's not like you to show jealousy about anything Tad does, Will. I am surprised that you would be upset about any happiness that Tad might have."

"But, Mr Landon, you don't understand. Ricky knows who he is and now Tad does. I still don't know who I am. It's not fair," Will burst out.

"Good heavens, Will. I'm surprised at you."

"I said you wouldn't understand," Will said sullenly.

"Now listen here, Will," said John sternly, "you say you don't know who you are. I say you are Will English. Someone I have watched grow to a man I respect and feel a great deal of affection for. I am surprised at you and can't believe what I am hearing."

"But you don't understand," Will protested.

"Look here, young fellow, who found you and dragged you off the street?"

"Tad, sir," Will said reluctantly.

"What did Tad do when he first brought you in?"

"He ... he gave me some food." Will was beginning to feel silly.

"He had a lot to share, didn't he?"

"No, he didn't," came the soft reply.

"What did he do next?" came the curt question. "Remember! for I am sure you do. I do and I am proud of him."

"He shared his clothes." By this time Will was hanging his head. "But he knows who his father was, and I don't?"

"For goodness sake, Will, pull yourself together. What was Tad last week when he didn't know who his father was? Was he any less than he is now?"

"No, sir, of course not."

"And if you never find out who your father was will it make you any less than you have been? Think, man." Landon shot at him.

"No," came the miserable reply.

"Will," John said more kindly, "don't think I don't know what you feel, I do. I will tell you that I too have tried to find out about you boys, and I have never been able to find out a thing. It didn't matter to me who your people were, I judged for myself and I never found anything in any one of you that I have disliked. I always have and always will judge a man as I find him and not who his parents were. I have known people with fine families who I would not give house room to and some who have had a family to be ashamed of who I have a great deal of time for. Do you really think it matters?"

"It does to me, Mr Landon. I would love to know whether my people were decent folk. That's all."

"Yes, I understand that, but remember one thing, Tad will never be able to prove his relationship to the Falconer-Meads. He will always wonder who he is for there is no proof, as you must know."

"But he knows who he is, even with no proof, Mr Landon. He apparently looks like them."

"Oh Will," Mr Landon said, "Will you are being unfair. Don't you think he wants proof, too. He will always wonder."

"Wonder?" Will threw to the man, " even if he has no proof he will know his mother wasn't a prostitute, and what if mine was?"

"Who says his mother wasn't a prostitute? Maybe his father was Falconer-Mead's son, but who can prove who his mother was? Who is to say he wasn't result of an alliance his father had with a street woman? Don't you think he is afraid that something like that happened? For goodness sake grow up, Will, and don't act like a spoilt child."

Hearing this Will looked up startled. "I didn't think of that, sir. You don't believe it do you, Mr Landon? How rotten if you do."

"Of course I don't, Will, I am sure he is their legitimate child. I am only telling you that he has and always will have a slight doubt in his mind. He would like proof just as much as you do.

Now for goodness sake have sense and a bit of sympathy." John leaned back in his chair and looked at the lad, who had been quite stunned at this conversation. "What a sensitive young man he is," Landon thought, "so thin, dark and frail." He said, "Can I say what I came to say or are you too upset to think straight, Will? Shall I come back another time?"

Will looked up, "I am sorry, sir. I guess I have been selfish. I could only look at it my way. Yes, I daresay you came to tell me something. I'm sorry. I thought Tad must have asked you to see me. Please do tell me."

"Well it will give you something to think about, Will, so perhaps I shall tell you."

"What is it, Mr Landon? Something I can do for you?" Will said eagerly.

"You know I have always wanted to send you to Paris to paint. Well, I have just heard of an opportunity that I don't think we can miss. Mrs Landon's brother Robert Cummins has just been posted to the embassy in Paris. He is a very pleasant man. I don't know his wife, but I do know her family and like them. I think it would be an opportunity to go while they are there. What do you think? Eh?"

Will was taken aback, just sitting there staring at his friend. "Well, I never," he said, "I always knew you wanted me to go, sir, but I must admit I have never thought deeply about it. But I don't think I would like to live at an embassy, sir, it sounds a bit formal. "

"No, I never intended you to, lad. But they could keep an eye out for you and they would be someone who you could turn to if you need. Think it over and talk it over with Ricky and Tad and let me know your decision."

"You've rather set me back on my heels, pinned my ears back and all that, Mr Landon. I'm just beginning to realise what a fool I've been. Thank you for coming, I'm sorry you had such a rotten reception from me." Will was looking very sheepish.

"Take my advice and speak to Ricky about it unless you have already. He is really the one you should listen to."

" But he doesn't seem to be around nowadays as often as he was and I daresay I have blamed him for that and I don't know why I should for he has a right to his own life. It's just that property, sir, he does spend a lot of time there and will do so more."

"You'd better sit down and think your life over my boy. I imagine you have felt rather neglected of late with Tad always haunting my home and Ricky with those schemes of his. I believe he has bought that place on the Hawkesbury. When I saw him about a month ago he told me he was thinking of it, but I thought he might have another interest out there, too."

"Oh, do you think so, sir? He does spend a lot of time at the Forrest's home," said Will innocently.

John Landon chuckled at this and said, "I presume you think he has Miss Elston in his sights, eh Will?"

"Well, I wouldn't be too surprised, he was rather bowled over when he first met her. Do you know anything about her, Mr Landon? Is she good enough for Ricky?" Will asked anxiously.

"I doubt if anyone would be in your eyes, Will, but whether we like it or not, I daresay Ricky will make up his own mind.'

"I suppose so."

"Will, if Ricky is serious about Miss Elston, he might be prepared to listening to my project with more calmness than if it had been at another time. I know he has never been keen about you leaving his protection and I am afraid this last episode of yours would not help. So if you do wish to go, approach the whole thing maturely. Show him you will be quite able to look after yourself. I have great faith in you Will. I always have."

"You are very kind, Mr Landon and I'll try to do as you say. But I must admit your proposal is a bit daunting. Paris is a long way away from home."

"Yes. Well you think it over carefully."

"Thank you, sir, I will."

Ricky had hoped to be home early but was not able to manage it. However he did eventually drive away from the office. He had little time to give to the problem he was to face but now as he drove through the quietening streets he was able to think. He did not like the prospect of facing Will but face him he must. It was not the problem of Will being upset about Tad, but, the fact that Will could so easily turn to alcohol when a problem arose. Seeing that heredity was the flavour of the moment he wondered whether this had been the trouble of either or both of Will's parents. Ricky had been hurt and sorry that had happened, and he was far from experienced in dealing with such. Drink had never had any pull for him and he had been amazed that it was the thing that Will had turned to. Perhaps he had been neglecting the lad of late. He made up his mind that he must remedy that in the future.

However it was a brighter Will than Ricky could ever have imagined who greeted him on his return. A subdued and sorry looking young man but one with a better attitude than he expected. Will followed Ricky to his room and asked if he might speak to him right away. Ricky was reminded of a chastened school child who knew punishment was on the agenda and the quicker it was over the better the child would feel.

He said, "Yes, Will. I was going to speak to you after dinner but if it can't wait. Fire ahead." Ricky sank down into one comfortable chair beside his bed and he motioned Will to take the other one.

"Ricky, you look fagged to death. Perhaps I should wait until you have dinner."

"It has been rather a difficult day, Will. But go on, I'm all right," replied Ricky.

"Mr Landon came to see me this afternoon, Rick," said Will.

"Did he, by jove?" Ricky opened his eyes wide, thinking that his friend had not wasted time.

"Yes," continued Will, "he made me feel terrible."

"No worse than you felt last night, I hope, Will?" laughed Ricky.

"Oh, Ricky, I am so glad you can laugh at it. It isn't really funny, you know, at least I don't think it is, but I am glad you are not mad at me."

"No, Will, I am not mad at you. I can see why you are upset but I am very disappointed that you turned to drink when something worried you. Why didn't you tell me?"

"But you weren't here, Rick. Anyway, I suppose I must have been ashamed of myself deep down. That's what Mr Landon thinks anyway."

"Do you mean you told Mr Landon what happened?"

"Yes, I did. He was very understanding, Rick, but he made me realise what a selfish brute I was and that I was being jealous of Tad. I hadn't thought of it that way. I can see it now."

"Will, I knew when Tad told us that you were thinking about your own folks. I know it is hard but you do realise don't you, that Tad will never be certain that he is the right grandson?"

"Yes, but I didn't, Rick. I didn't think there was any doubt about it, I didn't think anything could be more distressing than not knowing anything, I can see now that half knowing can be worse than that," said Will pensively.

"I am glad you see it and understand it," Ricky said.

"But, I didn't until Mr Landon pointed it out to me. He is a great gun isn't he? And do you know he tried on his own to find out who our people were Rick. Did you know that?"

"I didn't know, but I would have been surprised if he hadn't, you know, Will. He invested a lot in us, I hope you realise."

"I can't say I did. I am learning a fearful amount today. I guess it is a good thing I got drunk, it was worth it."

"For goodness sake, Will, don't get that idea. Nothing is worth repeating that exercise. Promise me you won't do it again?"

"You needn't worry, I'm not likely to do that again. Sorry, Rick. Any way I haven't told you what Mr Landon came to see me about and I'm most anxious to."

"What was it?"

"Mrs Landon's brother is at the embassy in Paris and Mr Landon thinks it would be a good time for me to go there and paint. He thinks that Mr Cummins would help me. What do you think?"

"Crikey, that's a surprise."

"Yes, I thought so too, but he's always been wanting me to go, so, I daresay we shouldn't have been. Surprised, I mean," Will said.

"No, he always had it in mind. It takes a bit of thinking about doesn't it." Ricky hesitated before adding, "Will, I have some news, too. I would have told you last night but I couldn't. I am going to get married."

"Great, Ricky. Miss Elston, I gather. Congratulations old boy."

"Come on you'd better get ready for dinner, I can see a long evening ahead of us to talk over lots. Tad will be here, too."

CHAPTER 16: *And then there was Dimity*

Mr and Mrs Forrest, with Jenny, came up to Sydney to arrange the ball which they were planning to hold when the engagement would be announced. They were finding it difficult to find a venue as the season was late and Christmas was very close. They had an almost fruitless search, for really Sydney did not boast of many places in which a fashionable ball could be held. They had almost decided on the room at the Royal, and were discussing this with the Landon's, when Mrs Landon said, "Oh, John, let's have it here." At first the Forrests would not hear of it, but their protests were quickly put aside.

"Nell, you had better let Sadie have her way, for once she gets an idea, as well we know, she will not give up, until you give way. So for a little peace please give in quickly." This brought a laugh and the decision was made.

It was not to be a very large dance, only fifty couples, and so the Landon ballroom was most suitable. Jenny soon found that the Landons were very happy to take over many of the arrangements which she and Mrs Forrest had been worried about achieving.

"We have so recently had Amabel and Tad's ball that all we have to do is repeat the orders for everything," said Sadie Landon. "The girls will help, won't you, my dears?"

"Oh, yes, mama, we had so much fun with Amabel's didn't we?" said Harriet.

"You see, Nell, you need not think about it at all, I have three good secretaries here and I will work them very hard. They do know how to work, believe me."

"She is a terrible taskmistress, Mrs Forrest. You should see how she makes us work at the hostel," put in Amabel. Then turning to her parents she said, "Mama, Papa, why don't we have Jenny to stay here until the ball and then we can do everything together."

"Oh, no I couldn't, but thank you very much all the same, I must go back to the children," said Jenny. "Thank you very much for the thought, Amabel."

Nell Forrest cut in, "Oh Jenny that is a lovely idea. It is so close to Christmas anyway that the children will love having extra holidays. In any case, my dear, we shall have to get used to not having you around, won't we, Ned?"

"Yes, we will miss our grown up daughter. I wish I could be annoyed at Ricky but I'm afraid we like him too much, even if he does take our Jenny away from us."

"You must tell us about your new home, too, Jenny," said Amabel.

So the conversation then turned to wedding dates and the new house that Ricky planned to build at Elizabeth Bay. They had studied plans for several weekends and had decided on a fairly large house that could be added to, as, and if, the English family increased. It was to be a two storied home in an acre of ground and had all the modern comforts that Ricky could think up. The block was gently sloping and with the house on a rise it would have a pleasant view of the harbour.

The girls decided that it would be a good idea to walk to the land to see it when the day became a little cooler for it was not far away from the Landon's own house. Then John suggested that they all go, saying, "It is good walking, ladies. Ricky took me to see it and I think you can manage all right, but we could drive if you would rather."

In the end the young ones walked and the four older folk drove, as the roads in the colony were still often either very dusty or very wet. They didn't attempt to walk over the land but were happy to look at it from the road. Jenny was able to point out where the house would be and tell how its aspect would be best to catch the summer breezes and be sheltered from the southerlies. It was all much admired, Jenny looking very wistful when thinking of setting up her own home and she wondered how successful she would be. Ricky seemed to her so perfect that she wondered whether she would be able to live up to his standard. It didn't occur to her that Ricky was thinking just the same about her.

Before the Forrests left they had decided that Jenny should remain with them at the Royal until their return home and for the next three weeks she would stay with the Landon's. Nell and Edward would return two days before the ball.

"I feel very mean leaving everything to you, Sadie. I seem to be walking away from my responsibilities," she said. "It is not what we planned, you know."

"I know, dear," said Mrs Landon, "John tells me I am a very managing female, don't you, John?"

"She certainly is, Nell. If I didn't have Charles to back me up, when he is home from school, I would be thoroughly hen-pecked," he replied. "Aren't you sympathetic, Ned?"

"Yes, I am in much the same boat, old chap. Women all round me. And James isn't old enough to stand up for me, yet. I must remember to train him to back me up in everything."

Their women folk all laughed at this and told them they had nothing to complain about. "Besides, you both look very happy about it," replied Sadie Landon.

So Sadie and the girls had a great deal of fun planning and choosing materials for gowns and having them made with a great deal of speed. The Landon's seamstress was not able to cope and so they employed two others to help. These women had things done so quickly and so well that Jenny decided to use them to make some other frocks while she had the opportunity.

"I need many more dresses now, Mrs Landon," she said, "for at home I don't need such fine ones, but here in town I will need them."

"You certainly will, Jenny. I am glad we have the opportunity for you to get them. Simpkins and her sister seem to be quite capable and have some lovely ideas haven't they?"

"Yes," she replied. "I suppose I will need a seamstress when I get married. I would like to have someone like that for I am sure there will be much to do."

"I daresay it will be a matter of who Ricky uses in the store to make curtains and drapes and things, otherwise they could do those too," Mrs Landon said.

"Yes, I must ask Ricky about that. Goodness there's such a lot to do."

The Forrests arrived two days before the ball and Nell was pleased that she was given some tasks to do. "Otherwise I will feel that I am just an ornament."

"You have no need to worry, Nell, Jenny has done more work than I could ever have expected a lass to do. My goodness that girl is a worker."

"Yes, she is," said Jenny's aunt. "She has that ability to get into a job without being asked. If she hadn't been like that I would never have left you with the task of getting the ball ready."

"All the girls have been marvellous. They have had such fun. I am sure Betsy has done no schoolwork since all this began. Truly I have done very little; they have done it all. It's good training for them, but I do think you and I should go over all the things just to make sure they haven't forgotten anything."

There was no need to worry for all seemed to be in readiness. The only thing that worried them was the weather. It was very hot and humid and not quite the best for dancing, but they all hoped that a cool change would come on the evening of the dance. They were very fortunate for as the three English men pulled up at the door for dinner they felt the first of a cool southerly breeze. Nell sent the servants to open all the doors and windows and fill the place with coolness.

Other guests were coming for dinner and twenty people sat down to a light but sumptuous meal. Sadie had suggested this as it would be difficult to eat a big meal and expect to be able to dance well after it. She was a skillful hostess and even though the meal was light it was very satisfying even for the men who were used to large hot dinners.

Ricky only had eyes for his Jenny. He couldn't remember afterwards what he ate, he just wanted to look at her and couldn't believe his good fortune in having such a wonder for his affianced wife. Tad was in much the same state over Amabel. Will had been partnered with a sweet little girl whose name was Dimity Roger. The Rogers had only just come to the colony and so the Landons had taken this opportunity of introducing them to the social life of Sydney.

Mr Falconer-Mead and Joshua were there, of course. Joshua partnering Harriet who was feeling very grown up. Poor Betsy was not allowed to come down to dinner but was to come and watch the dancing for a short time, later.

"They all look lovely," thought John Landon. "Like beautiful butterflies. But sensible ones," he assured himself. He felt very proud of his family.

His own Sadie looked magnificent in rich cream satin and lace. She wore a necklace of topaz which had belonged to his mother and grandmother. Nell was in pale mauve taffeta with a lace overdress which suited her prematurely grey hair. She looked regal in that colour and her necklace of amethysts was the same colour as her dress.

Jenny wore palest blue sprig muslin which made her blue eyes even bluer. She wore a string of pearls which had belonged to her mother. She also had a pearl bracelet which she wore over her blue lace mittens, a gift from Ricky.

Amabel was in plain pale green muslin with a deep green sash of wide satin. Her mittens were the same tone as the deep green sash. She wore an emerald pendant which was a present from her father on her eighteenth birthday. Harriet looked shy and sweet in her yellow Indian cotton, the neckline of which went right to her throat and so she wore no jewellery. Yes, a sweet bunch of blossoms John Landon thought.

Dimity Roger, the only other young lady at the dinner, was in beige. It did not really become her. She should have been wearing colours like the others but her mother had very strict ideas about girls wearing colours. She seemed to fade into the background of all the glitter and Will felt sorry for her. She seemed ill at ease but when he spoke to her found that she was a pleasant little person who was quite able to converse with a great deal of ease so he enjoyed their conversation. She had dark brown hair and brown eyes. She had an elfin appearance that attracted Will. Her face lit up when she smiled and from being a plain little thing, as Will had at first thought her, she became quite appealing.

During their various conversations she asked him if he liked dancing. "I think I would like it quite a lot Miss Roger, but you see I am crippled and I look awkward on the dance floor." Will surprised himself at this utterance for he rarely spoke so about his leg.

"But you can dance, Mr English? It doesn't hurt you?" Dimity asked.

"No, it doesn't hurt, Miss Roger. I just feel clumsy, that's all. Yes, I can dance. I have been well taught but it isn't my favourite occupation," he added with a smile.

"What is your favourite occupation then, Mr English?" she asked.

Then before he knew it Will found he was enjoying his speech with this little mouse of a girl. She seemed to have a knack of putting him at ease, and so he chatted about his painting, his going to Paris and about his two brothers of whom he sounded very proud.

It was time for the ball to commence and the four hosts stood at the door greeting their guests. There was a flurry of excitement among the young girls. Amabel noticed that Dimity was rather alone and took her to join the others. They all accepted her with interest and kindness. Each person was given a dainty program and pencil and it was hard for the girls to fit in all the names of the men who wished to dance with them. Of course Ricky wanted all of Jenny's dances as Tad wanted all of Amabel's but they knew better than that and had to be patient and share them out with others who had a call on them.

The orchestra set the music going and the dancing began, and they were soon swirling and waltzing and stepping out in country dances. A colourful scene. The great chandelier shone brightly and with bunches of candles in sconces along all the walls the whole place was shining. Will stood by a pillar watching it all and wishing a little that he was more nimble on his feet. His lameness didn't worry him often but on occasions like this it did. Both Mrs Landon and Mrs Forrest insisted on dancing with him, then Jenny and Amabel who assured him that they had kept dances for him, which pleased him mightily. He felt so confident after this that when he saw Dimity sitting out he asked her to dance and enjoyed it very much.

She was as light as a fairy and was able to praise him without making him feel embarrassed. He thought she was a very nice girl, unusual for Will. Ricky was pleased to see it.

At 11 o'clock the music stopped and supper was announced. The dining room had been set out for supper and the tables seemed to groan with the weight of various savouries and sandwiches, dainty pies and pastries, sweet meats, jellies, trifles, iced desserts, lemonade and fruit cup.

After this Mr Forrest stood up and asked to speak. He first thanked Mr and Mrs Landon for their hospitality and then asked Ricky to bring Jenny forward, he introduced them then as an engaged couple and that the wedding would take place the following December. This news was greeted with a great deal of applause and Ricky had to put up with a lot of back slapping from his friends and Jenny a great number of kisses. The already light and happy atmosphere seemed to become even lighter and happier. Jenny then folded her dancing mittens back so that all the girls could see her sapphire ring, which was much admired.

The dancing resumed and Ricky was able to claim most of Jenny's remaining dances as he now knew that everyone expected it. By one o'clock Jenny was feeling hot and rather tired and as Ricky noticed he asked Mrs Forrest if he might take her to the balcony and catch some of the cooler air. She agreed and as Tad was passing and heard the request he made haste to Mrs Landon and asked her permission to do the same for Amabel. The four young people went out on the terraces and looked over the lawns to the harbour below with the moonlight shining on the water. Several other couples joined them and Ricky was delighted that Will also had taken the opportunity to ask Dimity's parents if he may take her to join them. Apparently they had been reluctant to let their precious daughter go out with a stranger and so only agreed by accompanying them themselves.

The music resumed and the dancers returned to the ballroom to have the last of the dances. Ricky and Jenny lingered and he was able to catch her to him and say, "Oh, Jenny I love you so much. I cannot believe that you have promised to be mine. I wonder that

I have agreed to wait until December to truly claim you. I am most impatient, my darling." He gently folded his arms about her and kissed her softly on the lips. It was a precious moment and they forgot their surroundings and were only conscious of their love. Then they realised that the music was playing the finale; Ricky took her hand and laughing they returned to their guests not realizing how the time had slipped by.

Soon after the ball came Christmas. The Forrests had asked Ricky and Will to join them for the festive season and Tad and the Falconer-Meads went to the Landons. By this time Ricky had had apartments made for his and Will's use.

Will had not intended to come often but he found he liked being in the country and had spent some time painting pleasant country scenes, finding that this had been more of a challenge than he had ever imagined. He found he had to think in all sorts and new shades of greens, blues and greys that he had hitherto taken for granted. It was all very well to look at a lovely green hillside in real life, but to make it look good on canvas was an entirely different thing. He reveled in the challenge, and was turning out some quite satisfactory things. He was even making gum trees look really like gum trees and not the English trees that so many artists had made them look like. He thought he might do a very large canvas of the scene from the verandah for Ricky so he could have it in his new town house.

After a delightful and lazy week over the Christmas time the two young men returned to Sydney. Ricky was loath to leave his Jenny but there was much to do and a living to make and so he set off with a, for once, reluctant Will, who had announced that as soon as he got some gear ready he was returning to complete a big thing, about which he was rather secretive. Ricky recognised that there would be a surprise in store so said nothing.

Back in Sydney things had moved with the Falconer-Meads. The old man called a gathering of the senior Landons, Ricky, Tad and Amabel and also Will to attend him at the hotel over dinner. They dined this time in the main dining room and then retired to their host's suite. As soon as they had assembled and given the men a drink of rich old port he announced that he had called them together for he had much to tell them.

"I have decided that I should return to my home very soon. I am not getting younger and I find the summer heat a little trying. I feel as though I have achieved all that I can and so there is little use our staying any longer," he said.

Ricky saw that Tad had paled to such an extent that he thought the younger man would faint. He looked at the man again who continued. "I have not found any evidence to prove that Tad is my grandson and so must go home disappointed." If anything Tad looked even paler. "But on the other hand," the old man continued, "I am as convinced as I ever will be that he is my son's child." Tad let out a huge silent sigh. "I asked Tad, or may I now refer to him as Theodore? if proof were to be obtained would he change his name to the one he was born with and to my disappointment but not to my surprise, he assured me he would not. At first I was distressed about that but on thinking it over I can see that he had good reasons for this. Theodore, you might explain your reasons, please."

Will's eyes were glued to Tad as he rose to speak. "Yes, indeed, sir." Tad said, "Perhaps if you had found proof, sir, that I was your grandson I may have been tempted to change my name. If I had been going back to England to live I might also have been tempted to change my name. But as there is still no proof and as I am not going to live in England I do not think it would be right for me to change my name from the one I have lived with since I was a young boy. I owe everything to Rick, and that I know Will will agree with me. We have borne his name and deem it an honour that he wanted to share it with us all this time and I wish to continue to do so. I hope I shall never do anything to dishonour it. Thank you, Rick, but sir," Tad continued, turning to the old gentleman, "I do thank you and honour you for accepting me as your grandson even though there is no proof. I am sorry I cannot do as you ask but that is the way I feel. There is just one thing, and that is something I must ask Mr Landon." He turned to the Landons. "Sir, would you prefer it if Amabel married a Falconer-Mead rather than an English? For she comes first in my thinking."

"Mr Falconer-Mead," John Landon said, standing up. "I have told you how I watched these boys grow up. I have seen how they struggled to make ends meet. I have always felt a great deal of admiration for them, all three. And the fact that I have willingly agreed to give my precious daughter to Tad, no matter what he calls himself, is good enough for me, and I am sure my dear wife agrees." He sat down.

"Thank you sir," said Tad. "Please understand, Mr Falconer-Mead. Please don't be disappointed that I do not wish to do what you suggest."

"Come here, Theodore, my grandson." He took the young man's hand. "No, I am not disappointed, lad. I am proud of you. I will say that even though I have found no proof of our relationship I know you are Matthew and Martha's son and I am content, I need no proof. I go home content."

"Thank you sir," said Tad gripping the wrinkled hand. "I wish I could do something to show how grateful I am and what great pleasure you have given me."

Quickly Mr Falconer-Mead said, "There is something you can do for me, Grandson. I hope you will do it, and you too, Miss Amabel." They all waited to hear what was coming. He said, "Joshua and I are leaving in two weeks time when the "Redcoat" sails. She will get to England in time for spring and so we will miss the worst of the winter. But, I suggest that these two young people, Mrs Landon, marry as soon as it is possible and come to England and Mead Park for the northern summer. I would like Theodore to see the family home and meet our family. I hear that young Mr Will is about to head for Paris so why not combine the trips and come together. He can stay at Mead Park and have a small taste of England before carrying on to Paris. What do you say?"

The assemblage gasped at the thought, and at first were quite speechless. John Landon was the first to speak. "Sir, you have caught me, at least, unawares." There were murmurs of, "Yes." "That's so." "But, if you will give us all a little time to think about it we will certainly tell you as soon as possible. Isn't that right, dear?" he asked turning to Sadie, who was looking rather flustered.

"Yes, please, a little time to think about it," she said." There would be so much to do."

"Certainly, Mrs Landon. I wouldn't think that you could decide right away. But I would like to know before we leave if that is possible," their host said.

He was assured that they would make the decision before that. They spent the rest of the time together discussion possibilities. Ricky and Will drawing together while the others spoke of different things. "Puts you on the spot a little, Will. Looks as though you will have less time to think about going. What do you feel about it?" Ricky asked.

"As a matter of fact, Rick, I had thought I might go. The sea trip was a bit daunting for me but if Tad and Amabel are going it really makes things a bit easier for me. That is if they don't mind my tagging along."

Tad heard this last and assured him that they would be very happy to have him. "That is if Amabel is wanting to go," said Tad. "She might hate the idea, and I won't force her. I wonder if she wants to. You know I didn't even think of going, it never entered my head."

It certainly gave them all a great deal to think about but the decisions were made much quicker that Ricky could believe. Will was sure he wanted to go and the Landons and Amabel had agreed. Tad was, surprisingly, the only one who was dubious.

"Why so hesitant, Tad?" Ricky asked over dinner one evening. "It is a much faster voyage than it used to be in the old days. You may even get a steamboat and they are even faster. Are you worried about being seasick, or Amabel, Tad?"

"No, apparently Amabel is a good sailor, Rick. Of course I don't know whether I am, but I'm not worried about that. But, oh, I don't know whether we ought to."

"Why ever not, Tad?" asked Will. "Do you think you won't like the place or the people?"

"As a matter of fact, Will, "he answered, "it is just the opposite. What would happen if we liked it so much we didn't want to come home again. Or if they put so much pressure on us that we might have to stay. I don't want to get myself into a situation that I cannot handle. Do you see my point?"

"Yes, I do. I suppose you have to meet a lot of strange people you may or may not like, too. Yes, I do see. What do you think. Rick,?" asked Will.

"I just have to say that you must all make up your own minds. I am really happy with things as they are, but I can see that even if you don't go, Tad, things are going to be different. Will is going anyway. I suppose neither of you will be here when Jenny and I get married, will you? I will miss you both very much. But I still say you must do what you think is right."

"Gosh, Rick we can't do that. We can't leave you to get married all by yourself," said Will."I won't go. I'll go some other time. After you're married."

Ricky laughed and clapped him on the back. "You silly duffer I can get married without you. I'll miss you of course, but by the time you all return we'll be settled in our new house and be an old married couple."

Tad looked thoughtful. "I don't want to leave you in the lurch, Rick, either. Any way we might be home by the end of November. If we get married soon, we could go to England and return before you do the deed."

"For goodness sake, don't worry. I'll have others who will stand by me. Please don't put your trip off. Don't take me into your calculations, I really am happy for you to go. Just don't ask me to put the wedding off until you come back. I don't think I could wait."

"He really has it bad, Tad, hasn't he? But seriously, Rick, do you mind?" asked Will anxiously.

"No, you goat. Carry on with your plans. We only aim to have a quiet wedding at Windsor, anyway, not a hullaballoo like yours is going to be, Tad."

"Well, if we have to marry soon we may have a quiet one, too. But I don't really want to hurry it up and spoil Amabel's day. She is so looking forward to it."

This was the main topic of conversation at the Landon home, too. Sadie was on tenterhooks waiting for the young couple to make up their minds. She didn't want to hurry them and was quite determined to let them make their own decision. She hated the thought of her Amabel going so far away from her, but knew she just had to wait and try to be patient. She, too, was concerned that they might like the life in England so much that they may wish to stop. Mead Park sounded as though it would have a great deal to offer a young couple. "I mustn't think of that," she thought.

Tad and Amabel did decide to bring the wedding forward and take up Mr Falconer-Mead's offer of a visit to England. The date fixed was the last day in January. That would allow them to have two weeks at Rocklea before catching the ship for England. Will, too, decided to go with the young couple. So there was much hustle and bustle to get everything done in time. Seamstresses worked long hours at the Landon house and Tad spent a lot of time getting his affairs in order so that he could take a year off, which was the time they expected to be away. Mr Hughes had given him leave and told him to have some good stories to tell them all when he returned. He also gave him introduction to various friends and one who was editor of a large London Paper. Tad looked forward to presenting that.

As the time drew near, Ricky could see that Will was feeling very apprehensive about it and tried to spend time with him to allay his fears and show him as much brotherly concern as he could. It was difficult to find the time for so much was happening in his own life, with wanting to spend as much time with Jenny as he could; overseeing the plans and beginnings of their new home; settling things up for Rocklea and establishing the boys he sent there, as well as the normal business things he had to deal with for if he let his business run down there would be a fall in the cash flow and he would not be able to carry out the plans he had for his various schemes. If all this was not enough Tom became ill .

One night, on his return from the store he drove into the yard and as Joe, who was the stable hand that Tom had trained to look after the English stable, came out to take the horse, he said, "Mr English, could yer go an' see Tom? He ain't the best."

Ricky went to Tom's room and found the old man in bed.

He knew that things were pretty serious for he had never known Tom to take to his bed before. "Hello, Tom. Not feeling the thing?" he asked.

"It's me ol' ticker, Rick. It's gorn an' let me darn."

"What happened?" asked Ricky, sitting at his bedside.

"I just sorta collapsed wi' a pain in me chest. Frightened young Joe silly, I did. 'e ran for Mrs Keen and they got me 'ere, and then she sends 'im for the doc."

"And?" prompted Ricky.

"'E says its me 'eart and' I gotta stay 'ere." 'E give me some drops that ain't too good ter take, but 'e said it might 'elp."

"I'll get you moved into the house Tom, so I can watch over you."

"Thet yer won't, young Ricky. I don' wanna leave me beautiful room thet yer 'ad done fer me. I'm happy 'ere an' very comfortable and warm. Young Joe looks after me real good. 'E's in the room next door and I only have to knock and 'e comes quick."

"I take it, Tom, that you have had this pain before?"

"Yairs, Rick. I admit I 'ave, but it was real bad today."

"You silly fellow. Why didn't you tell me?"

"Yer got enough on yer plate, mate. I'll be all right, but I wanted yer to know." Tom looked up at his friend wistfully. "Mate, ah want yer ter know I think a lot 'o you. You've been thet good ter me, thet, well, if yer was me son yer couldn't 'ave done no more. In fact, I never known a son what did as much. I appreciate it, mate. I just wanna tell yer." Tom put his old gnarled hand out to the young man.

Ricky took it and held it. "Tom, when I think of how you helped me and sheltered me at the risk of your job, the little I've done never repays it. And who is talking of repayment anyway? You are my friend and always will be."

"Not for long, mate. I think I got me notice, this time."

"Not if I can help it, Tom. I'll see you have everything you can need."

"That's real good 'o yer, mate." He closed his eyes and then opened them again, looking up at Ricky. "Thenk yer."

"I'll come and see you later, Tom. I'd better tell Mrs Keen I am here."

Mrs Keen was able to tell him more and the news was not good. The doctor apparently thought that the old man's heart wouldn't serve him for much longer.

"But, don't you worry, Mister Rick. We'll look after him. But young Joe is very good to him and looks after him well."

"Let me know then if there is any change," he said.

So in between all the other things that Ricky had to do he sandwiched in as many visits to Tom as he could, seeing that his friend was getting weaker by day and not ever being really free of pain. His lips were very blue and he knew that it was only a matter of time. Tom was quite prepared and spoke openly to Ricky about his dying. Ricky found it a very moving experience and so was able to speak about it without reluctance. He had asked many times if there was anything Tom would like and was amazed when he told him one night, that he would very much like a real funeral with beautiful shining black horses with black plumes. "Thet would be real somethin'," he said with a smile. "I got a bit saved, Rick, and thet should pay fer it."

"You shall have it, old friend, and I won't be using your money," said Ricky, with a squeeze of Tom's hand. "It will be the best I can get for you. Just like I had for my father. Would that be all right?"

"I won't ask yer ter do thet," came the reply.

"Why not?" Ricky replied. "You have been a father to me for a long while, Tom."

Ricky didn't realise how soon it would be that he would have to arrange the funeral. Tom died that night. Joe had been sleeping in his room and early in the night he came to Ricky saying that he thought Tom was unconscious. All three of the boys went out to see him and he was certainly deeply asleep, at least. Ricky sent the others to bed and stayed with Tom until he saw that his breathing was getting shallower. He spoke to Tom at one stage and the response he got filled him with emotion. Tom opened his eyes and said "Hello, mate," faintly and gave Ricky's hand a slight squeeze. He just seemed to go into a quiet rest and then Ricky realised that he had gone. He took the pillows out and lay him flat. He covered him and blew the light out. Joe heard him moving and came in.

"He's gone, Joe," he said.

"I've lorst a real mate, Mr English. 'E were a real gentleman was old Tom."

"The best mate a man could have Joe. We will all miss him."

Tom had his funeral with black horses all decked with black plumes. Ricky made it as special as he could. Joe and the household staff attended with the three boys and several of Tom's ex-convict friends.

Ricky's next social occasion was a farewell to the Falconer-Meads. They were not waiting for the wedding but going in the new year. Ricky put on a dinner party for them and the Landon's. It happened that it was the day of Tom's funeral and Mr Falconer-Mead had heard about it. He thought it was very strange that Ricky had gone to the trouble of giving Tom the funeral he had and could not understand why he even attended it with Tad and Will.

Tad was about to say something and Ricky forestalled him by saying to the Englishman. "We all thought a great deal of Tom, Mr Falconer-Mead. He has been a friend for years and we will miss him greatly." Ricky frowned at Tad who took the hint and said nothing. Mr Landon changed the subject with quiet skill. Obviously Mr Landon thought these young men should look down upon Tom but they knew otherwise.

There was much chat about the various plans and it was mostly a pleasant evening, but Ricky wondered how his breezy Tad would fit into an English home that apparently was ruled with a rod of iron by this patriarch of a man.

Two days later they all went to see the ship sail, Tad assuring his grandfather that they would not be far behind them, just a few weeks. He seemed relieved when the ship sailed and grew smaller as it made its way down the magnificent Sydney Harbour.

The wedding day was as hot and humid as a summer day can be, and it was well that they had planned a morning wedding. Amabel wore a lovely white dress, for this reason. It was made of light weight cotton voile with an overdress of openwork lace. There were wide frills all round the hem. The neck line was demurely high and a wide swathe had been set around below the neckline covering the full sleeves. She wore a fetching flowered hat over her piled up golden hair.

Tad thought she was the loveliest thing he had ever seen. He quite gasped at her beauty and as he began to sway Ricky put a hand out to support him wondering what he would do with a swooning bridegroom, but he stood straight again and was able to receive his bride from her father without any further worry.

The Rector of St James married them smiling at this lad he had known for so many years, watching his growth from a small urchin to grown man and now seeing him marry one of the loveliest girls in the colony. He felt no doubts about this marriage for he felt it was truly one made in heaven.

A beautiful open carriage carried the couple to the Landon home where the reception was held. They were followed by the various members of the wedding party and family and friends all in like carriages. It was a grand procession to traverse the city streets on this hot Saturday morning. Tad and Amabel were little conscious of their surrounds but only of themselves, but they were duly admired by all who had lined the streets to watch. All crowds love a bride and even though this one was not looking their way they appreciated her beauty and knew the well known young reporter from the newspaper.

The reception took the usual form of magnificent food and many speeches and at last Tad began to realise that he should come out of his rosy cloud and demand that he take his love away to catch the train for Parramatta where they would spend the night. The whole gathering once more took to their carriages and set off to see the happy couple on to the train. By this time there was much merriment and jollying, Tad and Ricky being surprised at Will's frivolity. He had succeeded in tying all sorts of peculiar things to the train carriage that they were to travel in and eventually when the engine puffed its way along it was festooned with tins and ribbons and all sorts of bunting that Ricky was sure would not please the Railways staff.

Sadie Landon bid her Amabel a sad and damp farewell knowing that even though so far she would not be so far away, this was the beginning of losing her eldest and perhaps, dearest. She was on this day, anyway.

The party dwindled and the main guests looked at each other in that lost way that a group does when an exciting event is over. The Landons looked so bereft that Ricky took pity on them and suggested that they all go to his home and look at some of Will's pictures. He was about to package them for storage and had them out in the studio. Sadie had not seen them for some time and they jumped at the suggestion, and so spent a pleasant afternoon quietly recovering from what Sadie felt was almost a trauma.

John Landon was able to speak of Will to Ricky during the afternoon after seeing the portraits in the studio. "That boy really has something, Ricky. I hope he is able to benefit from some decent tutors in Paris. I feel confident he will and I hope you do to."

"Yes, I do, sir. I will miss him badly for I saw much more of Will than of Tad. Tad always seemed to be at your home, sir, but Will was always here. I am sure he will benefit, but I am concerned about his coping with being alone," said Ricky.

"I am sure my brother-in-law will look after him. He will like Robert and I am sure his wife will take to him," assured John. "I look forward to his letters eagerly. I imagine he will keep us informed."

"Of course, sir, I am sure he will do that. But it does take an age to hear if anything goes wrong," put in Ricky.

"Yes, but he will have Tad and Amabel near enough for him if he isn't happy. They will be there for some months at least, and he should know by then if he is going to settle."

"Yes, I suppose so," admitted Ricky reluctantly. "I am acting like a mother hen."

CHAPTER 17: *The Boys spread their wings*

Will was frantically busy during the last two weeks before they sailed. There was so much to do and organize but he was pleased to be busy, for if he ever did find time to sit and think he rather got cold feet about it all. He was thankful that in the end it had all happened quickly. He was forever running to Ricky and say, "Now don't forget, Rick, I want you to ..." and then go on to tell him about something he had been involved in. Ricky had no idea that the young man was involved in so much. He was learning to know Will better and better.

"Now Rick, you know that boy in the hostel, Cliff? Well, he wants to draw plans for houses and I have been teaching him the little I know. I would like him to get a draughtsman's job and so have been teaching him the basics of drawing. Can you see that he has an interview with an architect. Harvey, your architect, may give him a job. I have been meaning to see him myself but haven't had time. Would you see to it?" Another time was, "Rick, young Phil Yates is old enough now to be really getting out on his own. See about getting him a job somewhere where he can develop his sculpting skills will you? He's done some good work and I think he would like to work with a monumental mason. Jarvis might help."

Tad and Amabel came back full of love and good feelings for the world in general. They went to the Landon's house for the few days before sailing for Sadie wanted to have Amabel near for emotional reasons and also so that the final packing could be done more easily.

It was a forlorn group who wished 'bon voyage' to this party of travellers. It took at least ten weeks to sail to the homeland and it would be the same back and so even if they were to turn round and return quickly it would be many months before Sadie saw her Amabel again, and it would take that long to get the first news of her.

Ricky had such an empty feeling in his 'innards' as he called them. It was so long since he had been alone he wondered how he could cope without the boys. They always had some doings to tell him about each evening at home. He felt they kept him in touch with the world. Especially Tad with all his news. But at least the Forrests and Jenny were coming up to stay next week and that was something to look forward to. There was so much to do anyway and the foundations of the new house to go down when Jenny was here so she could see the first of her new home in place.

Ricky looked at Will. He was so pale and drawn. He hope he would keep well. He wondered if they would be seasick. "I don't think I was too bad when I came out." he mused. Tad and Amabel were still floating on a cloud. He thought he would float on a cloud when he married Jenny, too. Jenny was so lovely.

They suddenly realised that the ship was leaving the wharf. Last minute shouts were called and they all waved as the vessel slowly made her way up the harbour.

"Let us go along to Mrs Macquarie's Chair, John," said Sadie. "Then we could go along at other places and wave to them again," she added.

"No, we will not, Sadie," said John Landon in a stern voice. "You would have us go all the way to the Macquarie light and down the coast. No, we'll go home and quietly cry there," he added tenderly as he put his arm about her waist. "Come, let's go. In you get girls, wave your last waves." He bustled his family into the carriage and Ricky watched them drive off. He knew how they felt.

The house was quite as empty as Ricky had feared but he took out the plans of the house after dinner and tried to fill his mind with them. Mrs Keen kept popping in to see that he was all right and Ricky wondered whether she felt the loss of the boys, too. It was strange for they were so often out at their own things that he wondered why he missed them so soon, for he was used to them being away for an evening. He tried shaking it off by thinking of Jenny.

The Forrests and Jenny came a week later and settled into the house. They intended staying two weeks for business and pleasure. It was the first time they had stopped with Ricky and he was very pleased to have them. They had a busy round of social engagements and Ricky felt that the time was going too fast.

He noticed that Jenny was very quiet on the day they drove out to see the foundations laid for their new home. They had all been so busy that Ricky had little time alone with his love and he felt a great excitement that he at last had her on his own and they were going to see the beginnings of their future take shape. They walked up the slope of the house block to where the men were working, and watched as the men poured the first concrete into the trenches which would be part of the foundations of their home. There were massive stones cut and dressed waiting to be used for the bulk of the house. It would certainly be a substantial building.

They watched for a while and then Ricky led Jenny to a log where he lay a rug down suggesting that she sit in the shade. He ran down to the sulky and brought back a hamper of afternoon tea which Mrs Keen had prepared for them.

After serving Jenny he said, "Now, my dear, I want to know what is troubling you. I've noticed you have been very quiet and I'm wondering whether you are having second thoughts about our marriage. Please tell me. This is the time to say what is in your mind." Ricky felt his stomach tighten as he said this, but was determined. "I have felt that we haven't had as much time together as we should have but circumstances seem to have prevented that." Ricky took her hand and smiled at her encouragingly.

Jenny put her cup of lemonade down on the hamper and said, "Yes, Ricky, I have been a bit upset. I have had a great deal to think about and I am troubled. I know I have to speak to you about it, but haven't for the reasons you have said and also that I don't want to hurt you."

"Thank you for that, Jenny," he said, his heart in his mouth, by this time, wondering what was in her mind, fearful of what he was about to hear. Her sweet face looked so troubled but he continued to smile encouragingly at her. "Whatever you have to say must be said and now is a good time to say it as we will not be interrupted."

"Well," she said, sighing over her thoughts. "I think the first thing that upset me was that I had no idea what a big business man you are and what a busy life you lead and I wonder whether I could live up to you."

"Oh, darling," said Ricky, "You little darling. Life is not always as busy as it has been, for I have wanted you to meet my friends who I hope will be your friends. As far as business is concerned, I am not bigger, as you call it, than many other men in the city and we can live as quietly or as busily as you desire. I am not really a very social person, but I do enjoy dining with friends occasionally. Most nights I am home quite quietly. What else has been worrying you, my little one?"

"It's all the other things you do. I wouldn't know how to work with orphans, homeless people and the other things you do. I spent the other morning in the hostel with Miss Binks, as you know, and she told me such a lot about what you do. Ricky, I don't think I could keep up with you and all you do."

"But, Jenny, I wouldn't ask you to. I have only been interested in them because I wanted to pay back to society a little of what I have received myself. But I don't bring them home and they don't interfere with my home life at all. The boys rarely see my charges, as you once called them. I only want us to be happy in our own home and I want nothing more than to find you at home to greet me after a day at the office and settle down to just looking at you sitting opposite me each evening and every moment I can get to share with you. You will be and indeed are, right now, the most important thing in my life. I would lie down and let you trample on me, I think."

Jenny laughed at this, but said gravely, "I am a little frightened of that, too, Ricky. I am frightened that I will not be good enough for you and you will be disappointed in me."

"Jenny," said Ricky," it is my greatest fear that I will not be good enough for you and that you will be disappointed in me. We must work this out together and we will. I have never been married, either, and it is as big a mystery to me as it is to you, but, my very darling girl, we will work on it together. Will that do?"

"But you are so good at everything," she said, with her eyes full of tears.

Ricky took both her hands in his and said, "Jenny, look at me." She raised her eyes to his. "Do you love me, Jenny? Do you truly love me? Tell me honestly."

"Oh, yes, I do. I love you so much, but I am not good enough for you." With this the tears fell.

"And, my precious, I am not nearly good enough for you. I think that is a good start, don't you?"

"Yes, I suppose so," came the tearful reply.

"My darling, all I want is to look after you and shield you from all harm and hurt. I want to do that more than anything. I will take care of you, Jenny. Will you put yourself in my hands? Do you know, I do understand what you mean, I think. You can see that my daytime life will not alter that much, but yours will. I know you are a busy person who likes lots to do and that's why you took on teaching the Forrest children. But, darling, when we spend time together we will develop things for our mutual interest and you will see that we will have a new life but it will be shared. Does the thought of the big house worry you, dear? Do you think you will rattle around in it feeling lost?"

"No, not that. I am used to being in a house as large as ours will be but it seems a bit strange that I wonder what I will do with myself. You have everything so well organised, Ricky."

"Oh, my dear, have I not involved you enough in it? I am sorry. I have been thoughtless."

"No it's not even that, for how could you involve me more if I am not here?"

"I know what we'll do," said Ricky eagerly, "we'll only furnish the rooms that are necessary for what we need straight off, and then when you get a bit used to the place you can choose what you want for the rest. How will that be?"

Jenny gave her nose a ladylike blow and smiled a watery smile but said, "Thank you, Richard, that might be a good idea. I think now that everything will be all right."

"And we will promise to always tell each other when they have a problem, won't we?" Ricky asked.

"I'll try, really I will."

"Do you know, if you just set about to enjoy yourself all will be well, I am sure" said Ricky softly.

"No, I think there's more to it than that. I will just set about making you enjoy yourself, and then I am sure it will be all right. I'm sorry I have been so silly, but I do feel better now."

"And you always will be if we talk things over. Promise?" She nodded. "Well that's fine then. By the way, you called me Richard. Do you want to?"

"Yes, I often think of you as Richard. Have you ever been called that?"

"No, Jenny, I haven't, because my father was Richard and I've always been Ricky. Officially, of course I am Richard and always sign myself as such. Do you wish to call me that, darling? I don't mind if you do. As long as you want to call me something I don't mind what it is."

He set about chattering to try to get her mind settled. He realised what a big step it all was, but he knew her for a brave girl, otherwise she would never have been able to come to the colony to make a new life here in the first place. So they talked about the garden, the weather and everything else he could think of. He tried to put his mind on things that would interest her and soon she was chatting and laughing as easily as he was.

They packed the hamper up and Ricky asked her if she would like to go down to the point and watch the ships on the harbour for a while. She agreed to this and as he helped her into the sulky he said, "Do you know Jenny, Tad and Amabel were worried about the things you were. I suppose everyone is. Tad told me, so I was half expecting you to be concerned and was wishing you had a mother to talk things over with. They must have found everything was all right for I couldn't imagine anyone happier than those two when they set off for England. I don't think they would have cared where they were going as long as they were together." He looked up at her, "Jenny, my precious darling, it will be like that with us, too. I have pledged my life to do everything I can to make you happy."

"Oh, Richard, I would be a selfish beast if I ever wanted more than that. You are such a comfort and I do love you so." She reached down and kissed him on the lips. "Come on, find a ship for me to look at."

"Yes, ma'am," said Ricky jumping into the sulky and speeding the horse on its way.

Jenny excused herself from accompanying the Forrests when they set out next morning to visit old friends. She explained that she intended to go next door to the girl's hostel and see Miss Binks. Her heart was pounding a little as she knocked on the door. She had been in the hostel before, of course, so she knew the girl who opened the door.

"Would I be able to speak with Miss Binks, Please. Annie, isn't it?" she asked.

"Yes, Miss. I'll see if she is free. Please come in to the sitting room."

Jenny tried to relax in one of the armchairs but found it was not easy for now she was wondering what she was going to say when Binksie did come. However after being greeted with a broad smile and a bidding to sit and make herself comfortable until tea came she began to feel better. Binksie must have realised she was rather ill at ease and so sat and chatted to make her guest relax.

The tea arrived very quickly and as they sat over it Jenny said, "Binksie, I do hope I haven't interrupted your work. I don't want to be a nuisance, but I didn't know what time would be best to come."

"No trouble, my dear," Miss Binks assured her, speaking as though she had a troubled child in the schoolroom, and indeed she thought she did. "No trouble at all. I was only setting some work for one of the girls and she is quite capable of going ahead without me." She smiled at Jenny. "My child you look as though you have the cares of the world on your shoulders. Can I help? Is it in my line at all? Come on, tell me."

"Well, I will," said Jenny, "if you don't mind. You see I am worried about all this work that Ricky does and I don't quite know what I am going to do about it."

"Whatever do you mean, surely you don't mind what he does, girl?" Jenny was asked sharply.

"No, no. No I don't mind at all. Please, I am sorry, but I want to know how I can help too and I am scared to death of trying. Please help me."

With that Binksie roared with laughter. "What a silly goose you are to be sure. I daresay I am, too. I am sorry I laughed but it really was with relief, Miss Elston. I thought you were going to ask me how to stop him, and you know that would be impossible. For I find if someone has his sort of helping streak, there's nothing you can do about it but go along, too. Otherwise it would be rather like trying to turn a river back on itself."

"I know, or rather, that's what I thought it would be like. No, Miss Binks, I want to get into the river too, if you know what I mean. But I don't know how to. Please tell me how."

So talking it all over they sorted things out a little in Jenny's mind. Miss Binks told her how she could be most useful and take over some of the things that Amabel had done before she left. She suggested that once she got the feel of the place she would find how easy it would be to find a lot to do.

"You have apparently been teaching the Forrest children, Miss Elston, and so you won't find it much different for some of the girls have had no teaching at all and so have to learn their letters like the smallest Forrest. But it isn't much use you starting anything you could not carry through full time for you won't be here all that often, I suppose. At least, not yet. But there are other ways you could help. Just let me think a moment."

Jenny sat watching the capable woman for a while and said, "Miss Binks, I don't think it is what you do that is worrying me, but how you do it. I mean, I don't think I'll know how to talk to the girls."

"But, they are just girls, you know. You must be used to servants, you must know how to deal with them, "the older woman said.

"Oh, yes, of course I do. But when they are doing their work and I am doing my usual things it is easy. You see, all the servants we had at home were people I grew up with and I knew them well, but here I won't know what to say to them and they will know it."

"I daresay you are saying that the lower orders walk in a different world to those above. No, no, don't protest." Miss Binks held up her hand as Jenny was to protest that she wouldn't have put it like that. "I know you aren't thinking in those hard terms but I think I know what you mean. But remember that they may seem quite imperturbable when you see them doing their work around the house, but they are just as frightened of you and your world as you are of theirs. This is one of the things we try to break down here. Oh, we don't break down the barriers completely, but we teach the girls that we all have our values and whether we are doing something menial or something quite enlightening we must do our best."

"It all sounds very difficult. You see I think girls who have had a tough life would look at things differently and I know I have had a soft life. I know I have been spoiled, for I haven't had a hard life at all," said Jenny.

"Miss Elston, you lost your parents suddenly and you lost your home. You brought yourself out to the colony alone and that took a lot of courage. I don't think a few girls should fuss you, but I do understand and I am very pleased you have come to me. I know a little of the sort of person Mr English is and I wondered whether you understood. I see that you do and I admire you for admitting it. You will have no worries for you have faced it and are ready to do something about it. Many girls wouldn't. I have an idea," she added, "Can you sew?"

"Yes, I can. I particularly like doing white work and am embroidering pillow cases for my trousseau now."

"You see, you are an asset right away. We have a sewing circle each afternoon and most of the girls come and bring whatever craft work they are interested in. I believe that busy fingers, even in leisure hours, are fingers kept out of trouble and our sewing circle is a most important part of our training. Will you come, and bring your sewing?"

"Yes, most certainly I will. May I come this afternoon, please?"

"Yes, we would love you to come. You see this is the time that we want the girls to learn to be able to carry on what we would call a normal conversation and learn a few graces as well. While they are doing their work it's 'Yes, Miss Binks', and 'No, Miss Binks'.

I want them to be able to feel free to speak openly to us and they are learning how. You will find it is easier to get to know them when you are sharing something with them and them with you. I am sure it will be smooth sailing."

Jenny found that it was. She arrived at the stipulated time and joined the girls in the sitting room. Miss Binks was there, too, and Mrs Yates.

The girls were rather shy of Jenny at first and there seemed to be a few rather silent silences. Neither Miss Binks or Mrs Yates helped overcome this and so Jenny, taking a quiet deep breath, asked one of the girls who was doing white work like hers if she may look at her work and see if she could learn some new stitches. She marveled at the dainty work that some of the girls were doing. Two of them were doing white work and it was not long before young heads were together pouring over designs and new stitches. Binksie looked across at Mrs Yates and smiled and on receiving one back she winked a wicked wink as though to say, 'all is well.'

"Oh, miss," came the answer, "I am sure you know more'n me for I am jest larnin'. Please miss, kin I look at yours? Please?"

"Oh, yes. I've been dying to have a look at yours. May I come and sit with you? You're Millie, aren't you?"

"No, miss, I'm Sadie. But please, miss, come and sit 'ere. I mean here." Sadie indicated a chair at the table near her. "And please miss, this is Annie. She's doin' a rag rug."

This broke the ice rather and the girls unbent enough to start chattering. It seemed no time at all that Binksie stood up and said, "Come along, Miss Elston, this is where we get the afternoon tea and serve the girls." Turning to Mrs Yates she said, "Your turn to sit and receive today, Mrs Yates. Miss Elston will help me."

"That will be a pleasure," said Mrs Yates. "we will all wait in anticipation," and chuckled.

"I hope you don't mind that I shared with Mrs Yates what you told me this morning, Miss Elston. I don't know whether you have heard how Mr English found her in a destitute state and rescued her. She thinks the sun shines out of that young man and is very pleased indeed that he has found a young lady like you." Miss Binks looked straight at her. "We love your young man. We all think he is rather wonderful."

Tears flooded Jenny's eyes. "I do too, Miss Binks, and it is the worry of my life that I am not good enough for him."

"You'll do, my girl. You are going along the right track," Binksie assured her and gave her a big bear hug.

That was the first of many sessions and soon Jenny was able to walk into the hostel with no qualms at all. There she was made to feel useful and was able to find things that she could do and teach the girls that hadn't until then been done.

When she suggested that they should learn to dance, at first Binksie thought that might be going a bit far but after consultation with Ricky they thought they might try. It would be good for the girls to learn to have normal relationships with boys, so they invited the boy's hostel to partake in a little exercise one Friday night. Mr and Mrs Forrest and the Landons joined in with Ricky and Jenny and soon were teaching the boys that the art of dancing was not something to be looked down upon. At first the boys were horrified at touching the ladies hands and the girls very shy of twirling a waltz with the 'elderly' gentlemen. But when all the young folk saw that these people wanted them to have a good time they entered into the fun of it and began to take it seriously.

The boys had arrived looking well scrubbed and most reluctant. Mr Parker had to watch them in case any wanted to glide away to parts unknown or known as the case may be. Mr Brown, the joiner, turned out be a very fine dancer and soon was showing the girls how to do this dance and that. Jenny and Binksie took it in turn to play the piano and Ricky was good not demanding to dance with Jenny all the time even though he dearly wanted to. The girls had dressed with great care and the boys hardly recognizing these beauties who were 'just girls' in the daytime. There was not much to-ing and fro-ing between the hostels normally and at the end of the evening it was decided that the dance was a huge success and more should be planned. The supper that the girls provided just put the finishing touches on a pleasant evening for the boys.

All this helped Jenny and Ricky to know each other better and now that Jenny had lost her fear of the hostel she relaxed and just glowed. Being in love suited her as it did most young things. They spent much time writing to one another when they were apart and looked forward to the day when they would be together for always.

Writing to Jenny was not the only letter writing Ricky did now, for he had to keep letters from home continuously flowing towards England and Paris. He knew that Tad was better off than poor Will, for not only was he in a foreign land but in a very lonely state and that was ever a worry for Ricky. He didn't expect to hear for some months after they left and was happy to receive his first letters within a very short time.

His first from Tad was —

"Dear Rick,

I'll bet you didn't expect this so soon, but we had to call in at the Cape of Good Hope and there was a ship going to Sydney. So, we all took the opportunity to write home.

We are all very well. Will and I were sick all the way past the south coast of Australia. The old ship was absolutely horrible and so was being sick. Amabel wasn't a bit sick and has been my darling angel and looked after me marvelously.

Oh, Ricky she is wonderful. I don't know what I have done to deserve such a darling ..." The letter then contained such like remarks about the bride and her wonders but at least he finished the letter by saying, *"Will keeps well and appears to enjoy the voyage now that he isn't sick.*

Yours truly,
Tad"

Will's was much more interesting and a delight to Ricky.

"Dear Rick,

Now that I am no longer sick I am enjoying the voyage immensely. I was sick all the way across southern Australia. I don't know how Tad stood having Amabel fussing over him at that time for all I wanted to do was lie there and die and not be bothered with any one but the steward who looked after me.

I daresay you will be surprised to hear from me so soon, but a passenger was very ill and decided to get off the ship at Cape Town. This is a fine harbour with a number of ships, one of which is heading for Sydney and so we are able to send this off.

There are some very nice people aboard, and only a few that are not. The captain is a polite fellow to the passengers, but I believe not to the crew. Which side of him we don't see, but on occasions do hear.

The Marlings are aboard and are pleasant people. They have their two sons and a daughter travelling with them. The sons are about our age and good chaps. The girl is younger. The Richardsons are on too, and the Archibald Smiths. Several folk we have heard about but I have never met, the John James, the Heards from out near Bathurst and Gerald Cross from somewhere on the South Coast of N.S.W. Most of the cabin passengers got on in Melbourne. Two are absolutely awful. They are the Misses Agatha and Gertrude Pennefather. They complain about everything and are quite miserable. They don't like colony life and are going home to "culture." One wonders why such women bother to make the voyage out, it could never be to their liking. But several other families got on who are very good company and so you see I have a goodly number of people to while away my time with.

Melbourne is not as well developed as Sydney but is remarkable for its wide straight streets, not narrow ones like Sydney. The river is delightful and right in the city. Not as pretty as the harbour at home but very attractive. There are some good quality homes being built there for apparently there are some very rich people there. I suppose from the gold.

The Marling boys and I hired a cab to take us around to look at this place. We found it very interesting. You should see the black people here. Some of them are quite huge and very black. Everyone here seems to have black servants, they are everywhere. Not like at home where you never see black servants. Although I have heard people do have them in the country.

The town is well established and quite picturesque. There is a big mountain that they call Table Top that is flat and often has a cloud along it for all the world like a tablecloth. I think I must like travel.

I am not very good at sketching while the ship is going for sometimes it makes me a bit sick and when the deck is sloped it is difficult, but I am enjoying it and the Marlings are good company. But I have done some things that I really like of the big black fellows working on the wharf. They are so black and shiny that they reflect light on their skin.

Tad is well now, he was sick when I was but Amabel looked after him so he was all right. They spend their time ashore looking at shops and things so they go their own way. They don't mind me going off with the Marlings and I don't mind them going off. They have made friends with some other young couples and are happy with them. Occasionally Tad gets a feeling of brotherly remorse and wanders along to see how I am faring. He makes me chuckle, he is like an old uncle.

We all send our best wishes to you and the thing that would make this trip perfect would be to have you with us. Remember me to Jenny, I send her greetings.

Will."

With this were some funny caricatures of people who Ricky presumed were some of the passengers. Two sour looking females he took to be the Misses Pennefather, both with very long noses and droopy lips. Ricky thought he would carefully keep these and show them to Will when he got back. He might value the sketches some day, he thought.

The next mail from the boys came from London where apparently Joshua Falconer-Mead had met them and settled them in a hotel so that he could show them the sights before taking them to Sussex. Will wrote his usual glowing descriptions of all they saw and Tad his usual reports of his Amabel. One thing set Ricky thinking in Tad's letter was that Amabel apparently had lost her good sea-legs on the latter part of the trip and was quite peaky. Tad hoped it was not serious and that she would pick up soon. The next letter had Ricky in stitches for his thoughts of Amabel turned out to be quite right. She was enciente.[5]

[5] Pregnant

Tad wrote,

"Dear Rick,

Guess what! Amabel is increasing and I didn't even think about that. We are so excited that we can't think of anything else. She has been feeling quite poorly each morning, but is able to eat lunch happily each day. She is looking better now. I have insisted on her seeing a doctor, though, in case anything should be wrong. My grandfather insisted on her seeing Dr Light, who has been the family doctor here for generations I think. He brought my father in to the world. I cannot think that that is a good recommendation for I would like her to have someone more modern. However my grandfather says that having a baby is the same every generation and that doesn't change. But I do not want to risk Amabel.

I daresay I should tell you a bit about Mead Park and the people here. Well, it is a lovely home, and very large indeed. I have never seen such a big house, it's bigger than any we have at home. I don't know how many rooms it has but it is lots. I thought it was a castle when I first saw it. It has lovely gardens, too.

The people are, my grandfather, Joshua, his mother, my Aunt Mary, his father Uncle Cuthbert, my Aunt Jemima and all sorts of servants and things. They are a bit overwhelming and take a lot of getting used to but they are very kind to Amabel and that is what counts.

Grandfather took Amabel and me to see my other grandparents the day after we arrived. Their name is Stanthorpe, as I told you, and their place is called Hamilton. It isn't as big as Mead Park and it wouldn't want to be, but the gardens are absolutely lovely. I cannot get over this English spring, there seems to be blue plants all over the place. But Hamilton's gardens are simply lovely.

I cannot say enough about my Stanthorpe grandparents. I like them a great deal and somehow I felt at home right away and, of course, they loved Amabel. They have accepted me completely as I apparently have my mother's eyes, so my grandmother says, and of course, I look like Josh. She is a sweet, dainty little person and couldn't take me to see my mother's portrait soon enough. Ricky that made me quite emotional. In fact that state is, at this moment, quite

235

overwhelming. Me! hard-hearted, me! They asked Amabel and me to come to stay for a full day and this we did and thoroughly enjoyed it. We walked all over the simply acres of garden and it was astounding. My grandparents actually do some of it themselves. I think they would like us to take up residence there, but of course we cannot, but I would like to. We've been to see them several times.

They also have made Will very welcome which is more than I can say about the people at the Park. I think he will go on his way soon. But he is very well.

Grandfather sent us to see Amabel's relatives in Surrey and we had several days there. What a fine family I have married in to! Amabel was able to see all the young people she spent her girlhood with and I was able to meet all the people she has spoken of so much. Their homes are very lovely, too. None as big and grand as the Park but ever so homely. We took Will with us and they welcomed him as my brother's right, and that was good. Cheers!

Tad"

Will's letter was so different and much shorter;

"Dear Rick,

What a different place this is to what I have been used to. The colours of this northern spring are a delight. There are bluebells by the mile in the woods here.

I spend quite a lot of time wandering around sketching, and when they can Tad and Amabel take me with them to visit Tad's other grandparents who are very nice folks. At least they treat me like a human but I cannot say that about the people at the Park, as they all call it. They seem to think I am going to a den of iniquity by going to live in Paris to study painting. I must say, too, that these 'gentlewomen' don't really accept Tad either. Although, I don't think he is all that happy, he doesn't say anything. At least they are kind (too much) to Amabel so I suppose Tad thinks if they do that then he will put up with it. I think his grandfather is trying to make Tad settle here, I know Tad and I don't think there is a chance at all.

*I am going off after I visit Amabel's relatives. I hope they are like
the Stanthorpes for they are very kind people.*
Regards, Will."

This letter gave Ricky a great deal to think about and wondered
whether Mr Landon was correct in his assurance that Mrs Landon's
brother would give Will a welcome in Paris. He did hope so, for if
things didn't turn out well for Will he was not very happy to think
what the outcome would be.

From that time on only scrappy letters came from Tad and
the Landons were not very happy about Amabel being so far
from them while she was in her known condition. Mrs Landon,
especially worried about her and wished that the young people
would come home.

Will on the other hand wrote glowing letters of his time in Paris.
Mr Cummins had proved helpful. He met Will and settled him in
a decent apartment quite a distance from the embassy, explaining
that he knew that Will would want to be near the art school he was
to go to. Will hadn't met Mrs Cummins because the small children
were sick with the measles and so they couldn't have Will at their
home for a while. Will understood but as the weeks went by, seeing
only Mr Cummins occasionally, he wondered whether that was the
reason or was there another English 'gentle'-woman who would
not accept him. He found this was so, for when he at last was asked
to a meal at the Cummins home at the embassy he found she was a
cold unrelenting female who did not wish to be landed with a waif
from the colonies. This was not actually said, but Will was left in
no doubt, and it hurt.

But he wrote in glowing terms about the back alleys and streets
that gave him a great deal of scope for his particular type of street
scenes. He thoroughly enjoyed his school and found that without
a great deal of difficulty he could understand what the teacher was
saying. This man was as 'volatile as a steam train', said Will. He could
scream like a train whistle and often did, "at me," he said. He could
make himself understood easily but found that everyone spoke so
quickly that they were hard to follow, especially M. Jacques, who

was the teacher. The first weeks were a blur of misunderstanding and at times was very despondent, then two lively young Englishmen came to the class and he began to feel more settled. He found that he had more French than they did and so was able to feel a slight amount of superiority about his helping them. He found that they liked a rollicking night life that he was not able to keep up with, for his constitution was not up to it. But they were good company and it was hard to tear himself away from them.

Then in one letter Will told Ricky that he and his two friends had planned to take a walking holiday sketching through the country a little. He wondered whether he could keep up with them for they were athletic types and not too tolerant of his crippled leg, but he hoped that if he was not able he would find a good place to paint and settle there in a farm house.

"But the countryside is not like ours, Rick. There seems to be lots of open fields and no scattered houses like we know. The farmers seem to live in walled towns or something. But I must admit I don't really know but will find out. I hope I find something good to paint."

Surprisingly there were no more letters and Ricky began to worry. He knew he had to wait patiently for if anything was wrong Will would contact Tad and he thanked God that Tad was comparatively near. It was no use writing a worry letter for that would take months to get an answer and so he just had to wait. As time went by he was nearly frantic and he carried his concern to Mr Landon who was also a recipient of Will's mail.

"I was going to ask you the same thing, Ricky. I have been concerned for some time and did not like to tell you. I am sorry that Cummins has not been more helpful to the boy. I was so confident that he would be a great assistance to him. But apparently Agatha has taken a dislike to Will and takes every opportunity to write and tell me so. I had a disturbing one from her telling me that he has got into bad company and as she knew he was a useless type she was not surprised. Not what I planned, Ricky. I am so sorry."

"It isn't your fault, sir. I am sure he will be all right, but I wish I knew. If he is in trouble he wouldn't be likely to turn to the Cummins now, and I am sorry for it, but he is of age and should have enough sense to get himself out of any trouble he may be in. He has to go to Mr Cummins for his money anyway so surely he would see to him."

"Thank God he is close enough to England to keep in touch with Tad. But I have to tell you that in Tad's last letter he told us that he hasn't heard from Will either and was a bit concerned, but as he knew Will was going out to the country he didn't worry. Incidentally I wouldn't be surprised if Tad and Amabel came home, Ricky. I fancy they are not too happy there. What do you think?"

"I gathered that, too, Mr Landon. I presume Tad has found that having relatives is not all that marvellous. But he likes his mother's family. I am pleased about that."

CHAPTER 18: *Micky*

Ricky had a great deal to occupy his mind so had, at times, to put the thought of Will behind him. He was very busy with his town projects and his country ones, and tried to fit in seeing Jenny as often as he could. Their friendship grew as well as their love and they were beginning to feel they knew one another very well.

Rob Martin sometimes met Ricky in Windsor when he went down to Rocklea, but it was usually one of the grooms from the farm. When Rob came they were able to chat about the happenings of the place without any disturbance. So it was not a surprise to Ricky when he saw Rob sitting in the sulky when the coach pulled in.

"Hello, Rob. Hot, isn't it?" called Ricky.

"Gooday, Mr English. It certainly isn't a winter's day. Must be that spring is coming. Did you have a good trip down?" Rob asked.

"Yes, not too bad. But at times I wish I had time to come by ferry for the trip is much better that way. I can't say I like trains much. Too much stopping and starting." Ricky swung up into the sulky. "How is everything, Bob?"

"Not bad, Mr English, not too bad," was the reply.

Ricky looked around this small town and noted the changes each time he came. He was getting very fond of the place and knew quite a few of the residents. He doffed his hat at this one and that as they drove through. Soon they were out on the road to Rocklea and Ricky leaned back on the comfortable squabs and sighed a contented sigh. "I do enjoy this part of the trip. In fact I think I could easily live at Rocklea if it wasn't for my business. I look forward to the day when I will live here permanently, which I probably will do when I retire."

"You are certainly a country man at heart, aren't you?" Rob asked.

"Yes, I am. I miss it, and I didn't know how much I do until I bought Rocklea. Anyway, Rob, tell me about the place," Ricky said.

"The farm itself is going well. I feel sure we are keeping up the standard that Mr Raynes set." Rob chuckled. "You know Mr Raynes comes over sometimes to look the place over. Mrs Ormsby brings him. He doesn't stay but I always try to show him what we are doing. He never tells us when he is coming but just drops in. I hope you don't mind."

"Not at all, Rob. I told him to feel free to do it whenever he wishes to. I am glad he can come, for I know his heart is in the place. Is he happy with what you are doing?"

"He tells me so. What a nice old fellow he is," Rob said.

"He is that. Gosh, he got a fright when I told him that first time about the boys. He nearly had another stroke, I think. But he is happy about them now?"

"Yes, he has spoken to all of them, and particularly to young Micky. He seems to like the boy."

"What's on your mind Rob? you seem to be concerned about something."

"Well, yes, I am. I am a bit concerned about the boys. I think one or more of them are up to something and I don't know what."

"Why, what do you mean, Rob?" said Ricky.

"Well, as you know young Beetson is doing a great job with the boys. You certainly found a good'n in him. He knows how to handle them and is a good farmer. He's been very pleased with some of the boys. Micky stands out, because he came from a farm originally, but the other five are triers, and not bad lads. They are working as well as you could expect from town boys. It isn't that I am not pleased with their work, but something odd is happening. One of the ponies is being used illegally and we can't track down who is doing it. I think one of the boys is taking leave of absence at night and we do not know who."

"What, visiting some lass, do you think?" asked Ricky.

"It has to be that, Mr English, for there isn't a tavern near and I can't think what else it could be. And that's not all. I don't really know why but I have a feeling that Micky is something to do with it.

His work is dropping off and he doesn't have his heart in it as he used to."

"Have you spoken to him?"

"No, for I really don't have anything to go by, except that the pony is obviously being ridden, quite a way too. Both Beetson and I have tried to stay awake to catch the culprit but when we've been alert we've found nothing. And you know we need our sleep, we work hard enough and can't spend too many nights up on the prowl."

"No, of course not. Maybe I can help. I can take a turn to stay up at night."

"That would be good. But of course he doesn't do it every night. I think he just knows when we are on the alert."

"We'll give it a try anyway. I'd hate it if one of the lads is getting in to mischief, it's the thing that has worried me about taking half grown lads on. They are my responsibility and I don't want any of my boys to be a trouble to the neighbourhood."

"I have no reason to think there is trouble. I haven't heard of anything anyway."

"We'll just have to watch," said Ricky. "Now tell me about the rest of the place."

They chatted away very pleasantly and soon were at Rocklea. One of the boys saw him arrive and came to carry his bag into the house. "Thanks, Micky. How are you going out here?" Ricky asked. "Liking the place?"

"Yes, Mr English. It's a great place. I didn't think I would ever get to work on a place like this. Thank you."

"You grew up on a farm didn't you, Micky?"

"Yes, I did, until my people died, Mr English. Then I went to town to be with my uncle, and didn't have any chance then. Then he died too."

Ricky looked at the boy with red hair. He was about 15 and quite small for his age. "Well, make the most of it. Maybe you will get a good job and work for a place of your own one day. Make the most of the opportunity here, though, while you can," said Ricky.

"Thanks, Mr English," the boy said and left him to settle in.

Ricky had a busy day on Saturday but still felt fresh enough for his usual dinner with the Forrests. He never needed to be shown the way now for Ned Forrest had laughingly told him he had worn a track over to Claremont. He always enjoyed his time with Ned and Nell and, of course, Jenny.

As they settled down to talk after dinner, Ned said to Ricky, "Ricky, you told me you wanted to contact that black who helped your father."

"Yes, I did, Mr Forrest. Have you heard from him at last? It is a long time since he helped Father."

"Yes, it is, and I haven't heard a whisper of him since, until the other day. You know I told him to come to me if ever he needed me and he turned up here three days ago."

"Was he in trouble, Mrs Forrest?" asked Ricky.

"Yes, he was. Someone has been taking pot-shots at him and his people. He had a pellet in his arm and he was quite annoyed about it. Apparently some of the other blacks have been hit quite badly, and they are really ready to take reprisals. Durren apparently told them to hold their fire until he saw me. I went into Windsor and told the police there, they came out but they haven't been able to find the culprit."

Ricky somehow felt uneasy about this. "Tell me what Durren said, please."

"Well, it happens when the people go down to the river last thing at night. It is always after dark. I didn't think blacks were about much at night, but apparently they are. Someone sits up in a tall gum tree that overhangs the river opposite their camp, and as they come down he shoots at them. Not very accurately as it happens, which is a good thing. But something must be done for we don't want any reprisals here, I've my family to think of. Durren said that if we can find out who does it he can keep his people at bay."

"Didn't the police find any clues?"

"Only that a pony is tethered to a tree just near by. It is on my property, you know and I feel darned responsible."

Nell Forrest said, "I've never felt afraid of the blacks around here, Ricky, but I can understand them getting very annoyed about it. If, whoever it is, gets to be a better shot they might kill someone and then we would all be in strife."

"I'm seriously thinking of sending Nell, Jenny and the children away, Ricky, until it is sorted out. We are the nearest to their trouble and I won't risk my family."

Ricky said, "Indeed no! Do you think they should come up to Rocklea? They would be safer there."

Nell cut in, "No, not yet. I don't think anything will happen yet. I have great faith in that Durren of yours, Ricky."

"He's hardly mine, Mrs Forrest. I have yet to meet him."

Just then Jenny came into the room after settling the children down to bed. Nell said, "We are just telling Ricky about Durren, Jenny. Ned wants us to de-camp."

"I don't want you to be risked, Jenny. I think you should all come over to Rocklea," said Ricky anxiously.

"I'll not leave Ned, Ricky, so don't suggest it," said Nell.

"You'll do as I say, lass," said Ned, severely. "If I think you should go, you will."

"But Uncle Ned, you don't, do you?" asked Jenny. "I have great faith in Durren, Ricky. He is fine looking man."

"Just what Mrs Forrest says. I hope your faith is not misplaced. But seriously Mr Forrest, do you think there is a risk?"

"Well, I have a 24 hour watch all the time and I don't think anyone could slip through. All the men are alerted and are armed when on duty. So I really have faith that we will be all right. I do wish I could find the man who is doing it. I almost feel I could string him up. I think the men would do just that if I don't, for there are several families here and no-one wants to see them harmed."

Ricky found it hard to break away and leave his love in any danger, he realised that she was well protected, but he was uneasy. He thought deeply when riding home and as soon as he got to Rocklea sought our Rob and Beetson. He told them the story and he wasn't surprised when he found that they all came to the same conclusion. They worked out a plan, setting their ideas in motion, then they pretended to go to bed. Rob crept down to the paddock where the ponies were kept and hid behind a bush. Beetson lay in his bed snoring realistically, and Ricky waited in the stables with the three saddled horses. Ricky didn't think there was a chance of catching the culprit that night for it would be too good to be true. But it was not long before Rob slipped into the stables and said, "It's on, Mr English. I saw who I think is Micky slip onto the pony and head off down the paddock. I'll go and get Beetson."

"All right, Rob. As soon as you get back I will go for Ned Forrest for he must be in this too."

"Right-o." Rob slipped out again like a shadow. It was only a matter of minutes before he came back with Beetson and the three mounted and rode off a silently as they could, the two men following the rider and Ricky heading for Claremont.

Ricky didn't have to keep quiet for the lanes were away from the paddocks that the others were following and so he clattered into the yard at Claremont, pulling up with a start when one of Forrest's men on duty rushed out to meet him. He called to tell who it was and then asked the man to rouse Mr Forrest. But just then Ned put his head out of the top window. "Who's that?" he called.

"It's Ricky, Mr Forrest. Can you dress and come down? Rob and Beetson are following someone we think is the shooter."

"I'm on my way. Mason, get Jenson, and saddle horses," he called. Mason ran off. "And bring the gun, Mason," he called.

It was only a matter of minutes before Ned appeared, dressed, and very soon after Mason and Jenson came with horses. During that time Ricky explained what had happened. Ned in turn told the men.

"Lead off Mason. You have best night eyes. Follow him Ricky and Jenson and I will tag along. You know the tree Mason so move on a quietly as you can," instructed Ned.

They moved off into the night. Mason opening gates whenever needed, and soon they were cantering across the large river paddock. They left their horses at the far side and jumped over the post and rail fence. Just then they heard a scuffling and found Rob and Beetson's horses tethered under a gum tree. They walked silently towards a huge gum tree that Ricky could see against the moonlit sky. There was a clump of bushes near this and using this to hide behind they found that Rob and Beetson had had the same idea.

"He doesn't know we followed him Mr English, and now he is up in the tree, way up," whispered Rob.

"Is it Micky, Rob?" he asked.

Beetson whispered, "Yes, sir, it is. He's left the pony below the tree, and used him to hitch himself up to reach the first branch."

"I kin see the young varmint, Mr Forrest, kin I 'ave a pot shot at 'im?" asked Mason.

"You keep your fire, man. I'll deal with this. Give me the gun," Ned said.

"But, sir, I'd like to get me 'ands on 'im, and fill 'im with a few pellets first."

"Leave it to me, you can all come. If its a youngster I don't think we'll have much trouble," said Forrest.

"I don't think so either, Mr Forrest," said Beetson. "He's a good kid really, I don't know what's got into him. I'd like you to give him a chance, sir."

"We'll see what he has to say for himself. Now follow me." Ned walked openly to the foot of the eucalypt and stood looking up into the branches. "Hey, you up there. Micky. Come down out of that," he called.

There was silence.

Forrest called again, "Come on down we know you are there. Mr English, Mr Martin and Mr Beetson followed you here so we know where you are. Come down."

Again there was silence from the boy, but they could hear that he had moved a little.

"Give me the gun, Mr Forrest. I'll get the varmint down," said Mason. But Forrest kept a good hold of the weapon.

Ricky stood away from the tree and called, "Come on down Micky. You haven't a hope. All we have to do is wait and sooner of later you have to come. Come and talk it over and tell us what it's all about."

"Talk," said Mason indignantly. "Talk, Mr English. I'd like to bash 'im, getting us all upset, like."

"Quiet, Mason. If you can't control yourself you can go home," Ned said quietly.

Beetson called, "Micky, you've got to come down, lad. We'll give you a fair hearing."

"For goodness sake have sense boy," called Mr Forrest. "If you don't I'll put a shot of birdshot up the tree."

There was movement now and they could hear the lad coming down. As he reached the last branch he looked down and said, "Will you listen, Mr English. Will you give me a fair hearing?"

"Yes, of course, Micky," said Ricky, "we want to know what all this is about."

He jumped from the branch and Mason ran forward to grab him before anyone could stop him. There was a scuffle and the boy tripped over a root. The gun went off and there was a deafening silence to follow. Then they all rushed forward to see what the damage was, but all was well for the gun had gone off harmlessly.

"For goodness sake, Mason, hold your horses. You could have caused an accident," Forrest said.

"Sorry, sir. But I wanted to get him before he got away," Mason said indignantly.

"He's not likely to go far with all of us here." Turning he saw a small boy clutching a shot gun that looked almost as big as he was. "Good heavens your only a child," he said.

"No I'm not," came the cheeky reply, "I'm fifteen."

"Well you don't look it, and if you are you should have more sense. What's all this about?" he asked. Then hesitating he added, "No don't tell me here. Lets all go to my house and talk it over there."

"Good idea, Mr Forrest," said Rob, and led the way to the horses. Micky unhitched the pony and hopped on it's back.

"'ere you, don' run orf. Grab 'im sir," said Mason.

"It's all right Mr Forrest, I won't run away. You said you'd give me a fair hearing," he said petulantly.

"And so we will, lad," Ned assured him. "We left our horses the other side of the fence, so come along. Rob, you get yours and follow through the gate and take Micky with you. We'll see you at the house."

Ned dismissed Mason and Jenson when he reached the house and waited for the others to come. There was a light on in the house and Ned was not surprised to find Nell waiting up with tea and scones. They all went into the kitchen and Ned motioned them to sit round the big pine table.

He looked down at the boy and shook his head, "You've caused us a deal of trouble young fellow. What an infernal pest you are."

Micky was a slight boy with a shock of red hair. He had a pleasant pixie-like expression and a great number of freckles all over his face. He certainly did not look like a murderer, but apparently that's what he had intended to be.

Nell put cups of tea down in front of everyone and had buttered a huge plate of scones. She obviously thought that men work better on a full stomach. She sat on a vacant chair and listened intently.

Micky sat with head bowed and said, "I'm sorry I have caused trouble."

"That's all very well, Micky, but what on earth were you thinking of?" asked Ricky. "Did you feel you wanted to rid the place of blacks? Come on, out with it."

"I hate them, Mr English. I hate them because they killed my parents," said Micky.

"I know where I've seen you before," said Nell. "You're Micky Macksfield, aren't you?"

"Yes," answered Micky.

"Macksfield?" queried Ned. "Are you young Macksfield?"

Micky looked up as Ricky said, "Does the name mean anything to you, Mr Forrest?"

"Yes, it does," said Ned.

"It does to me, as well," said Rob. "I knew Macksfield well. I'm sorry Micky but I just didn't think. I always felt you were a bit familiar, but didn't think of you being Macksfield's son. Your not a bit like him but now I come to think about it you are the image of your mother. You see, my farm was next door to yours. Did you not remember me, Micky?"

"Well, I think I do, Mr Martin, but I was only very small when I left there," came the reply.

"What has that got to do with tonight then, young Micky?" asked Ricky.

Micky hung his head and refused to comment. But Rob was more forthcoming and asked, "Reprisals, Micky? Is that it?" he asked.

"They killed my parents, Mr Martin and I hate them," he shot out. "I hate them and I would do it again."

"Come on, that's no way to talk. Yes, your father was killed by some blacks but is that reason for taking it out on the ones that didn't?" asked Forrest.

"It must have been those, Mr Forrest. We are close enough here for it to have been them. Any way they're all the same."

"That they aren't, Micky, there are good and bad in any race. In any case I happen to know that these people near here had nothing to do with your father's death. That's right, isn't it Rob?" Ned turned to the man.

"Yes, it is sir," said Rob looking decidedly uncomfortable.

"They killed Ma too," burst out Micky.

Rob asked, "What makes you think that, lad?"

"'Cos Pa said, when I saw him last."

"Then what your father said, Mickey is wrong," Ned said quietly.

'I am sorry, Mr Forrest, but how would you know?" he contradicted.

"I know, son and so does Mr Martin, because we know exactly what happened to your mother, and I suppose I am a bit surprised that your uncle didn't tell you. But I suppose he thought that sleeping dogs ought to lie."

"Why? What do you mean, Mr Forrest?"

"I mean that your mother did not die from spears from blacks but from the way your father treated her."

"That's not true, Mr Forrest. It isn't true." The boy burst out.

"Yes, it is, Micky," said Rob Martin. "I was there and my wife sat with her while she lay dying. Your father ill-treated her, you know lad," he said softly. "That is why you were taken by your uncle as soon as your mother died. Your uncle didn't think you were safe with your father. He was a very devil when the drink was in him and was pretty hard to handle."

Micky burst into tears. A very hurt and mixed boy who was

really little more than a child. Ricky, Beetson and Nell sat quietly looking with compassion at the boy; Nell knowing the whole story, and Ricky and Beetson astounded at what they were hearing.

"Your father's brother knew what he was like, son, and he wanted to give you a chance to have a good life. He was a good man, George Macksfield," Rob told him. "And to finish the story," added Rob, who turned to Ned and said, "I'd better tell him the lot, sir, for he won't feel free of the problem until he does."

"Quite right Rob, carry on," he said but first addressed Micky again. "Micky you know Mr Martin well enough to know that he wouldn't say what was not true. In any case I was involved, too, so I can verify what he says, and Mrs Forrest, too. Do you wish to hear more, or will we leave it for now?" he asked.

Nell leaned over and took Micky's hand hoping he would not reject it. He didn't. "All right, Mr Forrest. I'll listen, but I should have been told before."

"I imagine your uncle would have told you as soon as he saw fit but died so suddenly that he may not have had the chance." Ned told him. "Would that be right? Go on Rob."

"Your father was drinking pretty heavily, Micky, and often didn't know what he was doing. He took to harassing the natives quite a bit and having pot-shots at them at times. One night it must have been too much for them and it was me who found him down at the river bank. His cows were bellowing and I could hear them from my place. I had often had to milk when he was unable and I just thought that it was the same as before, but he was dead and had been for some hours. I'm sorry Micky. I really am."

The boy sat quietly sobbing. Nell got up and made more tea. It is strange that in stressful moments how often one turns to tea, especially in the country kitchens of Australia where the tea seemed to relieve a strain even in the hottest weather. She made a cup of cocoa for Micky and placed it in front of him. "Drink that, laddie," she said, "We aren't going to talk any more tonight. You know the story now and I think you can ask anything more of Mr Martin another time. But I would suggest that you all go off home to your beds now."

"Yes, I think Micky has had enough for tonight. Drink up your tea, lad. Ricky, would you come with me for a minute before you leave."

"Ricky and Ned turned to go from the room when Micky said, "Mr English, I am sorry I have been a trouble. But I didn't know. What will I do now?" he asked passionately.

"We'll talk about it tomorrow, Micky. Drink up and we'll go home," said Ricky.

Ned led Ricky out and turning to him he said, "We are in a fix now, Ricky. I have reported this, as you know, so I will have to tell them something. Also I think we'll have to do something about the blacks."

"Yes, that's been worrying me," said Ricky. "What do you suggest."

"Well, first I thought we ought to drag young Micky over to make reparation, but I think that might make matters worse, for Macksfield's name was mud about here, and I don't think Micky would be believed. You know, like father like son, that sort of thing. Then I thought, if I take you over tomorrow and tell them a little we can work on the story, assuring them that it won't happen again. Then you can meet Durren and we can work on your part of the story for all its worth. What do you say?"

"Will it work, do you think, Mr Forrest?"

"Yes, I think it will. We have to protect all the women and children hereabouts and so a desperate deed needs a desperate solution. Will you come, boy?"

"Yes, of course. Like a shot."

"I know you were going home tomorrow. Can you put it off for a day?"

"Yes, I can and I will. I think what you suggest would work well," said Ricky. "It is as well that I have my part of the story to act out."

"Well, that's one way of putting it. Now I suppose you'd better take that brat home. I can't help feeling sorry for the kid, though. He had a very nice mother and an absolutely terrible father. It was gins he was after, you know. He used to use them and then toss them in the river. He did it once too often. Poor kid!"

"It's a pretty terrible story all round," said Ricky. "What about the police, though?"

"I daresay the best thing we can do is for me to drive you on your way on Monday into Windsor and sort it out then. They're pretty reasonable. If the boy had been pot-shotting whites there would be a lot more fuss, but some of these police think that getting a black or two doesn't matter. No wonder there are reprisals. One day they'll learn."

"Then, I'll collect my party and head for bed. I'll come after lunch if I may."

"You may as well come for lunch. Then we'll take Jenson and just the three of us, and see what we can do."

Ned and Nell saw them off and gratefully headed for bed.

The riding party was silent all the way. Micky attempting to say something but was cut short by Beetson who said, "No more tonight, Micky. Save it for another time."

They all fell into bed. But for Ricky, at least, to an uneasy sleep.

Jenson was quite amenable to accompanying Ned and Ricky to the blacks camp across the river. Ricky felt very apprehensive about it all and wished he was miles away. Never did he think he would meet up with Durren under these circumstances. He sat in the launch hoping for the best.

"Now, Jenson, I've asked you to come for you know the blacks better than any of us. I've brought the gun, but want it under cover unless there is any bother. Speak to them if you can and assure them that we are friendly. I daresay they will be very wary of us."

""Oi reckon they will be, surr," said Jenson. "Yer must admit they 'ave reason ter be."

"Yes, I agree. Let's hope for the best." said Ned. Turning to Ricky he said. "Jenson was here when they brought your father in, Ricky, and so knows the story. You've seen something of Durren, too haven't you, Jenson?"

"Yus surr. 'Es a good'n, Durren is, 'is name means messenger, and 'oi reckon thet's wot 'e is, a sort of messenger. 'E seems to know a lot of different tribes. 'Oi reckon it'll be orltight, surr. We'll watch fer weapons. If we sees them then'll it'll be all right."

"Whatever do you mean, Jenson? Do you want to see their weapons?"

"Yus surr. Weapons yer see is safer than them's what yer don't. When they are tetchy they drag 'em along the ground in the grass between their toes and 'ide 'em. They kin bring 'em up real quick an' get yer."

By this time they were getting closer to the far bank, Jenson rowing with even strides. Then he turned the boat so that he pushed the oars instead of pulling. This way he could see where they were going. "Wanna keep'em in sight, boss," he said.

"Good thinking, Jenson. You'd best get out further mid stream, though, or they will think we are creeping up on them. Speak in a normal voice, we don't want them to think we are doing that." So Ricky asked about the lovely trees that were growing along the banks and then about the fish one could catch. They could now see the clearing and a thin wisp of smoke from a fire.

"I'd call now, Boss. Call for Durren," said Jenson.

"Hello, there. Are you there, Durren?" called Forrest.

They saw a slight movement. Not much, but some. But there was not the normal camp life to be seen.

"Are you there Durren?" called Forrest again. "It's Mr Forrest, Durren. I have a visitor for you. Can we come ashore?"

This time they heard voices. There was quite a conversation going on and then Durren appeared with some men. He stood back and Ricky noticed that he and two companions stood in grass. No weapons were evident. Ricky felt rather chilled but tried to take it calmly.

"Hello, Durren. I have Mr English with me. You remember you looked after his father some time ago."

There was no movement from the black men, then Jenson called out in what Ricky thought was a jabber. This time there was interest and slowly the men came out of the grass and stood in a cleared patch. Durren spoke over his shoulder and soon several other people appeared. Men mostly, although Ricky could see a few women right at the back.

"It's all right, surr, we can land, now," said Jenson.

"You stay with the boat, Jenson," said Ned. "Keep the gun handy but don't use it unless I say."

"Too roight, 'oi won't surr. Oi'll keep it kivered."

Ned stepped out of the boat and Ricky followed. They offered their hands and greeted the men and smiled as widely as it was possible.

"This is Mr English, Durren. He has come to thank you for looking after his father. We haven't been able to find you, have you been walkabout?"

"Yus, boss. Me walkabout. Got wife." He called out and a gin came a step or two closer and giggled. "Wife," said Durren.

Ricky was amazed to see how young she looked. Durren was a big man and now seemed friendly enough. He came and shook hands with both the white men and spoke again to the other people. They turned and walked the few steps back to the camp, leading Ricky and Ned. Ned explained that Ricky lived in the big town, Sydney, much bigger than Windsor and was owner of Mr Raynes property now. The blacks seemed to understand, or at least did when Durren explained. Then they all sat down, Durren motioning to Ned and Ricky to sit on a log. Then he tried to explain to Ricky about finding his father and pointed to a cave nearby where Richard English's box with the papers was found. There was difficult chatter, but friendly enough, and after some time when everything seemed all right, Forrest said, "We found the man who was shooting, Durren, and took him away. You will not be troubled any more."

"What for he do?" asked Durren. He turned and explained this to the others. There was some hostile conversation, and a few started yelling about it. Then suddenly it quietened down and Durren repeated his question, "What for he do, boss?"

"He was a silly fellow, Durren. He was a town person who didn't know better. We fixed him and he won't do it again. I tell police and all is well. We want you to know we are sorry white man trouble black man. We all want to be friends." At that Forrest shook hands with Durren again and all the men came and shook hands again. There were smiles all round and all seemed to be settled.

"We'll go now, Durren. I did want to bring Mr English to you and also to tell you that the shooting man has finished."

"All right, now," said Durren.

"Thank you very much for looking after my father Durren. Could you show me the cave where my fathers things were?" asked Ricky.

"Come," said Durren. He led the way to the cave and Ricky agreed that it was a good place for keeping things. Then they turned and said "Good bye" to everyone and went back to the boat.

Ned told Jenson to tell them how much they appreciated Durren when he looked after Richard English. He did this and there were smiles and waves all round. Jenson picked up the oars and soon they were gliding downstream quite fast. When they got out of sight and well out of earshot they all sighed a great sigh and said," Thank goodness that's over."

"Oi thought it were a narrow squeak first orf, surr. They natives did 'ave spears in thet grass. Oi thought oi would 'avin spear for me dinner oi did. I were ready wi' gun, surr, but oi reckon it wouldn't 'ave been too good one gun agin orl them spears."

"Well, I think it was a good day's work Jenson. But I think Mr English saved the day for we had a good excuse and that paid dividends. Let's get home, I know the women are anxious."

"Not as anxious as I was, Mr Forrest. I must admit I never want to go through that again," said Ricky, wiping his brow.

Ricky thought the adventure was worth it though when they got back to Claremont for Jenny positively ran into his arms on their arrival. "Wow, darling that's a lovely reception," he said.

"Is everything all right, Ned?" asked Nell.

"Yes, all well, but as Ricky said, I wouldn't like too many adventures like that one." Turning to Jenson he said, "Thank you for your help, Jenson. I knew you were just the right person to take along."

Ricky also thanked the man and shook his hand. Then they turned and went inside to tea and the usual lovely scones. They explained all to their women folk and Ricky and Jenny were able to go up to the gazebo and chat until dinner. "I hope we don't have any more adventurous weekends like this, darling, I almost will be glad to get back to the safe and uninteresting town, this time. I hate the thought of leaving you here to face what might have been a sticky and nasty situation. Drat that Micky."

Ned picked Ricky up in the morning and both went to the police in Windsor. Ned had thought the best thing to do was to put their cards on the table and hope that nothing more would be done. The sergeant had known Macksfield and so was sympathetic to the boy. He was quite willing to do all he could about sorting it out so that Micky would be saved from trouble. Ricky and Ned were grateful that it seemed as though it would all come good in the end.

After all the excitement Ricky decided that a calm ferry ride up the harbour from Parramatta would be more pleasurable than riding in the dirty and dusty train and so by the time he arrived home it was all in the past. He only had his other worries to concern him again and that was bad enough, for he was very concerned about Tad and was more than concerned about Will. Mr Landon was quite sage about it all, though, and was a great aid to Ricky. He was determined that the young ones were all right and that they were old enough to sort themselves out. He still expected them to appear one day.

Mr Landon proved correct for out of the blue, there they were. For one September day Ricky came home to find several large trunks in the hall. He took one look at them and called, "Tad."

Tad appeared at the head of the stairs and said, "Hello, Ricky, we've come home."

"So I see and I am very glad to see you. Is everything all right? Come and tell me all about your trip. I thought you would turn into an Englishman, Tad."

"Not me, old boy, I am for Sydney. I feel at home here."

"How is Amabel? And I must tell you again I am very pleased with your news."

"So are we, Rick. That's one reason we came home. But I'll tell you all about it. Amabel is fine, but I sent her round to her mother, for she was most anxious to see her, naturally. I've asked them to come for dinner, I hope you don't mind.'

"Of course I don't, you melon. That's what I would expect."

" Let's go down and have a drink before they arrive. Rick you've done up the top floor for us, thank you. I knew you were going to but I really am pleased with it. Amabel is very excited about it. It's our first home. Rick, I think I will wait until Amabel's people come to tell you why we came home, if you don't mind."

"No, I don't mind. I expected that. It saves telling twice. But tell me, what of Will? Can you tell me about him and how he is?"

"Why, no. I thought you would have more news than me. To tell you the truth we rather stopped writing. So much was happening with all the relatives that I didn't write as often as I should have. How long is it since you heard?"

"Not since he went on that painting trip with his friends. I haven't had a letter since."

"Gosh, that's worrying. That makes me feel rotten, Rick. I was so full of my own problems that I guess I didn't think. I just expected him to be all right. But Mr Cummins would see to him, wouldn't he?"

"Apparently not. He didn't go down well with Mrs Cummins and he tried to keep his distance. I wish I could find out. I've written to the Cummins but it will take ages for us to hear. I must tell you that Mr Landon is very worried, too, for he has had some rather rotten letters from Mrs Cummins. She doesn't seem to be a gentle type, Tad. I would like to have a few choice words with that woman. Can you imagine anyone trying to take it out on a lonely lad just because he doesn't know who his father is?" Ricky could see the distress on Tad's face and said, "Don't worry. He's sure to be all right. Come on I think that's the Landon's."

CHAPTER 19: *Together Again*

It was a very happy dinner party. Ricky thought Amabel was glowing; so lovely in her advanced pregnancy. He couldn't help wondering what Jenny would be like in that state. As lovely and as happy as obviously Amabel was, he hoped. After dinner, they settled in the sitting room to hear the story. What they heard distressed the Landons and Ricky.

"First I want to say that my grandfather Falconer-Mead is a grand old man but I think he is very mistaken in liking the rest of the family. Josh, of course, was all right. I daresay he cannot be held responsible for his parents. His mother, Aunt Mary and his aunt, my Aunt Jemima are a pair of tartars. Aunt Jemima is the widow of my Uncle Henry who was the second son and is mother of one of the nastiest types I could ever wish to meet. His name is Horace. It should be "horrors". My Stanthorpe relatives are really grand people and we both like them very much." Tad took a deep breath and looked around him. "We are glad we went to England and always will be, but neither of us could stand the life there or stand having to try to fit into their way of life at Mead Park," said Tad.

"But surely your grandfather would have had a great deal to say about how they behaved to you, son," said Mr Landon.

"I can assure you, sir, that they all behaved very well when he was about, but unfortunately he rather kept to his rooms for I don't think he really liked them any more than we did. You see my Aunt Mary was quite convinced that I was an impostor and did not think she need accept me. Thankfully they were always very kind to Amabel. As a matter of fact, I think they were rather sorry for her, knowing something of your families and thinking she had thrown herself away."

"But Papa, they were absolutely horrid to Tad. They would look down their noses and call him, 'Theodore', in such a way that he would squirm and I would squirm with him."

"They accepted you as Theodore, son?" asked John.

"Yes, but to them it was an insult, you see. For I have an Uncle Theodore, or at least a great uncle. They don't like him. We thought he was rather grand, didn't we darling?" asked Tad.

"Yes. You see Papa he lives in the dower house and married his housekeeper. He really is very naughty for he is proud of it and keeps telling them. He loves to see them get haughtier, if that's possible," said Amabel.

"Dear, I think you should be more charitable," put in Mrs Landon.

"Oh, Mama, you wouldn't have been if you had seen it. They really did make things difficult," Amabel insisted.

"Is this why you came home, Tad?" asked Ricky.

"No, Rick, it wasn't. Actually Grandfather was the one who made us decide. He said that I would have to stay, change my name to Falconer-Mead and then I could sit in idleness and take an allowance. He expected me to just do that. He became rather abusive when I refused. He apparently thought I would jump at the chance."

"He was probably disappointed that you didn't, Tad," Mr Landon said.

"We both got a bit hot under the collar, sir, because he kept saying that this country had killed my father and so I shouldn't take the risk of it doing the same. I couldn't stand it, sir, I really couldn't. I couldn't ask Amabel to share a house with a lot of people who hated us."

"Surely that's a bit strong, Tad," said Rick.

"No it wasn't, really, sir, it wasn't. Horace didn't come very often, but when he did he was a rotter." At this Tad got rather red in the face.

"It was because of me, Papa. He just wouldn't leave me alone," said Amabel. "Tad had to knock him down one day, and his mother said it was my fault."

"I see," her father remarked. "At least, I daresay I can see. I am glad that Tad did knock him down then."

"He is poison, sir. He has wet lips and tried to put them on Amabel. I had to hit him and he went crying to his mother."

"How old is this toad, Tad?"

"He's about 27, I think. He's been about town forever and thinks he knows the lot. My Stanthorpe relatives don't like them at all. They say that my Uncle Cuthbert wasn't a bad sort when he was younger, but under Aunt Mary's care he has just withered and I wasn't going to stand for that happening to us. I consulted my Grandfather Stanthorpe and he agreed that it would be best if we came away. He has sent you a letter, sir, to explain. So once we decided to go and we just went as quickly as we decently could using Amabel's condition as an excuse saying that she was pining for you, ma'am."

"I was, too, Mama. I didn't want my baby to grow up there. You felt stifled all the time, not like being here at home."

"Well, we are very glad you came home. I imagine they have felt badly used but I daresay in the long run you've come out of it well, and no harm done."

"Well, I mean to write to my grandfather, Mr Landon, and apologize for not being able to do as he wished, for I do like him and I suppose he can't help his relatives. But really after one sees what life is like here, I couldn't be happy there. I really think that my father was a favourite, at least that is what we gathered from my Grandfather Stanthorpe, and I daresay my Grandfather Falconer-Mead hoped I would turn out like him."

"I would think there is a lot in that, son, and I am sure as he must have seen a great resemblance he would especially wish you to stay."

"I take it that both Josh and I look like our Grandmother. It is funny that we are both so alike, for there is not another who looks like us in the least."

"Family resemblances are strange, aren't they?" asked Ricky.

"Grandfather was so annoyed with us that he told me I could expect nothing at all from his will. I am sorry about that, Mr Landon. Not for me, for I honestly didn't think of it. But I would like Amabel to have what she has been used to. Now we will have to wait a while until I can do it. That shows you, though, how upset he was."

Amabel's mother said, "I am sure from what Amabel tells me that you spoil her enough as it is, young Tad. I am convinced it would do her good if she were really in want for a spell." She tried to look severe.

This brought a laugh for Tad was getting rather hot under the collar thinking she meant that as Amabel was in want it would do her good to stay that way for a while. He opened his mouth once or twice and then caught the twinkle in his mother-in-law's eyes. "You may well laugh about my lack of funds ma'am, but I would do anything to make your daughter comfortable."

"I am sure you would, Tad. But it wouldn't hurt the minx to have less of this world's goods," said her father. He then asked, "Did you spend much time in London, lad?"

"Not enough, sir. There is so much to see. But we had a good guide in Josh. He showed us such a lot. He even told us that in showing us the town he saw more of it than he had ever done himself. But, I only wish we could have seen more of the country, though, for what we saw we liked. It was good that we visited your people for we saw more then. And incidentally, sir, we did like meeting them. They made us very welcome."

"I do admit, I miss the hurly burley of family life a little." Amabel said to her father, who just smiled at her.

Her mother chipped in with, "Yes, I do miss the family for we always had such fun. I don't think I could have stood life at Mead Park either, my dears. I am so glad you came when you did. Think of all the plans Amabel and I are going to make. I have my first grandchild to look forward to. I was sad to think I may have missed out on that."

"Oh, mama, I was able to buy some lovely material for the baby and I am dying to talk plans over with you."

"Well we'll have to keep it until later, Amabel, I am sure we will not foist that conversation onto our menfolk."

Ricky said, "I am very glad you came home, Tad. I had visions of you staying, but at the same time really could not imagine you sitting doing nothing. I think I've been lonelier these months that I ever was as a boy."

"Glad to hear it, old son. We are certainly glad to be here. I just wish we knew about Will, though. I feel badly about him," said Tad.

"I am sure he will be all right," said John. "Rob might be under Agatha's thumb but he wouldn't neglect his duty to Will. I feel sure he will be safe and we'll soon hear from him."

They heard nothing! Several weeks went by with all three of the men writing to get news, but of course letters took so long to be answered that it would be months before they received any answers.

In the meantime a nursery was planned and the women folk had heads together over sweet little white dresses, drapes for the cradle and other things that women love to plan for new babies. The girls in the hostel were keen to be part of the planning and Jenny would not be left out when she came to town soon after Amabel's return.

Ricky came home, one day, to find, once more, a travelling trunk in his front hall. "It must be Will," he thought and called to Mrs Keen as obviously Tad and Amabel were out.

Mrs Keen came from the kitchen in great excitement followed closely by Will, himself. "It's Mr Will, Mr Rick. It's Mr Will," she cried.

"So I see, Mrs Keen," clutching Will's hand so tight he made the young man wince. He could see that Will's eyes were filled with tears and was very emotional. "You've given us some bad moments, young Will. Why didn't you write, you scallywag?" he asked slapping him on the back.

"I am so sorry, Rick, but I just couldn't. I have so much to tell you. I hope you will forgive me," Will said.

"I'll forgive you anything. I am just so glad you are safe. We have all been so worried about you, but all is well now. You look fine." He held him away. "But you are mighty thin, lad, what have you been doing with yourself?"

"I'll tell you all about it over some tea, if I may." He turned to the housekeeper. "Can we have tea, please, Mrs Keen?"

"You certainly can, Mr Will. Mr Ricky, he has just walked in and I was still getting over the shock. Maria will bring it in straight away."

"Come on Will," said Ricky leading the way to the sitting room.

Just then the front door opened and Amabel and Tad came in. "Will!" Tad called and gave him a great big bear hug. "You old horror, where have you been? You had us so worried."

Will greeted Amabel when he disentangled himself from Tad, and led the way into the sitting room. They chatted away about incidentals over the tea and when Amabel saw that they were not talking much about Will she stood up and said, "Would you please excuse me, I feel rather tired and wish to lie down." Turning to Will, she said, "I'm so glad to see you here, Will. Do you mind if I go? I will see you at dinner." With that she left the room.

"Tad, that was very thoughtful of Amabel. I must admit what I have to say is really for yours and Rick's ears at first. You may not wish to tell her what I have to say."

"Yes, she is grand, is my girl," said the ever loving Tad, "But what dark secret do you have to tell, young Will?"

Will was very hesitant about starting his story. Now that he was home he seemed to be reluctant about it. Now that he was here facing his two brothers, it was hard. He knew what he had to say would be a shock and above all he wanted their love and he couldn't help wondering if what he had to say would destroy that love.

"Come on, Will," said Tad. "What happened? We are waiting," urged Tad.

Ricky could see that Will was very upset and tried to calm Tad down from urging the boy to speak, but Tad was hard to stop once he got going on something. But he said, "Will, if you would rather wait and tell us later that's all right. Just take your time. We have all the time in the world."

"No, Ricky, I know that, but no, I must tell you. But I'm afraid you won't understand."

"We will, for sure, Will," said Tad persistently, with a grin.

So the story came slowly out.

During his first months in Paris Will was excited about and rather overcome with being there. When away from his art classes the street scenes so captivated him that he did little portraiture. He wandered the streets and painted picture after picture of back alleys and lanes, the people, children, old men and women and animals in the streets. He met a great number of painters and odd people living on the edge of the art world. At first rejecting their way of life. Then was inveigled into taking part in their party life, their seamy way of life. He started drinking to "be in it" with the others and owing to his frail constitution went down hill fast. He became ill and stopped seeing Mrs Landon's brother, Mr Cummins, who came looking for him. By this time Will's money was getting short and so he changed "digs" to a squalid place which suited his meagre purse. Mr Cummins found him and tried to knock some sense into him, but this had little effect, he thought. However, something of his state did filter through into Will's mind and he began to worry about it. He went down hill further. One night he had a dream ... this is what he told Ricky and Tad ...

"I must have been asleep or unconscious or something ... I don't know, but I really think I was dead. Whatever it was, I had a dream or a real experience, it really worried me. I found that I was in a place. I think it must have been just outside heaven. I was in a queue of people who were lined up to go in through a gate. It is peculiar that even though you had to queue to get through the gate or door, there didn't seem to be a fence to stop you from going round it. We were all standing on stuff that looked like cloud. There were two men at the gate letting a few people in and not letting others. It was Jesus and I think, and St Peter. As each person got to the gate they were asked about themselves, Jesus and Peter let only very, very few people through to heaven, I think it was."

"What a lot of rot, Will," said Tad, " I didn't think I would ever hear you being so fanciful."

"Quiet! Tad," demanded Ricky, "if you can't be quiet, leave the room." Ricky could see that Will was deeply moved. He was so pale and thin and quiet, he obviously expected to be ridiculed. Ricky could see that the young man was so deeply effected that he thought he didn't even care that he had been interrupted. "Go on, Will."

Will looked up and gave Ricky a weak smile. "I suppose I expected you to be disgusted, but I am only telling you what happened."

"Yes, I know," said Ricky, "go on."

"Well. I was very annoyed that so many people were lining up to get into heaven and not getting there. You see when they were rejected, they were made to go back to the world again and start all over again. And I was so annoyed to think that I would have to go back and be a cripple again and be lost without my own people and be so unhappy about it. You see I hadn't ever really thought about heaven before. I know you took us to church each week, Ricky, but I just thought it was a good place to learn to draw people. I suppose I heard what the chaplain said, but not consciously. I suppose I knew that there was a heaven and I just took it that was where I would end up, and I would have a nice new body. I suppose I had it in the back of my mind, although, I don't think I ever really took it out and looked at it properly. I think I believed it because you did. You had always led me right and I was content with that. I missed you a lot in Paris, Ricky, I truly did, and I know I've let you down. You've always been so straight with us." He looked rather stricken.

"You haven't let me down, Will. But go on, finish your story."

"Well, I got so flaming mad when I saw all these people being sent back to earth, and I don't know how I knew that, that I ran out of the queue and went up towards Jesus and Peter yelling that it wasn't fair, it would be terrible to have to start again and be a street kid again, I mightn't find you next time, and that would be awful. I might have to live a far worse life than the one I have and that would be terrible." Will shook with sobs. "When I ran up to get to Jesus, I didn't get there because everyone in the line started to sort of explode and being not there any more. I knew then they had been sent back to earth and I was, too."

Tad and Ricky were quiet now as Will finished speaking. He looked emotionally drained. They knew more was to come, Ricky just looked compassionate, and it was Tad who said, "What happened then, old man?"

Will looked up at him and said, "It was terrible, Tad. It was a nightmare. I began to hate the idea of going to sleep for it would all come back again. But then I realised that I was thinking of it all day, anyway, and that I was just letting it all drag me down further. I think I must have reached bottom. I tried to drink it away and it got worse. Then one day I think I must have reached as far down as I could go." He looked straight at Ricky. "I thought how I had let you and Tad and Mr Landon down and that I had to stop thinking of me and what I wanted and start thinking about you and all you've done for me. It didn't occur to me that it was the dream, or whatever it was that taught me to have a new beginning or anything. I didn't think of it in that light because it had just seemed like a nightmare. I knew then that I had to do something about it, so I started to eat better and I didn't drink any more. I cleaned myself up and when I felt a bit better and I went to see Mr Cummins. I asked him to give me my next allowance and I told him I was going home. He was very pleased at my decision and helped me all he could. So I got back to England and sailed on the next ship I could get on, and here I am. I haven't been able to paint at all since I had the dream, but I know that the first thing I have to do is paint it. I think it will stop haunting me when I paint it, and if I can have my old studio again I would like to move in. Can I please, Ricky?"

"Of course, it's yours. You'll find it very little changed, Will. We always hoped you would come home again sometime," assured Ricky.

"But, Will. What do you make of it? Do you really believe you were there in that place? It was just an awful dream, wasn't it, Will?" asked Tad anxiously.

Will looked straight at his brother. "No Tad, it wasn't a dream. I know I was there and our Lord gave me another chance to come back here and have another go at being a better person. He didn't want me start at the beginning again, to be born into the world again, He wanted to be born again right inside me. I never knew what that story about Nicodemus meant in the Bible, I didn't realise it myself until I was halfway home, when one night I was standing looking at the sea, leaning over the rail and I had nothing between God and me and I saw it in its proper perspective for the first time. I thank God that I can paint it and show it to you."

"You mean you have got religious or something? That's pretty rotten. I didn't think you'd ever become so silly," said Tad disgustedly.

"I hope you aren't going to preach at us. It is rotten isn't it, Ricky?"

"No, Tad. It isn't rotten, and I am not going to preach at you. I know now on that night I died and was given my second chance. I will probably never mention it again, except to Mr Landon and I owe him that. You'll find that I am just the same Will, but now I think I have got my self in order for the first time."

"But you said you would have to start again, didn't did you? You are just the same, you're not a little boy again," protested Tad.

"But I have started again, Tad. You'll see, I have made a fresh start and I don't think I'll ever be quite the same again. You'll just have to accept what I say, but I hope you will see that I am a better person to live with now." Will looked rather wistful.

Ricky didn't say anything, then giving him a nudge he said, "Take your things up, Will and settle in."

"I think I will, Rick. I'm sorry if I have hurt you and given you worry, but it will never happen again. I feel so free inside, I know that I am born all over again just like that man Nicodemus wanted to know about in the Bible."

Tad looked horrified, but didn't say so. It was just as well for he looked as though he would have said something very cutting.

"Is it all right, Rick?" Will asked.

"Yes, it is very right, Will. I understand. Now that you have told us, I look forward to having a long talk about it again. Go and settle in. We'll follow soon for it's nearly dinner time."

"Thanks, Rick," Will said, and turning to Tad he added, "Try to understand, Tad."

Tad looked up at him and gave him a weak smile. Ricky saw that Tad was deep in thought. "What do you make of that, Rick? You don't believe it do you? Do you think he is all right in the head?" Tad asked.

Ricky laughed, "Yes, he's all right, old chap. He has had a deep spiritual experience and it has affected him more than he ever thought such a thing could do."

"But do you go along with that sort of thing? Do you mean you believe in Jesus and all that they talk about in church?"

"Of course I do, Tad. Don't you?" asked the startled Ricky.

"Well, no, I don't think I ever thought about it much."

"Then why did you come to church every Sunday? Didn't anything you heard there touch you?"

"No I can't say it did, really. I suppose I went because you wanted us to, and that it was thing to do because everyone who was anything went to church on a Sunday and so if we wanted to better ourselves in people's eyes that's what we had to do."

"Oh, Tad. Where did I go wrong? Is that all it meant to you? I am so sorry," moaned Ricky.

"Well, you never talked about it much and so I don't suppose either Will or I ever thought about it. He only wanted to draw, anyway, and I always found someone interesting to look at. Why does it mean so much to you, Rick? What do you get out of it?" asked Tad.

"It isn't what I get out of it, Tad. I don't know, I suppose it is because I learned so much from Mother and Father. It meant so much to them that I just knew it had value and so I listened hard to what they were teaching in church and I found that it meant something to me, too. I am sorry, Tad, I suppose I felt that you would have the same feelings about it that I had because I have had them ever since I remember and I suppose I thought everyone did. Jesus is so real to me."

"Good heavens, is he? I thought he was some sort of myth or something. How can he be real to you when he has been dead for so long? Even if Will is right and he did see this Jesus, he saw that he was dead and in that other place, wherever that was. Anyway it was only some dream he had," Tad said with a disgusted look on his face. "Gee, Ricky, I just can't believe you'd go along with all that rubbish."

"Tad, it isn't rubbish. Jesus isn't dead, he is just in 'that other place' as you call it, but lives in all of us when we ask him to. If I didn't have Jesus in my life I would know that my life meant nothing at all. He helps me in everything I do. You'd better study your Bible and look for yourself."

"You make me sick. I've always thought you were such a practical person and now I find you are just a nothing." With this Tad walked out.

Ricky heard him go to the hall for his hat and then the front door slammed. "Oh, where have I gone wrong?" wailed Ricky as he sat with his head in his hands.

But Tad appeared later and at dinner he acted as though nothing was wrong but directed no conversation to Will. This didn't appear to have any affect on Will for he spent much of the time keeping the flow of talk going and keeping Amabel very amused with his 'take off' of some of the French people he had studied with. He told her of one man's over-gesticular speech and had her laughing merrily at the antics he used in illustration.

Ricky marvelled at the young man for, if anything, Will had always been rather reticent about his doings, however, he was the life of the party and Tad found that he could even smile at some of his antics.

They all settled in to the house very comfortably. They had to have more domestic help now that the family was enlarged. But soon Amabel found that walking up the stairs during her last weeks was an effort but everyone seemed to devote their lives to making her as comfortable as possible and the three young men, to whom babies were quite a mystery, were as helpful as they could be. They did view the prospect of the birth with something like horror. Tad was determined to stay with Amabel as long as he could when the time came but it was an ordeal that he did not look forward to, admitting as much to Ricky one evening. Ricky assured him he would be no help to him as he knew less about it all that Tad did.

"I don't know anything, Ricky. All the women say is, 'you'll be all right as long as you keep out of our way'. That's no help. Any way, old man, I hope you are here and can sit with me and help me through it. I gather it is a terrible thing for a woman, but darling Amabel is actually looking forward to it. Isn't she an angel, Rick? Not many women would tell their husbands that, would they?"

"I daresay she isn't really. Looking forward to the birth, I mean. She is, no doubt, looking forward to Tad junior but if what I've heard is true, I don't think a woman could look forward to such a thing as having it, would they, Tad?"

"I daresay we'll find out. You will promise me to wait with me won't you?

"Yes, but you do remember that in two weeks I have to be at Rocklea all week, don't you?"

"Oh that's all right the baby isn't due for four weeks yet, there is plenty of time."

Ricky was very pleasantly surprised at Will who was very busy painting every minute he could. He was not allowing anyone to see what he was painting but Ricky knew it was a huge canvas and that Will was filled with suppressed excitement at what he was doing. Ricky thought that it was probably the painting that would show the experience or dream or whatever it was that Will had had in France. Apart from painting, Will was much more cheerful and assertive than Ricky had ever known him. When anyone was around Will would take a smaller canvas and paint from some of the sketches he had made. They were delightful studies and Ricky felt that the lad had an inner something that had not been there before his overseas trip.

John Landon had noticed this too and came to Ricky one day in wonderment. "Ricky," he said, "have you seen that sketch of the little girl that Will is doing?"

"No, I haven't, but I saw the old black man he was painting the other day. Is the girl good, Mr Landon?"

"It is amazing, Ricky. That boy seems to have come alive. I always knew he was good but this is wonderful. Whatever happened to him over there has turned him into a genius. I saw that old man, too, it is marvellous. He seems to be painting faster than I have ever known him to do."

"Yes, it is as though he can't help himself. He is just on fire. You don't think he'll burn himself out do you, sir?"

"I don't know, but watch him. He is so cheerful I can't believe it. It is so good to see him so happy," said Landon concernedly.

"He really is happy, I am glad to say."

"We certainly started something sending him off like that, Ricky."

"I can't claim any credit for that, Mr Landon. I didn't want him to go, but you seemed so certain that it was the right thing to do and it was. You'd think he'd been there for years instead of months."

"What do you make of that experience he had, Ricky?"

"I can't say I really understand it but whatever it was it certainly touched something inside him. But, I am sorry to say that Tad doesn't accept it, though. He's being rather hard on Will and that worries me."

"Yes, I've tried to talk to Tad and got nowhere so decided to let it lie until it sorts itself out."

"Do you understand what happened to him, sir?"

"No, but I'm not dismissing it either. I hope it lasts for he is quite a changed person. All light and sunshine."

Tad had noticed this, too, but wouldn't try to understand. He never really taunted Will but was rather avuncular in all his dealings with the young man. Whenever he spoke to Will, which was no more often than he could help, he was rather patronizing. Ricky was wondering how they would get on while he was away, for he knew he could not depend much on Amabel at the moment for she was continually uncomfortable and her feet were so swollen that she could do little but sit in the dining room, which was the coolest room in the house, on a comfortable chair with a stool for her poor feet. She was very well except for her feet, and she was looking forward to the time when her babe would be born and she could resume her normal shape. The new nursery maid, Emma, attended to all her wants and was fast becoming an essential to Amabel in this male dominated house. Emma had been a hostel girl who had gone to the babies' home to learn to be a nursery maid.

Ricky had to be content that Tad would not start anything that would upset her but nevertheless set off for Rocklea with divided thoughts. He told himself not to worry about the home affairs and leave himself free to take pleasure in his visiting Jenny frequently. This he tried to do.

However, things took a different turn, for only the day after Ricky left Tad came to Will about 10am on that Saturday morning and asked him if he would send Joe for the doctor for it seemed as though Amabel's time had come.

"Yes, by all means, Tad. And what about Mrs Landon, would you like me to go for her?" he asked.

"Would you, Will? I would be most grateful. I don't like leaving her. I could send Joe, but it would be good if you could go while he is after the doctor. There's no knowing where he will be at this time. He may have to go looking for him. And Will, would you mind slipping in next door to get Binksie. And Will, you will hurry, won't you?"

"Yes I will, Tad, but I don't imagine there's much hurry. These things take time, I believe," said Will.

"A fat lot you know about it," said Tad bitingly, "it's Amabel, don't you realise?"

"Yes, all right, old fellow. I know you are worried and I'll be as quick as I can possibly be. I think I'll take the sulky, it will save Mrs Landon getting her carriage. I do hope she is at home."

"Oh ... Will, she's got to be. Amabel needs her."

"Don't worry, I'll find her where ever she is."

Will rushed downstairs and called for Joe to saddle a horse and go for the doctor and for the stable boy, Bill to get the buggy ready, calling for Mrs Keen to go upstairs to Amabel on his way through. Then to the girl's hostel to tell Binskie and out to the stables again to take the reins of the sulky and set off for Landon's.

Will was fortunate that Mrs Landon was at home and he soon had her packed into the vehicle and returned to the house as quickly as he could. There he wandered around for a while hoping he could do something then as no-one came to allay his concern he retired to the studio and began painting.

Tad came in some time later and said, "Can I stay for a bit?"

Will paused in the midst of a brush stroke and said, "Certainly, Tad. Make yourself comfortable. Is everything all right?"

"I suppose so," said Tad. "They won't let me in. The women, I mean. Will, this is horrible, to see Amabel in such pain. I'll never put her through it again, I will be sure. I was only thinking of myself."

Will just smiled for he really had no experience in saying the right thing to a man in such a situation. He looked at Tad and then went on painting.

Tad sat still for a while and then said, disgustedly, "You're no help," and left the room. Tad returned a few times during the afternoon, just coming in, sitting for a while and then leaving after saying a few pithy words. They had a rather silent dinner, for even though Will tried to make a little conversation Tad gave him only non-committal replies. Will felt sorry for him but said little knowing that whatever he said would not help.

At about eight o'clock, Tad burst into the studio and fired at Will, "Will you stop that infernal painting and pray or something? Don't you know that my wife is up there going through misery and all you do is paint ... paint ... paint."

"I am sorry, Tad. It is what I do best and I haven't seemed to give you any sort of comfort when I have said something to you. I thought it would be best if I just stayed here in case you want me."

"You call yourself a Christian. Can't you pray or something? You can't imagine what agonies Amabel is going through. Can't you pray for her? If there's such a thing as a God surely he will answer you. Why aren't you praying?"

"I am praying, Tad."

"I don't believe you. I haven't seen you."

"I haven't stopped praying since you first told me."

"I still don't believe you. I haven't seen you on your knees. Ever."

"Tad, there is more than one way to pray. I told you I haven't stopped praying for her and I feel a wonderful peace about Amabel. I am sure she will be all right, and the baby. I am praying for you, too, Tad."

"I don't want your prayers," Tad slung at Will. "I am all right, I just think you ought to pray for Amabel."

"I assure you, I am praying for her. In any case, why don't you pray for her yourself."

"How on earth can I? I've told you I don't believe in God, haven't I?" he almost sobbed.

"Do you know, Tad, I think you do believe in Him. You've just had everything go your way that you didn't think you needed Him."

"Well, I need Him now. For goodness sake, Will, help me," Tad sobbed.

"Before I can, you have got to tell me whether you do believe in Jesus, Tad. I know it is hard to admit to it after all this time, but I did and I am different, all through me. Tell me whether you have thought about it and what you truly believe."

"Yes, I do. I saw how changed you were and it really annoyed me, but I do have to admit that you are very changed and I do want to be like you."

"Not like me, like Jesus. You really mean it and not just because of Amabel?"

"Yes, I think so. I'm just so mixed up inside that all I want right now is for Amabel and the baby to be all right. I want to ask God for help and I can't do that unless you help me."

"Right let's kneel right down here." They knelt like two little boys and Will prayed for Tad to accept the Lord as his Master, and then encouraged Tad to say it himself. He stumbled over the words but said what Will had told him to. Then Will prayed for Amabel and the baby, speaking in such a way that Tad had never heard before. He spoke in prayer as though he was chatting away to his best friend and this surprised Tad a great deal. He had expected him to start intoning and almost groaning like some of the clergy were apt to do.

"Let's have a cup of coffee to buck us up, Tad," said Will, after they stood up, "we need it don't you think?" Will rang the bell and an excited Maria came to see their wants."

"Would you bring some coffee, Maria? I think Mr Tad is feeling a bit weak and needs some sustenance."

"Yes, Mr Will. Mr Tad, don't look so worried. It often takes this long the first time. Mrs English will be fine, you'll see."

"Thank you Maria. I must admit it is a trial. I do need the coffee, though."

The two brothers sat and looked at one another for a moment or two and then Tad said, "Thanks, Will. I don't know how I feel at the moment. All churned up, I think. But somehow I feel calmer."

"You certainly look a bit better."

Tad looked up at the easel where Will had been working. He could only see the back of the canvas that was there for Will had been facing Tad when he had come into the room. "What are you painting, Will? May I see it?"

Will indicated and he invited Tad to come and see. They walked together and stood before the canvas. Tad looked at it with surprise written on his face.

"What on earth have you been doing, Will? If I didn't know it I would say it was ... it is. It is Amabel's face. What's it all about?"

'Well, it's my way of praying, Tad. Just look at it and see what it tells you."

Tad looked and could see that Amabel's likeness was portrayed in a faint but light way amid the painting. She was smiling and yet there was concern. Tad could see love, anguish, joy and wonderment. Yes, all these things in the expression on his beloved wife's face. All across the painting were very misty figures, perhaps angelic ones, there were some sharp lines that didn't seem to be part of it and yet were. There were hazy shapes of baby figures and one stronger one that was painted in the Raphael style of a fat chuckling babe. There were arms reaching out for the baby who looked as though it was enjoying a big adventure coming into its unknown world.

Tad backed away from the picture and turned to bring a chair up. He brought it back, sat down, and gazed in rapture at the concept of it.

"Do you understand, Tad?"

"Yes," was all he said. Will was amazed at his stillness. Then Tad said, "This tells me more than you could ever say. It is your prayer, isn't it, lad?"

"It is," said Will, simply.

Maria bringing the coffee broke the spell a little, but Tad seemed to want to sit there, eyes glued to the painting as though he mustn't let go. Will was concerned that the painting might become too important to his brother but decided to worry about that later. They quietly spoke on occasions but the time didn't hang now and they were surprised to realise that it was ten o'clock, when they could hear Mrs Landon call, "Where are you, Tad?"

"Here, Mrs Landon." Tad shot to the door. "Is Amabel all right, is she all right?"

"Yes, she is fine and you have a lovely boy. And I have a lovely grandson," she said, giving Tad a bit hug.

"Will, did you hear that? I have a son."

"Yes, I heard it, old man. Congratulations."

"Are you sure Amabel is all right, Mrs Landon? When can I see her? Please?"

"Come on, you can see her now." She laughed as Tad was about to shoot up to their rooms. Remembering his manners, he turned to wait for his mother-in-law.

She just said, "Off you go and see her. Will, do you think we could all have something to drink?"

Will took her into his studio where they sat and quietly looked at one another and smiled, content with the results of the day. While they waited for their refreshments they wondered what Tad was thinking of his lovely, tired, Amabel and the scrap of humanity that was their son.

CHAPTER 20: *Dimity puts her foot down*

"Come along, Dimity, we are going to visit Mrs Thorne," said Mrs Roger.

"Oh, no I am not, mama," Dimity said petulantly. "I told you I am driving out with Mr English. He will be here soon."

"I am surprised at you speaking to me like that Dimity," said her amazed mother.

"I am sorry if I sounded rude, mama, but I did tell you."

"Tell me!" said the astounded mother. "Tell me! You should have asked me. In any case I would have said, no. I will not have you going about with that man. Alone, too."

"Oh, mama, you know it is all right for girls to go out in a carriage alone in the daytime. You have said so yourself," retorted Dimity. "Any way he is not 'that man', he is very pleasant, indeed."

"My dear, please don't get too fond of him. I am only thinking of you. I agree he is a personable young man, but, dear we don't know who his parents are."

"But that doesn't matter, mama. You were quite happy about him until that Mrs Thorne talked to you about him. Please mama, please let me go?"

"Your papa said I was not to permit you to have anything more to do with him. You will find you will forget all about him as soon as we return to England," said the distraught mother pulling on her gloves.

"But mama, I don't want to go back to England. I like it here much better. Oh why did papa have to have that row with Mr Pentacost. He liked it until then. Please make him stay."

"My dear I am unable to do that even if I wanted to. Once your father makes up his mind he is unchangeable. He is certainly unchangeable about that Mr English. He doesn't want him here. I must insist." She looked dubiously at her daughter. Mrs Roger was a small rather dumpy lady who liked to think she was very severe with her daughter. She thought she had won the day until she saw two tears squeeze from the big brown eyes. "Oh, Dimity, love, you haven't fallen in love with him, have you? You know that is not allowed. We will choose a nice husband for you in England and you will soon forget this man."

"I don't want a nice husband, mama. I love Will, and I won't forget him. I didn't while he was in France and I will never forget him," cried Dimity.

"Oh dear, oh dear, why did we ever come to this frightful place? We were so happy at home and now look what's happened. Oh dear, oh dear, come here and let me dry your eyes. Come on, now. There, there. A brave face. You know girls just cannot marry the first man they see, they have to remember their position. You must remember, dear, that you have a position to hold."

"Mama, he isn't the first man I ever saw, and I love him and I will have him. That is if he wants me," Dimity forgot herself so much as to stamp her foot.

"Dimity love, your father will be in a rage if he hears you say such a thing. Please don't mention it to him. I assure you that you will forget him when we leave. You must, dear, we won't allow you to marry him."

"But, mama, what is wrong with him? The Landons hold him in great regard," asked the weeping girl.

"Dimity," said her shocked mother, "he has apparently no background, as well you know. He is an artist, and perhaps you do not know what unsavoury reputations those sort of people have. For that matter I would not wish to tell you," Mrs Roger thought hard, "and he is a cripple, too, into the bargain. And ... I am sure there are lots of reasons, dear, why we would not want our only chick to marry such as he."

"Mama, you know he is not any of those nasty things you are thinking about. You liked him greatly until Mrs Thorne said all those terrible things. Don't you remember you said what a pleasant man he was and it was a pity he had such a bad leg? But that's all you could find wrong with him. And he is very well thought of here in the colony."

"But would not suit in England, I am thinking, dear," said her mother wishing she had not voiced her opinion of Mr Will English so well when they first met him.

"But he is not going to England, mama, and I will not either if he wants to marry me. Mama, I have made up my mind, I will not go back to England with you. I am staying." She stood in her full small height and looked down at her astonished mother.

"Dimity! Dimity!" was all her mother could say as she fell back on the cushions.

At that moment the door opened and the maid announced that Mr English was waiting for Miss Dimity below.

"Thank you, Barnes," said Dimity, "please ask him to wait a moment. Would you take him to the study."

"Yes, miss," said the maid and left.

"I am sorry, mama, but I am going out with Mr English. Please don't worry about me, I will be fine. I must get ready." She gave her mother a quick kiss and ran from the room.

Mrs Roger was left wondering about the waywardness of spoilt daughters. She sat for some time, then decided that she had no heart in visiting Mrs Thorne today, so sent a servant with a message to that lady, then returned to her room to remove her outer clothing and lay on the bed to recover from what she thought of, as a nasty experience.

Will greeted Dimity with a gayety that was a surprise. Dimity enquired, "You seem very happy Mr English?"

"Yes, Miss Roger, I have just become an uncle and I find I like the experience."

"Oh, has Amabel's babe come? Please tell me," exclaimed Dimity.

"Yes," laughed Will, "we all had a baby boy last evening. It was quite stressful."

"For your poor sister, indeed. But tell me is she well?"

"Yes, ma'am, very well considering the worrying day Tad and I had, and young Master English looks fine, too, if I am any judge, which I cannot claim to be."

"Have they chosen a name for him?" was the ever interested female's query.

"Yes, he is Master Henry English with a few extra names in the middle which I cannot remember. But on mature thought I would say John was one of them. Now, babies aside, where would my lady care to go on this warm spring day?"

"I have no preference, Mr English. Where would you suggest?"

"I believe there are some interesting ships in port Miss Roger and I have heard that one is a steamship, if that would interest you. We could go by the wharves and then to Mrs Macquarie's Chair. Perhaps if we have time you may care to walk in the Botanic Gardens. I have the hood up in the buggy which should shade you. If you are too warm we could pull up beneath the trees at the gardens."

"Thank you, you are most considerate," said the now prim Miss Roger.

Will swung himself up, in his usual style, into the carriage. He had an ability to do this down to a fine art. He was able to swing up so that he could land neatly into the vehicle without making it rock and at the same time protect his weak leg.

"You are very skilled at doing that, Mr English. I like to watch you. You make it look easy," said Dimity, admiringly.

"I hope it doesn't embarrass you. I try to manage without doing that," said Will shyly.

"No, I am not embarrassed. I think you have overcome something that at times must be quite irksome."

"You are most understanding. It is not every young lady who would be willing to be escorted by a cripple," said poor Will feeling his disability very much.

"I don't think of you as a cripple, Mr English. You are a friend who happens to have one shorter leg, that is all," declared Dimity, not knowing how much that made his heart glow.

"You make me feel very humble, and I thank you," Will said as he drove away.

They spent a pleasant time, finishing as Will suggested, shaded by the trees beside the Harbour where Will produced a hamper provisioned by Mrs Keen to aid a thirsty maid and her swain.

"I will miss all this when I leave," said Dimity pensively. If she said this for effect she couldn't be more pleased at the response to those words, for Will jerked so much that the horse plunged forward and Will had to put his mind on calming him before he had time to say a word.

When a little calmer he asked, "Miss Roger, what do you mean when you leave?"

"My parents and I are returning to England and we are to leave in four weeks." Dimity could see the muscles in Will's jaw tighten. "You see, they really do not like the life here and so have decided to return."

"Do you wish to go, too?" Will asked with his heart in his mouth.

"I must do as my parents wish," she answered demurely, but smiling to herself, for she could not be but gratified at the effect all this was having on her companion.

"Did you say you would be leaving in four weeks?" Will asked with anguish, and at her slight nod he burst out with, "But you cannot! You cannot!" Then recollecting himself he asked pardon and told her that he had been so surprised that he forgot his manners.

"I must," said the maiden, hopefully.

There was stunned silence for some time and then Will said, "Well, Miss Roger, I must take you home now as you must be feeling the heat." With that he stirred up the horse and set off for her home, saying very little on the way, but gently and tenderly helping her from the carriage at the door. He doffed his hat as she entered the house; she waved gaily, feeling rather pleased with herself.

Dimity was not usually a designing minx but she felt one now. She was not normally the type of girl who maneuvered people into her way of thinking, but she really loved her man and she was not going to lose him if it were at all possible. She felt rather quavery inside at the thought of tackling her father when the time came but she made up her mind that she would do it if she had to.

In the meantime her swain was heading for Landon's house as fast as his horse could properly go. He drew up at the main portico of the mansion and threw the reins to a groom who came to his aid. He ran up the steps and rang the bell impatiently. "May I see Mr Landon, please Tonkin?" he asked as the door was opened.

"I am sorry Mr Will but Mr and Mrs Landon have gone to visit Miss Amabel, or I mean Mrs English. They have not long gone, you must have passed them."

"I did not come from there, but I will go now. If I miss them would you please tell Mr Landon that I would like to see him and if it is possible he could wait to see me, it is urgent."

"Certainly, sir. I will tell him, but I am sure you will catch him at your home."

Back in the vehicle Will was forced to take it easier now for he knew his poor horse would be wondering why the haste. The usually patient Will was feeling decidedly impatient now, but he just gritted his teeth and forced himself to take it easy. He rushed in the door from the stables asking Maria if Mr Landon was still there, knowing that someone was for the Landon carriage was in the yard.

"Yes, Mr Will," said Maria. "They have all come to see the baby. Mr Landon was looking for you."

"Thanks, Maria, I'll go up." Will went up to where he could hear much laughter and found Tad entertaining all his in-laws but John. After a polite, quick greeting, Will asked with a sinking heart where Mr Landon was.

"Did you want John, Will?" asked Mrs Landon. "He is admiring his grandson. He'll be back in a moment. We are all allowed in one at a time and only for a short visit."

"Is everything all right?" he asked.

"Yes, fine," said Tad. "Have some tea, Will."

Will automatically took the cup. Tad looked at him with concern. He hadn't seen that look on Will's face since he came home and knew something was wrong. He sidled up to him as unobtrusively as he could and muttered, "Is everything all right, Will?"

"Well, yes, Tad, but I must see Mr Landon as soon as I can. Will he be long do you think?"

"No, the nurse will see that he isn't. Do you know she didn't want me to pick Henry up, she thought I might harm him. Isn't he wonderful, Will? You should hear him cry. Goodness he is noisy."

Will smiled and wondered how long Tad would think the little boy's cry would be wonderful. He imagined it would get louder as he grew older.

At last John Landon came, but then, after greeting Will he sat beside him slowly drinking his tea and Will had to listen to him extolling the beauties of his daughter and her babe. At last Will felt he could quietly say, "Could I have a private word to you, sir?"

"Yes, of course, lad, anytime you like." But he didn't move.

Mrs Landon moved quietly to her husband's side and said, "John, if you don't go and speak to Will he will eat a leg off that chair, I think." She laughed but smiled kindly at the impatient Will.

John turned and looked at Will, "You mean, now, lad? Right now?"

"If you please, sir." said Will.

"Right let's go to your studio." He picked up his tea and walked out with it leading the way to the studio where he wandered around as one who was used to knowing what went on in that place. He was most interested in the picture of Amabel and her pain. He looked at it and then at Will. "Tad told me about it. It has made a great impression on him."

"Yes, it has. I hope not too much. I painted it for my own benefit, really, not thinking that Tad would understand. At least I wasn't thinking of that at all, it was just something I had to do. I feel it helped her, Mr Landon. Can you understand that?"

"It's a bit deep for me but I think I do. You're no stranger to pain yourself are you?" He turned then to a huge shrouded canvas. "Is that the one you must paint?" And at Will's nod. "Not for viewing, eh, lad?"

"One day perhaps, sir. I don't know, yet. I have a long way to go."

John settled himself in one of the armchairs. "Well, now, what is it you so desperately want to see me about. You're like a cat on hot bricks."

"I feel it, too. Sir, I want to marry Dimity Roger."

"Do you now? Have you asked her? You surely don't want my advice on that do you? You are old enough to make up your own mind."

"No, of course I know that, sir. I want to marry her. But I had no intention of asking her until she knows me better, but she told me today that they are leaving the colony in a matter of weeks and I wanted to ask you whether it would be the right thing to approach her father and whether he would think me suitable. You know my background and I would have to tell him, of course. But sir, if he objects to me could I ask you to sponsor me, please?"

"Of course I would speak for you, Will. I daresay I know you as well as anyone and have always found that I can trust you, so that would be no effort on my part. Glad to, boy."

"Thank you, Mr Landon. I thought I may go and see him in the morning if he is at home. Do you think it will be a bit sudden for him. I daresay he won't like me as a suitor. What do you think my chances are?" asked Will anxiously.

"Will, I had no hesitation in letting my daughter marry Tad for I have known you since you were boys, and that may carry some weight, but I have to be honest with you, lad, he doesn't know you as I do. I am glad you spoke to me but I do believe you are going about it the right way."

"I hope so. This is where background counts, doesn't it? This is where Tad is fortunate."

John laughed, "I think you have no resentment to that, now, Will. You've thoroughly got over that."

"Yes, I certainly have. I was stupid and I realise that. At the same time I don't think Tad finds relatives are a great asset. But," he added wistfully, "it would be handy to have a few relatives right now."

"Remember, Will, I gave Amabel to Tad before I knew he had any."

"Yes, and that has worked out well, hasn't it?"

"Yes, I couldn't be more pleased. They are very happy. Do you know Miss Roger's feelings, Will? Have you given her a hint?"

"No, but I cannot help feeling she likes me."

"Well, all I can say, Will, is that you mustn't under estimate the power of woman. I hate to think what sort of performance I would have had to put up with if I had forbidden Amabel to have Tad. I think I would have had to leave home," he added with a chuckle. "If I am any judge I think your young lady might have a mind of her own so you may be able to bank a great deal on that."

Will chuckled, "I do think she may be a handful. She is only little but I think she does have a mind of her own. I'll be mindful of that."

"Well, best of luck, Will. I'll be waiting to hear from you. Come to the office after you have seen Roger. I didn't know he was leaving. He's not a close friend, you know. To tell you the truth, I didn't think he would fit in here. There is one thing you must think of, too, Miss Roger is their only child and she may miss her parents if she stays here alone. They would be very hesitant about leaving their one chick. I would be at any rate," said John the father.

"I realise that. I am very sorry they are thinking of leaving for it makes the decision so much harder for her. Do you think, sir, I am asking too much of her? Perhaps I shouldn't put it upon her." Will looked very worried.

"You must accept her word if that is so. She will have to weigh that up herself, but it is a great responsibility for you. Make sure you are able to accept that."

"Thank you, sir. I appreciate your friendship so much and I did want your opinion."

"Right, let's go back to the others, they will wonder what we are hatching up. Cheer up, Will, all is not lost yet."

Will was on the Roger doorstop as soon as it was acceptable, and was admitted to the study to await Dimity's father. He was rather surprised at the cool reception he got and couldn't work that out, for up till now the Rogers had always accepted him kindly. However, with a deep breath he launched into his plea not expecting the tirade he got when he finished.

"Mr English, you must know you could not be acceptable as a suitor to my daughter. I know nothing good about you and do not consider your pastime of painting to be a recommendation to me. I would be pleased if you would take yourself off and not darken my door again. I take it that you must have been making up to my daughter and I could not expect any better, from what I hear," said the irate father.

"Sir, please, I must protest. I have not indicated to your daughter anything but friendship and indeed would not have spoken until you knew me better but that I heard yesterday you were planning to leave the colony."

"The sooner the better as far as I can see. I will take my daughter as far away from you as I can. I will be pleased if you will leave now, sir."

"But please, sir, Mr Landon would speak for me. Please give me a hearing." Will felt like getting to his knees to plead the father even before he could plead the girl.

Roger walked to the bell and pulled it. As the manservant came in he said, "Mr English is leaving, Evans. Show him the door."

Will could do nothing but take his leave, bowing stiffly and turning to follow the man. He took his hat and cane and left quickly, his one thought was to get to John Landon as quickly as he could.

John could see what the lad had to tell him before he even spoke. "Come along in and tell me, Will. Or should I say that I see by your countenance you have not succeeded. Anyway sit down and tell me.

"Mr Landon, it was absolutely dreadful. Much worse than I ever thought. Mr Roger seems to think I am a blackguard or something. He was cold before I even spoke, as though he expected me to say what I did." Will explained all that had happened.

"Are you sure you did not upset Miss Roger yesterday, Will?"

"No, sir, I am sure I did not. She seemed to be very happy with me and is kindness itself."

"Perhaps that is what her attitude was, Will," Landon said gently. "Perhaps she was just being kind and not wishing it to go further. You must be prepared for that."

"Yes, I am prepared for that. If she does not want me then that is all there is to say to the matter but I would like to have the opportunity of hearing her say it."

"I can understand that. I feel that someone is behind this, for the man should have at least given you a hearing. I hear that Mrs Roger is thick with Mrs Thorne and that woman has a tongue like a snake."

"I don't think I know Mrs Thorne, Mr Landon, or at least I know of her but what would she know of me?" asked poor Will.

"I wouldn't know, lad, but some people don't have to know much to make a story. In any case I will go along and see Roger and try to undo what harm obviously has been done. I will go as soon as I can leave the office and call and see you after that. Try not to worry"

Little did they know but things were moving in Will's favour already for Miss Dimity Roger had caught sight of a man leaving the house and as she thought he limped, and presumed it was Will. She ran down stairs and into the study. "Was that Mr English, papa?" she asked. "Why did he not stop?"

"He didn't stop because I sent him on his way, Dimity," was the stern reply.

"Whatever do you mean, father?"

"I mean the man came to ask if he could pay his addresses to you and I told him to go."

With that Dimity burst into tears and berated her father. "Oh, father, what have you done? You don't mean it, say you don't?" she cried.

"I do, Dimity. I won't have him here and the sooner we leave this place the better I will like it. I told him to never come back."

'But why? what has he done?" she sobbed.

"He is not for you, my pet. Come here." She sat on his knee. "I want someone better for my little sweet," he cooed.

"I want him though, I love him, father. I want him, he is mine."

"Silly goose, you think you do, but he isn't for you. We'll find someone better for you." He patted her gently on the shoulder.

"Papa, I tell you I love him and he is mine. I want him and I don't want anyone else," she sobbed.

By this time Dimity's father was feeling a bit lost for he was not used to her acting like this. "Dimity, I forbid you to see him again. I will not have him in the house again.

Dimity stood up and, looking straight at her father she said, "Well, father, if that is so. I will see him away from the house."

Neither had heard the door open but they heard the gasp that came from Mrs Roger. "Dimity, did I hear right? Do you defy your father? I am surprised at you." With this she, too, burst into tears.

Mr Roger stood up pushing Dimity to one side. By this time was ringing his hands. His females had never acted like this before and he was stunned. "Now, now, dear, don't upset yourself ..." he said to his wife.

"Upset myself? Never did I think to hear my daughter say anything like that. Oh, dear." There came a renewed flood of tears.

Roger looked at them both, then at the door as though he expected a miracle to walk in, but as it didn't he cleared his voice and said, "Now stop it, both of you. This will not get us anywhere. Come along. Stop this and we'll see whether we can sort this out pleasantly." His women folk blew noses and dabbed at eyes and tried for some composure. "That's better," he said as the sniffs subsided a little. "Now Dimity dear, you have always been a good obedient girl who has never given us a moment's worry. What has got into you wanting a man such as this?"

"So unsuitable," her mother put in.

"Why is Mr English so unsuitable, papa? What has he done that's wrong? Why can't I see him?"

"Mrs Thorne says ..." started he mother.

"In fairness to the man, I think we will leave Mrs Thorne out of this, my dear," Roger said. Turning to Dimity he said, "Dimity, we do not know anything about this man's family. No one does. He was a street stray. Perhaps you did not know that?"

"Yes. I did, papa, and so were his two brothers," she quickly said.

"Not really a recommendation, my dear. But at least they have a background."

"But Tad didn't have a background when he became engaged to Amabel and she was allowed to marry him."

"Yes, but I am not Landon and I would not care to give my one and only chick to a nobody," he replied.

"We only want the best for you dear," said her mother. "You could marry anybody."

"Anybody but the man I love," Dimity said bitterly.

"You don't understand love, child. It is not necessary in a marriage. Why I ... but that doesn't matter," he said hastily. "Dimity, I do not want to be stern with you, for I have never had the need, but I forbid you to see this man again. We will be leaving on the 20th of next month and you will forget him before we have even got as far as Melbourne. I believe the Hardwickes are going home on the same ship and you know what a nice chap young Mr Hardwicke is. You will find his company most amusing."

"I won't papa, he has a wet sniff, and I cannot bear him. In any case I will not be going. I just refuse." Dimity stamped her foot again and looked straight at her father. Her parents said "Dimity!" almost in unison. "Sit down and listen papa, mama. You have had your say and now I will have mine."

"Dimity don't speak to your father like that. I think we have had enough of this Frederick. Dimity, go to your room!" Her mother rose rather like a plump bantam protecting her man.

"Hush, hush, dear. Do not let us remain fussed. Sit down again. Carry on then Dimity, what is it you have to say?" Her father said, calmly, although his colour showed that he was anything but.

"Father, I love Will. He has given me no encouragement, ever. He has always been very polite and very kind. So do not think he has ever done anything of which you would not approve." She warmed to her task. "I fell in love with him that first night I met him and he did me, too, I felt it. My heart nearly broke when he went away but I thought I would be able to wait and meet him again and so I tried to be patient. I agreed to go home when you suggested it because I thought I would be nearer to him, but since then he has come back and now I want to stay with him."

"Go on," prompted her father.

"All the time he was away I have gathered up any information I could about him."

"You should have not made yourself so conspicuous, Dimity. How could you?" asked her mother, bristling at the thought.

"I didn't make myself conspicuous at all, mama. I only had to listen to the young people speak of him. You may not know it but he is well thought of in town. He is very popular. He makes light of his deformity and is always cheerful, polite and considerate. Did you know that it was Mr Landon who sponsored him on his trip to Paris, papa?"

"No, but most penniless painters need a sponsor."

"He isn't penniless and there was no need for Mr Landon to do that but had always taken a great interest in him since a small boy and considered it his duty to guide him. You would be surprised at how well he is thought of. Mr Landon thinks he is a great genius. Please let him come and see me so you can get to know him? Please?" she pleaded. She rose and stood before her father. "I mean what I say, father. I have never wanted anything in my whole life like I want Will English. And papa," she said seriously, "papa, I mean to have him. I will not leave the colony with you unless he decides he doesn't want me." With that, she burst into tears once more and threw herself onto the couch and sobbed.

Her parents looked at one another. Her father said, "All right, Dimity, that's enough. I cannot agree, but I will promise you I will think hard about it and let you know what I have decided. It grieves me to hear you say what you say and I never thought to hear you defy me like this. But I can see that the fellow has you in his toils and I shall have to think deeply about what to do."

"But Frederick," wailed Mrs Roger, "you can't give in. We cannot leave our daughter to live in this place. You never would allow it. You wouldn't. Promise me you wouldn't?"

"For goodness sake, Matilda. No more fuss, I don't think I can bear it. I don't want to lose Dimity any more than you do and I said, I'll think about it, and I will. Now leave me, both of you and give me some quiet, please," he said tetchily, feeling near the end of his tether.

They left him but he found no quiet. He sat with his head in his hands until his butler came in to remind him that he had ordered the sulky to be at the door and it was now waiting. "Thank you, Evans."

He went about his business with a heavy heart all the time wondering what would be the outcome. He tried to put it aside but by mid afternoon gave up and went home with a feeling of foreboding. "You think you know people and you find you don't, especially your children," he mused. "I couldn't believe Dimity could act like that. There must be something good about the fellow.

I suppose I will have to find out what it is. But how on earth do I do that without anyone knowing what I am about."

He didn't have long to ponder over that for he found John Landon waiting for him when he got home. He groaned to himself, feeling he knew what was to come. He greeted John with the words, "I daresay I know why you are here, Landon, and I can't say I relish what you have to say. I imagine you are here to champion the fellow's cause and I must say at the outset that I am sick of his name, I've had it running around in my head all day."

"I am glad to hear that Roger, for at least it means you must be considering him."

"Not at all, man. I am not considering him at all but that dratted daughter of mine is. We've had floods of tears and vapours and the Lord knows what and I dislike scenes. And I am not used to them, what's more."

He didn't know what to expect from John but all he got was a chuckle. "Daughters can be a plague, can't they? I know, I have three. But nice to have around all the same. Keeps a man alive," said John.

"I might have agreed until today. I had no idea that my little Dimity could be such a virago."

"They all have a touch of it," John said, "I find they usually keep it hidden but they can bring it out at the most inconvenient times. Had a rotten day, have you?" he asked smugly.

"Yes, I have. She wants to marry that blighter and I just don't want her to. We plan to go home in a few weeks as my wife is not suited to this place. I cannot see myself leaving her here married to someone I cannot like."

"But be fair, man. You haven't seen enough of Will to like him or dislike him, have you?" came the swift query.

"Probably not, but I cannot say I want to."

"I can understand how you feel for I had to accept one of those boys taking my precious Amabel. You may believe I had to do some deep thinking when I saw what was afoot in that direction. It made me search as well as anyone could to find out about the boys but it defeated me and I could find no trace. So I had to fall back on my native instinct and take them as I found them. I did not go wrong."

"But your son-in-law did have a family. So you are all right."

"Yes, he has. But he didn't when I allowed them to be engaged."

"But he has now and that's the all important thing."

"Is it, Mr Roger? Is it the most important thing? I know several well-born people I would not give house room to, and many ill-born, if you like to put it that way, who I would share my life with willingly."

"You must be very happy that your daughter's in-laws are good people, though, Landon. You must feel some gratification that there is a family there. You cannot tell me otherwise."

"I was glad, I admit that," said John, amazed at the satisfied look on Roger's face. "I was glad, but mostly for Tad's sake, for one always wants to know about one's roots. But now. I think it has all proved my point. The young ones went, as asked by Tad's grandfather, and I was pleased to see them go, even though I thought we might lose them to a huge family estate and a loving family. I was never so wrong. They could not get home quickly enough, for they turned out to be a more stiff-necked lot of people, than you would ever find in this lovely place. They are so much so that all they seem to do is sit in their large mansion and pull the world to pieces. They certainly don't seem happy about it. Tad's maternal people are apparently the salt of the earth, but the more high-born ones, I wouldn't give a damn for."

"Oh," was all Roger said.

"Frederick, I have watched those three boys grow up and I am proud that they call me friend. You couldn't imagine what they went through, and I do not intend telling you, that's their story. But you couldn't find a straighter, nicer trio anywhere on earth and I'll back any one of them to keep to the line. If those two young things really love one another and want to marry, and if you give your blessing to it, I can assure you, you will not regret leaving Miss Dimity to Will's care."

"You speak of them as though they were perfection," Roger almost sneered.

"If I gave you that impression, I am sorry. There is no perfection, but they are good honest men. Will has been silly a couple of times, but who of us hasn't. It has all helped make him the man he is and that's a fine one." John looked straight at the man. "Roger, if Will had wanted to marry Betsy or Harriet and she loved him, I would give either of them to him most happily, and I cannot say more than that."

"No, I see you could not. I am really thankful you said that, for I see you feel strongly about this."

"Can you not give the boy a chance? Let him come here and get to know him. Must you go away so soon? Why not wait a while, if you can. Believe me, if they are matched nothing will separate them, if they are not, you will see that they will part all by themselves. Remember, that a little adversity often makes these young ones dig in their toes more than they should. Man, you do not want to lose your daughter, do you? And if I read Miss Dimity aright, I think there is metal in that little lady," John laughed.

"You speak sense, Landon. Metal? Yes, I had no idea it was there until today. I think I see what you mean."

"Will you give the lad a chance? Can I tell him to expect a word from you?"

"I suppose one has to bend to a woman's will. I daresay I will have to give way a little," Roger said reluctantly.

"It's hard the first time, but believe me, you get used to it," laughed the father of three girls. "Good night, Roger, and thank you for listening to me." John shook his hand.

"I suppose I must thank you for coming, but as yet I cannot decide whether I want to," said John's reluctant host.

"No, so I'll thank you instead. Good night."

CHAPTER 21: *The New House*

"**A**re you ready for dinner, Will?" called Tad. "Did I see Papa Landon? He didn't call to see Amabel." Tad stood at Will's bedroom door.

"Come in," called Will. "Yes, he was here, briefly, but was in a tearing hurry and couldn't wait."

"You look a bit more cheerful. What's been happening? Can you let me in on the secret?"

"Yes, I will tell you after dinner, if you can wait that long."

"All right, I'll wait but come along, I'm starving."

"You always are," said Will clapping Tad on the back.

The ease of past years had once again fallen on these two men and so it was easy for them to spend time alone. But they had to wait until after dinner before Will could share his problems. Tad was rather surprised at the suddenness of it all and was rather lost for words to begin with.

"Mr Landon seems to think that Mr Roger will give me a better hearing from now on. But I am rather anxious to see what happens. He told me that I was to try to wait patiently and see if Mr Roger will make a move to invite me to dinner or something. It will be hard, though," Will added.

"Have you told Ricky what's in the wind, Will?"

"No, I haven't, for I was going along slowly thinking I had lots of time to do my courting, but when Miss Roger told me they were going back to England I nearly died of fright."

"Then Ricky will get the surprise that I did?" asked Tad.

"In more than one way, won't he? For he doesn't know about young Henry yet, does he?"

"I sent a message telling him," replied Tad. "As a matter of fact I wonder whether he will come home a little sooner."

"He probably will, if I know Rick," said Will. "Goodness we will miss him when he gets married."

"Yes, he's going to move into the new house next week I think. It will seem peculiar. Will, if I can ever get a home of my own would you and Miss Roger want to stay here?" asked Tad.

"Yes, I daresay I would, Tad. My studio's here and I wouldn't want to leave that. Not for some time anyway. Are you thinking about leaving? Does Amabel like being here?"

"Oh, yes, she does. There's no worry about that, but some day when I can I would like to build my own house. Somewhere nice for children to grow up. This place is not all that good for little ones, is it?"

"Goodness me, we've been together for so long that it seems hard to think we'll all go our own ways, but I daresay that is what happens in life."

Ricky did come home two days early, bringing with him Jenny and Mr and Mrs Forrest. There now was not enough room in the house for all those visitors so Ricky had suggested that they stay in the new house, as the new servants were there and the place was ready for habitation. At first the Forrests objected thinking that they should allow the young couple to be the first residents, but when Ricky pointed out that as the servants were already in residence, surely they were the first. In any case Ricky had intended to move within a few days. So the Forrests and Jenny were able to move some of her belongings into the house as well as attend to business in the town. Jenny and Mrs Forrest were most anxious to see Amabel and Henry and so it was a good move for all. They would return home early the following week for that was the week before Ricky and Jenny's wedding at St Matthew's, Windsor.

Tad was in two minds as to whether he should leave Amabel to go to Ricky's wedding and worried about it quite a lot until Amabel put him right. She assured him that he should not miss the wedding as Ricky was depending on him and Will to support him at the church. She would be quite all right as Mrs Keen would watch over her, not to mention the nurse, Emma the maid and Binksie next door. She was upset at missing the ceremony but as her baby had been due about that time she hadn't thought she could attend in any case. She insisted that Tad go on the Friday before when Will was to leave but he assured her he would be back at home on Saturday night. She knew this was possible as they were to be married at eleven in the morning.

Ricky was, as Tad and Will surmised, quite surprised at Will's news and that the Rogers were anticipating a return "home". Will told him of his visit to the Roger's house and the reception he had received, and this annoyed Ricky quite a great deal, but tried not to let Will know how much. He had heard that Mr Roger was a quarrelsome man and that it didn't take much to make the man lose his temper. This worried Ricky, thinking that Will may becoming involved in a family that would prove hard to live with. However he encouraged Will to be as patient as possible and be guided by their ever loyal friend John Landon.

Ricky moved his gear to the new house as soon as the Forrests left and his two brothers helped him settle in, thinking it was hard to believe that Ricky was leaving them. But they were all very proud of the lovely house for it "had everything" according to Tad. Ricky was pleased with it and was in a fury of excitement getting it ready for his lovely Jenny and finishing off all the loose ends he had to tie up before taking Jenny away for two weeks on their honeymoon. They planned to be back in their own home for Christmas, alone, except for, perhaps, Will who would be the only single male left.

Other exciting things happened during that week, for Will had his long desired invitation to dine at the Roger's during the week following the wedding and Tad had a letter from his grandfather.

Tad came to dinner much excited on the evening on which Amabel made her first appearance since Henry's birth. He brought her into the dining room as the gong sounded, as though he was accompanying a queen, and indeed he thought he was. They chatted merrily all through the meal for it was to be Ricky's last, too, before moving, and then in the sitting room after dinner Tad announced, "I had a letter from Grandfather Falconer-Mead today. Guess, what? He has forgiven me and wants to make up for our unhappiness at Mead Park. Apparently Grandfather Stanthorpe called to see him and put him in the picture and got rather cross with his old friend.

Grandfather Falconer-Mead was not happy, apparently, at what he heard and caused quite a stir. I am afraid my name would not be a popular one, but I must admit I am pleased that my grandfather will not be so put upon in the future. He is now not at all annoyed with me and has sent me five thousand pounds to prove it. He said he had intended to give me money that would have come to my father and was glad to send it now. I was not at all happy to have it at first, but then I thought it would be rather ungracious not to accept it, and besides, I do like the thought of having it. Amabel and I will be able to build our dream house earlier than we hoped."

"What a good thing you wrote to him before you got that, Tad," said Ricky.

"Yes, by Jove. I am, too, for he knows that I hold no grudge against him, Rick. Yes, what a good thing I did. I have also written to him telling him, too, about Henry, and I think he would be pleased about that, don't you think?"

Will pounded him on the back and told him how pleased he was. Tad looked happy at that and asked, "You don't mind, Will?"

"No, not at all Tad. I am very pleased you have a fairy grandfather. Perhaps the time is right now to ask Ricky if it is all right if I can stay here if and when I marry?"

"Of course, it is all right. But you know, don't you remember? that all three of the houses are in all our names so we all have rights to them. If it is right with Tad it's all right with me."

"I am glad I told you the other day, Will, that I want to build our own house. I think that would be a grand arrangement. That is providing Miss Roger will like living here."

"I am sure she will. That is if she wants to marry me at all." But smiled as he said it. "Will I still be able to keep Mrs Keen , though?"

"I am quite sure if any one suggested to her that she should leave you she would just take a chair into the kitchen and sit there until we relented and told her she could stay," Ricky said, and chuckled as he added, "for some reason she thinks the world of you, Will." Will just smiled.

So they were three elated men who set off on Friday to go to Rocklea for the night before the wedding. The day was very hot and humid and Rick was a little worried about the weather holding. They did have a cool change that evening with no rain and Tad and Will assured him that the day would be all he hoped it would, and they were right.

On the wedding morning they were dressed in their best and waiting at St Matthew's a quarter of an hour before Jenny was due to arrive. They waited in the vestry and, with the Rector, kept Ricky chatting about everything they could think of for they could see he was very nervous. Then when they thought there was nothing else to say, the Rector got a message to say that Jenny had arrived so the three brothers went into the church and stood before the sanctuary steps. Ricky felt he couldn't look for he was quite overwhelmed at the thought of marriage to his lovely Jenny. Tad gave him a gentle nudge and there she was.

Jenny wore a long gown of white with very simple lines considering the fashion of the day. There was one full frill above the hem of the skirt and she wore a large hat which was trimmed with a filmy gossamer material. She carried a beautiful bouquet of white flowers. Ricky was almost breathless when he saw his bride coming towards him on her Uncle Edward's arm, and was not even conscious of the two little Forrest girls who preceded Jenny into the church, looking very proud of the attention they thought they were getting. But really very few people noticed the children for most eyes were on the bride.

Edward Forrest duly gave her to Richard and both bride and groom answered all the questions as though they were in another world. Too soon they were walking back up the aisle and it seemed to hit them only at that stage that they were married "for better or for worse".

There was not a large gathering, probably about fifty people. After all in the party were duly kissed and congratulated they all moved to the Bucks Head for luncheon, Ricky escorting Jenny to the new double seated buggy that he had bought for her. Joe, who took over from old Tom, was smartly dressed in fine new clothes and he proudly drove the married couple to the reception behind a lovely pair of grey horses.

There was a wonderful meal set out with food as only country folk can provide. With hams, beef and mutton from Rocklea and Claremont and all sorts of salad vegetables. Early peaches and apricots and every kind of sweetmeat one could think of. All very suitable for an Australian summer luncheon.

There were a few speeches, perhaps not really speeches but words that several of the men felt they must say. Toasts drunk and then while Jenny changed into travelling clothes people chatted happily for many had travelled far and saw friends only occasionally.

Jenny came out from changing amid much admiration and applause. She was dressed in a deep green. A silk dress with a coat of sturdier material of matching tones to protect her from the dust of the dirt roads. Her hat was much smaller than the bridal one and was anchored safely with a gauzy veil again of matching green.

Ricky handed her into the vehicle and climbed in beside her. They waved until they were out of sight of all their friends. Jenny looked at Ricky, and he to her, sharing a smile that almost said, "Well done. But now that's over let's get on with it."

After a few miles they came upon a man waiting in a sulky. Joe hailed him and pulled up. He hopped down and handed the reins to Ricky. "All right, Mr English? Will I leave you now?"

"Yes, Joe. All well, I can manage now. Thank you, you did your job well," said Ricky.

"Take care, Mr Rick, they are still pretty fresh, and are pulling a bit." Joe looked at Jenny. "Sorry, Mrs English," he said and then looked at Ricky, "Keep your mind on them, Mr Rick, we don't want to have any accidents."

"Stop fussing, Joe, you're as bad as old Tom. Believe you me I do not want any harm to come to Mrs English. I'll be very careful. Thanks again and goodbye."

Joe watched the buggy disappear from sight and climbed into the sulky. "Hope they're all right, Bill. I don't think Mr Rick is thinking of anything but his missus."

Ricky went on for a while and then pulled up again. "This is where I kiss my wife, young lady. I don't know how I have waited all this time." He performed the delightful task to their mutual enjoyment and set off again in a much freer frame of mind.

"How long will it take to get to Emu Plains, Rick?" asked Jenny.

"I don't know exactly but I want to drive as carefully as I can, but these fellows are wanting a gallop and are pulling my arms like mad. These roads are not the best but we'll get there, I promise you, well before dinner and in time to freshen up."

They were hot and dusty and very tired by the time they crossed the Nepean River and headed across Emu Plains to their friend's house. The Armitage's were in England and suggested that Ricky and Jenny spend their honeymoon there while they were away. The staff was in situ and were most welcoming to the young couple.

The housekeeper greeted them with a "Tch, tch, Mrs English, you are all dusty on your lovely clothes. Emmy can show you to your rooms and bring water for you to wash. I'll send up tea right away for I daresay you need it."

"Thank you, Mrs Bush, I think we do. We stopped and had some refreshment on the way but I really need hot tea."

Mrs Bush called to the men to bring up the trunks, called Emmy to show the guests their rooms and bustled off to get tea and everything else that was needed.

Their bedroom was huge and faced the lovely blue mountains. There was a lovely smell of orange blossom in the air and a cool breeze came in through the open window. Jenny leaned out of the window to catch the breeze and laughed gaily as Ricky came up behind her and put his arms around her.

"You are all mine, now, my darling, darling Jenny. Oh, I love you, I love you so much it jolly well hurts."

She turned round in his arms and put hers round his neck. "I love you, too, Mr Richard English and I am so happy that I could sing for absolute joy. Do you think anyone has ever loved as we do?" she laughed.

"I suppose so, but it is hard to believe," came the muffled reply as Ricky kissed his wife thoroughly.

They had an idyllic two weeks in that lovely place, often taking the buggy to have a picnic on the river bank. They gave up taking the greys on short runs for they were too frisky to want to wait for such dallying, but Ricky had the men take them for smart runs to keep them from being too fresh on the way home.

They had decided to spend their first Christmas in their own home and so started the long 36 mile journey home early one morning before it became too hot. They stopped at Parramatta for a long spell and lunch. Ricky had ordered a room so that Jenny could have a rest and freshen up. He expected to make the rest of the journey by the cool of the evening, but a cool change arrived early with some light showers and so the rest of the trip was made in comparative comfort. Nevertheless they were very pleased to get home.

As they pulled up Joe came to take the horses. "Everything all right, Mr English?

The horses go well?"

"Yes, everything is fine, Joe. They are very sweet goers, but very tired. It has been a long day but we took it slowly. Take them off and send our luggage up," said Ricky.

Ricky walked over to where Jenny was waiting and before the startled eyes of Mrs Breen, the new housekeeper, he swept her up into his arms and carried her into the house. Jenny laughed gaily and Mrs Breen joined in. "Welcome home, Mr and Mrs English," she said. "I hope you find everything to your liking."

"I'm sure we will," said Jenny between giggles. Then, looking around her noticed all the lovely flowers and the place looking so shining that it was startling. "Oh, Mrs Breen, the place looks lovely. Look at all the flowers. Look Ricky, aren't they beautiful?"

"They certainly are. Where did you get them all, Mrs Breen. Whose garden has been robbed?" he asked.

"Well, I had bought plenty myself Mr Rick, but that Edie Keen turned up with armloads. As though I wouldn't have enough," she said, and laughed. "I am sure she thinks I can't look after you both well enough. I told her to go home and look after her Mr Will and Mr Tad's family. I must admit, ma'am, she has been a great help though and was quite pleased with the result of our efforts."

"It's just as well you are friends," said Jenny, "for we might have had a battle on our hands."

"Yes, I am sure she would have tried to run both houses if she hadn't been able to persuade me to come. Even now she keeps a close watch over all I do."

"Come on Jenny, let's go up. You must have a rest before dinner and you must be very tired. Tea, I think, in our room, please, Mrs Breen."

"I'll send it right up, sir."

"I daresay we'll have to come down to earth Jen, now that we are home," said Rick as they walked upstairs. "I wonder how Will's romance is going. Not as good as ours." He squeezed her waist a little.

"Well, not yet, Ricky. But if I know anything about Dimity it soon will be. She is very taken with him. I could see that when they first met."

"Could you, love? All I could see that night was you," said Ricky. "I must admit that Will was furthest from my mind."

"And so it should have been, sir, on the night of our engagement." With that she flicked his tie and ran upstairs before he could catch her.

Will was filled with a great deal of apprehension as he rang the door bell of the Roger house. But he was received with courtesy by the stiff footman. He was surprised that he was shown in to the study. And further surprised when he found Dimity's father looking as friendly as he had been before he knew Will's intentions. This made Will feel a little more confident and he greeted him with careful courtesy.

"I have called you in here, Mr English, before the other guests arrive to speak to you about the situation we find ourselves in. I have asked you to dine with us only because we have considered that you may have the opportunity of social intercourse with us and to speak with our daughter in our presence." Roger said, pompously.

"Thank you, sir, you are most kind," said poor Will.

"I expect you to keep to that and not ask our daughter to meet you elsewhere. Do I make myself clear?"

"Yes, indeed, sir," said Will. "You may trust me to treat Miss Roger with the utmost respect, and I appreciate your kindness in allowing me to come tonight."

"Very well, then, see that I find no fault in your behaviour," was the curt reply.

Will began to boil inside his tight collar but kept a tight rein on his feelings. He was not used to being spoken to like this but tried to think of the end goal and not this silly little man's opinion of him.

Mr Roger then led him to the sitting room where two other guests were there with Mrs Roger. She greeted him coldly but politely and he moved to the couple, Ben and Isabel Grant whom he knew quite well. Soon four others joined the party and then Miss Dimity made her entrance. She was dressed in lovely pale daffodil which suited her brownness very well. She was careful to greet each guest in the same way and throughout the evening was the perfect daughter of the house.

Will wondered whether he would ever get to know her at this rate but on the whole enjoyed the evening. His hosts unbent somewhat as the night progressed but he was careful to not let his top quality manners slip one little bit. He was very pleased that the guests were friends of his and Ricky and he wondered whether Dimity had a hand in their choosing, for he didn't think that any of them were particular friends of the Rogers, and this proved to be so for the Grants took him home in their carriage and told him as much.

Will needn't have worried for Dimity often came to see Amabel and so he was able to see her without her mother's watchful eye. He was careful to never give one moment's concern, but Dimity appeared to give him some slight encouragement and he was content. Amabel gave him more to be happy about for she confided to him that Dimity had told her that she had her parents well in hand and that all would turn out well.

Will dined at their home several times before Christmas wondering about their plans to go to England. There had been no further mention of it and the date had passed when they were due to leave, but he didn't feel he could ask and so decided to just trust to luck that they had changed their minds, which indeed they had. For Amabel was able to give him the news that they had put off their trip until well into the new year. He thought this was a good sign.

He was very pleased with Dimity, and so indeed was Amabel, for she had been concerned that Dimity would turn out to be a wily miss and wondered whether her fostering of the friendship was the right thing, but she was pleased to report to Tad that Dimity was being very well behaved and not trying to be anything but a sensible girl who wished to know a man better. She felt confident that the romance was a good thing.

Ricky and Jenny spent Christmas in their new home and asked

Will to join them, but much to his pleasure the Rogers asked him to their home so he asked Ricky and Jenny to excuse him. Tad and Amabel and of course, Henry, spent the festive season with the Landons. So Ricky suggested to Jenny that they ask the Forrests to all come up and sample their skills in being hosts in their own home. Jenny was quite excited when they accepted and so planning for Christmas had to be enlarged quite a lot.

By the end of January Will found that the Rogers were relaxing in their vigilance of his friendship with Dimity and he began to feel that he was at last getting somewhere. One day he was waylaid by Roger and asked whether he was still of a mind about his precious girl.

"Yes, sir, I certainly am," came the ardent reply.

"Well," Roger said, "Mrs Roger and I plan to go ahead with our plans for England and as our daughter does not wish to accompany us we will now accept your suit, if that is agreeable to our daughter."

"Oh, sir. Thank you. Oh, I am overwhelmed, sir. Thank you." Will took his future father-in-law by the hand. "When may I speak, please, Mr Roger?"

"I believe she is in the sitting room, and you may go in."

Will tried not to hurry but bowed courteously and left with a broad smile on his face. He found his love, as her father had said, and she stood up, amazed at his presence, for she had apparently no knowledge of him being in the house.

"Mr English!" Dimity said with astonishment. "I had no idea you were here. I must tell Papa you are here."

"He knows, Miss Roger. I have already spoken to him, he gave me permission to come and speak with you."

Dimity looked up at him. "He did? Are you sure?" she asked.

"He certainly did and gave me permission to address you and ask you to be my wife. Oh, please Dimity, will you marry me, please? I want to more than anything."

Will took her in his arms and kissed her ardently and found that she was responding just as he had dreamed she would. "Will you, my darling girl? Please say you will."

"Yes, I do so want to. Oh-h-h." She put her face up to be kissed again and again.

After a respectable time Mr Roger made his appearance and found the couple sitting demurely, side by side, discussing wedding plans. "So you young things have decided to make a match of it?" he said.

Dimity flew to him. "Oh, papa, I am so happy. Thank you so much, I must tell Mama."

"She is coming down, pet. She won't be surprised, for we decided together that apparently only Mr English would make you happy, and we want our puss to be happy."

"Are you going to be content to leave her in my care, Mr Roger? If you do, I assure you I will take great care of her" said Will.

"Here is Mrs Roger now, we can all discuss it together. Come in, dear, these two young things are arranging dates. Come in and wish them happy."

Mrs Roger came in, tears streaming down her face, "Oh Dimity, I want you to be so happy, dear, but I can't bear to think of leaving you in this place."

"Cheer up, Mama. You may come back one day and you will find me a settled matron." Turning to her father she said, "Papa, do you really want to go? Please can't you stay? I am sure you will like it once you get used to it."

"Yes, sir, couldn't you stay?" put in Will. "I am sure Dimity will miss you a great deal and she will want to be near her mother so."

At this there was a fresh burst of weeping from Mrs Roger. "Dry those tears, dear for I have a plan," said the man. "I would suggest that the marriage takes place as soon as we can decently arrange it and then we go off to England, to return once my business is arranged, later in the year. How would that be?"

There were cries of approval from all three and so then they fell to making plans for these events. It was amazing how quickly the Rogers were willing to go along with Will's plans. He was so startled that it took him a while to sort out what he did want. He wondered what made such a change of heart in this couple and put it down to the iron will of his beloved, whom up until now showed very little signs of having such a one. Right in the back of his mind he wondered about this little brown lass of his and chuckled at the thought of the tussles he would have with her in the future, but in the way of youth, was sure he could handle whatever came.

It was a changed and happy Will who went home that day to tell Tad and then later Ricky what had befallen him. To tell them that his wedding day would be very soon and that he was the happiest man alive. Will's two brothers laughed and told him that they knew the feeling.

The wedding indeed, took place six weeks later when the weather was cooling a little. It was a very quiet affair for the Rogers did not have many friends, but the whole thing was done in the finest of styles for once they had made their mind up to accept Will then nothing was too good for him. Will, in fact, found their generosity embarrassing and found he had to put his foot down about accepting their largesse. This had amazed Mr Roger who told Will candidly that he did not expect refusal. "Will, my boy, I see more every day what a disservice I have done you over the months, for I thought you would wish to accept everything I could give you, and I might add that that is a considerable amount. But I find you reluctant to accept even the merest thing. I am gratified, but I wish you would accept."

"But sir, I would not have offered for Dimity if I hadn't felt I could support her. I may not be able to shower her with jewels and other such things, but if she truly loves me I am sure I can make her happy with what I can give her. I can support her well, sir, and I shall do so, even more, as time goes on."

"But, lad, will you not allow us to buy you a house?"

"No, thank you, sir. We will be happy in the house I am providing. Both my brothers have their own and the house we have been very happy in will suit us for some time to come."

"But isn't one brother still living there with his family?"

"Yes, at the moment he is, but will be moving in to his new home very soon and this will allow us to have the whole house to ourselves. Mrs Keen, the housekeeper and staff will remain with us and look after our needs very well."

"Well, if Dimity is happy with the arrangements then we will have to accept that, my boy. We will speak about this again when we return from England."

Will and Dimity were married at St James Church. Dimity

looking very sweet in a white velvet gown with a lovely matching bonnet. The reception, which was certainly in grand style, was held at the Royale. All sorts of exotic food had been procured from goodness knows where and the thirty or so guests felt it had been the most luxurious meal they had ever been asked to partake. The young couple spent their marriage holiday at Rocklea as Tad and Amabel had, for this lovely place spelt romance to all three couples, and Will could not think of a better place to take his bride.

Will was so taken with his love that even painting became secondary for some time after their return home. But one day, Dimity found him daydreaming in a way she had not experienced, although Tad and Ricky could have told her what was brewing. Will answered her only vaguely when Dimity spoke and muttering to himself after breakfast he headed for his studio. Mrs Keen saw him cross the hall and entered the dining room to find Dimity sitting non-plussed at the table staring at the door. She said, "Will, what's the matter?" thinking he was returning, and on seeing Mrs Keen she lamely said, "Oh."

Mrs Keen summed up the situation at a glance and brightly said, "I see Mr Will has taken one of his painting fits again, Mrs English. We won't see him all day if I am any judge. Did he say much this morning, ma'am?"

"No," said Dimity uncertainly, "no he didn't, Mrs Keen."

"Don't worry, my dear, he has the painting fit upon him. He'll paint like a mad thing for some hours and we will take sandwiches and tea in large quantities to him. He eats and drinks without being conscious of it, but at least he does take it. He isn't often like this but it seems as though the genius comes out in him and he just has to paint. Why don't you go in a watch him. He will like that. Just don't say anything, but just be there."

"Will he mind, Mrs Keen?"

"No, my dear, he will be very happy for you to be there. Mr Rick and Mr Tad would do that. He would throw them a smile occasionally and when he was finished what he is doing he will be wanting to show you what he has done."

"I daresay I have a lot to learn, Mrs Keen."

"You are doing very well, my dear. Mr Will is really very easy and he is always very kind."

"You are very fond of him, aren't you, Mrs Keen?" asked Dimity wistfully.

"Yes, my dear. I suppose because I have had to look after him more than the other boys, on account of him always being at home. He is a good boy." She smiled indulgently. "You will be very happy with Mr Will, my dear, he is very kind and considerate." Then suddenly realizing she may be speaking out of turn she added. "Oh, Mrs English, I do hope you will pardon me. I shouldn't speak so."

"That's all right, Mrs Keen. I understand. And," Dimity added, "I thank you for telling me, for I didn't know."

"Mr Will is a great genius, my dear, and I think geniuses are usually hard to live with, but we are lucky that Mr Will isn't really like that, just sometimes when he has to be."

Dimity did as she had been told and crept into the studio and sat in the chair that allowed her to watch Will. He turned as she entered and smiled. "I'm painting, love," he said unnecessarily. She didn't reply but watched the painting come alive at his hands.

His strokes were swift and sure. Dimity had never seen him paint before and was surprised at the way the whole thing was created. She could see why he had been only half aware of his surroundings for he had obviously been thinking of what he wanted to do for some time and now was all absorbed in the thing he was creating.

The canvas Will was using was not large, its wide side down. There was a background, but faint, of the bush and a river, reminiscent of Rocklea. In the foreground was a female figure, faceless so far. "I wonder who it is," mused Dimity. "Perhaps Will is trying to paint me, and cannot." Her gown was of deep green and the sheen of the material did not seem to fit in with a country background, but as Dimity was not versed in such things she thought she would wait for him to tell her. As the hours went by and she had come and gone several times, and his food had come and gone several times, then mid-afternoon he stopped, put his palette down and turned to look at her.

"It is all I can do today," he said, "until I can paint your face.

I must wait until it dries." Then he walked to her, not touching her. "Hello, darling, did you wonder where I've been?"

"No, Will, I knew. Mrs Keen explained. And I've been here."

"Yes, I knew, but I couldn't speak. Can you understand Dimity? I had to do what I had to do."

"It's all right, I do understand. Do you always paint like that?"

"No, not at all. I often paint and talk, but sometimes it seems to consume me and I can't think of anything but what I'm doing. Can you really understand, darling?"

"Yes, I think so. I've never seen you paint before, Will, and I didn't understand. I think I do know. We have to learn a lot about each other, don't we?"

"Yes, love, we do. Oh, Dimity love, I want to hold you and crush you to me, but I am sure I have paint on me and I daren't." He looked down at his hands. "This one's clean," he said and held out his left hand. "Come and see if you can tell what I have been doing. Maybe you won't, at first, but I hope you will one day without my explaining."

Will led her to stand right before the painting. "Can you see anything you recognise?" he asked.

"Yes, I think it is a misty scene of the view of Rocklea, but it isn't a clear one. Is it meant to be?"

"No it is a hazy background. Do you feel anything about it?"

"Well, without looking at the figure, I feel happy about it, but I don't really know why. Perhaps when she..."

"You," Will said.

"Perhaps when I have a face it may tell me more."

"Think some more, love. What else does it tell you?"

"I think it tells me that I make you happy and that we were so very happy at Rocklea. Is that it, Will?"

"You darling love, you darling little Dimity-mine. Yes, that is what I am telling you. The delirious happiness we are having, and did have at Rocklea. Darling, aren't we so fortunate, do you think anyone else has ever been as happy as we are?"

Dimity gurgled a laugh as he folded her into his painty arms. She didn't think anyone could be.

CHAPTER 22: *Dinner*

It was in July that Ricky suggested that the three couples get together and entertain several of their old and very dear friends. Of course the three had often dined and had become as close as any real family. The girls enjoyed each other's company and especially Jenny and Dimity enjoyed the unusual joy of having sisters. They had a great deal of fun together and were very keen to help Amabel choose materials and colour schemes for her new house. The house was not so far from her parents and Ricky and Jenny, and there was much too-ing and fro-ing between the houses. Will also encouraged Dimity to change the rooms around and re-decorate as she desired. She wisely decided to wait a while until she became more used to housekeeping and would learn about such things. In the meantime she listened intently to all the decisions made about Amabel's house and stowed it away in her brain for further consideration.

So it was not the usual dinner party that was planned but one that Ricky had in mind for quite some time. He wanted to formally thank all their old friends who had helped them so much in their growing years, and now that they were all married and settled he thought it would be a good idea to gather them together.

So the three young couples had dinner at Ricky's home to plan this special dinner party and it was not much of a surprise to them when their hosts announced that they were to be parents in the New Year. There was great jubilation and Ricky's thoughts of the previous year came true as he saw Jenny blooming, as only a happy, healthy, pregnant girl can look. She did have a torrid time for a few weeks but now was quite well and thrilled with her news. It was hard to keep their minds on the business on hand but after dinner settled down to working out who should be asked.

Each of the men wanted to host the dinner, but Will settled

that question by saying, "I will have my big painting finished and framed in three weeks, and I would like to have a viewing of it. Why don't you all come to us and Mr Landon can unveil the painting in my studio before the dinner? I do want your father to do that for me Amabel."

This was the decider. The girls talked over the actual dinner and then they settled down to work out the guest list. "Let's take them in order," said Ricky.

"In order?" queried his wife.

"Yes, Jen, in order of them appearing in our lives. What do you think, boys?"

"You mean start with Mr Hughes?" asked Tad.

"That's right," said Ricky. "Then Mr Landon."

"What a shame Mr Fraser is dead," said Will. "I never did feel I thanked him enough."

"Well he died pretty soon after we met him, didn't he?" put in Tad. "Who else, Rick?"

"Then comes Mr and Mrs Fishbon," said Ricky. "I think Mrs Fishbon is well enough to come."

"Particularly if she comes during the afternoon, Ricky, and rests before dinner. That's all right, isn't it Dimity?"

"Yes, of course. I love Mrs Fishbon. She tells me what a funny little boy you were and I love hearing about that."

"Then Tim Hinds, Rick. You'll have to have Tim," said Tad.

"Yes, and ..."

"I'm not having Patrick Thomas," said Will. "I know he taught me a lot, but I really don't think I want him."

"All right, Will. Anyone else?" asked Ricky.

"What about Mr and Mrs Forrest, Rick?" asked Will.

"Yes, I would like them to come, apart from wanting them for Jen's sake, I am very appreciative of what he did for Father."

The party was arranged for a month hence, to be held at Will and Dimity's home as suggested. The girls put their heads together working out all the little details needed for such an occasion. It was to be a special time, as Dimity knew, and she wondered what she would do without the support of her new sisters and Mrs Keen.

But she was happy with all the plans and looked forward to being hostess at a function that was so important to their menfolk.

As planned Mrs Fishbon came to the house during the afternoon and Dimity was pleased to fuss over her, between duties. She settled Mr Fishbon in the study to be free with the books there and later when she took him some tea she found him sound asleep in one of the large leather armchairs, so she crept silently out, knowing that the old man needed his rest as much as his lovely little dumpy wife. Mrs Fishbon had quickly become a firm friend of Dimity's, who had many anecdotes to tell her of Will's early days and the fun they all had teaching the boys how to be gentlemen. Mrs Fishbon had a very entertaining way of describing their antics and Dimity had visited her on many occasion. Perhaps Mrs Fishbon filled the niche of her own mother, but, mused Dimity, there could not be two women more different. No, they just found a mutual contentment in their friendship, she was probably more like a fond grandmother.

Mrs Fishbon was quite rested for the dinner and was looking quite spritely when they gathered before dinner. Dimity met her guests and led them all to Will's studio where there were chairs placed for everyone's comfort. There were several paintings to be seen one of which was that of Amabel on the day that Henry was born, this, he had given to Tad and Amabel, and another was the honeymoon painting. Will knew he could never sell those, they were too close to their hearts. Now that Dimity's figure was finished, the picture was an absolute delight. The portrayal of her was almost ethereal, she looked human but almost, no - not transparent but had a heavenly appearance, very hard to describe, but very pleasant to see. But the main thing in the studio was a shrouded painting that was absolutely huge. It seemed to take up the space of half a wall. Will asked all the guests to wander around and look at what they liked and when they were ready to be seated he would ask Mr Landon to come forward and unveil his big painting.

Will explained a little of the experience he had had in France, not expecting everyone to understand, but telling the bare bones of the story. He handed over to John who explained a little more than Will had done, also without going in to too much detail. He then moved over to the huge canvas and pulled a cord which moved to one side revealing a truly heavenly scene and those who knew the story could see what Will must have experienced.

There was absolute stillness in the room. No-one, for one moment doubted, that the main central figure was Jesus. A Jesus portrayed in a traditional form. The expression on his face was one of sheer love and acceptance of all those standing before him with not a hint of blame. There was sympathy, empathy, compassion and again an all embracing love. The figures of people before him showed bewilderment, sorrow, hurt, and even hate. There were some who were crippled, some with crutches and wheelchairs. The figure of Peter, slightly behind Jesus, showed him reaching out to the people with love and a helplessness that gave you the idea that he would love to help them but this must be between each one and Jesus. Beyond Jesus and Peter there was a fence that was not really a barrier, it was that the barrier was in the people's minds. Beyond that there were other people who had passed through the gate and their faces showed sheer joy and happiness. One of the people before Jesus was coming forward to protest that they would not be allowed to go through the barrier, but would have to return from whence they came and that person obviously hated the idea of it, not realizing that Jesus was not making them start from the beginning again, for some had very difficult lives, but to go back to learn a little more and have a second chance. A chance to be 'born again.'

After some minutes there seemed to be a sigh from all who looked at it, but still no-one spoke. It was very moving. Then Dimity quietly went over to Will and held his hand for she could see how deeply affected he was. He knew that their silence told him everything. But then John Landon said, "I think we all understand, Will. You have preached to us the sermon of life. I thank you." There were murmurs of, "Yes," "Indeed," "Yes, you have," "Marvellous". Nell Forrest sat gazing at the painting with tears running down her face not caring what she looked like, not being conscious of that at all, Ned held her hand tightly and was as moved as she.

Eventually they all, literally, came to earth. They congratulated Will but at the same time apologizing to him, for they all felt that congratulations were not warranted, they felt the inspiration had not come from him.

Maria came to announce that dinner was being served and so they all turned to leave the glorious thing that was there.

Will claimed Mrs Fishbon's arm to lead her to the dining room leaving Mr Fishbon to take Dimity in. Dimity had thought carefully about her placings but had to resort to consulting Ricky about some. However she soon knew that the dinner would be a success for all these people had a liking and respect for one another and it all seemed to flow well.

Jenny had met them all at one time or another but knew some of them only slightly, however she was seated between Tim Hinds and Mr Fishbon and thoroughly enjoyed herself. Amabel between Tim Hinds and Mr Forrest. Will was at the head of the table feeling very proud of the fact that he was in that place for such an occasion and Dimity was opposite him with John Landon and Mr Fishbon on either side of her. Tad and Mr Hughes, with Mrs Hinds between them.

The three girls felt very happy about the meal that they had planned and were content that they had not let their menfolk down. They could each of them see their husbands who gave them congratulatory smiles every now and then.

At the end of the meal, when the maids had left the room, Ricky stood up to speak. "Dear friends, we have asked you to be with us at this time, so that we could properly thank you for all you have done for us in the past. Now that we are all married, settled and on our way in our careers, we thought we would like to tell you that if it hadn't been your help in the days gone by we would never have got to this point in our lives. I would like to ask my brothers and our wives if they would all stand and drink a toast to our honoured guests."

The six young people stood and toasted their dear friends and families. There were murmurs of protest from the various men but they said little as Ricky proceeded. "It all started with Mr Hughes, who helped us immensely, by teaching us to be literate. Thank you, sir."

"My pleasure, Ricky. I'll have my say later," said Mr Hughes.

"Then Mr Fraser, Ricky. Do mention Mr Fraser," said Will.

"Yes, Will does feel eternally thankful to Mr Fraser and we are sorry we cannot thank him, for he died not long after we got to know him. But he certainly started something when he taught Will to draw. So in absence, we thank Mr Fraser. But before him came Tim Hinds who saved me from a real beating. And later he saved my father. Thank you, Tim, I shall always be grateful for what you did." Tim inclined his head, not wishing to comment on either episode that Ricky had mentioned.

"Then Mr Landon who has ever been our friend and mentor. You have done so much for the three of us, sir, that words cannot tell. We thank you." "Here, here." "Yes, indeed." Came from Tad and Will.

"Mr and Mrs Fishbon how can we thank you for all the wonderful things you have done for us. We were scrubby little urchins until you took us in hand and put some polish on us." "Very hard work," stated the old man with a grin. "I am sure it must have been," said Ricky with a smile, "you were patience personified. And when I think of the night that you and Mrs Fishbon began teaching us to dance. I can still laugh when I think of what our faces must have shown you."

"I would call it a disgusted look, I think Ricky," laughed Mr Fishbon, as all joined in. "But you always were quick learners, all three of you."

"Surely not me, Mr Fishbon?" asked Will. "When I think of the years it took to learn Latin verbs. Sir, why did I ever have to learn Latin?"

"Good discipline, apart from anything else," said Will's one-time teacher.

"Then Mr and Mrs Forrest, who did so much for Father. I can never thank you enough. You and Tim gave me back something which I had lost and then, sir, you allowed me to take my Jenny from you. You can see I am ever in your debt. Thank you both very much." Ricky then turned to look at each of their guests and bowed gracefully to each, Will and Tad quickly joined him in this little ceremony.

Mr Hughes then stood up and said, "For those who do not know it, I will relate a short story. One wintry morning when it was very cold and wet, I found an urchin asleep on the office step. When I woke him he told me a strange story, I asked him into the office and was able to act on what he told me and thereby was instrumental in having some very bad men arrested for robbery and the story was a scoop. This urchin interested me and I am happy to say we became friends. He became quite important to me for I had never met anyone quite like him. He wasn't content for me to have one urchin friend but soon had brought me another one to adopt, one who I have never been able to shake off in all these years. Later they brought in a third one, who did prove to be quite a trial until he found out what one could do with paper and pencil, then we couldn't stop him from using up all the scrap paper that the office could produce. Ladies and gentlemen, I would like to ask you to drink a toast to Ricky, Tad and Will." They did. "Thank you," said Mr Hughes and sat down.

"I hope I may say a few words now," said Mr Landon. "Charles, you may have found these three, but I claim them as mine as well. Friends," he said, looking around him, "I tell you that watching these three boys, and to me they always will be boys, grow up out of the life they were living, has been both a privilege and an example. A privilege to me for they were always so eager to make the best of adversity, and they had plenty of that, and an example to all who follow on in this new land of ours. As you know, so many of the population of this country started without any assets at all. So many have come here, many against their will, to make their way in the world. I call this the land of opportunity, a land that gives freedom and opportunity to everyone who will work, and I think that our three boys here are an example of what this land will be in the future. In England it is so hard for a working man to drag himself out of the state they were born in, but in this country it depends only on what a man puts in to life as to where he arrives. So I salute you, Ricky, Tad and Will as symbols of the future of this great nation. Friends, I ask you to drink a toast to "Terra Australis Espirito Santo" "The Great Southern Land of the Holy Spirit".

Ricky thanked John, for saying what he did, but suggested that it was not their collectives skills that had got them along in the world but their friends who had helped them. He continued, "I now have some proposals to make and I ask your permission to activate them. You know that we are interested in helping our young people to be better citizens and have several institutions where they can be fostered, be taught and to be encouraged, well, we would ask your permission to name the various places after you, our friends. You know we have three houses here, the boys hostel to our left and the girls hostel to our right. Dimity and Will wish to live here and will do so for as long as they desire. But I foresee that some day they will wish to live elsewhere and that Will shall begin an Art School here, then the three houses will be a whole. We would like to name these three, "The Fishbon Centre" with your permission, Mr and Mrs Fishbon."

"Oh, Ricky," Mrs Fishbon said.

"We do not deserve it, Ricky, but, yes, you may. We are honoured," said the old man, emotionally.

Ricky continued. "Sir," he said looking straight at John Landon, "we thank you for all your help over the years and ask you may we name our boys and girls orphanages the "Landon Homes"? The babies home we ask if we may call it "Sadie House"?"

"My dear boy, we are honoured, aren't we, Sadie?" Mr Landon said. Mrs Landon's eyes filled with tears. "Dear children," was all she said, smilingly.

"We are planning a training centre for boys that will be rather like a cadet training for the army and as Tim is about to retire from the regiment we are settling this centre up on the farm he is to live on and will be called "Hinds". Tim , of course, knows of this already."

Tim nodded agreement and said, "Yes, Jane and I were wondering what I would do when I left the regiment and this is a marvellous opportunity for us. Thank you, Ricky."

"We are also establishing a school for prospective writers and Mr Hughes will give his name, his talents and time to oversee this. Thank you Mr Hughes. And at Rocklea where we will have our country orphanages they will be called Forrest Houses.

So for those who didn't know of these proposals, I hope you will agree to all these, and I thank you."

"And, dearie," said Mrs Fishbon, "where will your names be on these wonderful projects of yours?"

"Dear Mrs Fishbon," said Will, "we will just be passing on the wonderful name of English that Ricky gave us, on to our children. You see, Tad and Amabel have started with Henry. Ricky and Jenny have already begun and Dimity and I now announce that we too are having a family and the Art School will not begin until we have filled this happy place with so many children that we can't fit in anymore."

Dimity laughed and then the friends too roared with laughter. It was so like Will to have the last word.

ABOUT THE AUTHOR
Sheila Hunter
1924-2002

Sheila Hunter was passionate about her family and loved to research their history. During this research she often read stories of street waifs who often got into trouble in Colonial Sydney. Ricky is a fictitious story centered around some of these street urchins. The convict towns of Sydney and Parramatta were dirty, smelly and dusty places with all sorts of desperate and despicable characters the street urchins were often caught pick pocketing or stealing from store keepers and street vendors. Occasionally these children were not really 'base born' or convict offspring, but just orphans left with no one to look after them! Life was very hard for them! No one looked out for them and it was survival by wits alone. Ricky is a child who stole Sheila's heart! He was the epitome of everyone or thing she would loved to have helped. If she had lived in this time I'm sure she too would have helped Ricky teach other children from the streets.

Sheila was born in New Zealand to Australian parents, Murdoch and Mabel McDonald (or Macdonald as they were known before they went to New Zealand) moved back to Melbourne Australia with her family when only 4 years old. She was a nurse by training, but an adventurer in her life! A wife and mother she was a great story teller, often making up very long stories for both her children and grandchildren. They would listen enwrapped within the stories of her telling.

In 1999 Sheila was awarded one of 20 Federal Recipients of the Year of the Senior Citizen Awards. She was an amazing woman! Life was tough - growing up during WW II in a single parent family (her dad had left them to beck to the two children in New Zealand, from his first marriage). They lived on the docks in Melbourne in a family Service Station. She went to school during the day and worked in the Service Station after school, weekends and at nights. She won a full 'Cello scholarship about this time but it was during the war and on arriving home one day found that her mother had sold her 'Cello to help pay the household bills! Yes life was hard! On leaving school she enrolled in Nursing only to be the butt of jokes from her family, but she not only succeeded but excelled at this caring role, ending up as acting Matron of "Roma" Private Hospital in East Gosford NSW.

Sheila, married Norman M Hunter in 1955 and they lived in Avoca Beach all their married life and had two children, Norman Jnr and Sara. Norman and Sheila were a well known couple on the Central Coast NSW with Norman a well know Real Estate Agent also owned and operated Avoca Beach Picture Theatre in Avoca, as well as amassing an amazing Natural History Collection that was known and studied world wide and together they were part of many groups and associations in the area. It was while researching Norman's Convict Family that she first came across the reference to street urchins in the many stories she read about.

In 2000, her beloved husband and fellow adventurer, Norman, died from Dementia and she unfortunately followed only two years later from Cancer.

Sara Powter 2017
  and I am proud to be her daughter!

See
www.sheilahunter.com.au

ALSO BY THIS AUTHOR

Part of the *Australian Trilogy*

"MATTIE - Coming of age in Convict Australia"

Woodslane/Hand in Hand Publications
ISBN: 9780994578204
by Sheila Hunter

Mattie aged 12 is convicted for petty theft, given the sentence of 7 years and is sent to Australia. She meets another convict woman who at her death gives Mattie a chance for a new life. Mattie makes the most of everything that comes her way. She earns her freedom, falls in love, marries and becomes a mother. Life is not kind to her. She meets bushrangers, moves to the Gold Fields in Bathurst, and starts a store. Mattie is the kind of woman that made Australia what it is today.

Child Convict, Wife, Bushrangers, Widow,
Bathurst Gold Fields, Shop Keeper, Town Builder ...
A remarkable woman!

Originally published on Amazon as
"Mattie" - the Story of an Australian Convict Child
ISBN: 1533458537
Large Print ISBN: 1533458537

Also available on Amazon/Kindle under the name of
MATTIE, The story of an Australian Convict Child

***

COMING SOON

Part of the *Australian Trilogy*

"THE HEATHER TO THE HAWKESBURY"

Follows four Scottish families from Skye to NSW
ISBN: 1533473641
Large Print ISBN: 1533473641
by Sheila Hunter

Follows Mary Macdonald and her family; her brother Fergus MacKenzie; sister-in-law Caro MacLeod; cousins the Fraser and all their families who have had to emigrate from the Isle of Skye during the "Clearances".

The story follows the four families from Scotland, on the ship out and to the NSW colony in 1850's. Mary does not cope with the changes and losses that occur in the first months in the colony. The other women in the family rely on her and she nearly crumbles. Through accidents, losses, trials, floods, and hard work the families struggle together and forge a strong bond with their new country.

The immigrants from Scotland helped make Australia what it is today!

Coming soon to Australian Bookstores &
Available on Amazon/Kindle

***

ALSO BY THIS AUTHOR

"REEF HOLIDAY"

Great Barrier Reef adventures in Queensland

ISBN: 1503298078
By Sheila Hunter

Sue White, aged 13, is excited that her parents are to take her on a holiday to the Barrier Reef. Her friend Alison advises her to speak to another girl in their school who lives on a Great Barrier Reef island, for tips about life in such a place. They are surprised to find that the White family is actually planning to holiday on the very island where Jess Carey and her family live.

The Whites, Phil, Sally & Sue, Jess Carey and her brother Lewis all travel to the reef together and so begins a great adventure for Sue and her new found friends. The Carey's are Alan and Bob, brothers, and their wives, Barbara and Win. Bob's son, Paul, is quite a skilled amateur naturalist and is most helpful and instructive when he takes parties of guests on to the reef.

The Carey youngsters and their extended family know their reef well and this holiday proves to be a learning experience for all at the resort. All the children get along well and have many adventures, including meeting some pirates.

This is a great introduction for kids to learn about life on the Great Barrier Reef in Queensland.

While this is not part of the Australia Colonial Trilogy you can trace the family to the end of 'The Heather to the Hawkesbury'. Sally, Sue's mother is a great great great granddaughter of the Macdonalds who arrived from Scotland in 1850's.

Available on Amazon/Kindle

***

COMING SOON

"AUTOBIOGRAPHY"

ANOTHER BLOOMING SHEILA! - the Early Years

VOL 1
by Sheila Hunter

Sheila Hunter (née Macdonald), spent her first years growing up in Ngakawau, a timber town on the North West Coast of the South Island of New Zealand.

Her beloved father, Murdoch Macdonald, although belittled by his wife Mabel, was a brilliant Engineer and built all sorts of mining and Timber equipment, including converting a tractor to a Locomotive and developing and Patenting a guy rope, pulley system to access tall trees in very steep valleys with minimal destruction. This system was used world wide, may still be, and was able to deliver full trees to the mill on the floor of the valley with safety and ease.

This takes the story through The Depression, her parents separation and divorce, and up to the beginning of the adventures that started with her marriage.

Sheila is the Author of an Australian Colonial Trilogy and a children's adventure story set on the Great Barrier Reef.

Co-Winner of *1999 NSW Senior Citizen of the Year* in the Year of the Senior Citizen.

VOL 2 LIFE WITH NORMAN
   - the Adventures begins

VOL 3 THE ECLECTIC ECCENTRIC COLLECTOR
   - the Museum Story

***

amazon REVIEWS FOR *"RICKY"*

5 stars ☆☆☆☆☆
B J Pierson on MARCH 21, 2016
Format: Kindle Edition

"What an amazing story of 3 urchins come to find themselves in growing up together and to make something of themselves with the help of others who formed themselves into fine young men. I look forward to reading "Mattie" and other books of this great country I hope someday to visit."

***

5 stars ☆☆☆☆☆
Jan Rouse on JANUARY 26, 2016
Format: Kindle Edition

"When is the next book available if there is one. I loved this one."

***

5 stars ☆☆☆☆☆
RoNnAleE on APRIL 25, 2016
Format: Kindle Edition

"Loved it!"

"A good story, well told! If a writer can develop a character so well as to have me shedding tears over their situation, I believe they have done their job well."

***